D1595633

DUMBARTON OAKS
MEDIEVAL LIBRARY

Daniel Donoghue, General Editor

THE BYZANTINE SINBAD

MICHAEL ANDREOPOULOS

DOML 67

The Byzantine Sinbad

MICHAEL ANDREOPOULOS

Translated by

JEFFREY BENEKER
and
CRAIG A. GIBSON

DUMBARTON OAKS
MEDIEVAL LIBRARY

HARVARD UNIVERSITY PRESS
CAMBRIDGE, MASSACHUSETTS
LONDON, ENGLAND
2021

First Printing

Library of Congress Cataloging-in-Publication Data
Names: Andreopōlos, Michaēl, active 11th century, translator. | Beneker,
    Jeffrey, translator. | Gibson, Craig A., 1968– translator.
Title: The Byzantine Sinbad / Michael Andreopoulos; translated by
    Jeffrey Beneker and Craig A. Gibson.
Other titles: Book of Sindbad. Greek. | Dumbarton Oaks medieval
    library ; 67.
Description: Cambridge, Massachusetts : Harvard University Press, 2021. |
    Series: Dumbarton Oaks medieval library; DOML 67 | Includes
    bibliographical references and index. | Greek text with English
    translation following; introduction and notes in English.
Identifiers: LCCN 2020036294 | ISBN 9780674251472 (cloth)
Subjects: LCSH: Fables, Syriac—Translations into Greek. | Byzantine
    literature—Early works to 1800.
Classification: LCC PN687.S6 B99 2021 | DDC 808.8/002—dc23
LC record available at https://lccn.loc.gov/2020036294

Contents

Introduction

The figure of the philosopher Sinbad, rendered in Greek as Syntipas, was introduced into the Byzantine literary tradition in the late eleventh century through two works translated from Syriac into Greek by Michael Andreopoulos. Both of these works, *The Book of Syntipas the Philosopher (BSP)* and a collection of sixty-two fables *(Fables),* are contained in this volume. Taken together, the *BSP* and *Fables* represent the character and the wisdom of Syntipas as they would become known to Byzantine readers. Although Andreopoulos translated both texts in the Middle Ages, they are distantly related to earlier Greek traditions as old as the fourth century BCE and, more immediately, to a complex development of medieval wisdom literature written in Persian, Arabic, and Syriac. The *BSP* and the *Fables* made their way into Greek by different paths, but once united by Andreopoulos's translations, they were probably assumed to belong together. Of the three oldest manuscripts that form the basis of our Greek texts, two transmit both the story of Syntipas and the fables that were attributed to him.

The Translator and His Patron

A dedicatory poem attached as an epigram to the *BSP* identifies the translator and the circumstances of his work.[1]

Michael Andreopoulos, speaking in the first person, claims that he translated the *BSP* as a commission from Gabriel, whom he identifies as the "revered governor of the city named for honey *(meli),*" that is, Melitene (modern Malatya in Turkey), a city in eastern Asia Minor located near the upper Euphrates River.[2] Gabriel was ruler *(doux)* of Melitene from the 1080s until 1101, a period when Turkish peoples were challenging Byzantium for control of the eastern territories. While remaining loyal to the Byzantine emperor, Gabriel also appears to have had good relations with the Seljuk Turks.[3] He had important local connections, as well. One of his daughters was married to the *doux* of neighboring Edessa in Syria, who ruled until he was overthrown in a coup led by the crusader Baldwin of Boulogne.[4] In 1100, when Baldwin became king of Jerusalem (as Baldwin I), he turned control of the city over to his cousin Baldwin of Bourcq (the future Baldwin II of Jerusalem). Gabriel then married another daughter, Morfia, to the second Baldwin, but he did not live long enough to profit from the alliance. Melitene was sacked in 1101 by Danishmendids, a Turkish group that was contending with the Seljuks, and Gabriel was executed.[5] Morfia, however, became queen of Jerusalem when Baldwin ascended the throne, and her progeny held powerful positions in the crusader states and the Byzantine empire.[6]

We know very little about Andreopoulos's life. In the same dedicatory poem, he identifies himself as a Christian and humbly calls himself "the least of the grammarians." A grammarian *(grammatikos)* was a literary scholar who often ran a secondary school. Andreopoulos, therefore, would have been an educated man, but one of relatively low social standing and perhaps financially dependent on Gabriel or

another member of the local nobility.[7] If he was in fact a teacher, his school would have served an important purpose. After students learned basic skills in reading and writing, the grammarian taught them more advanced topics, including grammar, literature, and prose composition.[8] Some students would go on to pursue further studies in rhetoric or philosophy. One obstacle to advancement seems to have been that Greek higher education was typically available only in Constantinople in the Middle Ages.[9] In many places outside the capital, however, a school run by a dedicated teacher, sometimes assisted by advanced students, could and did fill that need.[10] Andreopoulos's translations, like his presumed teaching, were probably intended for his local audience: the earliest manuscripts come from Trebizond, and the *BSP* and *Fables* do not appear to have reached Constantinople until well after their creation.[11]

The *Fables* are not explicitly connected with Andreopoulos in any sort of epigram or preface, but like the *BSP*, they were translated into Greek in eastern Asia Minor in the late eleventh century, and they are included with the *BSP* in two of the earliest manuscripts. Ben Edwin Perry originally suggested that they were written in Greek and then ascribed to Syntipas.[12] However, he later modified his position, arguing from characteristics of language that they were based on the Aesopic tradition, but that they had been written first in Syriac and then translated by Andreopoulos into Greek.[13] Andreopoulos appears to have believed that the *Fables* represented the teachings of Syntipas, much in the way that the Aesopic fables were thought to represent the teachings of Aesop and were frequently transmitted in books along with his Life.[14] Indeed, in the *BSP*'s dedicatory epigram, Andreo-

poulos identifies Syntipas as the "fable writer" *(mythogra-phos)*, assigning him to the same category of wise man as Aesop.[15]

The *BSP*, in its various forms, was, according to Ida Toth, "one of the most successful and most widely transmitted pieces of popular literature, and a true bestseller of medieval and early modern times."[16] Written in Persian in the sixth or seventh century, it was translated into Arabic in the eighth or ninth century, including a version by "Mousos the Persian," who has been identified as Mūsā b. ʿĪsā al-Kisrawī, a ninth-century Arabic scholar and translator of Persian literature.[17] An Arabic version was translated into Syriac sometime between the ninth and the eleventh centuries, and a Syriac version created during this period was most likely the exemplar used by Andreopoulos in approximately 1090 to create the first Greek version.[18] Translations from Syriac into Greek were relatively rare, but Andreopoulos made his translation at a time when the Byzantine Greeks were very interested in eastern art, architecture, and secular literature, and when patrons (such as Andreopoulos's own Gabriel) were sponsoring translations of eastern scientific texts and narrative fiction.[19]

The plot of the *BSP* involves a frame tale in which the Persian king Cyrus turns his son over to the famous philosopher Syntipas to be educated (on the structure, see below). Syntipas does indeed instruct the king's son, making him in turn the wisest of his peers, but before the son can demonstrate his wisdom, he is involved in a scandal. One of the

king's concubines falsely accuses him of rape, and he, sworn to silence for seven days because of an astrological warning, cannot defend himself. Cyrus believes his concubine's accusation and intends to execute his son. To delay this punishment, seven philosophers tell a series of stories over the seven days, and the concubine responds on most days with a story of her own. These interior tales are all aimed at influencing the king's judgment: the philosophers' stories are cautionary tales about the dishonesty of women, while the concubine warns of untrustworthy advisors. Once the son can finally speak, he clears his name and the concubine is punished. With the scandal resolved, the *BSP* concludes with a demonstration of the great wisdom that the son has acquired through the teaching of Syntipas.

Since the Persian, Arabic, and Syriac versions that lie behind the Greek *BSP* are not extant, Toth argues that "the 11th-century translation by Michael Andreopoulos most probably represents the oldest surviving witness of the earliest known eastern tradition."[20] Andreopoulos's version was later retranslated by an unknown author into the so-called *Retractatio,* a new Greek version whose grammar, syntax, style, and vocabulary were simplified in order to appeal to a wider contemporary readership.[21] Other simplified Greek translations were made from the fourteenth through the seventeenth centuries, and Greek versions were translated into Romanian, Bulgarian, and Serbian versions in the eighteenth and nineteenth centuries.[22]

Andreopoulos's eleventh-century Greek translation of the *BSP* is part of a family of so-called eastern versions of the Syntipas story, of which nine other versions are extant: one Syriac (which is later than the lost Syriac version trans-

lated by Andreopoulos, and breaks off at the beginning of the story of the old man, section 118 in this edition); three Persian (including two that appear, respectively, in *One Thousand and One Nights* and *One Hundred and One Nights*); three Arabic; one Old Spanish *(El libro des los engaños e los asayamientos de las mujeres);* and one Hebrew *(Mishle Sendabar).* The Old Spanish and Hebrew versions were each translated from Arabic.[23] The frame tale remains more consistent than the interior tales, which vary in number, order, and content across the eastern versions.[24]

While Andreopoulos's version belongs to this eastern medieval tradition, the tradition of seven wise men (or sages) as represented by the seven philosophers who tell the interior tales also has an ancient Greek analogue.[25] In his discussions of the origins of the *BSP,* Perry connects the seven philosophers to the "Seven Wise Men of Greece," a legend as old as the fourth century BCE, and perhaps older.[26] Perry also notes that three of the stories told in the *BSP* "can be traced to Graeco-Roman antiquity."[27] In his edition of the Greek life of Secundus the Silent Philosopher, Perry traces the translation of that second-century CE text into Arabic and argues that it influenced the development of the *BSP* and related works.[28] Likewise, the frame tale's theme of the young man falsely accused of rape has ancient antecedents, such as the Greek story of Hippolytus and Phaedra, and the biblical story of Joseph and Potiphar's wife. Though Andreopoulos rightly claims in his epigram that the *BSP* "did not exist among the Romans' books" before his translation, he nonetheless made himself part of a process of literary exchange that was much older than he likely knew.

The so-called western family of this tradition differs

greatly from the eastern family and therefore from Andreopoulos's Greek *BSP.* The location of the story is usually transferred from Persia to Rome; two versions place it in Constantinople, and the twelfth-century Latin version known as *Dolopathos* places it in Sicily during the reign of Augustus. The concubine from the king's harem in the *BSP* is transformed into the son's stepmother,[29] and the central Syntipas figure is removed (except in *Dolopathos,* which substitutes the Roman poet Virgil), leaving the seven sages to act alone. As for the structure, on each of seven days the stepmother tells a story and one of the seven sages responds with a story, and at the end the son tells a final story, for a total of fifteen stories, only four to six of which are arguably also found in eastern versions. This medieval tradition of *The Story of the Seven Sages* seems to begin in the mid-twelfth century in France, and French versions in both poetry and prose are known. French versions were later translated into Italian and into different Latin versions: the widely known *Historia septem sapientium,* and the apparently unique *Dolopathos.* The origin and early transmission history of the western family of the Syntipas story is still not well understood.[30]

The only named characters in the *BSP* are Syntipas the philosopher and Cyrus the king. The king's son, concubine, and royal philosophers are unnamed. Nor are the seven philosophers distinguished from one another except by ordinal number. Likewise, none of the characters in the interior tales is named. Cyrus is to be identified with Cyrus II, or the Great (r. ca. 557–530 BCE), but despite sharing a name and a title, he bears little resemblance to the historical Cyrus. The setting of the frame tale is Cyrus's palace in Persia; the settings of the interior tales are nonspecific. This lack of spe-

cificity, yet with a tinge of the exotic, probably contributed to the international, multilingual, and long-term appeal of the work.

The frame tale itself is a genre with ancient roots that was quite popular in the medieval period. It creates a narrative context for telling a series of interior tales. In the case of the *BSP*, the education of the king's son and the concubine's accusation against him provide the context for the seven philosophers, the concubine, and eventually the son himself to tell their stories. This type of tale, according to Bonnie Irwin, "is not simply an anthology of stories. Rather, it is a fictional narrative . . . composed primarily for the purpose of presenting other narratives. A frame tale depicts a series of oral storytelling events in which one or more characters in the frame tale are also narrators of the interpolated tales." These interpolated tales (also called interior, embedded, and nested stories or narratives) are told within the surrounding frame, which "provides a context for reading, listening, and, of course, interpreting the interior tales." Thus the surrounding frame depends on the interior tales to advance its plot, but the individual interior tales are essentially independent; they may be removed from any one particular frame to "stand alone or appear in a different frame, albeit with a different connotation."[31] As a frame tale is adapted or translated, its interior tales can be reordered, creatively reworked, or even replaced with other tales. In the *BSP* the interior tales are used, first (on days 1–7), to hasten or delay the king's decision to execute his son and, second (on day 8), as an opportunity for the king's son and Syntipas to demonstrate their wisdom and learning.

The following summary demonstrates the overall struc-

ture of the *BSP.* The numbers in parentheses correspond to the sections of the text and translation published in this edition.

Dedicatory poem of Michael Andreopoulos (1).

A brief prologue (2).

The frame tale begins: Syntipas educates the king's son and swears him to silence for seven days. One of the king's concubines falsely accuses the son of rape, and the king sentences him to death (3–11).

On days 1 to 7, the seven philosophers take turns telling the king two stories each that persuade him to call off the execution. On the following mornings of days 2 to 6, the concubine warns the king not to listen to the philosophers.

Day 1: The first philosopher tells the story of the lustful king, the resistant woman, and her suspicious husband (12–15), and the story of the adulterous woman, her suspicious husband, and a spying parrot (16–18).

Day 2: The concubine tells the story of the drowning of a fuller and his son (19–21). The second philosopher tells the story of the merchant, the girl, and the pure loaves of bread (22–25), and the story of the adulterous woman, her lover, his slave, and her husband (26–28).

Day 3: The concubine tells the story of the king's son and the female demon *(lamia)* (29–33). The third philosopher tells the story of the honeycomb that leads to a war (34–36), and the story of the woman, the lustful merchant, and the duped husband (37–39).

Day 4: The concubine tells the story of a prince who was transformed into a woman (40–45). The fourth philosopher tells the story of the greedy bath manager, his humiliated wife, and the son of a king (46–49), and the story of the lust-

ful man, the clever old woman, and the couple who break their mutual oaths of fidelity (50–55).

Day 5: The concubine tells the story of the pig, the monkey, and the figs (56–58). The fifth philosopher tells the story of the soldier and his faithful dog (59–62), and the story of the raped woman, her suspicious husband, and the burned cloak (63–69).

Day 6: The concubine tells the story of the thief, the lion, and the monkey (70–73). The sixth philosopher tells the story of the pigeons and the disappearing grain (74–77), and the story of the raped woman and the elephant-shaped honey cake (78–80).

Day 7: The concubine threatens to throw herself into a bonfire but does not tell a story (81–83). The seventh philosopher tells the story of three phallic wishes (84–89), and the story of the man who tried to compile all the vices of women in a book (90–95).

The eighth day dawns, and the son can speak again. He explains why he remained silent and why the concubine falsely accused him, and Syntipas accounts for his absence (96–99). Four of the philosophers debate who would have been responsible for the son's execution, and Syntipas explains why the woman is blameless (100–102). The son tells the story of the milkmaid who accidentally poisons her master's dinner guests, and he, four philosophers, and Syntipas debate who is to blame (103–7).

The son tells three stories of unexpectedly intelligent people: the three-year-old boy (108–10), the five-year-old boy (111–17), and the old man (118–26). He then explains to the king how Syntipas taught him (127–28).

The king asks his court how the concubine should be

punished (129–30). She tells the story of the mutilated fox (131–33). The son suggests that she be punished with the parade of infamy (134).

Syntipas tells the story of the philosopher's son who grew up to become a criminal (135–40).

The king's son repeats the earlier description of his education (see 128) and explains the ten ethical lessons that Syntipas also taught him (141–42). The king then asks his son twenty questions about fate, kings, philosophers, morality, and human relations (143–53).

A brief epilogue summarizes the subject matter and tallies up the twenty-seven stories of the *BSP* (154).

THE FABLES OF SYNTIPAS

The collection of sixty-two fables or "exemplary stories" attributed to Syntipas are descended from the Greek tradition. They began to appear in Syriac versions in the ninth century, and also found their way into Arabic. Andreopoulos translated them from Syriac into Greek at the end of the eleventh century, possibly at the same time that he translated the *BSP*.[32] They are generally considered to be part of the Aesopic corpus, and similar fables can be found in a variety of other sources. Perry identifies fifteen fables, however, that are unique to the collection. Thus, the collection ascribed to Syntipas is a significant contribution to the study of Greek fables because it expands the Aesopic corpus.[33]

How this collection came to be attributed to Syntipas is unknown. Perry hypothesized that the Syriac collection may have lost the page attributing the fables to Iosepos (Syriac for "Aesop"), the author to whom they are attributed in all

the Syriac manuscripts. Then, the proximity of the *BSP* to the *Fables* in the Syriac manuscripts may have led to the collection being attributed to Syntipas.[34] What seems clear is that, even in Syriac versions, the story of Syntipas was being collected together with Aesop's fables. Andreopoulos, moreover, appears to have accepted the attribution and, as mentioned above, considered Syntipas to be a "fable writer" along the lines of Aesop.

About These Texts and Translations

Our text and translation of the *BSP* are based on the edition of Viktor Jernstedt and Petr Nikitin (1912). Our text and translation of the Fables are based on the edition of Ben Edwin Perry (1952), with occasional preference given to the edition of August Hausrath and Herbert Hunger (1959). We have made few changes to these texts, which are documented in the Notes to the Texts. Biblical references are to *Septuagint with Apocrypha,* ed. L. C. Brenton (Peabody, Mass., 1986), and *The Majority Text Greek New Testament Interlinear,* ed. A. L. Farstad and others (Nashville, 2007). The Notes to the Translations do not constitute a full commentary, but are intended to clarify details and explain unusual features of the text. The Concordance lists the *Fables* and their corresponding numbers in Perry's catalog.

In rendering the *BSP* and *Fables* in English, we have attempted to preserve the sense of Andreopoulos's style and vocabulary. We have occasionally and very cautiously made use of the *Retractatio,* which Jernstedt–Nikitin print in parallel with the *BSP,* to interpret Andreopoulos's meaning, recognizing that the *Retractatio* is not merely a crib to the *BSP*

but a new work in its own right. In applying pronouns to animals in the *Fables,* we have preserved the gender from the Greek, rather than using "it" as is common in English.

We have benefited from examining Laura Gibbs, trans., *Aesop's Fables* (Oxford, 2002), and the brief selections of the *BSP* translated in Toth, "Authorship" (see n. 13). Raffaella Cribiore and Malcolm Heath kindly helped us better understand ancient and medieval education. We would like to thank Peter Miller and Rebecca Moorman for offering helpful advice on various aspects of the translation and notes, Kenneth Elliott for checking the Greek text, and John Kee for preparing the index. Louis-Patrick St-Pierre, a research fellow at Queen's University, helped review the proofs. We also thank Alice-Mary Talbot and Stratis Papaioannou for supporting this project in its early stages and offering countless improvements to the translation. We are especially grateful to Richard Greenfield and Alexander Alexakis for their meticulous editing that greatly improved the text and translation, and for their wise guidance in seeing the volume through to final publication. Any mistakes that remain are our own.

We dedicated our Dumbarton Oaks Medieval Library translation of Nikephoros Basilakes to the memories of our late fathers. In dedicating this volume to our beloved living mothers, Alice Beneker and Brenda Gibson, we blushingly apologize for the rampant misogyny and bawdy content of the *BSP,* and invite them instead to enjoy the *Fables,* omitting numbers 41 and 54.

Notes

1 This poem appears in the manuscript *Mosquensis Bibliothecae Synodalis gr.* 298 (*Vladimir* 436), which contains both the *BSP* and the *Fables.*

2 On the history of Melitene, see Bernd Andreas Vest, *Geschichte der Stadt Melitene und der umliegenden Gebiete: Vom Vorabend der arabischen bis zum Abschluß der türkischen Eroberung (um 600–1124)* (Hamburg, 2007). On the career of Gabriel, we follow Christopher MacEvitt, *The Crusades and the Christian World of the East: Rough Tolerance* (Philadelphia, 2008), 76–78, and Peter Frankopan, *The First Crusade: The Call from the East* (Cambridge, Mass., 2012), 50–55.

3 Alexander Beihammer, *Byzantium and the Emergence of Muslim-Turkish Anatolia, ca. 1040–1130* (London, 2017), 288; Frankopan, *First Crusade,* 55n65.

4 Christopher MacEvitt, "The Afterlife of Edessa: Remembering Frankish Rule, 1144 and After," in *Syria in Crusader Times: Conflict and Co-Existence,* ed. C. Hillenbrand (Edinburgh, 2020): 86–102, at 87–88.

5 Beihammer, *Byzantium,* 288.

6 MacEvitt, *The Crusades,* 77.

7 On the dependence of a *grammatikos* upon a patron, see Margaret Alexiou, "The Poverty of *Écriture* and the Craft of Writing: Towards a Reappraisal of the Prodromic Poems," *Byzantine and Modern Greek Studies* 10 (1986): 1–40, at 30.

8 Athanasios Markopoulos, "In Search for 'Higher Education' in Byzantium," *Recueil des travaux de l'Institut d'études byzantines* 50 (2013): 29–44, at 30.

9 Robert Browning, "Literacy in the Byzantine World," *Byzantine and Modern Greek Studies* 4 (1978): 39–54, at 46–47.

10 Markopoulos, "Higher Education," esp. 35–36. On Byzantine education in general, see Athanasios Markopoulos, "Education," in *The Oxford Handbook of Byzantine Studies,* ed. E. Jeffreys, J. Haldon, and R. Cormack (Oxford, 2008), 785–95, with further bibliography.

11 Charis Messis and Stratis Papaioannou, "Translations I: From Other Languages into Greek, III. Arabic," in *The Oxford Handbook of Byzantine Literature,* ed. S. Papaioannou (Oxford and New York, forthcoming). The turbulent situation in eastern Asia Minor may also have slowed their circulation beyond Melitene.

12 Ben Edwin Perry, *Studies in the Text History of the Life and Fables of Aesop* (Haverford, Pa., 1936), 185–90.

13 Ben Edwin Perry, *Aesopica: A Series of Texts Relating to Aesop or Ascribed to Him or Closely Connected with the Literary Tradition That Bears His Name,* vol. 1, *Greek and Latin Texts* (Urbana, Ill., 1952), 515–20. Perry's attribution is accepted by Laura Gibbs, trans., *Aesop's Fables* (Oxford, 2002), xxiv; and Ida Toth, "Authorship and Authority in the *Book of the Philosopher Syntipas,*" in *The Author in Middle Byzantine Literature: Modes, Functions, Identities,* ed. A. Pizzone (Boston and Berlin, 2014), 87–102, at 89n5.

14 For example, in the manuscript *Mosquensis Bibliothecae Synodalis gr.* 298 (*Vladimir* 436), the oldest extant copy of *BSP* and *Fables*. See Messis and Papaioannou, "Translations I," appendix.

15 Aesop is introduced as a "fable-story writer" (*logomythopoios*) in the anonymous *Life of Aesop 1* (in the Westermann recension, ed. Perry, *Aesopica,* 81–107).

16 Toth, "Authorship," 95.

17 On Mousos, see Toth, "Authorship," 95n15; Ben Edwin Perry, "The Origin of the Book of Sindbad," *Fabula* 3 (1959): 1–94, at 32–34. Perry, "Origin," 37–58, demolished the view of some earlier scholars that the *BSP* was Indian (Sanskrit) in origin. Stephen Belcher, "The Diffusion of the Book of Sindbād," *Fabula* 28 (1987): 34–58, at 48–49, suggests that the original may have been composed in Arabic rather than in Persian, but was inspired by or compiled from various Persian oral or written sources.

18 Messis and Papaioannou, "Translations I," noting the confusion of ethnic, religious, and linguistic nomenclature in the period, suggest that Andreopoulos's "Syrian" source may have been written in Arabic.

19 Ida Toth, "Fighting with Tales: 2 The Byzantine *Book of Syntipas the Philosopher,*" in *Fictional Storytelling in the Medieval Eastern Mediterranean and Beyond,* ed. C. Cupane and B. Krönung (Leiden and Boston, 2016), 380–400, at 387–91; Sebastian Brock, "Greek into Syriac and Syriac into Greek," *Journal of the Syriac Academy* 3 (1977): 1–17 (repr. in Sebastian Brock, *Syriac Perspectives on Late Antiquity* [London, 1984], chapter 2).

20 Toth, "Authorship," 94.

21 For discussion and criticism, see Perry, "Origin," 59–60.

22 Toth, "Authorship," 94–95, 100–101.

23 See Bettina Krönung, "Fighting with Tales: 1 The Arabic *Book of Sindbad*

the Philosopher," in Cupane and Krönung, *Fictional Storytelling,* 365–79, at 366, for the list of manuscripts. On the spread of the Syntipas story, see in general Krönung, "Fighting with Tales: 1," and Belcher, "Diffusion."

24 Perry, "Origin," 58. For a detailed comparison of the frame tale in the extant eastern versions, see Perry, "Origin," 66–84. For a concordance of the interior tales, see Krönung, "Fighting with Tales: 1," 378.

25 Andreopoulos's Greek translation is the oldest extant version of the *BSP* to refer to both Syntipas and the seven philosophers as "philosophers"; see Toth, "Fighting with Tales: 2," 391n32.

26 Perry, "Origin," 91, with further bibliography. Evidence for Greek conceptions of seven wise men is strongest in the fourth century BCE; for early traces and eastern influences of this phenomenon, see Richard P. Martin, "The Seven Sages as Performers of Wisdom," in *Cultural Poetics in Archaic Greece: Cult, Performance, Politics,* ed. C. Dougherty and L. Kurke (New York and Oxford, 1998), 108–28.

27 Perry, "Origin," 90.

28 Ben Edwin Perry, *Secundus the Silent Philosopher: The Greek Life of Secundus* (Ithaca, 1964), 1, 62. For critical discussion of Perry's arguments, see Belcher, "Diffusion," 34, 39.

29 She is called his stepmother in the prologue to the *BSP* and in sections 9–10; his birth mother is still alive (9).

30 Belcher, "Diffusion," 49–55.

31 Bonnie D. Irwin, "What's in a Frame? The Medieval Textualization of Traditional Storytelling," *Oral Tradition* 10 (1995): 27–53, at 28; see also H. Porter Abbott, *The Cambridge Introduction to Narrative,* 2nd ed. (2008), 28–30. For discussion of the framing of the *BSP* specifically, see Perry, "Origin," 16–17; Toth, "Authorship," 95–99.

32 On the *Fables of Syntipas,* see Gibbs, *Aesop's Fables,* xxiv; Francisco Rodríguez Adrados, *History of the Graeco-Latin Fable,* vol. 2, *The Fable during the Roman Empire and in the Middle Ages* (Leiden, 1999), 132–35; Perry, *Aesopica,* 511–28; Perry, "Studies," 185–90.

33 See the table at Perry, *Aesopica,* 524–26. The unique fables, which are numbered 401 to 415 in Perry, *Aesopica,* are numbers 4, 6, 10, 11, 16, 17, 19, 21, 30, 31, 38, 45, 48, 49, and 54 in the collection attributed to Syntipas.

34 Perry, *Aesopica,* 517–18, followed by Adrados, *History,* 133.

THE BOOK OF SYNTIPAS
THE PHILOSOPHER

Βίβλος Συντίπα
τοῦ Φιλοσόφου

Ἡ ἀρχὴ τῆς βίβλου ἔνε οὕτως·

Τοῦ μυθογράφου Συντίπα κατὰ Σύρους,
μᾶλλον δὲ Περσῶν τοὺς σοφοὺς λογογράφους,
αὕτη πέφυκεν ἢν βλέπεις δέλτος, φίλε.
Ἢν καὶ συρικοῖς τοῖς λόγοις γεγραμμένην
εἰς τὴν παροῦσαν αὐτὸς ἑλλάδα φράσιν
μετήγαγόν τε καὶ γέγραφα τὴν βίβλον,
τῶν γραμματικῶν ἔσχατός γε τυγχάνων,
Ἀνδρεόπωλος Μιχαήλ, Χριστοῦ λάτρις,
ἔργον τεθεικὼς προστεταγμένον τόδε
παρὰ Γαβριὴλ τοῦ μεγιστάνων κλέους,
δουκὸς σεβαστοῦ πόλεως μελωνύμου,
ὅς ἐστι Χριστοῦ θερμὸς ὄντως ἱκέτης.
Ὃς καὶ διωρίσατο γραφῆναι τάδε,
ὅτι γε μὴ πρόσεστι Ῥωμαίων βίβλοις.
Ἡ συγγραφὴ γὰρ ἥδε τοὺς κακεργάτας
διασύρει μάλιστα καὶ πρὸς τῷ τέλει·
πράξεις ἐπαινεῖ τὰς καλῶς εἰργασμένας.

2   Πρόλογος τοῦ πρωτοτύπου ἤτοι τοῦ ἀντιβολαίου, τῆς
Συρικῆς βίβλου τῆς λεγομένης "Συντίπα τοῦ Φιλοσόφου,"
ἔχων αὐταῖς λέξεσιν οὕτως· "Διήγησις ἐμφιλόσοφος, συγ-
γραφεῖσα παρ᾽ ἡμῶν περὶ τοῦ τῶν Περσῶν βασιλέως

THE BOOK OF SYNTIPAS
THE PHILOSOPHER

The book begins as follows:

This book which you see before you, my friend, is that of the fable writer Syntipas as told by the Syrians, or rather, as written down by the wise Persian authors. It was written in the Syrian language, and then I myself translated and wrote the book in the present Greek version, though I am the least of the grammarians. I, Michael Andreopoulos, a Christian, published this work as a commission from Gabriel, the glory of the nobility, the venerable governor of the city named for honey, who is truly a fervent suppliant of Christ, and who directed that this story be written because it did not exist among the Romans' books. For this book especially disparages evildoers, and, in its conclusion, praises deeds that have been nobly done.

Here is the prologue of the original, namely my exemplar, of the Syrian book entitled "The Book of Syntipas the Philosopher," which reads verbatim as follows: "A story imbued with learning, written by me, about Cyrus, king of the

2

3

Κύρου καὶ τοῦ γνησίου τούτου παιδὸς καὶ τοῦ αὐτοῦ διδασκάλου Συντίπα, ἔτι δὲ καὶ περὶ τῶν τοῦ βασιλέως ἑπτὰ φιλοσόφων καὶ τῆς μιᾶς αὐτοῦ τῶν ἄλλων πονηρᾶς καὶ ἀναιδοῦς γυναικὸς καὶ ἧς τῷ βασιλεῖ κατὰ τοῦ υἱοῦ προέθετο διαβολῆς καὶ σκαιωρίας οἷα τούτου μητρυιὰ τυγχάνουσα. Ἥντινα διήγησιν προϊστόρησε Μοῦσος ὁ Πέρσης πρὸς τὴν τῶν ἐντυγχανόντων ὠφέλειαν."

3   Βασιλεύς τις ἦν Κῦρος ὀνόματι, ᾧ καὶ ὑπῆρχον γυναῖκες ἑπτά. Ἦν δὲ ὁ τοιοῦτος ἄπαις καὶ τέκνων ἔρημος· ὅθεν καὶ παιδοποιίας ἐφιέμενος θερμότατα τὸ θεῖον ἐξελιπάρει τοῦ τῆς ἀτεκνίας λυθῆναι δεσμοῦ. Ἐπὶ πολὺ γοῦν περὶ τούτου δεόμενος ἔτυχεν τῆς ἐφέσεως, καὶ τούτῳ υἱὸς γεννᾶται· ὃς καὶ ἀνατρεφόμενος ηὔξανέ τε καλῶς καὶ ὡς δένδρον εὐ- θαλὲς ἐπεδίδου τῇ ἡλικίᾳ. Τοῦτον τοίνυν τῆς πρώτης ἤδη ἥβης τοῦ τέλους ἁψάμενον διδασκαλείῳ παραδέδωκεν ὁ πατὴρ πρὸς τὸ τοῖς σοφιστικοῖς ἐκπαιδεύεσθαι μαθήμασι. Τριετῆ δὲ διατρίψας ἐν τούτοις χρόνον οὐδὲν τούτων ὅλως ἐκαρπώσατο. Εἶτα διαπορούμενος ἐπὶ τούτῳ ὁ βασι- λεὺς ἔλεγεν ὡς· "Εἰ ἐπὶ μακρούς, τὸ τοῦ λόγου, ἐνιαυτοὺς παρὰ τῷδε τῷ διδασκάλῳ ὁ παῖς μου προσμείνοιεν, οὐδὲν τὸ παράπαν ἐξ αὐτοῦ μαθήσεται· ἀλλ᾽ ἐκδώσω αὐτὸν Συν- τίπᾳ τῷ φιλοσόφῳ, ὅτιπερ ἀκήκοα ὡς μάλα σοφιστικὸς ὁ ἀνὴρ καὶ τῶν ἄλλων ἁπάντων τοῖς λόγοις ὑπερτερῶν."

4   Καὶ ταῦτα εἰπὼν εὐθὺς τὸν Συντίπα μετεκαλέσατο καὶ φησι πρὸς αὐτόν· "Πῶς δοκεῖ σοι καὶ μέχρι πόσου τὸν ἐμὸν παῖδα ἐκπαιδεῦσαι, φιλόσοφε;" Ὁ δὲ ἔφη τῷ βασιλεῖ ὡς· "Τὸν παῖδά σου ἑτοίμως ἔχω ἐπὶ μῆνας ἓξ καὶ μὴ περαιτέρω τὸ σύνολον ἐκδιδάξαι καὶ ἐκπαιδεῦσαι καὶ

Persians, about his legitimate son, and about his son's teacher, Syntipas; and furthermore about the king's seven philosophers and about one of his several wives, who was wicked and shameless, and about the sorts of slander and intrigue that she used on the king against his son, because she was his stepmother. Mousos the Persian first wrote this story for the benefit of his readers."

There was once a king called Cyrus who had seven wives, but he was childless and bereft of offspring. And so, because he longed to have children, he fervently entreated God to be released from the bond of childlessness. Now when he had prayed for this for a long time, he obtained his desire, and a son was born to him. As the boy grew up, he became very strong and increased in height like a thriving tree. Accordingly, when he had just reached the end of his adolescence, his father sent him to a school to be educated in lessons about wisdom. Although he spent three years in his studies, the boy did not profit from them at all. Then the king, who did not know what to do about this, said, "Even if my child should remain with that teacher for many long years, as the saying goes, he will learn nothing at all from him. Instead, I will entrust him to Syntipas the philosopher, because I've heard that he is a very wise man and surpasses all others in his learning."

When he had said this, he immediately summoned Syntipas and said to him, "What do you think is the best way to educate my son, philosopher, and how long will it take?" And Syntipas answered the king, "I am ready to instruct your son in everything for six months and not a day longer,

τοσαύτης ἐμπλῆσαι φιλοσοφίας ὡς μή τινα ἕτερον εὑ-
ρίσκεσθαι τοῦ σοῦ υἱοῦ φιλοσοφώτερον. Εἰ δὲ μὴ οὕτως
ἔχοντα τοῦτον ἐντὸς τῆς διορίας παραστήσω σοι, ἀπο-
λέσθω μου τὸ ζῆν, ὦ βασιλεῦ, καὶ ἡ πᾶσά μου ὕπαρξις τῷ
σῷ κράτει προσγενέσθω· ἄτοπον γὰρ τηλικαύτην εὐθαλῆ
ἐπαρχίαν καὶ τοιοῦτον βασιλέα πλουτοῦσαν, πάσης συνέσεως καὶ ἀγχινοίας ἀνάπλεων, μὴ φιλόσοφον ἄνδρα
κεκτῆσθαι καὶ αὐτὴν δὲ τὴν ἰατρῶν τέχνην ἄκρως ἐξησκη-
μένον· εἰ γὰρ μὴ τοιοῦτος ἀνὴρ ἐν ἐπαρχίᾳ τοιαύτῃ ἐπι-
χωριάζοι, οὐ χρή τινα τὸ παράπαν ἐνδιατρίβειν αὐτῇ· με-
μύημαι γὰρ ὡς οἱ βασιλεῖς οὐδὲν τοῦ καυστικοῦ πυρὸς τῷ
θυμῷ διαφέρουσι καὶ δεῖ τούτοις καὶ φιλοσόφους ἄνδρας
προσομιλεῖν, ἵνα μὴ τῷ ζέοντι τῆς ὀργῆς παρὰ τὸ δέον
τινὰ τῶν ὑπηκόων ἀναλίσκωσιν. Εἰ τοίνυν, ὦ βασιλεῦ,
καθάπερ σοι ἐπαγγέλλομαι τέλειον ἐν φιλοσόφοις τὸν
υἱόν σου ἀποκαταστήσω σοι, χρὴ καὶ τὴν σὴν βασιλείαν,
εἴ τι δὴ καὶ παρ᾽ αὐτῆς ἐπιζητήσω, φιλοτίμως μοι
παρασχεῖν." Ὁ δὲ βασιλεὺς τῷ φιλοσόφῳ ἔφη· "Τί ἂν εἴη
τὸ ἐπιζητούμενον; Λέγε μοι, καὶ εἴπερ μοι πρόσεστιν εὐθέως σοι τοῦτο καθυπόσχωμαι· εἰ δὲ τῶν ἀδυνάτων μοι
ἔσται, οὐκ ὀφειλέτης σοι περὶ πράγματος ἀνυπάρκτου
γενήσομαι." Ὁ δὲ Συντίπας εὐήκοον καὶ καταπειθῆ τῷ
ἑαυτοῦ λόγῳ ὡς ἐν παραδείγματι τὸν βασιλέα καθιστῶν,
"Ὦ βασιλεῦ," ἔφη, "ὅπερ σοὶ παρά τινος οὐ χαίρῃ προσγενέσθαι, μηδὲ σὺ ἑτέρῳ τοῦτο πεποιηκέναι θελήσῃς."
Αὖθις δὲ ὁ βασιλεὺς τῷ τοιούτῳ λόγῳ λοιπὸν συγκατανεύων
καὶ χρησταῖς ταῖς ἐλπίσι τὸν φιλόσοφον ἐπερείδων, "Πᾶν
εἴ τι," φησίν, "αἰτήσει παρ᾽ ἐμοῦ, ἑτοίμως καί σοι δοθήσεται."

to train him, and to fill him with so much learning that no one else will be found to be more learned than your son. If I do not present him to you in this state within the specified time, my king, let me be deprived of my life, and let all my property be forfeited to your majesty. For it would be strange for so great and thriving a kingdom, one that is endowed with such a king who is filled with all intelligence and cleverness, not to possess a philosopher who is also perfectly practiced in the physicians' art. For unless such a man dwells in such a kingdom, no one at all should live there. For I have learned that kings in their rage are no different from burning fire and that philosophers must converse with them so that, when boiling over with anger, they do not wrongly destroy one of their subjects. And so, my king, if I return your son to you perfect among philosophers, as I promise you, then your majesty must generously provide me with anything I request." Then the king replied to the philosopher, "What would you ask for? Tell me, and if I possess it, I will promise it to you immediately. But if it is something impossible for me, I will not become indebted to you for something that I do not have." Syntipas, in order to make the king agreeable and obedient to his word, said by way of an illustration, "My king, do not wish to treat someone else in a way that you would not like to be treated by him." The king, in turn, ultimately agreed with this argument and, encouraging the philosopher with good hopes, said, "Whatever you ask of me, I will readily grant you." And with these

Καὶ τούτων οὕτως παρ' ἀμφοτέρων πρὸς ἀλλήλους λεχθέντων, συμβόλαιον ὁ φιλόσοφος τῷ Κύρῳ ἐξέθετο, ἐν ᾧ δὴ καὶ ἀνατέτακτο ὡς μετὰ μῆνας ἓξ καὶ ὥρας δύο εἰς τέλος δεδιδαγμένος ὁ παῖς τῷ βασιλεῖ παρ' αὐτοῦ ἀποδοθήσεται· εἰ δὲ πλέον τοῦ ἐμπροθέσμου τούτου καιροῦ τὰ τῆς συνθήκης παραταθήσεται, κεφαλικῇ ἐκτομῇ τὸν Συντίπαν ὑποβληθῆναι.

5   Ἐπὶ τούτοις τοιγαροῦν ὁ βασιλεὺς τὸν ἑαυτοῦ υἱὸν εἰς χεῖρας τοῦ φιλοσόφου παρακατέθετο. Παραλαβὼν δὲ ὁ Συντίπας τὸν υἱὸν τοῦ βασιλέως ἐκ τῶν χειρῶν αὐτοῦ ἐπὶ τὴν ἑαυτοῦ οἰκίαν ἀπήγαγεν. Εἶτα ἐν πρώτοις οἰκίσκον εὐρυχωρότατον νεωστὶ αὐτῷ ἐδείματο, καὶ τοῦτον ἔσωθεν εὐκόσμως περιχρίσας καὶ λευκότητι καταλαμπρύνας πᾶν εἴ τι τὸν νέον ἐκδιδάξαι ἔμελλεν ἐν τοῖς τοῦ οἰκίσκου τοίχοις εὐθὺς ἀνιστόρησε. Μετὰ δὲ ταῦτα, φησὶ πρὸς αὐτόν· "Πᾶσά σου ἡ διαγωγὴ καὶ ἡ δίαιτα, ὦ νεανία, ἐν τούτῳ ἔστω τῷ οἰκήματι, ἄχρις ἂν καλῶς ἐκμάθῃς ὅσαπερ ἐν τοῖς αὐτοῦ τοίχοις παρ' ἐμοῦ ἀνιστόρηται." Ἔκτοτε γοῦν ὁ φιλόσοφος τῷ παιδὶ παρεκάθητο, κἀκεῖσε αὐτῷ διόλου συνδιαιτώμενος ἐξεδίδασκεν αὐτὸν τὰ ἱστορηθέντα (ἥ τε βρῶσις αὐτῶν καὶ πόσις παρὰ τοῦ βασιλέως ἐστέλλετο), καὶ τούτου μεγάλως ἐπιμελησάμενος μέχρι τῆς τῶν ἓξ μηνῶν (καὶ μόνων) συμπληρώσεως τὰ τῆς διδασκαλίας ἀπήρτισεν, ὡς μηδεμίαν ὥραν περαιτέρω ταύτης τῆς διορίας τὸ πέρας αὐτῶν παρατεῖναι. Καὶ δὴ μεμάθηκεν ὁ παῖς ἅπερ οὐδεὶς ἕτερος μυηθῆναι δύναται.

6   Πρὸ γοῦν μιᾶς ἡμέρας τοῦ ἐμπροθέσμου καιροῦ ἐμηνύθη τῷ φιλοσόφῳ παρὰ τοῦ βασιλέως λέγοντος· "Τί

words exchanged by both parties, the philosopher set before Cyrus a contract in which it was stipulated that the boy, having been completely educated, would be returned by Syntipas to the king after six months and two hours; but if what he contracted to do was prolonged beyond this prescribed time, Syntipas would be subject to beheading.

And so, on these terms the king placed his son in the 5 hands of the philosopher, and Syntipas received the king's son from his father's hands and led him off to his own house. First of all, he constructed a new, very spacious room for him, and when he had beautifully painted the interior and made it a brilliant white, he immediately sketched on the walls of the room everything that he intended to teach the young man. After this, Syntipas said to him, "You must spend all your time and life in this room, my young man, until you have thoroughly learned everything I have sketched on its walls." And then the philosopher sat down with the boy, and by spending all his time with him there, he taught him what he had written. (Their food and drink were sent in by the king.) After thus devoting a great deal of attention to the boy until the six months (and no more) had passed, he completed his instruction in such a way that he did not prolong its conclusion a single hour beyond the deadline. And indeed, the boy had learned what no one else was able to learn.

Now on the day before the appointed time, the king sent 6 a message to the philosopher, asking, "What is the result of

ἄρα τῶν ὑποσχεθέντων παρά σοί ἐστιν;" Ὁ δὲ ἀντιμηνύει
τῷ βασιλεῖ ὡς· "Εἴ τί σοι ποθητὸν καὶ θυμῆρες καθέστηκεν,
ὦ κράτιστε βασιλεῦ· αὔριον γὰρ τὸν παῖδα ἐνέγκω σοι
ὥρᾳ τῆς ἡμέρας δευτέρᾳ καὶ ὄψει αὐτὸν ὡς ἐθέλει καὶ
ἱμείρεται τὸ κράτος σου." Ὁ δὲ βασιλεὺς ἐπὶ τῇ ἀγγελίᾳ
εὔθυμος λίαν καὶ περιχαρὴς καὶ εὔελπις γίνεται. Λέγει οὖν
πρὸς τὸν νέον ὁ φιλόσοφος· "Ἔδοξέ μοι ταύτῃ τῇ νυκτὶ
συζήτησιν ποιῆσαι τῆς ἀποκειμένης τῇ γενέσει σου τύχης
καὶ περὶ ταύτης ἀκριβῶς ἀστρολογῆσαι, ὡς ἂν εἰ ἔστιν σοι
συμφέρον, οὕτως τῷ πατρί σου παρ' ἐμοῦ προσαχθήσῃ
αὔριον." Τὴν οὖν τοιαύτην ἀστρολογικὴν συζήτησιν ὁ
φιλόσοφος ποιησάμενος ἔγνω ἐσύστερον ὅτι οὐκ ἔστιν
συμφέρον προσαχθῆναι τῷ βασιλεῖ τὸν υἱὸν αὐτοῦ, εἰ
μὴ ἄλλαι ἑπτὰ ἡμέραι μετὰ τὸν ὁρισθέντα παρ' αὐτοῦ
τοῦ φιλοσόφου καιρὸν τῷ παιδὶ ἀναλωθῶσιν· εἰ γὰρ μὴ
κἀκεῖναι παρέλθωσι, κίνδυνος περὶ τὸ ζῆν τῷ παιδίῳ
προσγενήσεται.

7   Ταῦτα γοῦν τῇ νυκτὶ μετὰ τὴν ἀστρολογικὴν συζήτησιν
ὁ φιλόσοφος κατανοήσας συνεχύθη τῇ λύπῃ. Ἰδὼν δὲ
αὐτὸν ὁ τοῦ βασιλέως υἱὸς οὕτω δεινῶς ἀθυμοῦντα ἐπηρώτα λέγων· "Ἵνα τί οὕτω στυγνὸς καὶ κατηφής, ὦ
διδάσκαλε, κατέστης;" Ὁ δὲ Συντίπας τὴν αἰτίαν δεδήλωκε
τῷ παιδί. Καί φησιν ὁ παῖς πρὸς αὐτόν· "Εἰ ἄρα σοι ἀρεστόν
ἐστι καὶ προστάττεις μοι, οὐδὲ παρ' ὅλον ἕτερον μῆνα τῷ
βασιλεῖ ὁπωσοῦν προσφθέγξομαι, ἀλλ' ἐφ' ὅσον βούλῃ
καιρὸν σιωπῶν ἔσομαι." Ὁ δὲ φιλόσοφος πρὸς αὐτόν,
"Ἀλλὰ τῷ πατρί σου," ἔφη, "συνθήκας ἐποιησάμην, ἃς
ἀδύνατόν ἐστι παραβῆναί με τὸ σύνολον· συνεθέμην γὰρ

your promises?" And Syntipas sent this message in reply to the king: "The very thing that you were longing for and that would please you, most powerful king. For tomorrow at the second hour of the day I shall bring your child to you, and you will see him as your majesty wishes and desires." When he received this reply, the king became very cheerful, exceedingly happy, and full of hope. Then the philosopher said to the young man, "I have decided that tonight I will inquire about the fortune that lies in store for you based on your horoscope. I will consult the stars carefully about this, so that I may deliver you to your father tomorrow, if it is advantageous for you." But then, when the philosopher made his astrological consultation, he learned that it was not advantageous for the son to be delivered to the king, unless the boy spent another seven days beyond the time that had been fixed by the philosopher himself. For if those days did not also pass, the boy's life would be in danger.

Now on that same night, after his astrological consultation, the philosopher realized his situation and was overcome by sorrow. When the king's son observed how terribly despondent Syntipas was, he asked him, "Why are you so gloomy and downcast, my teacher?" Syntipas revealed the reason to the boy, who replied to him, "If you like and you tell me to, I will not speak to the king at all for another whole month, but will keep silent for however long you wish." And the philosopher replied to him, "But I have made a contract with your father, which is absolutely impossible

7

αὐτῷ τῇ αὔριον ὑπ' ὄψιν αὐτοῦ παραστῆσαί σε καθ' ὥραν
τῆς ἡμέρας δευτέραν καὶ οὐ βούλομαι αὐτῷ τὸ παράπαν
διαψεύσασθαι. Πλὴν ἐγὼ μὲν τοῦ λοιποῦ κατακρύψω
ἐμαυτὸν καὶ διάγων ἐν τῷ λεληθότι ἔσομαι, σὺ δὲ ὥρᾳ
δευτέρᾳ τῆς αὔριον ἄπιθι πρὸς τὸν βασιλέα καὶ πατέρα
σου, καὶ παράστηθι μὲν αὐτῷ κατὰ τὰς ἡμετέρας συνθήκας,
μένε δὲ σιωπῶν ὑπὸ τὴν ἐκείνου ὄψιν καὶ παντελῶς ἄφωνος ἄχρι τῆς ἑτέρων ἑπτὰ ἡμερῶν παρελεύσεως."

8   Ἕωθεν οὖν πρὸς τὸν πατέρα ὁ παῖς κατ' αὐτήν που τὴν
δευτέραν ὥραν παραγίνεται καὶ τοῦτον ἐπὶ τῆς γῆς προσ-
κυνεῖ. Ὁ δὲ βασιλεὺς ἐγγυτέρω τὸν υἱὸν πρὸς ἑαυτὸν
καλέσας ποθεινότατα τοῦτον ἠσπάσατο καὶ προσφθέγ-
γεσθαι αὐτῷ χαριέντως ἀπήρξατο· ὁ δὲ υἱὸς οὐδὲν ἐλάλει
τῷ βασιλεῖ, ἀλλ' ἵστατο σιωπῶν καὶ ἀφθόγγως τῷ πατρὶ
ἐνατενίζων. Καὶ ὁ μὲν πατὴρ πάλιν τὸν παῖδα ἀποκρίσεως
χάριν ἐπηρώτα, ὁ δὲ παῖς ἄφωνος ὡσαύτως ἱστάμενος
οὐδὲν τὸ παράπαν ἀπεκρίνετο, καίγε τοῦ βασιλέως ὑπὸ
τῆς ἐπὶ τῷ υἱῷ περιχαρείας φαιδρὸν ἄγοντος σελέντιον
καὶ ἐφ' ὑψηλοῦ τοῦ βήματος κεκαθικότος καὶ πᾶσαν τὴν
ὑπ' αὐτὸν σύγκλητον εἰς ἀκρόασιν ὧν ἐδιδάχθη ὁ παῖς
ἑαυτῷ παραστησαμένου. Καταπληττόμενος τοίνυν ὁ βασιλεὺς ἐπὶ τῇ τοσαύτῃ τοῦ υἱοῦ σιωπῇ καὶ ἀφωνίᾳ ἔφη τοῖς
μεγιστᾶσι αὐτοῦ· "Κἂν γοῦν ὑμεῖς τῷ υἱῷ μου προσ-
φθέγξασθε· οὗτος γὰρ ἐμὲ δεδιώς, ὡς ἔοικε, σιωπᾷ." Τῶν
δὲ εὐθὺς τῷ νέῳ προσφθεγξαμένων ἐπαγωγά τινα καὶ
προσηνῆ ῥήματα καὶ ἀποκρίνασθαι αὐτοῖς λεγόντων αὐτῷ
ἐκεῖνος πάλιν ὡς τὸ πρότερον ἐσιώπα. Ὅθεν καὶ στρα-
τιώτας ὁ βασιλεὺς καὶ δραστικοὺς αὐτοῦ ὑπηρέτας εἰς τὴν

for me to break. For I agreed with him to deliver you into his presence tomorrow at the second hour of the day, and I do not wish to lie to him in the slightest. However, I will hide myself away for the time being and will live in secret, but as for you, at the second hour tomorrow go back to your father, the king. Present yourself to him according to our contract, but remain silent in his presence and completely mute until the seven additional days have passed."

The next morning, then, the boy came to his father at al- 8
most exactly the second hour, and prostrated himself on the ground. The king called his son closer, welcomed him enthusiastically, and began to speak kindly to him. The son, however, said nothing to the king, but stood there in silence, speechlessly fixing his gaze upon his father. So, the father once again tried to get a response from the boy, but he stood without a sound as before and gave no response at all, even though the king, overjoyed at the return of his son, was hosting a ceremonial assembly, was seated on a high rostrum, and had brought out his full senate to hear what his son had learned. The king, who was shocked at his son's persistent silence and speechlessness, said to his courtiers, "Perhaps you should address my son, for he is afraid of me, as it seems, and so remains silent." They immediately addressed the young man with encouraging and gentle words and kept asking him to respond to them, but once again, as before, he remained silent. So the king sent soldiers and his agents to search for the boy's teacher, but although they

τοῦ διδασκάλου αὐτοῦ ἀναζήτησιν ἐκπέμπει. Οἱ δὲ τοῦτον ἐπιμελῶς ἀναζητήσαντες οὐχ εὗρον. Πάλιν γοῦν ὁ βασιλεὺς λέγει τοῖς αὐτοῦ μεγιστᾶσι· "Τί ἄρα ὑμῖν εἶναι δοκεῖ τὸ τῆς σιγῆς ταύτης παραίτιον;" Εἷς δὲ τούτων ἀποκρίνεται τῷ βασιλεῖ λέγων· "Ἔοικεν, ὦ βασιλεῦ, ὡς τῷ υἱῷ σου πόματός τινος μετέδωκεν ὁ αὐτοῦ διδάσκαλος, ὥστε δι᾽ αὐτοῦ κραταιότερον τὴν διδασκαλίαν ἐν αὐτῷ παγιωθῆναι, καὶ στοχαζόμεθα ὡς ὑπ᾽ ἐκείνου τοῦ πόματος ἡ αὐτοῦ γλῶττα πεπέδηται, ἢ καὶ ἐκ σφοδρᾶς καὶ ἰταμωτάτης τοῦ μυσταγωγοῦ αὐτοῦ ἀπειλῆς τε καὶ ἐκφοβήσεως."

9   Ἐπὶ τούτοις οὖν τοῦ βασιλέως χαλεπῶς ἀνιωμένου μία τῶν αὐτοῦ γυναικῶν οὕτω δυσχερῶς ἔχοντα τὸν παῖδα θεασαμένη, φησὶ πρὸς τὸν βασιλέα· "Ἐπίτρεψον, ὦ βασιλεῦ, καταμόνας ἐμὲ καὶ τὸν υἱόν σου γενέσθαι, εἴ πως ἐμοὶ τὴν ἐνδομυχοῦσαν αὐτῷ αἰτίαν ἀνακαλύψειεν, ἐπεὶ καὶ πρὸ τούτου εἰώθει ἀνακοινοῦν μοι τὰ ἑαυτοῦ ἐγκάρδια, ἅπερ οὐδ᾽ αὐτῇ ἐφανέρου τῇ μητρί." (Ἡ μέντοι μήτηρ τοῦ παιδὸς καὶ αὐτὴ σφοδρότερον τοῦ πατρὸς τὴν καρδίαν ἐπὶ τῷ υἱῷ ἐτιτρώσκετο.) Φησὶν οὖν ὁ βασιλεὺς τῇ αὐτοῦ μητρυιᾷ· "Λάβε λοιπὸν σὺ τὸν υἱόν μου πρὸς ἑαυτὴν καὶ ὡς δυνατὸν θωπευτικῶς αὐτῷ προσομίλησον, εἴ πως διὰ σοῦ, ὡς ἔφησας, πρὸς τὸ λαλῆσαι κινηθείη καὶ γνῷς κἂν αὐτὴ τί τὸ τῆς σιγῆς αὐτοῦ καθέστηκεν αἴτιον." Ἡ δὲ τῆς χειρὸς τὸν παῖδα κρατήσασα πρὸς τὴν ἑαυτῆς οἰκίαν ἀπήγαγεν καὶ προσομιλεῖν αὐτῷ ὁμαλῶς ἀπήρξατο. Ὁ δὲ παῖς αὖθις τῇ ὁμοίᾳ καὶ πρὸς αὐτὴν σιωπῇ ἐκέχρητο, μηδόλως τοῖς μειλιχίοις αὐτῆς λόγοις ἐκμαλαττόμενος.

searched carefully, they could not find him. Then the king again addressed his nobles: "What do you think is the cause of this silence?" One of them answered the king, "It seems, my king, that your son's teacher has given him a potion so as to fix his teaching more strongly within him, and we surmise that his tongue has been bound by this potion, or by his teacher's vehement and very aggressive threats and intimidation."

While the king was terribly distressed at these events, 9 one of his wives, when she observed that the boy was being difficult, said to the king, "My king, allow me and your son to be alone, to see if he might reveal to me the hidden cause of his silence, since in the past he used to share with me the secrets of his heart that he would not reveal even to his own mother." (The boy's mother, however, was even more severely distressed in her heart over her son than his father was.) Then the king said to the boy's stepmother, "Take my son away with you in private, then, and talk with him using as much flattery as you can, to see, as you have said, if you might move him to speak and learn the reason for his silence." And so, she took the boy by the hand and led him to her apartment, where she began to talk gently with him. But the boy once again kept the same silence with her, and was not softened at all by her sweet words. Then the

Εἶτα λέγει πρὸς αὐτὸν ἡ γυνή· "Πέπεισμαι ὡς ὑπό τινα αἰτίαν οὐχ ὑπάρχεις, φίλτατε· ἵνα τί λοιπὸν ἐπὶ τοσοῦτον σιγᾷς; Ὅμως, εἴπερ τι τῶν ἀδοκήτων ἐπισυμβῆναί σοι δέδοικας, πρᾶγμα λυσιτελὲς συμβουλεύσω σοι, καὶ οὐ πρότερόν σου ἀπόσχωμαι, ἄχρις ἂν τὸ λεγόμενον ἐπ᾿ ὠφελείᾳ τῇ σῇ ἐκπληρώσῃς. Ὃ δέ φημι, τοῦτό ἐστιν· οἶδας ὅτι ὁ σὸς πατὴρ ἤδη τῷ γήρᾳ τετρύχωται καὶ ὅλως ἡ αὐτοῦ καταπέπτωκε δύναμις, σὺ δὲ σφριγᾷς τῇ ῥώμῃ καὶ ἀκμάζεις τῇ νεότητι· εἰ οὖν ἔστι σοι ἀρεστόν, ἐπιβουλήν τινα κατὰ τοῦ πατρός σου ἐκμελετήσω, κἀκεῖνον μὲν διαχειρίσομαι, σὺ δὲ ἀντ᾿ ἐκείνου τῆς βασιλείας ἐπιβήσῃ κἀμὲ εἰς γυναῖκα σεαυτῷ λάβῃς." Ταῦτα τῆς πονηρᾶς τῷ παιδὶ προσφθεγξαμένης σφόδρα ἐκεῖνος ἐπὶ τούτοις ἐχαλέπηνε καὶ τοσοῦτον τῷ θυμῷ καθ᾿ ἑαυτὸν διεταράχθη, ὡς καὶ αὐτῆς τῆς τοῦ διδασκάλου ἐπιλαθέσθαι ἐντολῆς, ἣν αὐτῷ περὶ τοῦ μέχρι ἑτέρων ἑπτὰ ἡμερῶν σιγᾶν δι-εστείλατο. Καί φησιν τῇ γυναικί· "Γίνωσκε, ὦ γύναι, ὡς τό γε νῦν ἔχον μέχρι συμπληρώσεως ἡμερῶν ἑπτὰ οὐδέν σοι περὶ ὧν εἶπας ἀποκριθήσομαι."

10   Καὶ τοῦτο τοῦ παιδὸς εἰρηκότος ἐκείνη περιδεὴς κατα-στᾶσα καὶ πολλῷ συσχεθεῖσα τῷ φόβῳ βουλὴν πονηρὰν καὶ σκαιωρίαν ἐπώλεθρον κατὰ τοῦ νέου ἐπινοεῖται, καὶ ἀθρόως διέρρηξεν ἑαυτῆς τὰ ἱμάτια καὶ τὴν ὄψιν τύψασα μεγαλοφώνως ἐκραύγασεν. Ὁ δὲ βασιλεὺς τῆς βοῆς ἀκη-κοὼς καὶ ἐπ᾿ αὐτῇ διαταραχθεὶς εὐθὺς προσκαλεῖται τὴν γυναῖκα καί φησι· "Τίς ὁ τρόπος, ὦ γύναι, τῆς τοσαύτης σου κραυγῆς;" Ἡ δὲ ἔφη τῷ βασιλεῖ· "Ἐγώ, βασιλεῦ, τῷ υἱῷ σου ἐμπόνως προσομιλοῦσα παρεσκεύαζον αὐτὸν τοῦ

woman said to him, "I believe that you have nothing to hide, dearest one. So why are you keeping silent for so long? Even so, if you really fear that something unexpected will happen to you, I'll suggest something advantageous to you, and I won't abandon you until you accomplish to your own advantage what I have suggested. This is what I propose: you know that your father is already worn away by age and that he has completely lost his potency, while you are vigorous in your strength and flourishing with youth. And so, if you like, I'll contrive a plot against your father and do away with him; then you may ascend the throne in his place and take me as your wife." When the wicked woman had explained her scheme to the boy, he became furious and was so roiled by anger inside himself that he even forgot his teacher's command to remain silent for another seven days. And so he said to the woman, "Know this, woman: I will not respond to you at present about your proposal, but only after seven days have passed."

When the boy had said this, his stepmother, who was 10 anxious and gripped by great fear, conceived a wicked plot and a destructive scheme against the youth. She suddenly ripped her own clothing, struck herself in the face, and cried out loudly. The king heard her cry and was disturbed, and so he immediately summoned her and said, "Why were you screaming like that, woman?" And she replied to the king, "I was talking patiently with your son, my king, and trying to

λαλῆσαί μοι, ἐκεῖνος δὲ αἰφνιδίως ἐπιπεσών μοι ἐνυβρίσαι μου τῷ σώματι ἐπειρᾶτο, ὡς καὶ τὴν στολήν μου δια-σπαράξαι τῇ πολλῇ βίᾳ, ὡς ὁρᾷς, καὶ τὴν ὄψιν μου τοῖς ἰδίοις κατατραυματίσαι ὄνυξι· κἀγὼ μὲν ᾔδειν ὡς ἑτέροις τισὶν ἐλαττώμασιν ὁ παῖς σου κατείχετο, τοιοῦτον δὲ αὐτὸν νενοσηκέναι ἀτόπημα οὐδόλως ὑπετόπαζον." Ὁ δὲ βασι-λεὺς τούτων τῶν ῥημάτων παρ' ἐλπίδα πᾶσαν καὶ προσ-δοκίαν ἀκούσας καὶ καταπλαγεὶς ἐπὶ τῷ παραδόξῳ τῆς ἀγγελίας, χαλεπῶς τὴν ψυχὴν κατὰ τοῦ υἱοῦ διετέθη καὶ παντελῶς αὐτὸν ἀπείπατο καὶ τῆς υἱότητος ἀπεκήρυξεν. Ἐπὶ πολὺ δὲ τὴν καρδίαν νυττόμενος καὶ πικρῶς τῇ ἀθυμίᾳ βαλλόμενος ποικίλους τε καὶ ἀλλοκότους λογισμοὺς ἀνα-κινῶν ἐν ἑαυτῷ κατὰ τοῦ υἱοῦ, τέλος τῇ ἀνίᾳ καταποθεὶς θάνατον καταψηφίζεται τοῦ παιδός.

11   Ὑπῆρχον οὖν τότε τῷ βασιλεῖ σύμβουλοι φιλοσοφώτατοι ἑπτά, οὓς καὶ εἰώθει ἐπὶ πᾶσι τοῖς παρ' αὐτοῦ πραττομένοις συνίστορας παραλαμβάνειν. Οὗτοι τοίνυν ἐνωτισθέντες τὴν ἐξενεχθεῖσαν παρ' αὐτοῦ κατὰ τοῦ υἱοῦ ἀπόφασιν καὶ ὅτι δίχα τῆς αὐτῶν συμβουλῆς θάνατον ἐκείνου κατεψηφί-σατο, συλλογισάμενοι καθ' ἑαυτοὺς ἔγνωσαν ὡς τῷ σφοδρῷ καὶ ὑπερβάλλοντι τῆς ὀργῆς καὶ τῆς λύπης ὁ βασιλεὺς ἡττηθείς, ἐφ' ᾧ τὴν τῆς γυναικὸς κατηγορίαν ἀληθῆ ἐλογίσατο, τεθνάναι τὸν υἱὸν ἀνεξερευνήτως κατ-εδίκασε καὶ ὡς "Οὐ δίκαιόν ἐστιν οὕτως ἀνεξετάστως τὸν βασιλέα διαχειρίσασθαι τὸν υἱὸν αὐτοῦ, καὶ ὅτι ἐσύστερον πικρῶς μεταμεληθεὶς ἡμᾶς," ἔλεγον, "αἰτιάσεται καὶ ὡς ἐχθροὺς μᾶλλον ἀποστραφήσεται, ὅτι μὴ τοῦ ἐγχειρήματος αὐτὸν διεκωλύσαμεν. Φέρε δὴ λοιπὸν μέθοδόν τινα πρὸς

make him speak to me, but then he suddenly attacked me and attempted to rape me, so that he ripped my dress very violently, as you can see, and wounded my face with his nails. I knew that your son was suffering from other defects, but I never suspected that he would be sick with such perversity." The king heard her words, which were contrary to all his hopes and expectations, and was shocked by her extraordinary claim. He became deeply angry with his son, rejecting him completely and renouncing him as his son. Profoundly stung and cast into bitter despair, he turned over in his mind various outlandish schemes against his son. Finally, consumed by grief, he condemned the boy to death.

At that time the king had seven advisors, the most learned of men, whom he was accustomed to consult in all of his undertakings. These men heard about the judgment that the king had pronounced against his son and that, without their advice, he had sentenced the boy to death. And so they consulted among themselves and decided that the king, overcome by the vehemence and excess of his anger and grief, in the midst of which he had reckoned that the woman's accusation was true, had condemned his son to die without an investigation. "It is not just," they said, "for the king to kill his son in this way without examining the evidence. Later, when he has repented, he will blame us bitterly and instead turn away from us as though we were his enemy because we did not stop him from acting. Come now, let us

τὸν βασιλέα ὡς δέον ἐπινοησώμεθα, πῶς ἄρα τὸν αὐτοῦ υἱὸν τῆς τοῦ θανάτου τομῆς ἐξαρπάσωμεν." Εἶτα ἐβουλεύσαντο ἕκαστον αὐτῶν ἐφ᾽ ἑκάστῃ ἡμέρᾳ περὶ τοῦ υἱοῦ προσομιλῆσαι τῷ βασιλεῖ.

12 Καὶ δὴ θάτερος τῶν ἑπτὰ φιλοσόφων, ὁ καὶ πρῶτος, φησὶν ὡς· "Τὴν σήμερον ἡμέραν ἔγωγε τῷ βασιλεῖ παραστὰς τὸν υἱὸν αὐτοῦ κατὰ τὴν ἡμέραν ταύτην τῆς σφαγῆς ἀπαλλάξω." Εὐθὺς γοῦν ἐκεῖνος παραγίνεται πρὸς τὸν βασιλέα καὶ ἐπὶ τῆς γῆς προσκυνήσας ἔφη· "Βασιλεῦ, οὐ δίκαιόν ἐστι τοὺς βασιλεῖς πρὸ τῆς ἀληθείας τι πράττειν."

13 Εἶτα καί τινος ἀπαρξάμενος διηγήματος ἔφη· "Ἦν γάρ τις βασιλεύς, ὃς τοσοῦτον ὑπῆρχεν θηλυμανὴς καὶ φιλογύναιος, ὡς μηδὲν ἕτερόν τι τῶν γυναικῶν ἡγεῖσθαι ποθεινότερον. Οὗτος οὖν προκύψας τῶν βασιλικῶν ἀκουβίτων ὁρᾷ γυναῖκά τινα σφόδρα περικαλλῆ τε καὶ ὡραίαν, καὶ ταύτης ἥλω τῷ κάλλει καὶ σφοδρὸς αὐτῷ πρὸς αὐτὴν ἐντέτηκεν ὁ ἔρως. Ὅθεν καὶ τὴν ἰδίαν ἔφεσιν ἐκπληρῶσαι μηχανώμενος τὸν αὐτῆς ἄνδρα μεταστέλλεται καὶ ἐπί τινα βασιλικὴν ὑπηρεσίαν ἐκπέμπει, αὐτὸς δὲ νυκτὸς πρὸς τὴν γυναῖκα παραγενόμενος εἰς συνουσίαν ταύτην ἠρέθιζεν. Ἐκείνη δὲ συνέσεως καὶ ἀγχινοίας πλήρης τυγχάνουσα καὶ τῇ σωφροσύνῃ μᾶλλον σεμνυνομένη, 'Δούλη μὲν ἐγὼ τοῦ κράτους σου,' ἔφη, 'ὦ δέσποτα βασιλεῦ, καὶ πρὸς τὴν τῶν σῶν προσταγμάτων ἐκπλήρωσιν ἑτοιμοτάτη, ἀλλ᾽ ἐν πρώτοις δέομαι μίαν κἀμοῦ γενέσθαι παρὰ τῆς βασιλείας σου αἴτησιν.' Καὶ τοῦτο εἰποῦσα δείκνυσιν αὐτῷ βίβλον τινὰ τοῦ ἰδίου ἀνδρός, ἐν ᾗ περὶ σωφροσύνης διείληπτο καὶ τῆς τῶν αἰσχρῶν καὶ ἀλόγων ὀρέξεων ἀποτροπῆς, καὶ

contrive some stratagem against the king, as we must, to rescue his son from the mortal blow." Then they planned that each of them on successive days would converse with the king about his son.

Then one of the seven philosophers, the first one, said, 12 "Today, when I come before the king, I will deliver his son from execution for one day." Then he immediately approached the king, prostrated himself on the ground, and said, "My king, it is not right for kings to do anything before they know the truth."

Then he began to tell a story: "There was once a king, 13 who was so crazy about the female sex and so in love with women that he considered nothing else more desirable than women. And once, peeping out from the royal bedchambers, he saw a woman who was very gorgeous and beautiful. He was captivated by her beauty, and a passionate desire for her melted his heart. Then, as a scheme to fulfill his longing, he summoned her husband and sent him on a royal mission while he himself went to the woman by night and began attempting to seduce her. But the woman was very intelligent and clever, and rather prided herself on her chastity, and so she said, 'I am a slave to your majesty, my master and king, and I am fully prepared to fulfill your commands. Nevertheless, I ask first that your majesty grant me one request.' When she had said this, she showed him a book belonging to her husband, which contained chapters on chastity and the rejection of shameful and irrational appetites, and

ταύτην προτειναμένη, Ἀνάγνωθι, βασιλεῦ,' ἔφη, 'ἐν ταύτῃ
τῇ βίβλῳ μικρὸν καὶ ἐξ αὐτῆς κατανόησον πῶς χρὴ τοὺς
κατὰ σὲ βασιλεύειν καὶ κρατεῖν ὡς δέον τῶν ἡδονῶν.' Ὁ
δὲ βασιλεὺς ἀφέμενος τὰ ἐν τῇ βίβλῳ ἐκείνῃ κατανοῆσαι
προσπαίζειν ἀσχημόνως ἐπεχείρει τῇ γυναικὶ καὶ ἀτάκτως
αὐτῆς περιάπτεσθαι, οὐδὲν δὲ τῆς οἰκείας ἀναιδείας ἀπώνατο, ἀλλ' ἐσύστερον ἐκεῖθεν ὑπανεχώρησε μηδὲν ὅλως
ἐπ' αὐτῇ διαπραξάμενος ἄτοπον. Τὸ δέ γε τούτου βασιλικὸν
δακτύλιον τῆς χειρὸς ἐξολισθῆσαν, ὅτε ἀτάκτως τῆς
γυναικὸς περιήπτετο, ὑπὸ τὴν ἐκεῖσε κλίνην ἀποπέπτωκεν,
μὴ εἰδυίας τῆς γυναικός.

14   "Ὅτε δὲ ὁ αὐτῆς ἐπανέκαμψεν ἀνὴρ καὶ εἰς τὸν αὐτοῦ
εἰσελήλυθεν οἶκον, καθεσθεὶς συνήθως ἐπὶ τῆς κλίνης
ὁρᾷ τὸ βασιλικὸν δακτύλιον ὑπὸ τὴν κλίνην κείμενον, καὶ
τούτῳ τοὺς ὀφθαλμοὺς περιεργότερον ἐπιβαλὼν βασιλέως
ὄντως τυγχάνειν παραχρῆμα ἐπέγνω. Καὶ τοῖς λογισμοῖς
ταραττόμενος ἔφη ὡς, Ὁ βασιλεὺς ἐλθὼν τῆς γυναικός
μου κατεξανέστη καὶ αὐτῇ πάντως συνεφθάρη.' Ἔκτοτε
γοῦν δέος αὐτὸν τοῦ βασιλέως εἰσέδυ καὶ τῇ γυναικὶ συγ-
κοιτάζεσθαι οὐκέτι τὸ παράπαν ἐτόλμα, ἀλλ' οὔτε τι πρὸς
αὐτὴν περὶ τούτου λελαληκέναι. Ἐπὶ πολὺ δὲ αὐτοῦ ταύτης
ἀφισταμένου πέμπει πρὸς τὸν ἑαυτῆς πατέρα ἡ γυνὴ καὶ
αὐτοὺς δὲ τοὺς ὁμαίμονας καὶ δεδήλωκεν αὐτοῖς ὡς· Ὁ
σύνευνός μου παντελῶς ἀπεστράφη με.' Ὁ δὲ πατὴρ αὐτῆς
καὶ οἱ αὐτάδελφοι ἅμα τῇ ἀγγελίᾳ ταύτῃ πορεύονται πρὸς
τὸν βασιλέα ἐκεῖνον καὶ καταβοῶσι τοῦ ἀνδρὸς λέγοντες
οὕτως· Ἀγρὸν ἡμῶν, ὦ βασιλεῦ, τῷδε τῷ ἀνδρὶ ἐκδεδώ-
καμεν, ὃν καὶ ἐπὶ πολὺν ἐργαζόμενος καιρὸν νυνὶ τοῦτον

handing it to him she said, 'My king, read a little in this book and learn from it how those like you ought to rule and should master their pleasures in the right way.' The king, however, neglected to learn the lessons in the book and tried instead to joke indecently with the woman and to embrace her lustfully, but his shamelessness got him nowhere. Rather, he later left her house without having accomplished any wicked deed. Nonetheless, while he was lustfully embracing the woman, his royal ring had slipped from his hand and fallen off under the bed without her noticing.

"When her husband returned, he entered his house and 14 sat down on the bed as usual, and he saw the royal ring lying underneath. When he cast his eyes upon it rather curiously, he realized immediately that it actually belonged to the king. Disturbed by this realization, he said to himself, 'The king came here and overpowered my wife and surely corrupted her.' From that point on, he became afraid of the king and he no longer dared to go to bed with his wife at all, nor even to discuss the matter with her. When he had been aloof from her for a long time, the woman sent a message to her father and brothers and disclosed the situation to them: 'My husband has completely rejected me.' As soon as they heard this news, her father and brothers made their way to the king and lodged a complaint against her husband: 'My king, we have given our field to this man here, which he worked for a long time but has now abandoned and, in

καταλέλοιπε καὶ τούτου καταμελήσας ἀποχερσωθῆναι πάλιν ὡς τὸ πρότερον πεποίηκε. Διὸ καὶ δεόμεθα τοῦ κράτους σου, εἴτε τὸν ἀγρὸν ἐργαζέσθω εἴτε ἡμῖν τοῦτον ἀποκαταστησάτω.' Ὁ δὲ βασιλεὺς ἐκεῖνος ταύτης ἀκρο- ασάμενος τῆς ἐγκλήσεως, 'Τί οὗτοι λέγουσι;' πρὸς τὸν ἄνδρα τῆς γυναικὸς ἔφησεν. Ὁ δὲ ἀποκριθείς, 'Ἀληθῶς,' εἶπεν, 'ὦ βασιλεῦ, ταῦτα καὶ εὐλόγως φάσκουσιν· ἀγρὸν γὰρ ἡμῖν ἐκδεδώκασιν, ὅνπερ καὶ καλλιεργεῖν ὅση δύναμις οὐδόλως παρημέλουν· ἀλλ' ἐν μιᾷ τῶν ἡμερῶν ἐν αὐτῷ με ἐργαζόμενον ἴχνεσιν λέοντος ἐντυχεῖν συμβέβηκεν, ἃ καὶ θεασάμενος οὐκέτι τὸ ἀπ' ἐκείνου προσπελάσαι τῷ ἀγρῷ τετόλμηκα.' Ὁ δὲ βασιλεὺς ἐκεῖνος ἀκούσας τῶν τοιούτων ῥημάτων ἔφη τῷ ἀνδρὶ τῆς γυναικός· 'Ἀληθῶς ταῦτα λέγεις, ὦ ἄνθρωπε· ὁ γὰρ λέων ἐν τῷ ἀγρῷ πάντως εἰσελήλυθεν· ἀλλ' οὐ κατά τι τοῦτον ἐλυμήνατο, οὐδ' οὐκέτι ἐκεῖσε εἰσελθεῖν ἐπιχειρήσει. Τὸ λοιπὸν οὖν ὡς τὸ πρότερον κάτεχε τὸν ἐκδοθέντα σοι ἀγρὸν καὶ ἀφόβως ἐργάζου.'"

15   Ταύτην οὖν ὁ θάτερος τῶν φιλοσόφων τὴν διήγησιν τῷ βασιλεῖ ἀνενεγκών, λέγει· "Ταύτην τὴν διήγησιν, ὦ βα- σιλεῦ, τῷ σῷ κράτει παρεισήγαγον, ἵνα γνῷς ἐξ αὐτῆς ὡς οὐ πάντα δὴ τὰ ἑκάστῳ κατηγορούμενα καὶ ὑποπτευόμενα τῆς ἀληθείας ἔχονται, οὔτε χρή τινα διαβολαῖς εὐχερῶς πείθεσθαι καὶ ἀνεξετάστως καταδικάζειν. Καὶ ἄλλην δὲ διήγησιν ἀκουτισθεῖσάν μοι παρίστημι.

16   "Ἀνὴρ γάρ τις ἦν φυλῆς ὑπάρχων τῆς Ἀγαρηνῶν. Οὗτος περιέργως τὰ ἐν τῇ αὐτοῦ οἰκίᾳ καὶ ποικίλως ἀκριβολογῶν

neglecting it, he has made it dry up again as before. So, we ask of your majesty, either let him work the field or let him restore it to us.' When the king heard this accusation, he said to the woman's husband, 'What do these men mean?' The husband answered, 'Truly, my king, they are speaking reasonably. For they did hand over a field to me, which I in no way neglected to cultivate as well as I could. But one day when I was working there, I happened to encounter the tracks of a lion, and since seeing them, I have never again dared to approach the field.' When the king heard this explanation, he said to the woman's husband, 'You say these things truly, sir. For a lion surely did enter your field. But he did not damage it in the slightest, and he will never again attempt to enter it. And so, for the future, as before, keep possession of the field that was given to you and work it without fear.'"

After he told this story to the king, the first of the philosophers said, "I have introduced this story to your majesty, my king, so that you may learn from it that not every accusation or suspicion against someone is true, nor should one readily believe slander or condemn someone without examining the evidence. Now I will present another story that I have heard.   15

"There once was a man from the race of the Hagarenes. In the course of his various and inquisitive investigations   16

ὄρνεόν τι θαυμαστότατον ὠνήσατο ἐνάρθρως φθεγγόμενον, ὅπερ ψιττακὸν οἶδεν ἡ συνήθεια καλεῖν. Καὶ τοῦτο βαλὼν ἐν κλωβίῳ ἐν τῷ αὐτοῦ οἰκήματι ἔθετο καὶ παρήγγειλε τῷ ὀρνέῳ προσεκτικῶς αὐτοῦ τῇ γυναικὶ ἐνορᾶν· 'Καὶ εἴ τι δ' ἄν,' φησί, 'μέχρι τῆς ἐμῆς ὑποστροφῆς ἡ σύζυγος διαπράξηται, παρατήρει τοῦ ἀπαγγεῖλαί μοι.' Οὕτως οὖν τῷ ψιττακῷ παραγγείλας ὁ ἀνὴρ ἐπί τινα ὁδοιπορίαν τῆς οἰκίας ὑπανεχώρησεν. Ἔκτοτε δὲ ξένος τις ἐκεῖσε παραγενόμενος τὴν τοῦ ἀνδρὸς γυναῖκα μοιχεύων διετέλει, συνειδυίας αὐτῇ καὶ τῆς ἐν τῇ οἰκίᾳ δούλης. Ὅτε δὲ τῆς ὁδοιπορίας ὁ ἀνὴρ ἐπανῆκε, προσκαλεῖται τὸν ψιττακὸν καὶ ἐπερωτᾷ αὐτόν, τί ἄρα τὴν γυναῖκα θεάσαιτο πράξασαν. Ὁ δὲ πάντα τὰ τῇ γυναικὶ ἀκολάστως πραχθέντα τῷ κυρίῳ αὐτοῦ ἐξεφώνησεν. Ὁ δὲ ἀνὴρ δεινοπαθήσας ἐπὶ τοῖς ἀγγελθεῖσιν αὐτῷ περὶ τῆς ἰδίας συζύγου οὐκέτι αὐτῇ εἰς κοίτην συνήρχετο. Ἡ μέντοι γυνὴ ὑπέλαβεν ὡς ἡ αὐτῆς δούλη τῷ ἰδίῳ ἀνδρὶ τὰ γεγονότα ἀπήγγειλεν, καὶ ταύτην προσκαλεσαμένη ὀργίλως αὐτῇ καὶ πικρῶς ἔλεγεν ὅτι· 'Ὄντως σὺ τὰ πραχθέντα μοι τῷ ἀνδρί μου δεδήλωκας;' Ἡ δὲ δούλη τὴν ἔφορον ὤμνυε Δίκην ὡς οὐδὲν αὐτῷ περὶ τῆς κυρίας ὁπωσοῦν λελάληκεν· 'Ἀλλ' ὁ ψιττακός,' φησί, 'μᾶλλον τὰ περὶ σοῦ τῷ ἀνδρί σου διετράνωσεν.'

17   'Ἡ δὲ γυνὴ τούτου ἀκούσασα τοῦ ῥήματος καὶ συνεῖσα παρὰ τοῦ ὀρνέου μᾶλλον ἑαυτὴν κατηγορηθῆναι ἐμηχανήσατο ψευδῆ τόν ψιττακὸν τῷ ἀνδρὶ ἀποδεῖξαι. Αὐτίκα γοῦν πρὸς ἑαυτὴν τοῦτον λαβοῦσα παρ' ὅλην τὴν ἐπιοῦσαν νύκτα ἐντὸς τοῦ ἰδίου κλωβίου τοῦτον παρακατεῖχεν ἔνθα δὴ καὶ συνήθως ἡ γυνὴ ἐκοιτάζετο, καὶ δὴ τὰ τῆς μηχανῆς

26

into the goings-on in his house, he bought a most marvelous bird that could speak articulately, which in everyday language is called a parrot. He put the bird into a cage and placed it in his room, ordering the parrot to watch over his wife attentively. 'And if my spouse should engage in any mischief while I'm gone,' he said, 'take notice and report it to me.' Having thus instructed the parrot, the man departed from the house on a trip. Then a stranger arrived and repeatedly committed adultery with the man's wife, whose handmaid was in the house and knew what was going on. When the man returned from his trip, he called the parrot and asked what he had seen his wife doing, and the parrot divulged to his master all of his wife's licentious activities. The man suffered acutely at this report about his spouse, and so he stopped sharing a bed with her. The woman, in turn, suspected that her maid had reported her adultery to her husband. She summoned her and said angrily and bitterly to her, 'Was it really you who revealed what I did to my husband?' The maid swore by Justice which watches over everything that she had said nothing at all to him about her mistress. 'It was the parrot,' she said, 'who told your husband about you.'

"When the woman heard this explanation and understood that she had been accused by the bird instead, she schemed how to expose the parrot to her husband as a fraud. She took the bird to her own room straightaway and kept him in his cage all that night in the place where she herself usually slept. She carried out her scheme against him like

17

ἐπ᾽ αὐτῷ οὕτω πως διεπράξατο· χειρόμυλον γάρ τινα
πλησίον τοῦ ψιττακοῦ διετέλει συστρέφουσα, ἐξ οὗ καὶ
ἦχος βροντώδης εὐθὺς ἀπετελεῖτο· πρὸς δὲ καὶ κάτοπτρον
ἀπέναντι τῶν τοῦ ὀρνέου ὀφθαλμῶν περιέστρεφεν, ὅπερ
δὴ ἀποστίλβον ἀστραπηβόλοις αὐγαῖς ἀφομοιοῦτο. Σὺν
τούτοις καὶ σταλαγμοὺς ὕδατος τοῦ ψιττακοῦ μακρόθεν
κατέσταζεν. Ὁ δὲ ψιττακὸς τούτων οὕτω τελουμένων
ἐδόκει ὡς ἀληθῶς δι᾽ ὅλης τῆς νυκτὸς ἐκείνης ὑετὸν
καταφέρεσθαι καὶ βροντὰς ἀπηχεῖσθαι καὶ ἀστραπὰς
ἀπαυγάζεσθαι. Ἕωθεν οὖν ὁ ἀνὴρ τῆς γυναικὸς ἐπιστὰς
τῷ ψιττακῷ, φησὶ πρὸς αὐτόν· ᾽Τί δήποτε ταύτῃ τῇ νυκτὶ
ἑώρακας;᾽ Ὁ δὲ τῷ αὐτοῦ κυρίῳ ἀντέφησεν· ῾Τῆς νυκτὸς
ταύτης ὁ ὑετὸς καὶ αἱ συνεχεῖς βρονταὶ καὶ ἀστραπαὶ οὐκ
εἴασάν με τὸ παράπαν ἑωρακέναι τί ἄρα τῇ νυκτὶ ταύτῃ
γεγόνει.᾽ Ὁ δὲ ἀνὴρ τούτων παρὰ τοῦ ὀρνέου ἀκούσας
καθ᾽ ἑαυτὸν ἔλεγεν· ῾Ὄντως οὐδὲν τῶν τοῦ ὀρνέου τούτου
ἀγγελιῶν ἀληθές ἐστιν τὸ σύνολον, ἀλλὰ πάντα δὴ τὰ
παρ᾽ αὐτοῦ μοι φθεγγόμενα ψευδῆ καὶ ἀπατηλὰ πεφύκασιν,
ὃ καὶ δῆλον ἐξ ὧν μοι τανῦν ἀποφθέγγεται, ὅτιπερ οὐδὲν
τούτων τῇ νυκτὶ ταύτῃ συμβέβηκεν· οὔτε γὰρ ὑετὸς
κατηνέχθη οὔτε βρονταὶ ἀπηχήθησαν οὔτε ἀστραπαὶ
ἀπηύγασαν. Ὅθεν,᾽ φησί, ῾καὶ ὅσα μοι περὶ τῆς συζύγου
παρὰ τοῦ ψιττακοῦ ἠγγέλη ψεῦδός τε καὶ ἀπάτη τῷ ὄντι
ἐτύγχανον.᾽ Ταῦτα οὖν ἡ πονηρὰ ἐκείνη γυνὴ πανούργως
μηχανησαμένη, ἤδη, βασιλεῦ, ὡς ἀκούεις, τὸν ἄνδρα
ἠπάτησεν καὶ τὴν ἐκείνου φρόνησιν κατὰ κράτος νενίκηκε
τόν τε ψιττακὸν ψευδῆ ἀπέδειξεν, καὶ οὕτως αὐτῇ ὁ ἀνὴρ
διηλλάγη.

this: she continuously turned a hand mill near the parrot, which immediately produced a sound like thunder; in addition, she rotated a mirror before the bird's eyes, which shone like flashes of lightning; and in combination with these things, she sprinkled drops of water on the parrot from a distance. As a result of her actions, the parrot truly believed that rain had fallen all that night, thunder had rumbled, and lightning had flashed. The next day, the woman's husband stood beside the parrot and said to him, 'What did you observe last night?' And the parrot replied to his master, 'Last night the rain and continuous thunder and lightning completely prevented me from observing what was going on during the night.' When the man heard the bird's words, he said to himself, 'In reality, nothing that this bird has reported to me is true, but everything that he has said to me is false and deceptive. This is clear from what he has just told me, because none of those things happened last night: no rain fell, nor did thunder rumble, nor did lightning flash. And so,' he said, 'what the parrot has reported to me about my spouse is in reality false and deceptive too.' That wicked wife, then, maliciously contrived this scheme, and in the end, as you hear, my king, deceived her husband, outwitted him, and exposed the parrot as a fraud. And in this way, the man was reconciled to her.

18 "Γνῶθι τοιγαροῦν, ὦ βασιλεῦ, ὡς οὐδεὶς δεδύνηται κατά τι τῶν πονηρῶν γυναικῶν τὸ σύνολον περιγίνεσθαι." Τούτων ὁ βασιλεὺς Κῦρος παρὰ τοῦ θατέρου συμβούλου τε καὶ φιλοσόφου ἀκηκοὼς εὐθὺς ἀναβάλλεται τὴν ἀπόφασιν, μᾶλλον δὲ αὐτὴν ἀνατρέπει καὶ κελεύει μὴ ἀναιρεθῆναι τὸν υἱὸν αὐτοῦ.

19 Ἡ μέντοι τοῦ βασιλέως πονηροτάτη παλλακὴ τῇ ἐπαύριον πάλιν πρὸς αὐτὸν παραγεναμένη καὶ παραστᾶσα τούτῳ σὺν δάκρυσιν ἡ κατάρατος ἔλεγεν· "Οὐ πρέπον ἐστίν, ὦ βασιλεῦ, τὸν ἅπαξ γεγονότα κατάδικον καὶ τοῦ θανάτου ἔνοχον μὴ εὐθὺς ἀπολέσθαι· εἰ γὰρ μὴ τὸν τοιοῦτον ἀναιρεῖσθαι προστάττεις, οὐδεὶς ἔσται πεποιθὼς ἐπὶ τὴν τοῦ κράτους σου δικαιοσύνην.

20 "Ἦν γάρ τις γναφεὺς ἀνήρ, ὃς ἔν τινι πλύνων ποταμῷ εἶχεν σὺν αὐτῷ καὶ τὸν υἱὸν αὐτοῦ. Ὁ δέ γε τούτου υἱὸς ἐν τοῖς ὕδασι τοῦ ποταμοῦ παίζων καὶ νηχόμενος διετέλει, εὐθὺς δὲ αὐτὸν τὰ ὕδατα κατακλύζοντα ἀπέπνιγον. Εἰσελθὼν δὲ ὁ πατὴρ αὐτοῦ τὸν παῖδα ἐξελέσθαι ἐκεῖθεν ἠπείγετο, σφοδρὸς δὲ τῷ ῥεύματι φερόμενος ὁ ποταμὸς ἀμφοτέρους κατακλύσας εὐθὺς ἐναπέπνιξεν.

21 "Οὕτως καὶ σὺ ἀπολῇ, βασιλεῦ, εἰ μὴ προαπολέσεις θᾶττον τὸν υἱόν σου. Εἰ γὰρ ὑπέρθῃ τὴν ἐκείνου ἀναίρεσιν μικρὸν ὅσον, τραχηλιάσας σου πάντως κατεξαναστήσεται καὶ μετά γε τῆς βασιλείας καὶ αὐτῆς σε τῆς ζωῆς ἀπορρήξει." Τούτων ἀκούσας τῶν ὀλεθρίων ῥημάτων παρὰ τῆς γυναικὸς ὁ Κῦρος πάλιν τὸν υἱὸν ἀποκτανθῆναι διακελεύεται.

"Know, therefore, my king, that no one is able to prevail 18 at all against anything that comes from wicked women." When king Cyrus heard this story from the first advisor and philosopher, he immediately put off his decision, or rather he overturned it and ordered that his son should not be executed.

On the next day, however, the king's most wicked concu- 19 bine came to him once again. Appearing before him with tears in her eyes, the accursed woman said, "My king, once a man has been found guilty and condemned to death, it is proper for him to be killed immediately. For if you do not order such a man to be executed, no one will have faith in your majesty's righteousness.

"For there was once a fuller, who had his son with him as 20 he was washing clothes in a river. This man's son was playing and swimming in the waters of the river, when they suddenly overwhelmed him and began to drown him. The father rushed into the water to rescue his son, but the river, sweeping along with its fierce current, overwhelmed them both and drowned them immediately.

"You will die in the same way, my king, if you do not kill 21 your son first. For if you postpone his execution even for a second, he will surely exalt himself and rise up against you and bring an end not only to your reign but also to your very life." When he heard the woman's deadly words, Cyrus again ordered his son to be killed.

22 Ἕτερος δὲ τῶν ἑπτὰ σοφωτάτων τοῦ βασιλέως συμβούλων ὁ δεύτερος παραστὰς αὐτῷ καὶ ἐπὶ τῆς γῆς συνήθως
προσκυνήσας ἔφη· "Βασιλεῦ, εἰς τὸν αἰῶνα ζῆθι. Ἠκηκόειν
αὖθίς σε κατὰ τοῦ σοῦ υἱοῦ θάνατον ἀποφήνασθαι. Διὸ
καὶ δουλικῶς ἀναφέρω τῷ κράτει σου ὡς εἰ ἑκατὸν σχεδὸν
προσυπῆρχόν σοι παῖδες, οὐκ ἔδει σε πάντως ἕνα τούτων
καὶ μόνον θανάτῳ ὑποβαλεῖν· πόσῳ γε μᾶλλον ἕνα ἔχοντα
παῖδα φιλοστόργως χρὴ τῆς αὐτοῦ ζωῆς περιέχεσθαι; Σὺ
δέ, βασιλεῦ, τοὐναντίον, κελεύεις αὐτὸν ἀναιρεθῆναι,
ὅπου γε δεῖ μᾶλλον συζητῆσαι πρότερον εἰ ἀληθὴς ἄρα
καὶ οὐ δολερὰ ἡ κατ᾽ αὐτοῦ προτεθεῖσα διαβολὴ πέφυκε.
Σκέψαι τοιγαροῦν, ὦ δέσποτα, μήπως ἀδίκως τὸν υἱόν σου
ἀνέλῃς καὶ πικρῶς ἐσύστερον μεταμεληθεὶς σεαυτὸν
ἀνωφελῶς αἰτιάσῃ, καὶ ζητήσεις πάλιν τὸν υἱόν σου μάλα
ἐμπόνως καὶ οὐχ εὑρήσεις αὐτόν. Συμβήσεται γάρ σοι
ὥσπερ τινὶ ἐμπόρῳ συμβεβηκέναι λέγεται.

23   "Φασὶ γὰρ περὶ ἐκείνου ὡς ἐάν τι ῥυπῶδες ἑώρα, εἴτε
τῶν ἐσθιομένων εἴτε δὴ τῶν πινομένων εἰδῶν, οὐδόλως
αὐτοῦ μετελάμβανε. Μιᾷ γοῦν τῶν ἡμερῶν ἐπ᾽ ἐμπορίαν
ἐστέλλετο, καί τινα πόλιν καταλαβὼν ἐν αὐτῇ κατέλυσεν.
Εἶτα τὸν αὐτῷ ὑπηρετοῦντα νεανίσκον ἐπὶ τὴν ἀγορὰν
ἐκπέμπει ὄψα αὐτῷ ὠνησόμενον. Ὁ δὲ ἀπελθὼν ἐντυγχάνει
τινὶ νεάνιδι δύο καθαροὺς ἄρτους ἐπιφερομένῃ καὶ τούτους εἰς ὤνησιν τῷ βουλομένῳ προτεινούσῃ. Τῇ γοῦν
αὐτῶν καθαρότητι καὶ τῷ τῆς θέας ἐπαγωγῷ ἡσθεὶς ὁ
ὑπηρέτης εὐθὺς τοὺς ἄρτους ὠνήσατο καὶ τῷ αὐτοῦ κυρίῳ
ἀποκεκόμικεν. Ὁ δὲ ἔμπορος τούτους φαγὼν ἐνηδύνθη
μᾶλλον τῇ αὐτῶν μεταλήψει, καί φησι τῷ νεανίσκῳ·

Another of the seven very wise advisors to the king, the 22
second one, appeared before him, made the customary
prostration, and said, *"My king, may you live forever.* I have
heard that you have once again condemned your son to
death. As your servant I thus suggest to your majesty that
even if you had nearly one hundred sons, you should not by
any means put even a single one of them to death. But since
you have just one, how much more lovingly ought you to
protect his life? But you, my king, on the contrary, are ordering his execution, whereas you should instead investigate
first whether the slander leveled against him is true and not
treacherous. Therefore, master, consider that you will perhaps execute your son unjustly and then, when you have bitterly repented, will blame yourself to no avail, and though
you will look very hard for your son again, you will not find
him. For what is said to have happened to a certain merchant will happen also to you.

"They say about this merchant that if he ever noticed 23
that any food or drink was unclean, he would never eat it.
Now one day he was traveling on business and came to a certain city, where he stopped to rest. Then he sent his young
servant boy into the marketplace to buy food for him. The
servant went off and encountered a girl who was carrying
two white loaves of bread and offering them for sale to
anyone who wanted them. Pleased by their cleanliness and
their attractive appearance, the servant immediately pur-
chased the loaves and brought them back to his master.
The merchant ate them and was quite pleased with what
he had eaten, and so he said to the young man, 'Buy some of

Ἑκάστην ἀπὸ τούτου ἐξωνοῦ μοι τοῦ ἄρτου καὶ ἄγε μοι τοῦ φαγεῖν.' Ὁ δὲ νέος οὕτω κατὰ τὸ διαταχθὲν αὐτῷ ἐποίει καὶ διόλου τοὺς ἄρτους ἀπ' ἐκείνης ἐξωνεῖτο τῆς νεάνιδος καὶ τῷ αὐτοῦ κυρίῳ ἀπεκόμιζεν.

24 "Ἐν μιᾷ δὲ πρὸς τὴν ἀγορὰν ἀπελθὼν εὑρίσκει τὴν νεάνιδα ἐκείνην μηδὲν συνήθως ἀπεμπολοῦσαν, καὶ πρὸς τὸν ἔμπορον ἐπανακάμψας λέγει αὐτῷ· Γνωστὸν ἔστω σοι, κύριέ μου, ὡς οὐκέτι ἐξ ἐκείνου τοῦ ἄρτου ἠδυνήθην σοι ἐφευρεῖν· νεᾶνις γάρ τις τοῦτόν μοι ἐπίπρασκεν καὶ νῦν οὐδὲν οὐκέτι τοῦ διαπωλεῖν κέκτηται.' Ὁ δὲ ἔμπορος τῷ ὑπηρέτῃ φησί· Κάλεσόν μοι λοιπὸν ἐκείνην τὴν νεάνιδα, ὅπως ἡμῖν διασαφήσει πῶς τὸν ἄρτον ἐκεῖνον μέχρι τοῦ νῦν παρεσκεύαζεν καὶ εἰς τὸ ἐξῆς ἡμεῖς τοῦτον καθιστῶντες τοιόνδε ἐσόμεθα καὶ οὐκέτι τοῦ ὠνεῖσθαι προσδεηθῶμεν.' Ἄγει οὖν παρὰ τὸν ἔμπορον τὴν κόρην ὁ ὑπηρέτης, καί φησιν αὐτῇ ἐκεῖνος· Λέγε μοι, ὦ νεᾶνι, πρὸς αὐτῆς τῆς ἀληθείας, πῶς τὸν ἄρτον ὃν ἐπώλεις τῷ ἐμῷ ὑπηρέτῃ οὕτως ἡδὺν παρεσκεύαζες; Γλιχόμεθα γὰρ καὶ ἡμεῖς αὐτὸν παρομοίως σοι καθιστᾶν, ὅτιπερ ἡδὺς μάλα τῇ γεύσει ἡμῖν ἀποκατεφάνη.' Ἡ δὲ πρὸς αὐτόν, 'Τραῦμά τι,' φησίν, 'ἐνεφύη τοῖς νώτοις τῆς κυρίας μου, περὶ οὗ δὴ πρὸς αὐτὴν ὁ ἰητρὸς ἔφησεν· "Ἄλευρον, ὦ γύναι, καθαρώτατον ἄγουσα καὶ τοῦτο βουτύρῳ τε καὶ μέλιτι φύρουσα ἐπιτίθει σου τῷ τραύματι, μέχρις ἂν αὐτῷ παντελὴς ἡ ῥῶσις προσγένηται." Ἡ δέ γε κυρία μου λοιπὸν κατὰ τὴν τοῦ ἰητροῦ ἐποίει διάταξιν. Ὁσάκις δὲ παρ' ἡμῶν ἐξῄρετο τῆς πληγῆς ἐκεῖνο τὸ φύραμα, αὐτίκα ἀπέρριπτο. Ἐγὼ δὲ τοῦτο μετὰ ταῦτα τῆς γῆς ἐξαίρουσα

this bread for me every day and bring it to me to eat.' The young man did as he was commanded and always bought the loaves of bread from that girl and brought them back to his master.

"One day, however, he went off to the marketplace only to find that the girl was not selling the bread as usual, and when he returned to the merchant he said, 'I am sorry to report, my lord, that I can no longer find any of that bread, for a girl was selling it to me, but she no longer has any to sell.' And the merchant said to his servant, 'Summon that girl for me, then, so that she may reveal to us how she has been making that bread up to now, and in the future we'll make bread like that ourselves, and no longer have to buy it.' So the servant brought the girl to the merchant, who said to her, 'Tell me in all truthfulness, my girl, how did you make the bread that you were selling to my servant so delicious? For we long to make bread like yours, because it was ever so delicious to our palate.' And she answered him, 'My mistress developed a sore on her back, for which the doctor gave her these instructions: "Take the purest flour, mix it with butter and honey, and apply the dough to your sore until it is completely healed again." And so, my mistress followed the doctor's orders, and whenever the dough was taken off her sore, it would immediately be thrown away. But afterward I would pick it up from the ground and use it to make loaves of

εἰς ἄρτους παρεσκεύαζον, καὶ ἐρχόμενος ὁ σὸς ὑπηρέτης
ἐξ αὐτῶν ὠνεῖτό σοι. Νυνὶ δὲ τοῦ τῆς δεσποίνης μου
τραύματος τέλεον ὑγιάναντος οὐκέτι μοι χρεία ἐστὶν
ἐκεῖνόν γε τὸν ἄρτον παρασκευάζειν.' Τούτων οὕτω παρὰ
τῆς κόρης ῥηθέντων πρὸς τὸν ἔμπορον εὐθὺς ἐκεῖνος
πικρότατα μυσαχθεὶς τὸν θάνατον αὐτὸς καθ' ἑαυτοῦ
ἐκαλεῖτο, καὶ διαπορούμενος θεραπείαν ἐπιθεῖναι τῷ
πράγματι καθ' ἑαυτὸν ἔλεγε· 'Τὸ μὲν στόμα καὶ τὰς χεῖράς
μου ἤδη εὐχερῶς ἀπονίψασθαι ἔχω, πῶς δὲ καὶ τὴν κοιλίαν
ἔσωθεν ἐκκαθάρω;'

25   "Οὕτως οὖν, ὦ βασιλεῦ, δέδοικα μήπως καὶ τῷ σῷ
κράτει ὡς τῷ ἐμπόρῳ ἐκείνῳ συμβήσεται, καὶ ζητήσεις ὡς
προεῖπόν σοι τὸν σὸν υἱὸν καὶ οὐκέτι εὑρήσεις." Ταῦτα ὁ
δεύτερος φιλοσοφώτατος σύμβουλος τῷ βασιλεῖ εἰρηκὼς
προσέθετο τοῖς αὐτοῦ λόγοις καὶ τοῦτο ὡς· "Τῶν γυναικῶν
τοὺς δόλους πολλούς τε καὶ ποικίλους, ὦ βασιλεῦ, τυγχάνειν ἀκήκοα. Ἐξ ὧνπερ νῦν μίαν σοι παρατίθημι διήγησιν.

26   "Γυνὴ γάρ τις ἦν ἐραστήν τινα κεκτημένη, ὃς καὶ τῶν
τοῦ βασιλέως εἷς ἐτύγχανε δορυφόρων. Καὶ ἐγένετο ἐν
μιᾷ τὸν ἐραστὴν ἐκεῖνον πρὸς τὴν ἐρωμένην ἀπεσταλκέναι
τὸν ἑαυτοῦ οἰκέτην τοῦ θεάσασθαι εἰ ὁ ἐκείνης σύνευνος
ἐν τῇ οἰκίᾳ πάρεστιν. Ἡ δὲ γυνὴ θεασαμένη τὸν τοῦ
ἐραστοῦ δοῦλον κατέσχε τοῦτον καὶ πρὸς συνουσίαν
αὐτῆς ἐβιάσατο. Ὁ δὲ εὐθὺς αὐτῇ συγγινόμενος ἐχρόνιζεν
πρὸς τὴν ἐπάνοδον. Εἶτα ὁ αὐτοῦ κύριος εἰς ζήτησιν τοῦ
δούλου ἐκεῖσε παραγέγονεν. Γνοῦσα δὲ ἡ γυνὴ ὡς ὁ
ταύτης ἐραστὴς τὰ ἐκεῖσε κατέλαβεν, λέγει τῷ αὐτοῦ

bread, and your servant would come along and buy some of them for you. Now, however, that my mistress's sore has completely healed, there is no longer any need for me to make that bread.' When the girl had explained this to the merchant, immediately he felt bitterly disgusted and began to pray for his own death. Unable to treat his condition, he said to himself, 'I can quite easily wash my mouth and my hands now, but how am I to cleanse the inside of my belly?'

"And so, my king, I am afraid that your majesty will suffer 25 the same fate as that merchant, and you will seek your son, as I said before, but you will no longer find him." After saying these words to the king, the second of his most learned advisors also added this to what he had said: "I have heard, my king, that the deceptions of women are many and varied. I now offer you a story about one of them.

"A woman once had a lover, who was also one of the king's 26 bodyguards. One day it so happened that that lover sent his servant to his mistress to see if her husband was at home. When she saw her lover's slave, the woman grabbed him and forced him to have sex with her. And, of course, because he was having sex with her, his return was delayed. Then his master arrived there in search of his slave. When the woman realized that her lover had arrived, she said to the

οἰκέτῃ· Εἴσελθε σὺ λοιπὸν πρὸς τὸν ἐνδότερον οἰκίσκον.' Καὶ τούτου γενομένου εἰσέρχεται πρὸς αὐτὴν ὁ ἐκείνου κύριος καὶ αὐτίκα ἐπ' αὐτῇ ἀκολασταίνειν ἀπήρξατο.

27 "Ἐκείνων γοῦν ἀλλήλοις οὕτως συμφθειρομένων καὶ τοῦ δούλου ἐνδότερον προσκαρτεροῦντος ἀθρόον ὁ τῆς γυναικὸς ἀνὴρ παραγίνεται. Ἡ δὲ μοιχαλὶς ἐδεδίει τῷ ἐραστῇ ἐξειπεῖν ἐνδότερον αὐτὸν εἰσιέναι, μήπως ἐκεῖνος τὸν ἑαυτοῦ οἰκέτην ἐκεῖσε θεάσαιτο· ὅθεν ἄλλως τὰ καθ' ἑαυτὴν διαθέσθαι ἐπινοησαμένη λέγει πρὸς τὸν μοιχόν· Ἀπογύμνωσόν σου τὴν σπάθην καὶ τῶν ὧδε φάνηθι μετὰ θυμοῦ ἐξερχόμενος καὶ προσποιητῶς καθυβρίζων με, μὴ μέντοι γε τῷ ἀνδρί μου προσφθέγξῃ.' Ὁ δὲ πεποίηκε καθάπερ αὐτῷ ἡ γυνὴ ἐπετείλατο καὶ ξιφηφόρος τῆς οἰκίας ἐξερχόμενος τὴν γυναῖκα θρασέως καθύβριζεν. Ὁ τοίνυν τῆς γυναικὸς ἀνὴρ εἰσελθὼν ἔνθα ἡ γυνὴ ἐτύγχανεν, ἐπηρώτα αὐτὴν λέγων· Τίς ὁ τρόπος τῆς ἐνταῦθα τοῦ ξένου τούτου παρουσίας, ὦ γύναι, καὶ τῆς μετὰ ξίφους πρὸς σὲ αὐτοῦ ὕβρεως;' Ἡ δὲ τῷ ἀνδρὶ ἔφη· Τούτου τοῦ ξένου ὁ δοῦλος, ἄνερ, ἀποδιδράσκων αὐτὸν σύντρομος ἐνταῦθα κατέφυγεν, καὶ παρ' ἐμοῦ ἔνδον κατακρυβέντος ἐκείνου οὗτος ὁ αὐτοῦ κύριος βιαίᾳ χειρὶ πειρᾶται αὐτὸν ἐντεῦθεν ἐκβαλεῖν τε καὶ ἀπολέσαι· ἐμοῦ δὲ αὐτῷ ἀποτειχιζούσης τὴν εἴσοδον ἵσταται μετὰ θράσους, ὡς ὁρᾷς, καθυβρίζων με.' Ὁ δὲ ἀνὴρ πρὸς αὐτήν· Ποῦ ἐστιν ὁ οἰκέτης;' Ἡ δέ, "Ἐν τῷ ἐνδοτέρῳ οἰκίσκῳ τυγχάνει,' φησίν. Ἐξῆλθεν οὖν ὁ ἀνὴρ θεάσασθαι εἰ ὁ τοῦ δούλου δεσπότης ὑπανεχώρησεν καὶ τοὺς ὀφθαλμοὺς τῇδε κἀκεῖσε περιστρέφων οὐχ ἑώρακεν αὐτόν. Στραφεὶς οὖν καλεῖ τὸν δοῦλον

slave, 'Go into the back room.' After this happened, his master came in, and he began to fool around with her straightaway.

"Now while they were thus engaged in their corrupt embrace and the slave was waiting in the back room, the woman's husband suddenly arrived. The adulterous woman was afraid to tell her lover to go into the back room because he would see his slave there. So she devised a different solution: she said to the adulterer, 'Draw your sword and make it look as if you're angrily storming out of here and pretend to curse me, but don't say anything to my husband.' He did just as the woman ordered him, and brazenly cursed her as he came out of the house brandishing his sword. The woman's husband came in to where his wife was and asked her, 'Why was this stranger here, and why was he cursing you while brandishing his sword?' And she said to her husband, 'This stranger's slave, my husband, ran away from him and took refuge with me in fear. After I hid him inside, that one, his master, tried violently to force him out of there and kill him. As I blocked the entrance against him, he stood there insolently cursing me, as you saw.' Her husband said to her, 'Where is the slave?', and she replied, 'He's in the back room.' So, the husband went out to see if the slave's master had left and, looking all around, did not see him. After returning, he

27

καί φησιν αὐτῷ· "Ἄπιθι λοιπὸν ἐν εἰρήνῃ· ὁ γὰρ κύριός σου τῶν ἐνταῦθα μακρὰν γέγονεν." Τότε λέγει πρὸς τὴν ἑαυτοῦ σύζυγον· 'Μεγίστην, οἶμαι, ὦ γύναι, τῷδε τῷ δούλῳ τὴν εὐποιΐαν εἰργάσω.'

28   "Ἰδοὺ τοιγαροῦν, ὦ βασιλεῦ, ἀποδέδεικται τῷ κράτει σου ὡς οὐ χρὴ τὸ παράπαν τοῖς τῶν γυναικῶν ἀπατηλοῖς ὑποσύρεσθαι λόγοις." Τούτων πάλιν ὁ βασιλεὺς παρὰ τοῦ δευτέρου συμβούλου ἡδέως ἀκροασάμενος, μηδαμῶς αὖθις κελεύει τὸν υἱὸν αὐτοῦ ἀναιρεθῆναι.

29   Ἡνίκα δὲ τοῦ προστάγματος ἡ πονηρὰ τοῦ βασιλέως ᾔσθετο παλλακή, παρέστη εὐθὺς αὐτῷ κατὰ τὴν τρίτην ἡμέραν, καί φησιν πρὸς αὐτόν· "Οἱ σοφώτατοί σου δῆθεν σύμβουλοι, ὦ βασιλεῦ, σκαιότατοι μᾶλλον καὶ κακότροποι πεφύκασι καὶ πολλήν σοι τὴν βλάβην ἐμποιῆσαι πειρῶνται." Ὁ δὲ βασιλεὺς ἔφη τῇ γυναικί· "Καὶ πῶς, ὦ γύναι;"

30   Ἡ δέ, "Ἦν γάρ τις," φησίν, "βασιλεύς, ὃς ἐκέκτητο υἱόν, καὶ τοῖς κυνηγεσίοις ἐκεῖνος σφόδρα ἐτέρπετο. Καὶ ἐν μιᾷ φησιν ὁ υἱὸς τῷ τοῦ βασιλέως καὶ πατρὸς αὐτοῦ σοφωτάτῳ συμβούλῳ· 'Αἴτησαι τὸν πατέρα μου καὶ βασιλέα ἵνα μοι ἐπιτρέψῃ πρὸς θήραν ἐξιέναι.' Ὁ δὲ βασιλέως σύμβουλος αἰτεῖται τοῦτο παρὰ τοῦ βασιλέως. Ὁ δὲ βασιλεὺς ἐκεῖνος ἔφησε τῷ συμβούλῳ· 'Εἰ ἄρα συνεξέλθῃς αὐτῷ καὶ σύ, γενέσθω τὸ αἴτημα.' Ἐξέρχεται οὖν μετὰ τοῦ υἱοῦ τοῦ βασιλέως ὁ τοῦ πατρὸς σύμβουλος, καὶ ἀμφότεροι ἐπὶ τὴν θήραν πορευόμενοι ὁρῶσί τινα ὄναγρον. Εἶτά φησιν ὁ σύμβουλος τῷ παιδί· 'Καταδίωξον ὀπίσω τούτου τοῦ ὀνάγρου καὶ μόνος σὺ τοῦτον θήρευσον.' Ὁ δὲ εὐθὺς κατεδίωκε τὸν ὄναγρον. Ἐσύστερον δὲ μονωθεὶς τῶν

summoned the slave and said to him, 'Go in peace now, for your master has gone a long way from here.' Then he said to his wife, 'In my opinion, you have done the greatest kindness to this slave here.'

"See then, my king, that I have proved to your majesty 28 that one should not be seduced even in the slightest by the deceitful words of women." The king again gladly heard these words from the second advisor, and once more ordered that his son should in no way be executed.

When the king's wicked concubine learned of his com- 29 mand, she immediately appeared before him on the third day, and said to him, "Your so-called very wise advisors, my king, are really crooked and malicious, and are trying to cause you great harm." Then the king said to her, "How so?"

And she replied, "A king once had a son who took great 30 pleasure in hunting. One day the son said to the very wise advisor of his father the king, 'Ask my father the king to allow me to go hunting.' The king's advisor asked this of the king, who replied to his advisor, 'I grant his request on the condition that you accompany him yourself.' His father's advisor then went out with the king's son, and as the two of them were making their way to the hunt, they saw a wild ass. Then the advisor said to the boy, 'You chase after this ass and hunt it by yourself.' The boy immediately began to pursue it, but later found himself separated from his fellow

ἄλλων συνθηρευτῶν καὶ μὴ εἰδὼς ὅποι τὸν ἑαυτοῦ ποιεῖται δρόμον εὑρίσκει ὁδόν τινα καὶ ταύτην πορεύεται.

31 "Εἶτα καί τινι νεάνιδι θρηνούσῃ κατ' ἐκείνην τὴν ὁδὸν ἐντυγχάνει, καί φησιν αὐτῇ· Τί, ὦ νεᾶνι, ὀδύρῃ; Καὶ πόθεν ἄρα τυγχάνεις;' Ἡ δὲ λέγει πρὸς αὐτόν· "Ἐγὼ βασιλέως εἰμὶ θυγάτηρ, καί τινι ἐλέφαντι ἐπωχούμην καὶ τούτου ἐξολισθήσασα οὐκ ᾐσθόμην τὸ σύνολον, καὶ ἀναβλέψασα θεάσασθαί τινα τῶν ἐμῶν οἰκετῶν οὐδαμῶς τινα τούτων ἑώρακα. Μετὰ δὲ ταῦτα πλανηθεῖσα οὐκ ᾔδειν ὅποι πορεύομαι, ἀλλ' ἔτρεχον σφοδρῶς, ἄχρις ὅτου τανῦν ἰλιγγίασα.' Ταῦτα οὖν τῆς κόρης εἰπούσης ὁ τοῦ βασιλέως ἐκείνου υἱὸς κατοικτείρας αὐτὴν εὐθὺς ταύτην ἐπεβίβασεν ὄπισθεν. Ἡ δὲ κόρη τοῖς τοιούτοις λόγοις ἤδη αὐτὸν ἀπατήσασα παρεσκεύασεν πλανηθέντα διά τινος καταλύματος διελθεῖν, καὶ λέγει τῷ νεανίσκῳ· Χρεία μοί ἐστι τοῦ εἰσελθεῖν ἐν τούτῳ τῷ καταλύματι.' Τοῦ δὲ καταγαγόντος αὐτὴν τοῦ ἵππου κἀκείνης εἰσελθούσης ἐκεῖσε ἀκούει ὁ τοῦ βασιλέως υἱὸς θορύβου τινὸς καὶ ἀλαλαγμοῦ ἐν τῷ καταλύματι γινομένου. Καὶ ἀπελθὼν προκύψαι καὶ κατιδεῖν τί τὰ ἀκουόμενα, ὁρᾷ τὴν κόρην ἐκείνην ὡς λάμια μᾶλλον ἐτύγχανεν καὶ ὅτι ἑτέραις δυσὶ λαμίαις προσομιλοῦσα ἔλεγεν αὐταῖς ὡς· "Ἰδοὺ ἤγαγον ὑμῖν νεανίσκον τινὰ ἔφιππον.' Αἱ δὲ πρὸς ἐκείνην ἀντέλεγον· Ἀπάγαγε λοιπὸν τοῦτον ἐπὶ τὸ ἕτερον δεῖνα κατάλυμα.'

32 "Ὁ νέος τοίνυν τούτων οὕτω λεγομένων ἀκούων ἐπαναστρέφει εὐθὺς ἐπ' αὐτὸν δὴ τὸν τόπον, ἔνθα τὴν δῆθεν κόρην τοῦ ἵππου κατήγαγεν. Ἐκείνη δὲ πρὸς αὐτὸν

hunters and, not knowing which direction to take, he found a road and followed it.

"Along the road he came upon a girl who was weeping bit- 31 terly and said to her, 'Why are you grieving, my girl? And where are you from?' She replied to him, 'I am a king's daughter. I was riding on an elephant, and I didn't even realize that I had slipped off. When I looked around to find one of my servants, I saw none of them. After that, I wandered about without knowing where I was going, and I kept running hard until I felt faint.' When the girl had said this, the king's son took pity on her, and immediately sat her behind him on his horse. But the girl, having now deceived him with this story, managed to lead him astray to an inn. She said to the young man, 'I need to go inside this inn.' When he had set her down from the horse and she had gone inside, the king's son heard a commotion and loud noises coming from within. When he went to peek in and see what he was hearing, he observed that the girl was actually a lamia and was talking with two other lamias, to whom she said, 'Look, I've brought you a young man on horseback.' But they replied to her, 'Take him away to that other inn.'

"When the young man heard this exchange, he returned 32 immediately to the very spot where he had taken the supposed girl down from the horse. She returned to him quickly

τὸ τάχος ἐπανῆκε καὶ ἐπέβη τούτου ὄπιθεν ὡς τὸ πρότερον.
Ὁ δὲ αὐτὴν σφόδρα ἐδεδίει καὶ ὑπέτρεμε. Καὶ λέγει αὐτῷ
ἐκείνη· 'Τί οὕτως, ὦ νεανίσκε, ὑποτρέμεις καὶ δέδοικας;'
Ὁ δὲ τοῦ βασιλέως υἱὸς πρὸς αὐτὴν ἀντέφησεν· 'Τινὸς
τῶν ὁμηλίκων ἐπιμνησθεὶς τανῦν ἐκεῖνον πτοούμενος
ὑποτρέμω.' Ἡ δέ, 'Ἀλλὰ σύ,' φησίν, 'ἵνα τί μὴ δωρεαῖς τὸ
ἐκείνου θράσος κατακοιμίζεις; Βασιλέως γὰρ υἱὸς εἶναι
λέγεις καὶ χρυσίου δαψιλοῦς εὐπορεῖν.' Ὁ δὲ πρὸς αὐτὴν
λέγει· 'Ἀλλ᾽ οὐ διὰ δώρων ἐκεῖνός μοι σπένδεται.' Αὖθις δὲ
ἡ λάμια πρὸς αὐτόν, 'Δεήθητι τοῦ πατρός σου κατ᾽ αὐτοῦ,'
ἔφη, 'κἀκεῖνός σε τῆς αὐτοῦ κακίας λυτρώσεται.' Ὁ δὲ
νέος, 'Ἀλλ᾽ οὐδ᾽ ὁ πατήρ μου περιγενέσθαι αὐτοῦ δεδύνηται.' Ἡ δέ, 'Λοιπὸν τοῦ Θεοῦ,' φησί, 'κατ᾽ αὐτοῦ δεήθητι
καὶ ἀπαλλαγήσῃ τῆς τούτου σκαιότητος.' Ὁ δὲ τοῦ
βασιλέως υἱός, 'Καλῶς εἶπας καὶ προσηκόντως,' ἀπεκρίνατο
καὶ εὐθὺς εἰς οὐρανὸν τὰς χεῖρας ἅμα καὶ τοὺς ὀφθαλμοὺς
ἀνατείνας, 'Δέσποτα Θεέ,' ἐδυσώπει λέγων, 'δός μοι τῷ
οἰκέτῃ σου κατισχῦσαι τούτου τοῦ πονηροῦ δαιμονίου καὶ
τῶν αὐτοῦ με μηχανημάτων ἐξάρπασον.' Καὶ ταῦτα αὐτοῦ
εὐξαμένου ῥίπτει ἐκείνη ἑαυτὴν κατὰ τοῦ ἐδάφους καὶ τῷ
χοῒ ἐνεκυλίετο, καὶ πειρωμένη αὖθις ἀναστῆναι οὐδόλως
ἠδύνατο. Ὁ δὲ νέος παραχρῆμα χαλινὰ πάντα χαλάσας
ἀκρατῶς ἐκεῖθεν τὸν ἵππον ἐξήλαυνε καὶ τὸ κάκιστον
διαδρὰς δαιμόνιον μέχρι τῆς πατρῴας διασῴζεται οἰκίας,
ἔτι σύντρομος ἀπὸ τῆς λαμίας τυγχάνων.

33 '''Ἐκ ταύτης τοίνυν τῆς προτεθείσης σοι παρ᾽ ἐμοῦ, ὦ
βασιλεῦ, διηγήσεως γνῶθι ἀκριβῶς τὸ σκαιόν τε καὶ ἀπα-
τηλὸν τῶν συμβούλων σου καὶ ὅτι σὲ αὐτὸν φενακίζοντες

and got up behind him as before. Then he became very afraid of her and began to tremble. She said to him, 'Why, young man, are you trembling? What are you afraid of?' And the king's son answered her, 'Just now I recalled one of my companions, and I am trembling because I am afraid of him.' She said, 'But why don't you soften that man's arrogance with gifts? For you say you're a king's son and that you have lots of gold.' And he replied to her, 'But that man will not make peace with me in return for gifts.' In turn the lamia said to him, 'Appeal to your father against him, and he will set you free of his wickedness.' The young man said, 'But not even my father has been able to overcome him,' to which she replied, 'Then appeal to God against him, and you will be delivered from his wickedness.' Then the king's son replied, 'You have spoken well and appropriately.' Immediately he raised his hands as well as his eyes to heaven, and began to say reverently, 'Lord God, grant to me, your servant, to overcome this wicked demon and rescue me from its wiles.' When he had made this prayer, the lamia threw herself to the ground and began to roll in the dirt, and though she tried, she was completely unable to stand up again. The young man immediately slackened the reins and drove the horse pell-mell from that place. He escaped that most evil demon and got himself safely back to his father's house, though he was still terrified by the lamia.

"From this story that I have related to you, my king, you 33 may know well the crookedness and deception of your advisors, and that they trick you with words, wanting in no way

λόγοις τὸ συμφέρον τῷ κράτει σου οὐδόλως ἐθέλουσιν. Ὅθεν κἀγὼ διὰ τὸ τὴν ἐπ᾽ ἐμοὶ καὶ σοὶ τοῦ υἱοῦ σου ἀτοπίαν ἐᾶσαί σε ἀνεκδίκητον γνωρίζω τῇ σκηπτουχίᾳ σου ὡς ἐξ ἅπαντος τρόπου ἐμαυτὴν διαχειρίσομαι." Τούτων πάλιν ἀκούσας ὁ βασιλεὺς Κῦρος παρὰ τῆς γυναικὸς ἀναιρεθῆναι τὸν υἱὸν αὐτοῦ κελεύει.

34   Κατ᾽ αὐτὴν δὲ τὴν τρίτην ἡμέραν παραστὰς τῷ βασιλεῖ ὁ τρίτος τῶν αὐτοῦ σοφωτάτων συμβούλων προσεκύνησε συνήθως ἐπὶ τῆς γῆς, καί φησιν πρὸς αὐτόν· "Βασιλεῦ, ζῆθι εἰς τὸν αἰῶνα. Γινώσκειν ἀξιῶ σου τὸ κράτος ὡς συμβαίνειν τι τῶν ἐλαχίστων πράξεων ἐν τῷ βίῳ εἴωθεν, ὅπερ οἱ ἄνθρωποι μηδαμινὸν τυγχάνον ἐπὶ μέγα πολλάκις αἴρουσι καὶ ὡς ἐξαίσιον διατρανοῦσιν. Καὶ ἄκουσον διηγήσεως τῷ λόγῳ μου συμμαρτυρούσης.

35   "Δύο γάρ τινα περιφανῆ χωρία ὑπῆρχον, ἃ καὶ διὰ μόνον μελίσσιον κηρίον ἄλληλα διώλεσαν." Ὁ δὲ βασιλεύς· "Πῶς; Καὶ τίνι τρόπῳ;" Καὶ ὁ φιλόσοφος πρὸς αὐτόν· "Ἦν γάρ τις θηρευτὴς ἀνήρ, καὶ ἐγένετο αὐτὸν ἔν τινι ὄρει μελίσσιον ἐφευρεῖν βοράδιον, ὅπερ ἐκεῖθεν ὁ ἀνὴρ ἄρας πρὸς διάπρασιν διεκόμιζεν. Ἔτυχε δὲ ἕνα τῶν αὐτοῦ θηρατικῶν κυνῶν συμπορεύεσθαι αὐτῷ. Μετὰ δέ γε τὸ διακομισθῆναι παρ᾽ αὐτοῦ τὸ μελίσσιον ἐκεῖνο βοράδιον ἐντυγχάνει τινὶ τῶν ἐν τοῖς ἐδωδίμοις εἰωθότων ἐμπορεύεσθαι καὶ δείκνυσιν αὐτῷ τὸ τοιοῦτον. Αὐτίκα γοῦν ἐκεῖνος ἐντὸς αὐτοῦ τὴν χεῖρα ἐμβαλὼν ἐκβάλλει μικρόν τι τοῦ μέλιτος· εὐθὺς δέ τι ἐξ αὐτοῦ ἐπὶ τῆς γῆς ἀπεστάλαξε. Καί τις μέλισσα ἐλθοῦσα ἔστη ὡς ἔθος ἐπ᾽ ἐκείνου τοῦ μελισσίου στάγματος. Ἦν δέ γε μία γαλῆ τῷ ἐμπόρῳ

what is advantageous to your majesty. For this reason I myself am telling your royal highness that, if you allow your
son's crime against both me and you to go unavenged, I will
certainly kill myself." When king Cyrus heard these words
once again from the woman, he ordered that his son be
executed.

On the third day, the third of the king's very wise advisors 34
came to him, made the customary prostration on the
ground, and said to him, "*My king, may you live forever.* I think
your majesty should know how it usually goes with the
smallest events in life: though something may be insignificant, people often elevate it to great importance and turn it
into something extraordinary. Hear now a story that bears
witness to my statement.

"There were two eminent villages that destroyed each 35
other on account of a single honeycomb." The king said,
"How? In what way?" And the philosopher said to him,
"There was once a hunter, who happened to discover a beehive on a hill, which he picked up from there and carried off
to sell. One of his hunting dogs was accompanying him. After he had carried off that beehive, he encountered a man
who traded in foodstuffs and showed it to him. Straightaway, then, that man put his hand inside it and pulled out a
little bit of the honey, and immediately some of it dripped
on the ground. Then a bee came and alighted, as they typically do, on that drop of honey. Now that merchant had a

ἐκείνῳ, ἥτις θεασαμένη τὴν μέλισσαν ἁρπάσαι αὐτὴν ὥρμησεν. Ἰδὼν δὲ τὴν γαλῆν ὁ τοῦ θηρευτοῦ κύων ἐπιδραμὼν κατέσχε ταύτην καὶ ἀπέπνιξεν· ὁ δὲ ἔμπορος εὐθὺς τὸν κύνα σφοδρῶς πλήξας ἀπέκτεινε. Παραχρῆμα γοῦν ὁ θηρευτὴς τὸν ἔμπορον ῥάβδῳ ἔτυψεν. Καὶ γέγονεν μεταξὺ τούτων ἰσχυρὰ διαμάχη. Οἱ δέ γε κάτοικοι τῶν δύο χωρίων ἐκείνων ἀκούσαντες τὰ γενόμενα καὶ μεγάλως κατ᾽ ἀλλήλων διαταραχθέντες, ὅτιπερ ὁ μὲν θηρευτὴς ἐκ τοῦ ἑνὸς ὥρμητο χωρίου, ὁ δὲ ἔμπορος ἐκ τοῦ ἑτέρου, ἐπαναστάντες ἀλλήλοις μαχαίρας ἔργον ἐγένοντο.

36 ῾"Ἴδε οὖν, ὦ βασιλεῦ, ἐκ μηδαμινῆς ἀφορμῆς πηλίκα δὴ τὰ δεινὰ ἀπετελέσθησαν. Καὶ νῦν ἐπάκουσόν μου, παρακαλῶ, καὶ μὴ ἐκ ψιλῆς καὶ ἀπατηλῆς σκαιωρίας καὶ διαβολῆς τὸν υἱόν σου ἀσυζητήτως ἀνέλῃς, ἄχρις ἂν τὸ ἀληθὲς περὶ αὐτοῦ σοι βεβαιωθείη. Καὶ ἄλλην δέ σοι διήγησιν ἀκουτισθεῖσάν μοι παρατίθημι.

37 ῾Ἀνὴρ γάρ τις τὴν ἑαυτοῦ σύζυγον ἐπὶ τὴν ἀγορὰν ἔστειλε τοῦ δὴ ἑνὸς ἀργύρου ἐλειόγενες ὠνήσασθαι, ὅπερ σύνηθες καλεῖσθαι ὀρύζιον. Ἡ δὲ πορευθεῖσα ἐφίσταταί τινι τῶν κατὰ τὴν ἀγορὰν ἐμπόρων καὶ δοῦσα αὐτῷ τὸν ἄργυρον ἐξωνεῖται τὸ ὀρύζιον. Ἐκεῖνος δὲ ἔφη πρὸς αὐτήν· ῾Οὐδαμῶς, ὦ γύναι, τουτὶ τὸ ὀρύζιον ἡδύσματος δίχα τοῦ καλουμένου σάχαρος ἐσθίεσθαι εἴωθε· τί σοι ὄφελος λοιπὸν τοῦτο μόνον ὠνησαμένῃ;' Ἡ δὲ πρὸς τὸν ἔμπορον ἔφη· ῾Οὐκ ἔστι παρ᾽ ἡμῖν τὸ τοιοῦτον ἥδυσμα.' Ὁ δὲ πρὸς αὐτήν, ῾Ἀλλ᾽ εἴπερ,' φησίν, ῾εἰς τὸ ἐνδότερον συνεισέλθῃς μοι ἐργαστήριον, καὶ ἐξ ἐκείνου παράσχω σοι.' Ἡ δὲ ἀντέφησεν· ῾Δός μοι πρότερον καὶ εἰθούτως συνεισελεύσομαί

cat, which saw the bee and rushed to grab it. When the hunter's dog saw the cat, it attacked, caught, and throttled the animal. The merchant immediately struck the dog violently and killed it. Then the hunter at once started beating the merchant with his staff, and a mighty struggle broke out between them. And, when the inhabitants of those two villages heard what had happened, they became very upset with each other, because the hunter came from the one village, and the merchant from the other. So they attacked each other and all fell victim to the sword.

"And so, you may see, my king, how such great evils resulted from a trifling cause. Now listen to me, I beg you, and do not execute your son without an investigation, just because of some alleged and deceptive intrigue and slander, before you have confirmed the truth about him. Let me relate for you also another story which I have heard. 36

"Once a man sent his wife to the marketplace to buy grain grown in a paddy, which in everyday language is called rice, for a single silver coin. She went to the market and, going up to one of the merchants, gave him the silver coin and bought the rice. He said to her, 'This rice is not usually eaten without a sweetener called sugar. What good is it, then, for you to buy only the rice?' And she answered the merchant, 'We don't have that sort of sweetener at my house.' 'Well,' he said to her, 'if you come with me into the back room of my shop, I'll give you some.' She answered him, 'Give it to me first, and then I will go inside with you, for I know well the 37

σοι· ἐπίσταμαι γὰρ κἀγὼ τὴν τῶν ἀνδρῶν πανουργίαν.' Ὁ δὲ εὐθὺς σταθμήσας δέδωκεν αὐτῇ ἐκ τοῦ σάχαρος. Ἐκείνη δὲ αὐτό τε καὶ τὸ ὀρύζιον ἐν ᾗ καὶ περικεκάλυπτο ὀθόνῃ ἐνθεῖσα κατέδησε καὶ τὴν ὀθόνην παρέθετο τῷ εἰς ὑπηρεσίαν τοῦ ἐμπόρου ἐκεῖσε προσκαθημένῳ παιδί, καὶ αὐτίκα συνεισῆλθεν τῷ ἀνδρὶ ἐπὶ τὸ ἐνδότερον ἐργαστήριον τοῦ ἐκπληρῶσαι χάριν τὰ τοῦ ἀνδρὸς καταθύμια. Ὁ δὲ ἐκείνου ὑπηρέτης λύσας εὐθὺς τοὺς τῆς ὀθόνης συνδέσμους ἀποκενοῖ μὲν ἐξ αὐτῆς ἀμφότερα τὰ εἴδη, χοῦν δὲ ἀντ' αὐτῶν ἀγαγὼν τῇ ὀθόνῃ ἐναπέδησεν. Εἶτα ἡ γυνὴ θᾶττον ἐκεῖθεν ἐξελθοῦσα, σύντρομός τε ὑπὸ τῆς αἰδοῦς καὶ κατάφοβος τυγχάνουσα, εὐθὺς ἄρασα τὴν ἑαυτῆς ὀθόνην ἐπὶ τὴν οἰκίαν ἐπανέκαμψεν.

38 "Εἰσελθοῦσα δὲ παρὰ τὸν ἴδιον ἄνδρα ἐγγὺς τούτου τὴν ὀθόνην τίθησι καὶ εἰσέδυ ἐνδότερον τοῦ ἀγαγεῖν χύτραν εἰς ἕψησιν τοῦ ὀρυζίου. Ὁ μέντοι ταύτης ἀνὴρ λύσας ἐν τῷ μεταξὺ τοὺς καταδέσμους τῆς ὀθόνης ὁρᾷ αὐτίκα τὸν χοῦν, καί φησι τῇ γυναικί· 'Τί ἐστιν τοῦτο, ὦ γύναι; Χοῦν ἡμῖν ἀπεκόμισας ἢ μᾶλλον ὀρύζιον;' Γνοῦσα δὲ καθ' ἑαυτὴν ἡ γυνὴ ὡς ὁ τῷ ἐμπόρῳ ἐξυπηρετῶν παῖς τὸ δρᾶμα εἰργάσατο, τὴν χύτραν ἐάσασα σινιατήριον τῶν ψιλῶν ἀντ' αὐτῆς κεκόμικεν, ὅπερ ἡ συνήθεια καθαρώτατον κόσκινον ὀνομάζειν εἴωθεν, καὶ λέγει πρὸς τὸν ἄνδρα· ''Εν τῇ ἀγορᾷ, ὦ ἄνερ, πορευομένης μου ὑπό τινος ἵππου λὰξ πληγεῖσα πέπτωκα καὶ εὐθὺς τὸν ἄργυρον ἐν ἐκείνῳ τῷ τόπῳ ἀπώλεσα· διὸ ἐκεῖθεν τουτονὶ τὸν χοῦν συλλέξασα ἤγαγον, ὅπως αὐτὸν σινιάσασα τὸν ἄργυρον ἴσως εὕροιμι.' Ταῦτα αὐτῆς τῷ ἀνδρὶ προβαλλομένης ἐκεῖνος εὐθὺς τοῖς

craftiness of men.' He immediately measured out some sugar and gave it to her. And she put it together with the rice into the linen cloth that she was wearing as a shawl, and after tying up the cloth, she handed it to the servant boy who was sitting alongside the merchant. Then straightaway she accompanied the man into the back room of his shop to fulfill his desires. Meanwhile his servant immediately untied the binding of the cloth, emptied the package of both goods, replaced them with dirt, and bound up the cloth again. Then the woman quickly emerged from the back room, trembling and frightened because of her shame, and immediately picked up her cloth package and made her way back home.

"And after she returned to her husband, she placed the 38 package near him and went into a back room to fetch a pot so she could boil the rice. Her husband, meanwhile, untied the strings of the package and straightaway saw the dirt, and he said to his wife, 'What is this? Have you brought us dirt instead of rice?' When the woman realized what the merchant's servant boy had done, she left the pot and brought out a sifter with fine holes, which in everyday language is called a very-fine-grained sieve, and said to her husband, 'As I was going to the marketplace, I was struck by a horse's hoof and knocked down, and I immediately lost the silver coin in that place. And so, I collected this dirt from there and brought it home, so that I might sift it and perhaps find the coin.' When she had told this story, her husband imme-

λαληθεῖσι πεπίστευκε καὶ αὐτὸς τὸν χοῦν αὐτοχείρως ἐσι-
νίαζεν, ὡς καὶ τὴν αὐτοῦ γενειάδα ὑπὸ τούτου κονιορ-
τοῦσθαι.

39 "Γνῶθι τοιγαροῦν ἐντεῦθεν, ὦ βασιλεῦ, ὡς τῶν γυναικείων μηχανημάτων καὶ τῶν ποικίλων αὐτῶν βουλευμάτων
οὐδεὶς περιγίνεται." Τούτοις τοῖς λόγοις ἡδέως προσσχὼν
ὁ βασιλεὺς κελεύει αὖθις σχολάσαι τὴν ἀναίρεσιν τοῦ υἱοῦ
αὐτοῦ.

40 Ἡ δέ γε πονηρὰ γυνὴ κατ' αὖ τὴν τετάρτην ἡμέραν
πάλιν παρέστη τῷ βασιλεῖ μάχαιραν κατέχουσα τῇ χειρί,
καί φησι πρὸς αὐτόν· "Βασιλεῦ, εἰ μὴ ἀπὸ τοῦ παιδός σου
θᾶττόν με διεκδικήσεις, ταύτῃ δὴ τῇ μαχαίρᾳ ἐμαυτὴν
ἀνελῶ. Πέποιθα δὲ ἐπὶ Θεὸν ὅτι κατὰ τῶνδε τῶν ἐχθρῶν
σου μᾶλλον καὶ οὐ συμβούλων νίκην τοιάνδε δῴη μοι,
ὁποίαν δὴ καί τινι βασιλέως υἱῷ κατὰ τοῦ φιλοσόφου
συμβούλου τοῦ πατρὸς αὐτοῦ βραβευθῆναι λέγεται." Ὁ δὲ
βασιλεὺς λέγει τῇ γυναικί· "Καὶ τίς ἦν ἡ ἐκείνου ὑπόθεσις;"

41 Ἡ δέ, "Ἦν γάρ τις," φησί, "βασιλεὺς καὶ ἐκέκτητο υἱόν,
ᾧ τινι θυγατέρα βασιλέως ἑτέρου περικαλλῆ ἐμνηστεύσατο.
Ἧς ὁ πατὴρ δεδήλωκε τῷ τοῦ παιδὸς φυτοσπόρῳ λέγων·
'Στεῖλον πρός με τὸν ἐμὸν γαμβρόν, ὡς ἂν ἐνταῦθα
ἐκτελέσω ἀμφοτέρων τῶν μνηστήρων τοὺς γάμους, καὶ
εἰθούτως ὁπότε καὶ βουληθῇ ὁ υἱός σου ἀράτω τὴν ἑαυτοῦ
σύζυγον καὶ πρὸς σὲ ἀμφότεροι ἐπανελθέτωσαν.' Ὁ δὲ τοῦ
γαμβροῦ πατὴρ κελεύει αὐτῷ εὐθὺς πρὸς τὸν πενθερὸν
ἀπιέναι.

42 "Εἶχεν δέ τινα σοφώτατον σύμβουλον ὁ βασιλεὺς
ἐκεῖνος καὶ ἐπέτρεψε κἀκείνῳ μετὰ τοῦ υἱοῦ ἀπελθεῖν. Καὶ

diately believed what she had said, and he began to sift the dirt himself, with the result that his beard became covered with dust.

"Therefore, know from this, my king, that no one can 39 overcome the wiles of women or their diverse schemes." The king accepted this argument, and so he again ordered a halt to his son's execution.

On the fourth day the wicked woman again appeared be- 40 fore the king, holding a knife in her hand, and said to him, "My king, unless you avenge me quickly against your son, I will kill myself with this knife. I am confident that God will grant me victory against these advisors, or rather enemies, like the one they say was declared for a king's son against his father's advisor." The king said to the woman, "And what happened with that man?"

And she said, "There was once a king, and he had a son, to 41 whom he had betrothed the very beautiful daughter of another king. Her father communicated with the young man's father, saying, 'Send my son-in-law to me, so that I may celebrate the wedding of the betrothed couple here, and then, whenever your son wishes, let him take his wife and let them both return to you.' And so the father of the bridegroom ordered him to go immediately to his father-in-law.

"Now that king had a very wise advisor, whom he en- 42 trusted to go with his son. In the course of their journey, the

δὴ ἀμφότεροι τῆς ὁδοῦ ἐχόμενοι παντὸς τοῦ συμπαρομαρ-
τοῦντος ὄχλου ἦσαν προπορευόμενοι. Καὶ οὕτω τὴν ὁδὸν
ἀνύοντες ὑπὸ δίψης ὕδατος προσεδεήθησαν, καὶ περιερχό-
μενοι πηγὴν ἐφευρεῖν μιᾷ μόνῃ πηγῇ ἐντυγχάνουσιν, ἧς ἡ
φύσις τοιῶσδε ἦν ἔχουσα· εἴ τις γὰρ ἀνὴρ ἐξ αὐτῆς
ἐπεπώκει, εὐθὺς εἰς γυναικείαν ὄψιν μετεμορφοῦτο. Ὁ
μέντοι τοῦ βασιλέως ἐκείνου φιλοσοφώτατος σύμβουλος
ἠπίστατο πρὸ τούτου τὴν τῆς πηγῆς ἐκείνης συνήθειαν,
οὐδὲν δὲ περὶ ταύτης τῷ παιδὶ διεσάφησε· τοὐναντίον δὲ
λέγει πρὸς αὐτόν· 'Μεῖνόν με παρὰ τῇδε τῇ πηγῇ, ἄχρις
ἂν ἐγὼ μόνος περαιτέρω μικρὸν προελθὼν γνώσομαι
εἴπερ ἄρα τὴν ὁδοιπορίαν ἡμῶν ἐπευθείας πορευόμεθα.'
Καὶ καταλιπὼν ἐκεῖσε τὸν τοῦ βασιλέως υἱὸν πρὸς τὸν
αὐτοῦ πατέρα ἐπανέκαμψεν καί τινα λυπηρὰν ἀγγελίαν
περὶ τοῦ υἱοῦ πλασάμενος ἀπήγγειλεν αὐτῷ λέγων· 'Βασιλεῦ, ὁ υἱός σου, οἴμοι, ὑπὸ λέοντος κατεβρώθη.' Ὁ μέντοι
παῖς τὸν τοῦ πατρὸς πονηρότατον σύμβουλον παρὰ τῇ
πηγῇ προσμένων διετέλει. Εἶτα ἐν τῷ μεταξὺ τῆς δίψης
αὐτὸν σφοδρότερον φλεγούσης ἐγερθεὶς αὐτίκα ἐξ ἐκείνης
τῆς πηγῆς ἔπιε καὶ ἅμα τῇ πόσει εἰς γυναικείαν ὄψιν
νεάνιδος μετεμορφώθη, καὶ διηπόρει τί ἄρα καὶ δράσαιτο.

43   "Φυτηκόμος δέ τις ἀνὴρ ἐκεῖσε παραγενόμενος ἐπηρώ-
τησε τὸν παῖδα λέγων· 'Πόθεν εἶ σύ, καὶ τίνος υἱός; Καὶ
τίς ἐνταῦθά σε ἤγαγεν;' Ὁ δὲ παῖς τῷ ἀνδρὶ ἀπεκρίνατο·
'Ἐγὼ βασιλέως τοῦ δεῖνος τυγχάνω υἱὸς καὶ ἀπηρχόμην
κατ' ἐντολὴν τοῦ ἐμοῦ πατρὸς πρὸς βασιλέα ἕτερον τὸν
δεῖνα χάριν τοῦ γάμους παρ' αὐτῷ ἐκτελέσαι, καὶ προπο-
ρευόμενος τοῦ συνεπομένου μοι ὄχλου μακρὰν ἐκείνου

two were traveling ahead of the whole group that was accompanying them. And thus, as they made their way, they became thirsty and needed water, and as they went around looking for a spring, they found only one, whose nature was as follows: if any man drank from it, his appearance was immediately changed into that of a woman. The king's most learned advisor, however, already knew the character of that spring, but he did not inform the boy about it. On the contrary, he said to him, 'Wait for me by this spring, while I go a little bit ahead by myself and find out if we are making our journey by the most direct route.' And leaving the king's son there he returned to his father. After inventing a sad tale about the son, he reported it to him: 'My king, your son was, alas, eaten by a lion.' The boy, however, continued to wait by the spring for that most wicked advisor of his father. In the meantime, because he was extremely parched by thirst, he got up and straightaway drank from that spring. As soon as he drank, he was transformed and took on the feminine appearance of a young girl, and had no idea what he should do.

"A vinedresser came along and questioned the boy, asking, 43 'Where do you come from, and whose son are you? And who brought you here?' And the boy answered the man, 'I am the son of King So-and-So, and at my father's command I was going to another King So-and-So in order to celebrate my wedding in his kingdom. As I traveled out in front of the group that was accompanying me, I became separated from

γέγονα, εἶτα μονωθεὶς ἀπεπλανήθην, δίψῃ δὲ σφόδρα κατεχόμενος τῇδε τῇ πηγῇ ἐνέτυχον, καὶ ἐξ αὐτῆς πιὼν εὐθύς, ὡς ὁρᾷς, εἰς γυναικείαν μετεποιήθην ὄψιν.' Ὁ δὲ ἀνὴρ ἐκεῖνος τῶν ῥημάτων τοῦ νέου ἀκούσας κατῴκτειρε τοῦτον τῆς κατεχούσης συμφορᾶς, καί φησι πρὸς αὐτόν· 'Ἐγὼ ἀντὶ σοῦ εἰς γύναιον μεταμειφθήσομαι καὶ ἐπὶ μῆνας τέσσαρας τῇ γυναικείᾳ μορφῇ ἐπιμενῶ, ἄχρις ἂν σὺ τοὺς γάμους σου ὡς αἱρετόν σοι ἐκτελέσεις· πλὴν ὄμοσόν μοι ὡς μετὰ τὸ πέρας τῶν τεσσάρων μηνῶν πάλιν ἐλεύσῃ πρός με.' Ὁ δὲ τοῦ βασιλέως υἱὸς ὤμοσε τῷ φυτηκόμῳ ἐκείνῳ ὡς ἐκ παντὸς τρόπου πρὸς αὐτὸν ἐλεύσεται. Ὁ δὲ ἀνὴρ παραχρῆμα εἰς γυναῖκα μετεμορφώθη καὶ ὑπέδειξεν αὐτῷ καὶ τὴν πρὸς τὸ ζητούμενον κατευθύνουσαν ὁδόν.

44   "Μετὰ δὲ ταῦτα τῶν τεσσάρων μηνῶν περαιωθέντων ἐμνήσθη ὁ τοῦ βασιλέως υἱὸς τῶν ἐν ὅρκῳ συνθηκῶν καὶ πρὸς τὸν φυτηκόμον εὐθὺς παραγίνεται τὴν γυναικείαν ἔτι μεταμόρφωσιν ἔχοντα. Εὑρίσκει δὲ αὐτὸν καὶ κατὰ τὴν φύσιν τῶν γυναικῶν ἐν γαστρὶ συλλαβόντα, οἷα τῆς αὐτοῦ γαστρὸς ἡρμένης οὔσης πρὸς ὄγκον. Καί φησιν αὐτῷ ἐξ εὐλόγου τῆς προφάσεως· 'Πῶς ἄρά γε τανῦν ἀντὶ σοῦ εἰς γυναῖκα μεταμειφθήσομαι; Καὶ γὰρ ὅτε με πλησίον τῆς πηγῆς ἐν τῇ γυναικείᾳ μορφῇ εὕρηκας παρθένος ἐγὼ τὸ σῶμα ἐτύγχανον, καὶ σὺ νῦν κατὰ γαστρὸς ἔχεις· πῶς οὖν λοιπὸν κατὰ σὲ γενήσομαι;' Οὕτως οὖν αὐτῶν ἀλλήλοις διαλεγομένων ὁ τοῦ βασιλέως υἱὸς ἐκεῖνον τὸν ἄνδρα τῇ τοῦ λόγου πιθανότητι νενίκηκε, καὶ πρὸς τὸν ἴδιον πατέρα καὶ βασιλέα σὺν τῇ συζύγῳ ἄσμενος ἀνέκαμψεν καὶ δεδήλωκε τῷ βασιλεῖ ὅσα παρὰ τοῦ σοφοῦ—τὴν κακίαν

them; then, finding myself isolated, I wandered off, and while I was very thirsty I came upon this spring. As soon as I drank from it, I was transformed, as you see, and took on a female appearance.' When the vinedresser heard the young man's words, he pitied him for the disaster that had befallen him and said to him, 'I will change into a woman instead of you, and I will keep my female shape for four months, until you celebrate your wedding according to your wishes. But swear to me that after the four months have passed you will come back to me.' The king's son swore to the vinedresser that he would by all means come back to him. The man was immediately transformed into a woman and also showed him the road which led directly where he wanted to go.

"After the four months had passed, the king's son remem- 44
bered the agreement that he had made under oath and immediately returned to the vinedresser, who still retained his
female form. He discovered, however, that he had conceived
in his womb, as a woman naturally would, seeing that his
belly was swollen up. And so he made a sensible suggestion
to him: 'As things are now, how could I be changed into a
woman in your place? For when you found me near the
spring in the form of a woman, I had the body of a virgin,
but now you are pregnant. So how could I become like you?'
After they had discussed the matter with each other in this
way, the king's son won that man over with his persuasive
argument, and he happily returned to his own father the
king together with his wife and revealed to the king all he
had suffered on the journey at the hands of his wise—wise in

μᾶλλον—συμβούλου αὐτοῦ ἐν τῇ ὁδῷ πέπονθεν. Ὁ δὲ βασιλεὺς ἐκεῖνος δεινοπαθήσας ἐπὶ τῇ τοῦ πονηροῦ καὶ σκολιοῦ συμβούλου δολιότητι εὐθὺς αὐτὸν ἀναιρεθῆναι προσέταξεν.

45 "Οὕτως οὖν κἀγώ, βασιλεῦ, ἐπὶ τῇ θείᾳ πέποιθα δίκῃ ὅτι δῴη μοι ἐκδικηθῆναι ἀπὸ τούτων τῶν σκαιῶν σου καὶ σοφῶν τῇ κακίᾳ συμβούλων. Εἰ δ᾽ οὖν, ἐμαυτὴν δια- χειρίσομαι καὶ ἔσται τὸ τοῦ κρίματός μου αἴτιον ἐπὶ σέ, ὅτι γε μὴ ἀπὸ τοῦ υἱοῦ σου ὡς ἔδει με ἐξεδίκησας, ὃς εἰς τοσοῦτον ἀπηνείας κατ᾽ ἐμοῦ ἐτρέπετο ὡς καὶ τῷ σώματί μου ὕβριν πειρᾶσθαι ἐπενεγκεῖν." Αὖθις δὲ ὁ βασιλεὺς τούτοις τοῖς λόγοις συναρπαγεὶς κελεύει τὸν αὐτοῦ παῖδα ξίφει ὑποβληθῆναι.

46 Μετὰ δὲ τὴν τοιαύτην ἑτέραν ἀπόφασιν εἰσέρχεται κατὰ τὴν τετάρτην ἡμέραν πρὸς τὸν βασιλέα ὁ τῶν φιλοσόφων αὐτοῦ καὶ συμβούλων τέταρτος, καὶ συνήθως αὐτῷ προσκυνήσας, "Βασιλεῦ," ἔφη, "ζῆθι εἰς τὸν αἰῶνα. Γνωρίζω τῷ κράτει σου ὡς οὐ χρή τινα τῶν κατὰ σὲ βασιλέων κατὰ συναρπαγήν τι τὸ σύνολον διαπράττεσθαι, ἄχρις ἂν ἐμπόνως τὸ προτεθὲν συζητήσας οὕτως ἐσύστερον τῇ ἀληθείᾳ ἐπισταίη· ὃς γὰρ ἂν μὴ πρότερον μέχρι τῆς ἀληθείας τὸ ἀκουτισθὲν ἐξετάζοιε, συμβήσεται αὐτῷ ὥσπερ τινὶ τῶν βαλανέων προσγενέσθαι λέγεται." Ὁ δὲ βασιλεὺς ἔφη· "Καὶ πῶς γε; Σαφήνισόν μοι."

47 Ὁ δὲ σοφώτατος σύμβουλος τῷ βασιλεῖ ἀπεκρίνατο· "Ἦν γάρ τις υἱὸς βασιλέως, καὶ ἐγένετο ἐν μιᾷ πορευθῆναι αὐτὸν ἐπί τι βαλανεῖον τοῦ περιχρῖσαι ἅμα καὶ ἀπολοῦσαι τὴν σάρκα. Ἦν δὲ ὁ αὐτὸς εὐμεγέθης καὶ πολύσαρκος τῷ

wickedness, that is—advisor. That king was greatly distressed by the deceit of his wicked and crooked advisor, and so ordered that he be executed immediately.

"Thus I, too, my king, am confident that divine justice 45 will grant me to take vengeance on these crooked advisors of yours who are also wise in wickedness. If not, I will kill myself and the blame for my condemnation will be on you, because you did not avenge me against your son as you should have done, when he has turned against me so roughly that he even tried to rape me." And once again, carried away by these words, the king ordered his son to be put to the sword.

After another such decision, there came to the king on 46 the fourth day the fourth of his learned advisors, who made the customary prostration and said, "*My king, may you live forever.* I will tell your majesty that no king such as you ought to do anything at all in haste, but only after he has examined the matter painstakingly and thereafter is certain about the truth. For someone who does not first examine a rumor to determine whether it is true will suffer the same fate as a certain bath attendant." And the king said, "How so? Explain it to me."

Then the very wise advisor answered the king, "There 47 once was a king's son, who happened one day to go to a bath house to anoint and wash his body. Now the young man was very big and fat, so that you could not see his genitals at all.

σώματι, ὡς ἐντεῦθεν μὴ καθορᾶσθαι τὸ παράπαν τὰ τοῦ νέου αἰδοῖα. Τοῦτον οὖν ἑωρακὼς ὁ βαλανεὺς περιπαθῶς ἀπωδύρετο. Ὁ δὲ τοῦ βασιλέως υἱὸς ἔφη πρὸς αὐτόν· Ἵνα τί οὕτως οἰκτρότατα δακρύεις; Ὁ δὲ ἀπεκρίνατο· Ὅτιπερ υἱὸς μὲν βασιλέως πέφυκας, υἱὸν δὲ σεαυτῷ οὐ δυνήσῃ κτήσασθαι· ὁρῶ γάρ σε μὴ τὰ ἀνδρῶν τὸ σύνολον ἔχοντα, καὶ πῶς γυναικὶ συγγενέσθαι σοι γένηται; Ὁ δὲ νέος τὰ ῥήματα τοῦ βαλανέως ἡδέως δεξάμενος δέδωκεν αὐτῷ χρυσὸν ἕνα, φήσας πρὸς αὐτόν· Γινώσκειν σε λοιπὸν βούλομαι ὡς ὁ βασιλεὺς ὁ πατήρ μου γυναῖκά με ἀγαγέσθαι βούλεται, καὶ τοῦτο ὅπερ ἔφης κἀγὼ ἐπιστάμενος διηπόρημαι τὰ μέγιστα, πῶς ἔσται μοι τῇ γυναικὶ ἐκείνῃ κατὰ τοὺς ἄνδρας συναφθῆναι· ἀλλά μοι λάβε τουτονὶ τὸν χρυσὸν καὶ ἀπελθὼν ἔνεγκέ μοι περικαλλῆ τινα γυναῖκα, ὡς ἂν ἐπ᾽ αὐτῇ τὰ τῆς συνουσίας διαπράξασθαι πειράσομαι.᾽ Ὁ δὲ βαλανεὺς κομισάμενος τὸν χρυσὸν ἐν ἑαυτῷ ἔλεγεν· Ἐνέγκω λοιπὸν τῷδε τῷ νεανίσκῳ τὴν ἐμὴν ὁμόζυγον, ἐπειδή, ὡς ὁρῶ, οὐδὲν τῶν ἀνδρῶν ὁ τοιοῦτος πρὸς συνουσίαν κέκτηται.᾽

48   Καὶ ταῦτα συλλογισάμενος, ἀπελθὼν ὁ μάταιος ἤνεγκεν αὐτῷ τὴν ἑαυτοῦ σύζυγον. Ὁ δὲ τοῦ βασιλέως υἱὸς πρὸς ἑαυτὸν τὴν γυναῖκα λαβὼν εἰσήγαγεν αὐτὴν ἔνθα ἡ αὐτοῦ στρωμνὴ παρὰ τῷ βαλανείῳ ἐφήπλωτο καὶ παρ᾽ ὅλην τὴν νύκτα ὡς ἀνδράσι εἴθισται ταύτῃ συνεγίνετο. Εἶτα περὶ τὴν πρωΐαν προκύψας ὁ βαλανεὺς ὁρᾷ τὸν νεανίσκον τελείαν συνάφειαν ἐν τῇ αὐτοῦ γυναικὶ κατὰ τοὺς ἄνδρας πράττοντα, καὶ πικρᾷ τῇ μεταμελείᾳ πληγείς, Δείλαιος ὄντως ἐγώ,᾽ καθ᾽ ἑαυτὸν ἔλεγεν, ὅτιπερ τούτου

When the bath attendant saw him, he was deeply upset and lamented bitterly. The king's son asked him, 'Why are you weeping so pitifully?' And he answered, 'Because you're the son of a king, but you will not be able to have a son yourself. For I see that you don't have any male parts at all, and so how will you be able to have sex with a woman?' The young man was glad to hear the bath attendant's words, and he gave him a gold coin and said, 'Well, I want you to know that my father the king wants me to take a wife, and I too am aware of what you've just said, and I have absolutely no idea how I'll be able to have sex with that woman in the way that men do. So take this gold coin and go bring me a very beautiful woman, so that I may attempt to have sex with her.' But the bath attendant, after he had taken the gold coin, said to himself, 'Well, let me bring my own wife to this young man, since, as I can see, a person like him possesses no male parts with which to have sex.'

"And with this reasoning the fool went off and brought 48 his own wife to the king's son. The latter took the woman off privately and led her to where his couch had been made ready in the bath house, and all night long he had sex with her in the way that men do. Then, when it was almost morning, the bath attendant peeked in and saw the young man having actual sex with his wife in the way that men do. Struck by a bitter sense of regret, he said to himself, 'Truly am I wretched, for I myself am the perpetrator of this

τοῦ δράματος αὐτὸς αὐτόχειρ γεγένημαι.' Οὕτως οὖν τοῦ
ἀνδρὸς τῇ ἀθυμίᾳ τιτρωσκομένου μετὰ μικρὸν ἡ γυνὴ
ἐκεῖθεν ἐξέρχεται· καί φησιν πρὸς αὐτὴν ὁ ματαιόφρων
ἀνήρ· 'Ἄπιθι τοῦ λοιποῦ, γύναι, πρὸς τὴν οἰκίαν ἡμῶν.' Ἡ
δὲ πρὸς αὐτὸν ἀντέφησεν· 'Πῶς ἄρα προθύμως ἐπὶ τὴν
οἰκίαν πορεύσομαι οὕτως παρὰ σοῦ ὑβρισθεῖσα ἐφ' ὁλό-
κληρον νύκτα, ὅς με τὴν σὴν γυναῖκα τῷ τοῦ βασιλέως
υἱῷ συγκοιτάσαι οὐκ ἐρυθρίασας;' Τούτοις τοῖς λόγοις ὁ
βαλανεὺς σφοδρότερον τὴν καρδίαν νυγεὶς καὶ τῇ ἀνίᾳ
καταποθεὶς ἀγχόνῃ τὸν ἑαυτοῦ βίον κατέστρεψε.

49 "Καὶ σὺ τοιγαροῦν, ὦ βασιλεῦ, μακροθύμησον καὶ μὴ
σπεύσῃς οὕτως ἀσυζητήτως ἀπολέσαι σου τὸν υἱόν, μήπως
καὶ αὐτὸς κατ' ἐκεῖνον πικρότατα μεταμεληθεὶς οὐδὲν
σεαυτὸν ὀνῆσαι δυνήσῃ. Πῶς γὰρ ἕνα σε παῖδα καὶ μόνον
κεκτημένον οὕτως συναρπάζεσθαι χρεὼν εἰς τὴν ἐκείνου
ἀναίρεσιν, καὶ ταῦτα μήπω εἰδότα κἂν ἀληθὴς κἂν ψευδὴς
ἡ κατ' ἐκείνου προτεθεῖσα διαβολὴ πέφυκε; <. . .>

50 "Γυνὴ γάρ τις ἦν ἀνδρὶ νομίμῳ συζῶσα, ὃς δὴ καὶ ἐπί
τινα ἐξεδήμει ὁδοιπορίαν καὶ μέλλων τῆς ἑαυτοῦ ἐξιέναι
οἰκίας συνθήκας ἐνόρκους τὴν γυναῖκα ἀπήτησεν, ᾧ καθ'
ὁμοιότητα καὶ αὐτὸς αὐτῇ συνετάξατο ὡς τὴν πρὸς ἀλλήλους ὁμόψυχον πρόθεσιν ἀπαράτρωτον τηρήσουσιν καὶ
σωφρονοῦντες ἔσονται ἄχρι δὴ τῆς τοῦ ἀνδρὸς πρὸς αὐτὴν ἀνακάμψεως. Εἶτα καὶ δεδήλωκε τῇ γυναικὶ ὡς· 'Μετὰ
τόσας ἡμέρας πρὸς τὴν οἰκίαν ἐπανελεύσομαι.' Μετὰ δέ
τινα καιρὸν τῆς διορίας τῶν ἡμερῶν περαιωθείσης προ-
έκυπτεν ἡ γυνὴ τῇ ὁδῷ προσέχουσα, εἴπερ ἄρα ὁ ἀνὴρ
αὐτῆς καθορᾶται ἐρχόμενος. Νέος δέ τις αὐτὴν θεασάμενος

crime.' With her husband thus overcome by despair, his wife emerged a little later, and the foolish man said to her, 'Go back to our house for now.' But she answered him, 'Why should I want to go to our house after being violated in this way for a whole night on account of you, who were not ashamed to make me, your own wife, sleep with the king's son?' The bath attendant was badly stung by these words and took them to heart; consumed with grief, he took his own life by hanging himself.

"And therefore, my king, be patient and do not be in a 49 hurry to kill your son without an investigation, so that you yourself do not most bitterly regret what you have done to him but be unable to help yourself. For how is it right that you, who have one and only one child, should so rashly order his execution, and do this without yet even knowing whether the slander made against him is true or false?

"There was once a woman who lived with her lawful hus- 50 band. He was departing on a trip, and when he was about to leave his house, he demanded that his wife should make an agreement under oath, and in the same way he himself also made an agreement with her that they would keep their fidelity to each other unsullied and remain chaste until the husband returned to her. Then he also explained to his wife, 'After so many days I will return home.' After some time, when the set number of days had passed, the woman peeked out and looked at the road to see if indeed she could see her husband coming. A young man saw her and fell in love with

καὶ ταύτης ἐρασθεὶς ἤρξατο αὐτῇ περὶ συνουσίας δια-
λέγεσθαι· ἡ δὲ οὐδόλως ἠνέσχετο. Ὁ δὲ τὴν καρδίαν δεινῶς τῷ ἐκείνης ἔρωτι τιτρωσκόμενος πορεύεται πρός τινα
γραΐδα γυναῖκα ἐγγύς που τῆς ἐρωμένης γυναικὸς ἐκείνης
τὴν οἴκησιν ἔχουσαν, καί φησιν πρὸς αὐτὴν ὡς· Τήνδε τὴν
γειτνιῶσάν σοι κόρην ἀθρόον προκύπτουσαν ἰδὼν καὶ
σφοδρῶς αὐτῆς ἐρασθεὶς πρὸς συνουσίαν ἐβιασάμην,
οὐδαμῶς δέ μοι τὸ παράπαν πειθομένην ἐφεῦρον, ἀλλὰ καὶ
βαρέως ἐνεγκοῦσαν τὸ εἰρημένον. Εἰ οὖν σὺ ταύτην
πεισθῆναί μοι παρασκευάσεις, ὃ ἂν ἐξ ἐμοῦ θελήσῃς ζήτησον καὶ δώσω σοι.' Ἡ δὲ γραῦς τῶν τοιούτων ῥημάτων
ἀκούσασα, "Ἐγώ,' φησίν, 'τὴν κόρην εὐήκοον καταστήσω
σοι.'

51   "Καὶ τοῦτο εἰποῦσα ἐγείρεται εὐθὺς καὶ μηχανικῶς τὰ
τοῦ πράγματος συσκευάζει· ἄλευρον γὰρ ἀγαγοῦσα καὶ
τοῦτο ζύμῃ δι' ὕδατος φύρασα, πιπέρεως ὕστερον ἐμπιπλᾷ
τὸ φύραμα καὶ οὕτως αὐτὸ εἰς ἄρτον παρασκευάζει, εἶτα
τόν τε παρασκευασθέντα ἄρτον καὶ ἣν ἔτυχε κεκτῆσθαι
κύνα μεθ' ἑαυτῆς λαβοῦσα πρὸς τὴν κόρην ἐκείνην
πορεύεται. Ἦν δὲ ἡ κύων κατόπιν τῆς γραΐδος ἀκολουθοῦσα
καὶ αὐτῇ τότε πρὸς ἐκείνην συνερχομένη. Ὅτε δὲ ἡ γραῦς
τῇ οἰκίᾳ τῆς κόρης ἤδη προσεπέλασε, ῥίπτει τῇ κυνὶ αὐτῆς
ἐκ τοῦ ἄρτου ἐκείνου, ἡ δὲ κύων φαγοῦσα τοὺς ὀφθαλμοὺς
εὐθὺς δακρύων ὑπὸ τοῦ πιπέρεως ἐμπίπλαται καὶ σφοδρῶς
δακρυρροοῦσα τῇ γραΐδι συνείπετο. Ἐκείνης δὲ εἰσελθούσης πρὸς τὴν ἐρωμένην νεάνιδα ὁρᾷ ἡ κόρη τὴν κύνα
δακρύων ὀχετοὺς τῶν ἑαυτῆς προχέουσαν ὀφθαλμῶν καί
φησιν πρὸς τὴν γραΐδα· Τίς ἡ αἰτία τῶν τῆς κυνὸς ταύτης

her, and began trying to sweet talk her into having sex with him; but she completely rebuffed him. Since he was terribly heartsick with love for her, he went to an old woman who had her house somewhere near the woman he loved, and he said to her, 'When I saw this neighbor girl of yours suddenly peeking out, I fell passionately in love with her and tried to get her to have sex with me. But I found that not only did she completely refuse me, but she even took offense at what I suggested. So, if you can make her compliant to me, ask of me whatever you want and I will give it to you.' When she heard what the young man said, the old woman replied, 'I will make the girl obliging to you.'

"After she said this, she got up immediately and craftily 51 assembled what she needed for the task. She took flour and mixed it with yeast and water, and then she filled the dough with pepper and thus baked it into a loaf. And then, taking with her both the loaf that she had made and a dog that she happened to own, she went to visit the girl. The dog followed the old woman and accompanied her on the way to the girl. When she came near the girl's house, she threw the dog a bit of the bread, and when the dog ate it, its eyes were immediately filled with tears from the pepper, and in this state it followed the old woman, shedding copious tears. The woman arrived at the house of the girl whom the young man loved and, when the girl saw the dog with streams of tears pouring from its eyes, she said to the old woman, 'What's the cause of this dog's tears?' The old woman, with

δακρύων;' Ἡ δὲ γραῦς αὐτῇ σὺν δάκρυσιν ἀπεκρίνατο·
Αὕτη ἡ κύων θυγάτηρ μου, φεῦ, ἐτύγχανέν ποτε· καί τινος
νεανίσκου ἐρασθέντος αὐτῆς καὶ ποικίλως αὐτὴν πρὸς
συνουσίαν ἐκβιάζοντος, αὕτη οὐδόλως ἠνέσχετο· ὁ δέ γε
νέος ἐκεῖνος ὑπὸ τῆς σφοδρᾶς ἀθυμίας κατηράσατο ταύτην ἐκ κατωδύνου καρδίας, καὶ εὐθὺς ἡ θυγάτηρ μου εἰς
κύνα, οἴμοι, μετεμορφώθη, ἥτις αὕτη ἡ δακρύουσα κύων
ἐστίν, ὡς ὁρᾷς· ὁσάκις γὰρ τῆς οἰκίας ἐξέρχομαι, οὕτω
πικρῶς ὀλοφυρομένη κατόπιν μου βαδίζει.' Ταῦτα τῆς
γραῖδος ἐκείνης μετὰ δακρύων πρὸς τὴν κόρην εἰπούσης,
ἐκείνη καταπλαγεῖσα ἐφ' οἷς ἠκηκόει τε καὶ ἑωράκει
παλλομένην ἔσχε τῷ φόβῳ καὶ ἄττουσαν τὴν καρδίαν, καὶ
τῇ γραΐδι ἔφη· Δέος λοιπόν, ὦ γύναι, κἀμοὶ ἐπεισέρχεται·
νέος γάρ τίς με προκύπτουσαν θεασάμενος ἑάλω μου τῇ
θέᾳ, καὶ πρὸς συνουσίαν με τοῦ τοιούτου βιασαμένου
ἔγωγε τοῦτον μετὰ θυμοῦ ἀπεσεισάμην· καὶ νῦν ταῦτά σου
ὁμιλησάσης μοι δέδοικα μὴ καὶ αὐτὴ ἐκείνου μοι ἐπαρα-
σαμένου τῷ αὐτῷ πάθει περιπετὴς γένωμαι. Ἀλλά γε
λοιπὸν ἀναστᾶσα ἄπιθι καὶ ἀναζήτησον τὸν νεανίσκον
ἐκεῖνον καὶ εὑροῦσα μέχρις ἐμοῦ ἄγαγε, καί σοι φιλότιμον
τὴν δεξίωσιν ποιήσωμαι.' Ἡ δέ γε μηχανικωτάτη ἐκείνη
γραῦς, ''Εγώ,' φησίν, 'ἀπελθοῦσα τὸν νεανίσκον ἐκεῖνον τὸ
τάχος ἀγάγω σοι· πλὴν σὺ ἐν τῷ μεταξὺ σαυτὴν κατα-
κόσμησον.' Ἡ δέ γε κόρη εὐθὺς ἐγερθεῖσα ἑαυτήν τε
ἀγλαομόρφῳ στολῇ κατελάμπρυνε καὶ τὴν οἰκίαν περι-
εκάθηρέ τε καὶ κατεκάλλυνε καὶ τὰς ἐν αὐτῇ στρωμνὰς
κοσμίως κατέταξεν, εἶτα καὶ δεῖπνον πολυτελῆ παρητοίμασεν. Ἡ δέ γε προαγωγὸς ἐξελθοῦσα εἰς τὴν τοῦ

tears of her own, answered her, 'This dog, alas, was once my daughter. And when a young man fell in love with her and was trying in various ways to get her to have sex with him, she completely rebuffed him. That young man in his excessive despondency cursed her from his grieving heart, and immediately my daughter was, alas, transformed into a dog, which is this very same crying dog, as you see. For whenever I leave the house, she walks behind me, lamenting bitterly in this way.' When that old woman had tearfully said these things, the girl was astounded at what she had heard and seen, her heart began to quiver and leap with fear, and she said to the old woman, 'Now I'm terrified too. For a young man saw me peeking out and was captivated by the sight of me, and when he tried to get me to have sex with him, I angrily refused him. But now that you have shared this story with me, I fear that I myself may also fall victim to the same fate, if that man curses me. But now get up, go off and search for that young man, and when you find him bring him right to me, and I will give you a generous reward.' That very crafty old woman said, 'I will go off and quickly bring that young man to you. But you, in the meantime, make yourself beautiful.' The girl immediately brightened herself up with a beautiful gown, thoroughly cleaned and polished her house, arranged the dining couches in an orderly fashion, and then prepared a lavish dinner. When the procuress went out in

ἐραστοῦ ἀναζήτησιν ἐκεῖνον μὲν ἐφευρεῖν οὐκ ἠδυνήθη, συλλογισαμένη δὲ καθ᾽ ἑαυτὴν ἔφησεν ὡς· Ἡ νεᾶνις ἐκείνη δωρεαῖς φιλοτίμοις ὑπέσχετό με δεξιώσασθαι· λοιπὸν οὖν ἕτερόν τινα νεανίσκον εὑρήσω καὶ πρὸς αὐτὴν ἀπάξω.᾽ Περιερχομένη δὲ ἐντυγχάνει τῷ τῆς γυναικὸς ἀνδρί, καὶ πρὸς αὐτόν, Ἀκολούθει μοι,᾽ ἔφη, μὴ εἰδυῖα πάντως ὡς ὁ ἀνὴρ ἐκείνης ἐστί, ῾καὶ ἀποφέρω σε,᾽ φησίν, ῾εἰς οἰκίσκον λίαν εὐκοσμότατον, ἐν ᾧ τις γυνὴ προσκάθηται περικαλλὴς σφόδρα καὶ ὡραιοτάτη καί σοι τῷ ὄντι εἰς συνουσίαν ἐφαρμόττουσα.᾽ Ὁ δὲ ἀνὴρ τούτοις τοῖς λόγοις τῆς προαγωγοῦ καταθελχθείς, Πορεύου μου ἔμπροσθεν,᾽ ἔφη. Αὐτῆς δὲ τούτου προπορευομένης κἀκείνου συνεπομένου αὐτῇ παραγίνονται πρὸς τὴν τοῦ ἀνδρὸς οἰκίαν.

52   Ὁ δὲ τὸν ἑαυτοῦ οἶκον ἑωρακὼς καὶ ὅτι πρὸς ἐκεῖνον ἡ γραῦς αὐτὸν ἐκάλει συνεχύθη τῇ λύπῃ καὶ καθ᾽ ἑαυτὸν ἔλεγεν· Ἔοικεν ὄντως ὅτι τοιαῦτα ἡ σύζυγός μου διεπράττετο ἐξότου αὐτῆς ἀπεδήμησα.᾽ Εἰσαγαγοῦσα δὲ αὐτὸν ἡ προαγωγὸς καθεσθῆναι ἐπὶ τῆς αὐτοῦ συνήθους κλίνης πεποίηκε. Θεασαμένη δὲ ἡ γυνὴ ὡς ὁ αὐτῆς γε ἀνὴρ ἐκεῖνος ἐτύγχανεν εὐμηχάνῳ τινὶ πρὸς αὐτὸν τῇ πανουργίᾳ ἐχρήσατο, καὶ εὐθὺς ἀναστᾶσα χεῖρας τῷ ἀνδρὶ ἐπέβαλεν καὶ τῆς αὐτοῦ γενειάδος ἀναιδῶς ἐφαψαμένη πλήττει αὐτοῦ τὴν ὄψιν καὶ σὺν δάκρυσιν ἐβόησε λέγουσα· Ὦ ἀκόλαστε καὶ διεφθαρμένε, αὗται ἡμῶν αἱ πρὸς ἀλλήλους συνθῆκαι τυγχάνουσιν, οὗτοι οἱ ἔνορκοι δεσμοί; Οὐ σωφρονεῖν ἐπηγγείλω μοι μέχρι τῆς οἴκαδε ἀνακάμψεως; Ἵνα καὶ τί λοιπὸν παρ᾽ οὐδὲν πάντα θέμενος εἰς ζήτησιν μᾶλλον ἐξῆλθες τῆς προαγωγοῦ ταύτης;᾽

search of the lover, she could not find him; after pondering for a while, she said to herself, 'That young woman promised to reward me with generous gifts. So then, I'll find another young man and bring him to her.' As she was going around, she encountered the woman's husband, and said to him, 'Follow me,' completely unaware that he was the girl's husband. And she said, 'I'm taking you to a very lovely house, in which there resides a woman who is gorgeous and very beautiful and, in fact, just right for sex with you.' Beguiled by the procuress's offer, the man said, 'Lead me there.' While she walked ahead of him and he followed her, they arrived at the man's house.

"When he saw his own house and that the old woman was 52 beckoning him toward it, he was overwhelmed with grief and said to himself, 'Truly, it seems, my wife has been behaving like this ever since I left her.' After leading him inside, the procuress made him sit down on his own usual couch. When the woman saw that that man was her husband, she used wickedness as a trick against him. She immediately got up and assaulted her husband, and audaciously grabbing his beard, she struck his face and shouted tearfully, 'You licentious and corrupt man, is this the agreement we made with each other? Are these our sworn bonds? Didn't you promise me to remain chaste until your return home? Why did you set all that aside now and go out in search of this procuress instead?'

53 "Ὁ δὲ ἀνὴρ ἔκθαμβος λίαν γεγονὼς ἐπὶ τῇ τοῦ γυναίου τοσαύτῃ ἀναιδείᾳ καὶ ἀθρόᾳ ἰταμότητι, ‘Καὶ τί τὸ συμβεβηκὸς αἰτίαμα πέφυκε;’ πρὸς τὴν σύζυγον ἀπεκρίνατο. Ἡ δέ, ‘Σήμερον,’ φησίν, ‘ἠκηκόειν τῆς ὁδοῦ σε καταλαμβάνειν καὶ σοῦ τῆς πρός με διαθέσεως ἐποιησάμην ἀπόπειραν, εἰ ἄρα τετήρηκας τὰς συνθήκας ἀπαραβάτους, καὶ τὴν οἰκίαν σαρώσασα καὶ ἐμαυτὴν κοσμίως στολίσασα προσποιητῶς ταυτηνὶ τὴν γραῖδα πρός σε ἔστειλα, ὥστε δι' αὐτῆς δοκιμάσαι τὴν τῆς γνώμης σου ἔκβασιν καὶ εἴπερ πρός με σωφροσύνην συνετήρησας ἢ τοὐναντίον δι' ἀκολάστου πράξεως τὴν ἐμὴν κοίτην διέφθειρας, καὶ ἰδού σε δολιόφρονα καὶ ἀκόλαστον εὕρηκα καὶ τῶν ἐνόρκων συνθηκῶν ἀναμφίλεκτον ὑπερόπτην. Λοιπὸν γοῦν οὐκέτι σοι φιλιάζουσαν ἕξεις ἐμὲ τὴν ὁμόζυγον, οὐδεπώποτε, δόλιε, διαλλαγήσομαί σοι.’

54 "Ὁ δὲ ἀνὴρ ἔφη πρὸς αὐτήν· ‘Ἐγὼ μᾶλλον, ὦ γύναι, τἀναντία δὴ ταῦτα κατὰ σοῦ ὑπόπτευον καὶ ὅτι μεθ' ἑτέρων τοιαῦτα εἰ ἀκολασταίνουσα· ἐπεὶ δὲ οὕτως, ὡς ἔφης, ἔχειν σε διϊσχυρίζει, δῆλά σοι καὶ τὰ κατ' ἐμὲ παριστῶ, ὡς τῇ γραΐδι ταύτῃ τούτου χάριν ἠκολούθηκα, ἐφ' ᾧ πρὸς τὴν ἐμήν με προσεκαλεῖτο οἰκίαν· εἰ γὰρ πρὸς ἕτερόν τι μέρος ἀπάγειν με ἐπεχείρησεν, οὐδὲ προσεσχηκέναι τῷ λόγῳ αὐτῆς ἠνεσχόμην ἂν τὸ σύνολον.’ Ἡ δὲ γυνὴ ὥσπερ τοῖς ῥηθεῖσι διαπιστοῦσα καὶ σφοδροτέρῳ δῆθεν τῷ θυμῷ κατ' αὐτοῦ φερομένη καὶ ἑαυτῆς πλήττει τὴν ὄψιν τήν τε στολὴν διαρρήξασα πάλιν αὐτοῦ κατεκραύγαζε λέγουσα· ‘Ὢ δολίων ἀνδρῶν δολιώτερε καὶ σκολιῶν σκολιώτερε, ὁ κατ' ἐμοῦ δολερᾷ τῇ γνώμῃ

χρησάμενος, οὐκέτι σου τοῖς ὅρκοις πεποιθῶσα ἔσομαι, ὅτιπερ αὐτοῖς οὐδεμία πρόσεστιν ἀλήθεια.' Ταῦτα πρὸς τὸν ἄνδρα διαπραξαμένη ἐπὶ χρόνον ἱκανὸν αὐτῷ δῆθεν ἀπεχθάνετο καὶ οὐ πρότερον αὐτῷ διηλλάγη, ἄχρις ὅτου ἐκεῖνος πολυτελῆ αὐτῇ κόσμον κατεσκεύασεν χρυσοῦ ἅμα καὶ ὑφάσματος.

55 "Καὶ νῦν, ὦ δέσποτα βασιλεῦ, ἀπὸ ταύτης δὴ γνῶθι τῆς διηγήσεως ὡς οὐδεὶς τῶν ἀνθρώπων ταῖς τῶν γυναικῶν μηχανουργίαις ἀντικαθίστασθαι δύναται." Τούτων παρὰ τοῦ τετάρτου καὶ σοφωτάτου συμβούλου ὁ βασιλεὺς ἀκρο-ασάμενος κελεύει τὸν υἱὸν αὐτοῦ μηδαμῶς ἀποκτανθῆναι.

56 Ἡ δέ γε αὐτοῦ μιαρωτάτη παλλακὴ τῆς ἐπὶ τῷ υἱῷ ἀναβολῆς τοῦ βασιλέως αἰσθομένη παρέστη αὐτῷ κατὰ τὴν προρρηθεῖσαν τετάρτην ἡμέραν ἀπόδεσμόν τινα τῇ χειρὶ κατέχουσα, καί φησιν πρὸς αὐτόν· "Ἰδού, βασιλεῦ, φάρμακον δηλητήριον, ὡς ὁρᾷς, ἐπιφέρομαι, καί σοι τὸν ζῶντα Θεὸν ἐπόμνυμι ὡς εἰ μὴ ἀπὸ τοῦ σοῦ παιδὸς θᾶττον ἐκδικήσεις με καὶ ξίφει αὐτὸν ἀναλώσεις, ὅτι ἐνυβρίσαι μοι ἀναιδῶς ἐπειρᾶτο σώφρονί τε οὔσῃ καὶ σωφρόνων τῶν γεννητόρων, ἐξ αὐτοῦ δὴ τοῦ δηλητηρίου ἀνυπερθέτως πίομαι καὶ βιαίως τῆς ζωῆς ἀπορραγήσομαι καὶ ἔσται σοι θεόθεν τῆς ἀπωλείας μου ἕνεκεν ἀσύγγνωστος ἡ κατά-κρισις. Οὐδὲν δὲ τὸ παράπαν οἱ σοφοὶ οὗτοι σύμβουλοί σε ὠφελήσουσιν, ἀλλὰ μᾶλλον συμβήσεταί σοι ὑπ' αὐτῶν ὥσπερ καί τινι τῶν χοίρων ἐπισυμβέβηκεν.

57 "Ἔθος γὰρ ἦν ἐκείνῳ ἐπί τινα συκῆν παραγίνεσθαι καὶ τὰ τοῦ δένδρου ἀποπίπτοντα σῦκα ἑκάστοτε ἐσθίειν. Μιᾷ γοῦν τῶν ἡμερῶν παρ' αὐτὴν ἀφίκετο κατὰ τὸ αὐτοῦ

treacherous mind against me, so I'll no longer have any faith in your oaths, because there's no truth in them.' After she had outmaneuvered her husband in this way, she pretended to be mad at him for a long time and did not reconcile with him until he had provided her with expensive finery of both gold and woven cloth.

"And now, my king and master, know from this story that   55
no man can oppose the machinations of women." Having heard these words from the fourth very wise advisor, the king ordered that his son by no means be killed.

When his most foul concubine learned of the king's de-   56
ferment in the case of his son, she appeared before the king on that same fourth day with a package in her hand, and she said to him, "Look, my king, as you see, I'm carrying a poisonous drug, and I swear to you by the living God that unless you avenge me quickly against your son and put him to death by the sword, because he shamelessly attempted to rape me, although I am chaste and come from chaste parents, I will drink this poison without delay and violently take my own life, and God will condemn you without forgiveness because of my death. Nor will these wise advisors be of any benefit to you, but rather you will suffer from them the same fate as a certain pig.

"For there was once a pig that was in the habit of going to   57
a fig tree and eating the figs that would fall. Now one day it arrived there as usual and saw a monkey climbing up into

σύνηθες καί τινα ὁρᾷ πίθηκα τῇ συκῇ ἐπαναβάντα καὶ ἐκ τῶν σύκων ἐσθίοντα. Ὁ δέ γε πίθηξ τὸν χοῖρον ἑωρακὼς ῥίπτει αὐτῷ ἓν σῦκον ἄνωθεν, ὅπερ ὁ χοῖρος τῶν πιπτόντων ἡδύτερον τυγχάνον ἡδέως καὶ ἤσθιε. Καὶ τούτου χάριν ἕτερον σῦκον ῥιφθῆναι παρὰ τοῦ πίθηκος ἐξεδέχετο. Ἐκείνου δὲ οὐδὲν ἔτι τῷ χοίρῳ προσρίπτοντος ἵστατο οὗτος κάτωθεν ἐκτεταμένον κεκτημένος τὸν τράχηλον καὶ πρὸς τὸν πίθηκα ἀδιακόπως ἠτένιζεν. Ἐπὶ πολὺ δὲ αὐτοῦ ἄνω τοὺς ὀφθαλμοὺς ἀνατείνοντος αἱ τοῦ τραχήλου αὐτοῦ φλέβες ἀπεψύγησαν, καὶ παραχρῆμα ὁ χοῖρος τῆς ζωῆς ἀπερράγη."

58   Τούτων ὁ Κῦρος παρὰ τῆς γυναικὸς ἀκούσας καὶ δεδιὼς μήπως ἑαυτὴν τῷ δηλητηρίῳ κτείνῃ φαρμάκῳ καὶ αὐτὸς ἀποδειχθῇ τοῦ θανάτου αὐτῆς αἴτιος, κελεύει αὖθις τὸν υἱὸν ξίφει ἀναλωθῆναι.

59   Τῆς τοιαύτης οὖν ἀποφάσεως αὖθις ἐξενεχθείσης, εἰσέρχεται πρὸς τὸν βασιλέα κατὰ τὴν πέμπτην ἡμέραν ὁ πέμπτος αὐτοῦ φιλοσοφώτατος σύμβουλος καὶ τὴν συνήθη αὐτῷ ἀπονείμας προσκύνησιν, "Δέσποτα," φησίν, "βασιλεῦ, ζῴης εἰς τὸν αἰῶνα. Ἐπίσταμαι σὺν ἀκριβείᾳ ὡς ἀνάπλεως σοφίας καὶ συνέσεως πέφυκας· ἵνα τί τοίνυν ὁ ἀγχινοίᾳ κατάκομος οὕτως ἀσυλλόγιστον ἀποφαίνῃ τὴν καταδίκην καὶ μὴ πρότερον συζητεῖς καὶ ἐρευνᾷς τὸ προκείμενον; Ἀλλ᾽ ὅμως ἄκουσόν μου τῆς παρούσης διηγήσεως.

60   "Ἦν γάρ τις στρατιώτης ἀνήρ, ὃς τῷ βασιλεῖ καὶ τοῖς ὑπ᾽ αὐτῷ μεγιστᾶσι τῆς οἰκείας ἕνεκεν ᾠκείωτο γενναιότητος. Κύνα δέ τινα ὁ τοιοῦτος ἐκέκτητο ἀπ᾽ αὐτῆς τε

the tree and eating the figs. When the monkey saw the pig, it threw one of the figs at him from above, which the pig gladly ate because it was sweeter than the ones that fell. And for this reason, he waited for the monkey to throw another fig. But the monkey threw no more figs down to him, and the pig was left standing below with his neck stretched out and his gaze fixed steadily on the monkey. Because he was lifting his eyes upward for a long time, the veins in his neck froze and the pig immediately lost his life."

When Cyrus heard this story from the woman, he was 58 afraid that she would kill herself with the poisonous drug and that he himself would be found guilty of her death, and so he ordered again that his son be put to death by the sword.

When this sentence was again pronounced, the fifth of 59 the king's most learned advisors came to him on the fifth day and, after performing the customary prostration before him, said, "*My* master and *king, may you live forever.* I know very well that you are filled with wisdom and intelligence. Since you abound in cleverness, why then do you pronounce such an irrational sentence without first inquiring into and investigating the case before you? But still, listen to the story that I am about to tell you.

"There was once a soldier, who was an intimate friend of 60 the king and his noblemen on account of his valor. This man owned a dog that he had raised from birth and that did

τῆς γεννήσεως παρ' αὐτοῦ ἀνατραφέντα καὶ τὰ παρ' αὐτοῦ
τούτῳ ἐπιταττόμενα ὥσπερ τις τῶν λογικῶν πράττοντα·
ὅθεν καὶ προσπαθῶς ὁ στρατιώτης περιεῖπε τὸ κυνάριον.
Ἐν μιᾷ γοῦν ἡ τοῦ ἀνδρὸς σύζυγος πρὸς τοὺς ἑαυτῆς
ἀπῄει γεννήτορας, καὶ τὸν ἑαυτῆς νηπιάζοντα παῖδα παρὰ
τῷ πατρὶ λιποῦσα ἀκριβῶς αὐτῷ προσέχειν τῷ ἀνδρὶ
παρήγγειλεν· 'Ἐγὼ γάρ,' φησίν, 'οὐ χρονίσω τοῦ ἐπανελ-
θεῖν.' Καὶ ταῦτα εἰποῦσα κεκοίμηκεν τὸ παιδίον πρότερον
καὶ εἰθούτως ἐκεῖθεν ὑπανεχώρησεν. Τοῦ δέ γε ἀνδρὸς τῇ
οἰκίᾳ προσκαρτεροῦντος καὶ τοῦ παιδίου ὑπνώσαντος,
ἀθρόον τις τῶν τοῦ βασιλέως παρεγένετο δορυφόρων.
Καὶ τὴν θύραν τοῦ τοιούτου κρούσαντος ἐξῆλθεν ὁ στρατιώτης θεασόμενος τὸν κρούσαντα. Ἑωρακὼς δὲ αὐτὸν
ἐκεῖνος, 'Ὁ βασιλεὺς καλεῖ σε,' πρὸς αὐτὸν εἴρηκεν. Ὁ δὲ
στρατιώτης ἅμα τῷ λόγῳ τὰ ἑαυτοῦ στρατιωτικὰ περιβάλ-
λεται ἄμφια, καὶ τὴν σπάθην ἀράμενος καὶ τῷ δορυφόρῳ
μέλλων ἀκολουθῆσαι, προσκαλεῖται τὸν κύνα καὶ παραγ-
γέλλει αὐτῷ τά τε ἐκεῖσε καὶ τὸ παιδίον τηρεῖν, 'Τοῦ
μηδένα,' φησίν, 'τὸ παράπαν προσπελάσαι τῷ οἰκήματι.' Ὁ
μὲν οὖν στρατιώτης τῷ κυνὶ ταύτῃ παραγγείλας πρὸς τὸ
τοῦ βασιλέως ἀπῄει παλάτιον.

61 'Τοῦ δέ γε κυνὸς τῷ παιδὶ παρακαθημένου κἀκείνου
ὕπνῳ κατεχομένου, ὁρᾷ ὁ κύων ὄφιν τινὰ παμμεγέθη
κατὰ τοῦ παιδὸς ἕρποντα καὶ αὐτὸν ἐκλαφύξαι σχεδὸν
ἐπειγόμενον. Αὐτίκα γοῦν ἐγερθεὶς πόλεμον πρὸς τὸν
ὄφιν συνέστησεν καὶ καταδακὼν αὐτὸν παραχρῆμα νε-
κρὸν ἀπηργάσατο. Κατ' αὐτὴν δὲ τὴν ὥραν ἐπανῆκεν
ὁ στρατιώτης, καὶ τούτου εἰσερχομένου ὁ κύων αὐτῷ

whatever he commanded as though it were a creature endowed with reason, and because of this, the soldier treated his little dog with great affection. Now one day the man's wife was going to see her parents, and she left her infant son with his father and ordered her husband to pay very close attention to him. 'For I'll be back,' she said, 'before very long.' After she had said this, she first put the baby to bed and then left. As the man was waiting at home and the child was sleeping, one of the king's bodyguards suddenly arrived. This man knocked on the door, and the soldier came out to see who was knocking. When the bodyguard saw the soldier, he said to him, 'The king summons you.' As soon as the bodyguard said this, the soldier put on his military uniform, and as he took up his sword and was about to follow after the bodyguard, he called for his dog and ordered it to watch over both the property and the child, 'So that no one,' he said, 'comes near the house at all.' And so, when the soldier had given this order to the dog, he went away to the king's palace.

"Now as the dog was sitting beside the boy, who remained 61 fast asleep, it saw an enormous snake slithering toward the child, practically rushing to devour him. Straightaway it jumped up, joined battle with the snake, and killed it at once with its fangs. At that very moment the soldier returned, and as he was coming in, the dog joyfully came to meet him.

χαριέντως προσαπήντησεν. Θεασάμενος δὲ ἐκεῖνος αἵματι τὸ τοῦ κυνὸς στόμα λελυθρωμένον, ἐδόκει περὶ αὐτοῦ ὡς τὸν παῖδα βέβρωκε, καὶ θυμωθεὶς κατ᾽ αὐτοῦ τῷ ξίφει τύψας τὸν κύνα ἀπέκτεινεν. Εἶτα ἐντὸς τῆς οἰκίας γενόμενος ὁρᾷ τὸν παῖδα καθεύδοντα, καὶ μὴ κατά τι τὸ σύνολον παραβλαβέντα, ἑωράκει δὲ καὶ τὸν ὄφιν ἀποκτανθέντα καὶ πρὸς τῇ κεφαλῇ τοῦ παιδίου κείμενον, καὶ εὐθὺς ἔγνω ὡς ὁ κύων τὸν ὄφιν ἀπέκτεινεν. Εἶτα πικρῶς μετεμέλετο ὅτιπερ ἀναιτίως τὸν κύνα ἀνῄρηκεν, οὐδὲν δὲ πάντως τῆς μεταμελείας ἀπώνατο.

62   "Καὶ σὺ οὖν, ὦ βασιλεῦ, μὴ οὕτως ἀκόπως τὸν υἱόν σου ἀνέλῃς, μήπως καὶ τῷ σῷ κράτει ὡς ἐκείνῳ δὴ τῷ στρατιώτῃ συμβήσεται, καὶ μεταμελόμενος ἐπευχαῖς οὐδὲν σεαυτὸν ὀνῆσαι δυνηθήσῃ. Καὶ ἄλλης δέ μου διηγήσεως ἄκουσον.

63   "Ἀνὴρ γάρ τις ἦν τὸν τρόπον ἀκόλαστος, ὃς ἡνίκα περί τινος εὐειδοῦς ἠκηκόει γυναικὸς πάντα λίθον ἐκίνει, τὸ τοῦ λόγου, ἄχρις ἂν αὐτῇ ἐκ παντὸς τρόπου συνεμίγη. Τῷ γοῦν τοιούτῳ ἀνδρὶ περί τινος ἐδηλώθη γυναικὸς σφόδρα ὡραιοτάτης, ἥτις ἔν τινι χωρίῳ τὴν κατοίκησιν ἐκέκτητο. Καὶ μαθὼν τὰ κατ᾽ αὐτὴν ὁ ἀνὴρ ἀπέστειλεν βιαζόμενος ταύτην εἰς συνουσίαν αὐτῷ συνελθεῖν· ἡ δὲ σωφρόνως καὶ σεμνῶς βιοτεύουσα ὡς ἀπηχές τι καὶ ἄτοπον τὴν τοῦ ἀνδρὸς βίαν ἀπεσείσατο. Ὁ δέ γε θηλυμανὴς ἐκεῖνος μηδ᾽ οὕτως παυόμενος ἐπ᾽ ἐκεῖνο παρεγένετο τὸ χωρίον καὶ καταλύει ἀναιδῶς παρ᾽ ἐκείνῃ τῇ γυναικί, εἶτα ὡς τὸ πρότερον βιάζειν αὐτὴν ἐπεχείρει· ἡ δὲ οὐ τὸ παράπαν ἠνέσχετο. Σφοδρῶς δὲ ἐκεῖνος τῷ ἔρωτι σφαδάζων

But when the man saw the dog's mouth stained with blood, he thought that it had eaten the boy and, in his anger at the dog, he struck it with his sword and killed it. Then, once he had entered the house, he saw the boy sleeping and completely unharmed, and he also saw the snake lying dead near the child's head, and he realized immediately that the dog had killed the snake. Then he bitterly regretted that he had killed the dog for no reason, but he gained absolutely nothing from his regret.

"And so, you, my king, do not heedlessly execute your son 62 like this, or else your majesty may suffer the same fate as that soldier and, despite your regret, be unable to help yourself with prayers. But hear another story from me, also.

"There once was a man whose behavior was lascivious, 63 and whenever he heard of some beautiful woman, he moved every stone, as the saying goes, until he had sex with her by any means he could. Now an exceedingly lovely woman who had taken up residency in a certain village came to this man's attention. When he learned about her, he sent a message to her and tried to get her to have sex with him, but because she lived her life chastely and respectably, she rebuffed the man's pressure as disgraceful and inappropriate. That lecherous man did not stop there, but went to that village and shamelessly found lodging with the woman, and then kept trying to force her as before. She, however, would not give in at all. As he was in a frenzy due to his lust, the man went off

ἀπέρχεται πρός τινα γραΐδα γυναῖκα καὶ αὐτῇ ἀνακοινοῖ
τὰ τοῦ πράγματος. Ἡ δὲ γραῦς τῶν ῥημάτων τοῦ ἀνδρὸς
ἀκούσασα, 'Μάτην,' φησί, 'κάμνεις, ὦ ἄνθρωπε· ἦν γὰρ
ζητεῖς γυναῖκα τῶν πάνυ σωφρόνων καὶ κοσμίων καθέστηκεν, οὐ μέντοι μᾶλλον τῶν ἀκολάστων ὡς ὑπετόπασας.' Ὁ
δέ γε ἀνὴρ αὖθις, 'Ἀλλ' εἴπερ,' φησίν, 'ἀπελεύσῃ πρὸς
αὐτὴν καὶ τῷ θελήματί μου στοιχῆσαι ταύτην παρασκευάσεις, εὐθὺς εἴ τι δὴ καὶ παρ' ἐμοῦ ἐπιζητήσεις ἑτοίμως
παράσχω σοι.' Ἡ δὲ γραῦς τοῖς τοιούτοις συγκινηθεῖσα
ῥήμασι, 'Ἐγὼ μέν,' ἔφη, 'τὰ καταθύμιά σοι διαπράξωμαι,
σὺ δὲ λοιπὸν ἄπιθι πρὸς τὸν ἐκείνης ἄνδρα, καὶ εὑρήσεις
αὐτὸν καλυψάμενον ἐπιβλήματι τῶν εἰς στρωμνὴν χρη-
ματιζόντων· ζήτησον γοῦν ἐκεῖνο τοῦ παρ' αὐτοῦ ἀπεμπο-
ληθῆναί σοι, καὶ λαβὼν μέχρις ἐμοῦ διακόμισον.'

64 "Ὁ δὲ καθάπερ αὐτῷ ἡ γραῦς διεστείλατο πορεύεται
πρὸς τὴν ἀγοράν, διδαχθεὶς παρ' ἐκείνης καὶ τὰ τοῦ ἀνδρὸς
σύσσημα. Περιερχόμενος δὲ τοῖς ἐκεῖσε προσεῖχε ὡς δεδίδακτο ἐργαστηρίοις τὸν ἄνδρα ὀψόμενος, ἰδὼν δέ τινα
τὰ τῇ γραΐδι λεχθέντα κεκτημένον σήμανδρα, ἐπέγνω
εὐθὺς ἐκεῖνόν τε τυγχάνειν τὸν τῆς γυναικὸς σύνευνον,
καὶ πρὸς αὐτὸν ἀφικόμενος, 'Πώλησόν μοι,' ἔφησεν, 'τόδε
σου τὸ ὕφασμα.' Ὁ δὲ τοῦτο τῷ ἀνδρὶ διέπρασεν. Ὃ καὶ
λαβὼν ἐκεῖνος τῇ γραΐδι ἀπεκόμισε. Ἡ δὲ τούτου ἀσμένως
δεξαμένη αὐτίκα τινὰ τούτου τρία μέρη τῷ πυρὶ κατέκαυ-
σεν καὶ τῷ ἐραστῇ ἔφησεν· 'Καθέσθητι τοῦ λοιποῦ ἐν τῷδε
τῷ οἰκήματι, καὶ μηδεὶς τὸ παράπαν τῶν ἔξω κατίδῃ σε.'
Εἶτα τὸ ἔπιπλον ἐκεῖνο μεθ' ἑαυτῆς λαβοῦσα ἐπὶ τὴν
τῆς γυναικὸς οἰκίαν ἐπορεύθη, καὶ εἰσελθοῦσα ἀθρόως

to an old woman and shared his problem with her. But when the old woman heard the man's story, she said, 'You're wasting your time, sir, for the woman that you're pursuing is very chaste and decorous, not licentious, as you've assumed.' The man replied, 'Even so, if you go to her and make her compliant to my desire, I'll gladly get you whatever you ask from me right away.' The old woman was excited by the man's offer and said, 'I'll make happen what you have in mind. Now you go to the woman's husband, whom you will find wrapped in a bedspread. Then ask him to sell it to you, and when you have it, bring it back to me.'

"The man did precisely as the old woman had ordered   64 and went to the marketplace, having also been instructed by her as to the man's distinguishing features. As he walked around, he gave his attention to the workshops there, as he had been instructed, in order to look for the husband, and when he saw someone who had the features the old woman had described, he recognized him immediately as the young woman's spouse. He approached him and said, 'Sell me this blanket of yours.' The husband sold it to him, and he took it and brought it back to the old woman. She received it happily, and straightaway burned it in three places in the fire. Then she said to the lover, 'Stay for now in my house, and let no one from outside see any sign of you.' Then she took the blanket with her and made her way to the woman's house. She quickly went inside and, craftily escaping the woman's

μηχανικῶς ἐκείνης τὴν ὅρασιν διαλανθάνει καὶ ὑπὸ τὸ τοῦ ἀνδρὸς αὐτῆς προσκεφάλαιον τὸ ἔπιπλον τίθησι, καὶ μικρὸν τῇ γυναικὶ μετὰ ταῦτα ὁμιλήσασα ἐξέρχεται ἐκεῖθεν. Ἡ μέντοι γυνὴ μὴ εἰδυῖα τὸ δρᾶμα οὐδὲν ὅλως περὶ τῆς γραΐδος ὑπετόπασεν.

65 "Περὶ δὲ τὴν τοῦ ἀρίστου ὥραν ὁ τῆς γυναικὸς ἀνὴρ παρεγένετο, καὶ εἰσελθὼν κατεκλίθη ἐπὶ τῆς κλίνης αὐτοῦ. Τοῦ δὲ προσκεφαλαίου μετεώρου τυγχάνοντος, διάρας τοῦτο τοῦ καλῶς διαθέσθαι, ὁρᾷ ὑπ' αὐτῷ τὸ ἔπιπλον ἐκεῖνο ὃ πέπρακε κείμενον. Καὶ πρὸς μὲν τὴν σύζυγον οὐδὲν ὅλως περὶ τούτου ἀπεφθέγξατο, ἐγερθεὶς δὲ ἀθρόως χεῖρας αὐτῇ θρασέως ἐπέβαλεν καὶ σφοδροτάταις ταύτην πληγαῖς περιέβαλεν. Ἡ δὲ δεινοπαθήσασα τὴν καρδίαν αὐτίκα τῆς οἰκίας μετ' οἰμωγῆς ἐκπορεύεται καὶ πρὸς τοὺς αὐτῆς παραγίνεται γεννήτορας. Διηπόρει δὲ καθ' ἑαυτὴν ἐξότου χάριν ἠκίσθη.

66 "Ταῦτα δὲ ἡ γραῦς παρά τινων ἐνωτισαμένη πορεύεται καὶ αὐτὴ ἔνθα οἱ τῆς γυναικὸς διῆγον γεννήτορες, καὶ πρὸς ἐκείνην εἰσελθοῦσα περιπαθῶς αὐτῇ ἔλεγεν· 'Ἠκηκόειν ὅπως σε ὁ ἀνὴρ σφοδρῶς κατῄκισε καὶ τὴν σὴν ὀδύνην οἰκείαν, ἴσθι, ἐλογισάμην.' Ἡ δὲ τῇ γραΐδι ἀντέφησεν· 'Ἐκεῖνος μὲν ἤδη χαλεπῶς ἡμᾶς ἔτυψεν, ἐγὼ δὲ οὐκ ἐπίσταμαι διὰ ποίαν γε αἰτίαν.' Ἡ δὲ γραῦς, 'Ἀλλ' εὖ ἴσθι,' ἀπεκρίνατο, 'ὡς ἐκ γοητείας τινῶν χαιρεκάκων ταῦτα συμβέβηκε· πλὴν εἴπερ σοι δοκεῖ ἐλθὲ ἐπὶ τὴν ἐμὴν οἰκίαν· ὑπάρχει γὰρ ἐκεῖσε ἰητρός τις ἀνήρ, οὗπερ οὐδεὶς ἰητρῶν δοκιμώτερος καθέστηκε, κἀκεῖνος δὴ παντοίαν εὖ ποιήσει θεραπείαν, καὶ μᾶλλον τὰ τῆς πείρας καὶ αὐτὴ διδαχθῇς.'

notice, placed the blanket under the husband's pillow, and then after conversing briefly with the wife, she left the house. The woman, however, since she had no knowledge of the scheme, was not suspicious of the old woman at all.

"Around lunchtime, the woman's husband arrived, and 65 going inside he lay down on his bed. Now his pillow was elevated, and when he lifted it to arrange it comfortably, he saw the blanket that he had sold lying underneath it. He said nothing at all about it to his wife, but getting up suddenly he rashly grabbed her and beat her with very violent blows. His wife was heartbroken, and straightaway she left her house in tears and went to her parents. She had no idea why she had been mistreated.

"When the old woman learned of these events from some 66 others, she too made her way to where the woman's parents lived, and going in to her, said with great emotion, 'I've heard that your husband has seriously mistreated you. You should know that I count your grief as my own.' The woman replied to the old woman, 'He struck me badly just now, but I have no idea why.' And the old woman answered, 'You must clearly realize that this was caused by the sorcery of some spiteful people. But if you agree, come to my house. For there is a doctor there, who is more skilled than any other doctor; he will indeed perform all sorts of treatment, and you will learn for yourself about their sorcery.' The woman

Ἡ δὲ τοῖς λόγοις τῆς γραῖδος συγκατέθετο καὶ ὥσπερ ἔνθους ὑπ' αὐτῶν γενομένη, "Ἐγὼ μέν,' ἔφη, 'ἑτοίμως ἀκολουθήσω σοι, σὺ δὲ εἴπερ μοι ἐκείνου τοιαύτην ἐμποιήσεις ἀσφάλειαν, κἀγὼ φιλοτίμως σε καὶ δεόντως δεξιώσω.' Εἶτα ὀψίας γενομένης λαβοῦσα αὐτὴν ἡ γραῦς ἐπὶ τὴν ἑαυτῆς οἰκίαν ἀπήγαγεν, καὶ τῷ ἐραστῇ ἔφησεν ὡς· "Ἰδοὺ ἐντὸς ἀρκύων τὸ θήραμα καὶ ἤχθη σοι ἡ γυνή.' Ὁ δὲ εὐθὺς ἀναστὰς κατέσχε τὴν γυναῖκα καὶ βιαίως αὐτῇ συνεγένετο. Ἐκείνη δὲ οὕτως ἐνυβριζομένη καὶ πικρῶς ἄγαν τὴν ἀσχημοσύνην φέρουσα ἐκινεῖτο μὲν εἰς τὸ κραυγάσαι, ἐσιώπα δὲ διὰ τὴν αἰσχύνην. Ἐσύστερον δὲ σύντρομος ἐξελθοῦσα πρὸς τοὺς γεννήτορας τὸ τάχος ἐπανῆκε.

67 "Πρωΐας δὲ γενομένης ὁ ἐραστὴς τῇ γραῖδι ἐκείνῃ, 'Τοῦ μὲν ἤδη γεγονότος ἕνεκα μεγάλας σοι, ὦ γύναι, ὀφείλω τὰς χάριτας, ἐπὶ δέ γε τοῖς τῇ γυναικὶ συμβεβηκόσι παρὰ τοῦ ἀνδρὸς αὐτῆς οὐ μικρῶς λελύπημαι, ὅτιπερ ἐγὼ πάντως αὐτῶν αἴτιος γεγένημαι.' Ἡ δὲ γραῦς, 'Μὴ λυποῦ,' φησίν· ἐγὼ γὰρ διά τινος εὐμεθόδου μηχανῆς παρασκευάσω ἐκείνους ἀλλήλοις διαλλαγῆναι. Σὺ δέ μοι λοιπὸν ἐπὶ τὴν ἀγορὰν ἄπιθι πρὸς τὸν τῆς γυναικὸς σύνευνον καὶ ἐπὶ μικρὸν ἐκεῖσε παράμεινον· κἀκεῖνος εὐθὺς περὶ οὗ σοι ἐπώλησεν ἐπίπλου ἐμμελῶς πρός σε ἀνεξετάσει· εἶτα αὐτὸς τοῦτο ἀποκρίθητι, ὡς· "Τῷ πέπλῳ σου καλυψάμενος ἐπί τινος ἐκαθέσθην κλιβάνου καὶ κατὰ λήθην ἐμοῦ τῷ πυρὶ προσεγγίσαντος ἐν τρισὶν ἐξεκαύθη μέρεσι. Ἐγὼ δὲ ἀνιαθεὶς ἐπὶ τῷ γεγονότι παρέσχον τὸ ἔπιπλον πρὸς γραῖδα τινὰ γνωστήν μοι, ὅπως τοῦτο ἀπαγαγοῦσα πρός τινα τῶν ὑφαντῶν τὰ ἐκκαυθέντα τούτου μέρη ἀνυφανθῆναι

agreed with what the old woman said, and as though inspired by her words, she said, 'I will happily follow you, and
if you can get him to create that kind of security for me, I
will pay you a generous and fitting reward.' Then when evening had come, the old woman took her and led her away to
her own house, and she said to the lover, 'Look, the prey is in
the net: the woman has been brought to you.' The man got
up immediately, grabbed the woman, and raped her. As she
was being violated like this and was enduring the disgrace
with great misery, she wanted to cry out, but instead kept
quiet because she was ashamed. Afterward she left, trembling, and returned quickly to her parents' house.

"When morning came, the lover said to the old woman, 'I   67
owe you great thanks for what you just did, but I feel very
sorry for what the woman's husband has done to her, because I myself am entirely to blame for it.' And the old
woman said, 'Don't feel sorry, for I myself will bring about
their reconciliation through a well-designed scheme. Now
leave me and go off to the woman's husband in the marketplace and stay there for a little while. That man will immediately question you carefully about the blanket he sold you,
and you should answer him as follows: "I wrapped myself in
your robe and sat upon an oven, and when I absent-mindedly
got too close to the fire, it was burned in three places. I was
upset by what had happened, so I gave the blanket to an old
woman I know, so that she would take it to a weaver and

παρασκευάσει. Ἐξότου δὲ τὸ τοιοῦτον ἡ γραῦς ἐκείνη παρέλαβεν, οὐκέτι αὐτὴν ὁπωσοῦν ἑωράκειν, ἀλλ᾽ οὐδὲ τὸ παράπαν ἐπίσταμαι τί ἄρα καὶ γένοιτο." Ταῦτα οὖν,' φησί, 'τῷ τῆς γυναικὸς ἀνδρὶ λάλησον· καὶ εἰθούτως ἔγωγε ἐμαυτὴν ἐμφανίσω καὶ πρὸ τῶν ὀφθαλμῶν ὑμῶν διερχομένη ἔσομαι· καὶ ἅμα τῷ θεαθῆναί με, σήμανον εὐθὺς τῷ ἀνδρὶ ὡς· "Ἰδοὺ ἐκείνη ἥν σοι ἔφην γραΐδα, πρὸς ἥν καὶ τὸ ἔπιπλον ἐνεχείρισα." Καὶ σὺν τῷ λόγῳ φώνησόν με εὐθὺς καὶ ἐπερώτησον τί τὸ ἔπιπλον γένοιτο. Ἐγὼ δὲ ἐξ ἑτοίμου ἐπ᾽ ἀκροάσει τοῦ ἀνδρὸς εὐλογοφανῶς μάλα περὶ τούτου ἀποκριθήσομαι.'

68   "Ἀναστὰς οὖν ἐκεῖνος μετὰ ταύτας τὰς τῆς γραΐδος ὑποθήκας πορεύεται καὶ ποιεῖ ὅσαπερ καὶ δεδίδακτο, καὶ τῷ συνεύνῳ τῆς γυναικὸς διωμίλησεν ἅπαντα. Ἐσύστερον δὲ καὶ ἡ γραῦς κατ᾽ ὄψιν αὐτῶν διήρχετο· καὶ καλέσας αὐτὴν ὁ τῆς μοιχείας ἐργάτης ἀνηρώτα περὶ τοῦ πέπλου. Ἡ δὲ γραῦς τῷ τῆς γυναικὸς ἀνδρὶ ἐνατενίσασα πρὸς ἐκεῖνον ἐποιεῖτο τὸν ἀπόλογον καὶ ἔλεγεν· Ἀπάλλαξόν με τῶν τοῦ ἀνδρὸς τοῦδε ἀδίκων ὀχλήσεων· καὶ γάρ μοι πέπλον ἐνεχείρισεν, ἀπαγαγεῖν τοῦτό τινι τῶν ὑφαινόντων εἰς τὰ τούτου διαφθαρέντα μέρη ὡς δυνατὸν ἐπισκευάσαι. Ἔγωγε κατά τινα τύχην παρὰ τὴν σὴν εἰσῆλθον ὁμόζυγον, καί με παντελῶς λέληθε κἄν ἐν τῷ σῷ οἰκίσκῳ κἄν ἐν ἑτέρῳ τόπῳ παρ᾽ ἐμοῦ κατελείφθη, ὡς μὴ δύνασθαι μνη-σθῆναί με τί ἄρα καὶ γένοιτο.' Τούτων οὕτω ῥηθέντων τῷ τῆς γυναικὸς ἀνδρί, ἐκεῖνος τῇ γραΐδι ἀντέφησεν· Ἀλλὰ σοὶ γνωστὸν ἔστω, ὦ γύναι, ὡς ἐκείνου τοῦ ἐπίπλου ἕνεκεν οὐ μικρὸς χόλος καὶ θόρυβος ἐν τῷ οἴκῳ μου γέγονεν.'

have the burned portions rewoven. Since that old woman took it from me, I haven't seen her at all, nor do I have any idea what has become of her." So, say that to the woman's husband,' the old woman said, 'and just then I will appear and pass right before your eyes. And as soon as you see me, indicate to the man, "Look, there's the old woman whom I was telling you about, to whom I handed over the blanket." As you say this, call to me immediately and ask me what has happened to it, and I will be ready to say something quite convincing about the blanket within earshot of the man.'

"After hearing the old woman's suggestion, the man got 68 up and went and did all that he had been instructed to do, communicating everything to the woman's husband. After that, the old woman came into view, and that adulterer called her over and asked about the robe. The old woman fixed her gaze on the woman's husband, however, and made her defense to him: 'Stop this man from unfairly pestering me! He gave me a robe to take to a weaver to repair the ruined parts, as best he could, but by chance I ran into your wife, and I completely forgot whether I left the robe in your house or in some other place, and so I can't recall what actually happened to it.' When she had said this to the woman's husband, he replied to her, 'Well, you should know that this blanket has caused considerable anger and uproar

Καὶ ἐκβαλὼν αὐτίκα ἐπιδέδωκεν ἀμφοτέροις τὸ τοιοῦτον ἔπιπλον, εἶτα πορευθεὶς οἴκαδε τῇ ὁμοζύγῳ ἐσπείσατο καὶ δωρεαῖς αὐτὴν φιλοτίμως ἐδεξιοῦτο, ἀξιῶν αὐτῇ διαλλαγῆναι· ἡ δὲ μόλις τῷ ἀνδρὶ διηλλάγη.

69 "Καὶ νῦν γίνωσκε λοιπόν, ὦ βασιλεῦ, ὡς ἀπέραντος ἡ τῶν γυναικῶν μοχθηρία καὶ δι᾽ αὐτῆς οὐκ ὀλίγοι ἀδίκως ἀπόλλυνται, ὥσπερ δὴ καὶ τὴν τοῦ ἀνδρὸς ὁμόζυγον συνέβαινεν τῇ τῆς γραΐδος μηχανουργίᾳ." Τούτοις αὖθις προσσχὼν ὁ Κῦρος τὴν ἀναίρεσιν τοῦ παιδός ἀναβάλλεται.

70 Ἡ δέ γε τοῦ βασιλέως παλλακὴ ταῦτα ἐνωτισθεῖσα εἰσέρχεται πρὸς αὐτὸν κατὰ τὴν αὐτὴν πέμπτην ἡμέραν καὶ μετὰ οἴκτου αὐτῷ ἔφη· "Ἐπὶ τῷ Θεῷ πέποιθα, ὦ βασιλεῦ, ὡς τοιαύτην μοι δίκην κατὰ τῶνδέ σου τῶν φιλοσόφων δῆθεν συμβούλων βραβεύσοιεν, ὁποίαν δὴ καί τινι κατὰ λέοντος καὶ πίθηκος βραβευθῆναι λέγεται." Ὁ δὲ βασιλεὺς ἔφη· "Καὶ πῶς τὰ κατ᾽ ἐκεῖνα συμβέβηκε τὰ ζῷα;"

71 Ἡ δὲ ἀπεκρίνατο· "Ἦν γάρ τις ὄχλος ἐμπόρων, οἵ καὶ ἐπί τινα ἐμπορίαν συνήθως ἐστέλλοντο. Ἐτύγχανον δὲ ἐκείνοις οὐκ ὀλίγα ὑποζύγια. Καὶ ὀψίας γενομένης ἐπί τι κατέλαβον πανδοχεῖον, ἐν ᾧ κατέλυσαν· τὸν δέ γε τοῦ πανδοχείου πυλῶνα κατασφαλίσαι ἐπελάθοντο. Εἶτα λέων εἰσελθὼν εἰσέδυ τὸ οἴκημα καὶ ἑαυτὸν ἀταράχως τοῖς ὑποζυγίοις ἐγκατέμιξε, μή τινος περὶ αὐτοῦ αἰσθομένου τὸ σύνολον. Μετὰ μικρὸν δὲ παραγίνεταί τις τῶν κλεπτῶν συλῆσαι ἐκ τῶν ὑποζυγίων. Καὶ δὴ σκοτίας οὔσης ἀναψηλαφῶν αὐτῶν ἕκαστον τῇ χειρὶ διετέλει, ὅπως τὸ πολυσάρκως ἔχον τῶν ἄλλων συλήσειε. Τὴν δέ γε ψηλάφησιν ἀπαρχόμενος ποιήσασθαι, ἐκτείνας αὐτοῦ τὴν χεῖρα τοῦ

in my house.' And straightaway he took out the blanket and handed it over to the two of them. Then, after he had gone home, he made peace with his wife and generously rewarded her with gifts, thinking it right that they should be reconciled. And she was reconciled with her husband, but only with difficulty.

"So now, my king, know that the mischief of women is 69
boundless, and many men have been unjustly destroyed by it, just as indeed happened to that man's wife through the old woman's machinations." Cyrus paid attention once again to these words and postponed his son's execution.

When she heard about this, the king's concubine came 70
before him on the same fifth day and with piteous wailing said to him, "I trust, my king, that God will decide this case in my favor against these supposedly learned advisors of yours, just as they say a case was once decided in a certain man's favor against a lion and a monkey." And the king said, "And what happened with those animals?"

She answered, "There was once a large group of mer- 71
chants, who were traveling as usual on business. They had with them quite a few pack animals. When evening came, they arrived at an inn, in which they took up lodging, but they forgot to secure the gate of the inn. Then a lion came along, slipped inside the establishment, and calmly intermingled with the pack animals, none of which noticed him at all. A short time later a thief came to steal one of the pack animals. Since it was dark, he went around examining each of them by hand, so that he might steal the fattest one. But as he began to make his examination, he stretched out his

λέοντος ἀνεπαισθήτως ἥψατο. Καὶ τῶν μὲν κτηνῶν εὐτρα-
φέστερον αὐτὸν εἶναι κατενόησεν, ἕνα δὲ τοῦτον τυγχάνειν
τῶν ὑποζυγίων ὑπετόπασεν. Καὶ αὐτίκα τούτου ἐπιβὰς
ἐξήει τοῦ πανδοχείου. Αὐτοῦ δὲ ἐξερχομένου καθ᾽ ἑαυτὸν
ὁ λέων ἐφθέγγετο· ῾Οὗτός ἐστιν ἀληθῶς ὃν τῆς νυκτὸς
φύλακα λέγουσιν καὶ αὐτός μου ἐπιβέβηκεν.᾽ Καὶ ταῦτα
λέγων ἐδεδίει μᾶλλον τὸν κλέπτην καὶ παρ᾽ ὅλην τὴν
νύκτα τοῦτον διαβαστάζων δρομαῖος ἐπορεύετο. Καὶ ὁ
ἀνὴρ δὲ λέοντι ἐποχεῖσθαι διαγνούς, τοῦτον ἐπτοήθη τὰ
μέγιστα μήπως αὐτοῦ κατάβρωμα γένηται. Πρωΐας δὲ γενομένης ἔτυχε τὸν λέοντα ὑπό τι δένδρον διέρχεσθαι· καὶ
δὴ τὸ τάχος ὁ ἀνὴρ τὴν δεξιὰν ἐκτείνας τοῖς τοῦ δένδρου
κλάδοις ἑαυτὸν ἀπηώρησεν, ἔπειτα δὲ καὶ τοῦ δένδρου
ἐπαναβὰς τὸν τοῦ λέοντος διέφυγε κίνδυνον. Καὶ ὁ λέων
τὸν τοιοῦτον ὑποδειλιῶν φυγὰς εὐθὺς ᾤχετο.

72   ῾Τούτου πορευομένου πίθηξ αὐτῷ συναντᾷ, καὶ ἐπηρώτα τὸν λέοντα· Τί οὕτω περιδεὴς καὶ ἔμφοβος τυγχάνεις;᾽ ῾Ο δὲ λέων ἀπεκρίνατο· ῾Ο τῆς νυκτὸς φύλαξ
λεγόμενος κατασχών με καὶ ἐπιβάς μου παρ᾽ ὅλην δι-
ήλαυνεν τὴν νύκτα.᾽ ῾Ο δὲ πίθηξ, ῾Καὶ ποῦ ἐστιν,᾽ ἔφη,
῾ἐκεῖνος;᾽ ῾Ο δὲ λέων, ῾Απέναντι τῶν ὀφθαλμῶν ἡμῶν ἐπ᾽
ἐκείνου,᾽ φησί, ῾τοῦ δένδρου κεκάθικεν.᾽ ῾Ο δὲ πίθηξ εὐθὺς
ἐπ᾽ ἐκεῖνο ἐπορεύθη τὸ δένδρον τὸν ἄνδρα ὀψόμενος. ῾Ο
δὲ λέων μακρόθεν ἑστὼς ἐνητένιζεν τῷ πίθηκι, τοῦ ἰδεῖν
τί ἐκεῖνος παρὰ τῷ ἀνδρὶ δράσαιτο. Τοῦ μέντοι πίθηκος τῷ
δένδρῳ ἐπαναβάντος, ὁ ἀνὴρ ἀμφότερα ἐπτοήθη τὰ ζῷα
καὶ ὑπὸ τοῦ συνέχοντος αὐτὸν δέους ἀγωνιῶν τὴν τοῦ
δένδρου σχισμάδα παραχρῆμα εἰσέδυ. ῾Ο δὲ πίθηξ τῇ χειρὶ

hand and touched the lion without realizing it. He could tell that it was the most well-nourished of the beasts, but he was also under the impression that it was one of the pack animals. Then straightaway he mounted it and rode it out of the inn. As the man was riding off, the lion said to itself, 'This must be the one they call the night watchman, and he has mounted me.' And thinking this he feared the thief even more, and thus he carried him at a run all night long. As for the man, once he realized that he was riding on a lion, he also became terrified that he would become the animal's dinner. At daybreak it so happened that the lion passed under a tree, and so the man quickly stretched out his right hand and suspended himself from its branches, and then, climbing up to the top of the tree, he escaped the danger from the lion. And the lion, still terrified of the man, immediately made its escape, too.

"As the lion was going on his way, a monkey met him, and asked the lion, 'Why are you so scared and afraid?' And the lion answered, 'The one they call the night watchman seized me, mounted me, and rode me all night long.' And the monkey said, 'Where is he?', to which the lion replied, 'He's sitting at the top of that tree right in front of us.' And the monkey immediately made its way to the tree to see the man. The lion stood at a distance and watched the monkey carefully, to see what it would do when it encountered the man. When the monkey climbed up the tree, the man became terrified of both animals, and overcome by the fear that possessed him, he immediately got into a hole in the tree trunk.

72

τῷ λέοντι ὑπεσήμανε, τοῦ αὐτὸν παραγενέσθαι καὶ ἀποκτεῖναι τὸν ἄνδρα. Καταλαβὼν δὲ τὰ ἐκεῖσε ὁ λέων ἔστη
κάτωθεν τοῦ δένδρου. Ὑπῆρχεν δὲ ὁ πίθηξ τοὺς τῶν
ἀναγκαίων διδύμους εὐμεγέθεις ἔχων, οὓς καὶ ἰδὼν ὁ ἀνὴρ
μικρὸν ἀνεθάρσησε, καὶ ἄφνω τούτους περισχὼν δεσμοῖς
περιέσφιγξεν. Καὶ αὐτίκα ὁ πίθηξ τῆς ζωῆς ἀπερράγη καὶ
τοῦ δένδρου ἀποπέπτωκεν. Ὁ δὲ λέων ἰδὼν αὐτὸν πικρῶς
ἀπολωλότα καθ᾽ ἑαυτὸν ἔλεγε ὡς· Ἀληθῶς ὁ τῇ νυκτὶ
ἐλάσας με <τοῦτον ἀπέκτεινε.᾽ Καὶ> ὀξύτατα ἀπέδρα. Καὶ
οὕτως ἀμφοτέρων ζῴων ὁ ἀνὴρ περιεγένετο.

73   "Καὶ κατ᾽ αὐτὸν γοῦν τὸν τρόπον κἀγώ, βασιλεῦ, πέποιθα ἐπὶ τὴν θείαν δύναμιν ὡς δῴη ἡμῖν κατὰ τῶν φιλοσόφων περιγενέσθαι, ὅτιπερ σοῦ καὶ ἐμοῦ τοσαύτην μέσον
τιθέασι σύγχυσιν. Τοῦτο δέ μοι θεόθεν εὔχομαι, εἰ μή τί
γε, βασιλεῦ, σύ με διεκδικήσεις ἐφ᾽ οἷς ἐνυβρισθῆναι παρὰ
τοῦ υἱοῦ σου ἐβιαζόμην." Τούτοις τὴν καρδίαν ἀλγήσας ὁ
βασιλεὺς κελεύει τὸν υἱὸν αὐτοῦ ξίφει ὑποβληθῆναι.

74   Ὁ δὲ τοῦ βασιλέως ἕκτος φιλόσοφος σύμβουλος τὴν
τοιαύτην κατὰ τοῦ υἱοῦ αὐτοῦ ἐξενεχθῆναι ἀπόφασιν μαθὼν εἰσέρχεται πρὸς αὐτὸν ὥρᾳ ἕκτῃ, καὶ προσκυνήσας
φησί· "Βασιλεῦ, ζῆθι εἰς τὸν αἰῶνα καὶ ἐπὶ μακροὺς χρόνους
ἡ ἐξουσία σου διαμείνοιε. Γνῶναι δέ σου τὸ κράτος δουλο-
πρεπῶς ἀξιῶ ὡς εἰ μὴ τὸ παράπαν υἱός σοι ἐτύγχανεν, ἔδει
σε διαπύρως ἔτι δυσωπῆσαι τὸ θεῖον τοῦ παιδίον γεννη-
θῆναί σοι ὥστε τοῦτον κληρονόμον τῆς βασιλείας κατα-
λιπεῖν· νυνὶ δὲ παῖδα ἔχων πειρᾶσαι τοῦτον ἀνελεῖν σκαι-
οτρόπου γυναικὸς διαβολῇ, καὶ ταῦτα μήπω εἰδὼς κἂν
θανάτου ὁ παῖς ἔνοχος κἂν ἀθῶος πέφυκε· καὶ ὅτιπερ εἰ

The monkey waved to the lion to come over and kill the man and, when it arrived, it stood beneath the tree. Now the monkey happened to have enormous testicles, and when the man saw them, he gained a bit of courage, and he quickly grabbed them and bound them up tightly. And straightaway the monkey lost its life and fell out of the tree. When it saw the monkey suffer this miserable fate, the lion said to itself, 'For sure the one who rode me in the night must have killed the monkey,' and it ran away very quickly. In this way the man prevailed over both animals.

"And in this very way, my king, I too trust that divine 73 power will grant that I prevail against the philosophers, since they have created such great turmoil between you and me. I pray that God will grant me this, if you do not, my king, avenge me somehow for being forcibly raped by your son." Pained in his heart by these words, the king ordered his son to be put to the sword.

When the king's sixth learned advisor heard that this sen- 74 tence had been pronounced against his son, he came to the king at the sixth hour, and after making his prostration, said, "*My king, may you live forever* and may your power endure for many long years. As your servant, I think your majesty should know that if you had no son at all, you would still have to beseech God fervently for one to be born to you, so that you could leave him behind as heir to your kingdom. As it is, you have a son but are attempting to execute him on the basis of the slander of a wicked woman, and you do this without knowing whether your son is guilty of a capital crime or is innocent. And you should know that, if you de-

τοῦτον ἀσυζητήτως ὀλέσεις, καιρίαν ἐσύστερον ἐπισπάσῃ
τὴν λύπην, καί σοι προσγενήσεται ὥσπερ δή τινι ἐπισυνέβη
περιστερᾷ.

75   "Λέγεται γὰρ περὶ ἐκείνης ὅτι τοῖς γηδίοις παρεδρεύουσα
καθ᾽ ὃν καιρὸν ἐθερίζοντο διετέλει κατόπιν τῶν θεριστῶν
τὸν ἀποπίπτοντα σῖτον συλλέγουσα καὶ ἐσθίουσα, ἡνίκα
δὲ ἐκορέννυτο, τὸ περιττεῦον τῆς συλλογῆς ἐπί τινα θυρίδα μετακομίζουσα. Μιᾷ γοῦν κατὰ τὸ αὐτῆς σύνηθες
μετεκόμιζε τὸν αὐτῇ περιττεύσαντα σῖτον καὶ τῇ θυρίδι
τοῦτον ἐναπετίθει, ἕως οὗ πλήρης ἡ θυρὶς ἐγεγόνει· εἶτά
φησι πρὸς τὴν ἰδίαν ὁμόζυγον ὡς· Ἡ Μηδεὶς ἡμῶν προσεγ-
γίσῃ τῷδε τῷ ἀποτεθέντι παρ᾽ ἐμοῦ σίτῳ ἄχρις ἂν ὁ τοῦ
χειμῶνος ἐπισταίη καιρός, ὅτε μὴ ἔσται τὸ παράπαν ὁ
σῖτος ἐφευρισκόμενος καὶ ἐκ τούτου τοῦ ἀποτεθέντος
ἀμφότεροι διατραφῶμεν.᾽ Ἡ δέ γε ὁμόζυγος πρὸς τὸν
ἄρρενα ἔφη· Ἡ Καλῶς τοῦτο καὶ συμφερόντως μεταξὺ ἡμῶν
διεστείλω καὶ οὕτως ὡς ἔφησας γενέσθω.᾽ Ἔκτοτε γοῦν
ἀμφότεραι αἱ περιστεραὶ ἐν τοῖς ἔξω διόλου περιήρχοντό
τε καὶ ἐνέμοντο.

76   "Τοῦ δὲ ἡλίου διηνεκῶς ἐκείνῃ τῇ θυρίδι ἐπιλάμποντος
ἀπεξηράνθη ὁ ἐν αὐτῇ ἀποτιθέμενος σῖτος, καθότι ἐν τῷ
θερισμῷ ποσῶς ὑπῆρχεν ὑποχλοάζων. Καὶ δὴ ἐν μιᾷ τῶν
ἡμερῶν ἡ ταῦτα κομίσασα περιστερὰ τῇ θυρίδι ἐφίσταται
τοὺς ἐκεῖσε κόκκους θεασομένη καὶ εὑρίσκει τούτους ἐλ-
λιπεῖς κατὰ πολὺ γεγονότας ὑπὸ τῆς ξηρότητος. Λέγει οὖν
πρὸς τὴν ὁμόζυγον· Ἡ Τί ἐστι τοῦτο ὅπερ νῦν τεθέαμαι;
Οὐ διενετειλάμην σε μηδόλως τούτοις ἡμῶν προσψαύειν
τοῖς σιτίοις;᾽ Ἡ δ᾽ ὁμόζυγος, Ἡ Καὶ οὐχ ἡψάμην αὐτῶν,᾽

94

stroy him without an investigation, you will bring grievous sorrow upon yourself in the future and will suffer the same fate as a certain dove.

"For they say that this dove would frequent the fields at 75 harvest time, collecting the wheat that would fall behind the reapers and eating it. Whenever the dove was full, he would carry the surplus that he had collected to a small opening in a wall. Now one day the dove was carrying the surplus wheat, as was his habit, and storing it away in the opening, until the opening became full. Then the dove said to his spouse, 'Let neither of us touch this wheat that I have stored away until wintertime is upon us, when wheat can't be found at all, and we may both feed upon this stockpile.' The female dove replied to the male, 'What you've commanded is in our best interests, and so let's do what you have said.' From that time, then, both doves always went around and fed themselves outdoors.

"But the sun shone continuously on that opening, and so 76 the wheat stored there dried up, since it had still been somewhat green when it was harvested. And then one day the dove that had carried the wheat perched upon the opening to look at the grains that were there, and he found they had shrunk a lot by being dried out. He said then to his spouse, 'What have I just seen? Didn't I tell you not to touch our wheat at all?' His spouse answered, 'And so I didn't touch it.'

ἀπεκρίνατο. Ἡ δὲ οὐδαμῶς τῇ ὁμοζύγῳ πεπίστευκεν, ἀλλὰ μᾶλλον κατ᾽ αὐτῆς ἀγριάνασα πλήττει θρασέως ταύτην καὶ τῆς ζωῆς ἀπορρήγνυσι, καὶ μονωτάτη καταλιμπάνεται. Ἐπιστάντος δὲ τοῦ χειμῶνος καὶ πολλῶν ὑετῶν τε καὶ νιφετῶν καταφερομένων πάλιν ὁ ἀποτεθεὶς σῖτος ἐκεῖνος τῇ τοῦ ἀέρος ὑγρότητι νοτισθεὶς ὅλην ἐκείνην ὡς τὸ πρότερον τὴν θυρίδα πεπλήρωκεν. Ὅπερ θεασαμένη ἡ περιστερὰ τὴν αἰτίαν τῆς ἐλλείψεως καὶ τῆς ὡς πρῴην ὑστέρας ἀναπληρώσεως καθ᾽ ἑαυτὴν ἐπέγνω, καὶ τὸ ἀπ᾽ ἐκείνου πικρῶς ἐπὶ τῇ ἀπωλείᾳ τῆς ὁμοζύγου μετεμέλετο, οὐδὲν δὲ τῆς μεταμελείας ἀπώνατο.

77   "Οὕτως οὖν ἐπίσταμαι, ὦ βασιλεῦ, ὡς εἴπερ καὶ σὺ τὸν υἱόν σου διαχειρίσῃ ἐκ ψιλῆς διαβολῆς τοῦ καταράτου τοῦδε γυναίου, καὶ ταῦτα μὴ εἰδὼς εἰ ἐκεῖνος κατάκριτος ταῖς ἀληθείαις πέφυκεν, συμβήσεται καὶ τῷ σῷ κράτει ὡς ἐκείνῃ τῇ περιστερᾷ συμβέβηκεν, καὶ τοῖς κέντροις τῆς μεταμελείας χαλεπῶς ἔσῃ νυττόμενος καὶ οὐδέν σοι ἐντεῦθεν γενήσεται ὄφελος. Καὶ ἄλλης δέ μου διηγήσεως ἄκουσον, ὦ βασιλεῦ, περὶ τῶν γυναικείων δηλούσης σοι πανουργευμάτων.

78   "Ἀνὴρ γάρ τις ἦν γεωργικὴν μετερχόμενος ἐπιστήμην. Οὗτος οὖν ἐν μιᾷ ἐξέρχεται ἐπὶ τὸν αὐτοῦ ἀγρὸν κατασπεῖραι αὐτόν. Περὶ δέ γε τὴν ὥραν τοῦ ἀρίστου ἡ τοῦ γεωργοῦ σύζυγος ὄψα αὐτῷ παρητοίμασεν ὄρνιθός τε καὶ μελιπήκτου ἐδέσματος, ἃ καὶ σπυρίδι ἐνθεῖσα πρὸς τὸν ἄνδρα ἐκόμιζεν. Συνέβη δὲ πορευομένην αὐτὴν διά τινος καταλύματος διελθεῖν. Εὐθὺς δέ τινες ἐκεῖθεν ὁδοστάται ἐξορμήσαντες κατέσχον τὴν γυναῖκα καὶ ἐν ἐκείνῳ

But the dove did not believe his spouse in the least. Instead, he became enraged at her, beat her impetuously, and took her life, and so he was left utterly alone. When winter came, there was much rainfall and snow, and that stored-up wheat became damp from the moisture in the air and once again filled the entire opening as before. When the dove observed this, he realized the cause of the shrinkage and of the subsequent restoration, and from then on bitterly regretted the loss of his spouse, but he got no consolation from his regret.

"And so, my king, I understand that if you too kill your 77 son on the basis of mere slander from this accursed woman, and if you do this without knowing whether he is truly worthy to be condemned, your majesty will suffer the same fate as that dove, and you will be stung by pangs of regret, and nothing will help you then. And let me tell you another story, my king, that will reveal to you the wicked ways of women.

"There was once a man who practiced the art of farming. 78 And so, one day, this man went out to his field to sow it. Around lunchtime the farmer's wife prepared a meal for him of both fowl and honey cake; she put this in a basket and was carrying it to her husband. It so happened that while she was on her way she passed by an inn. Immediately some highwaymen rushed out, seized the woman, took her

εἰσαγαγόντες τῷ καταλύματι βιαίως αὐτῇ συνεγένοντο καὶ ἃ διεκόμιζεν ὄψα ἀφελόμενοι κατέδοντο. Μικρὸν δέ τι τοῦ μελιπήκτου ἐδέσματος ἐσύστερον λιπόντες καὶ εἰς μόρφωσιν ἐλέφαντος τὸ καταλειφθὲν ἐπισκευάσαντες τῇ σπυρίδι ἐναπέθεντο, μηδέν τι περὶ τοῦδε εἰδυίας τῆς γυναικός, καὶ τὴν σπυρίδα κατεκάλυψαν. Ἡ δὲ γυνὴ ταύτην ἀνελομένη κεκαλυμμένην ὡς τὸ πρότερον τυγχάνουσαν καὶ ἀγνοοῦσα ὡς τὰ ἐν αὐτῇ ὄψα παρ' ἐκείνων ἐβρώθησαν πρὸς τὸν ἄνδρα ἀπεκόμισε.

79 "Καὶ τὴν σπυρίδα πρὸ τῶν ἐκείνου ὀφθαλμῶν αὐτῆς καταθεμένης, ἐκεῖνος αὐτὴν εὐθὺς ἀνακαλύπτει, καὶ ὁρᾷ μηδὲν ἕτερον ἔχουσαν ἢ μόνον τὸ μελίπηκτον ἔδεσμα τὸ τὴν μορφὴν φέρον τοῦ ἐλέφαντος. Ὅπερ ἰδών, 'Τί τοῦτο, γύναι;' πρὸς τὴν σύζυγον ἔφησεν. Ἡ δὲ ὄψεις τῷ ὁρωμένῳ ἐπιβαλοῦσα εὐθὺς τὸ αὐτῇ συμβεβηκὸς δρᾶμα διαμηχανᾶται καί φησι πρὸς τὸν ἄνδρα ὡς· 'Τῇ νυκτὶ ταύτῃ καθευδούσης μου ἔδοξα κατ' ὄναρ ἐλέφαντι ἐποχεῖσθαί με καὶ τούτου ἐξολισθήσασαν τοῖς αὐτοῦ ποσὶν συμπατηθῆναι. Ἔξυπνος δὲ γενομένη πολλῷ τῷ φόβῳ συνειχόμην καὶ αὐτίκα πρὸς τὸν ὀνειροκρίτην τὸ τάχος ἐπορεύθην καὶ αὐτῷ τὰ ὁραθέντα διηγησάμην· ὁ δὲ εὐθὺς τὸ ὄναρ διέλυσεν καί μοι ἐνετείλατο εἰπών· "Ὡς ἐλέφαντος μορφὴν χρή σε, ὦ γύναι, ἐκ μελιπήκτου παρασκευάσαι ἐδέσματος καὶ τῷ ἀνδρί σου εἰς βρῶσιν ἀποκομίσαι, ὅπως τὸ ὄναρ τοῦτο ἀκινδύνως σοι διαλυθείη." Καὶ ἰδοὺ κατὰ τὰς ὑποθήκας ἐκείνου, ὡς ὁρᾷς, πεποίηκα, σὺ δὲ λοιπόν, ὦ ἄνερ, προθυμότατα φάγε, ὡς ἂν μηδείς μοι προσγενήσεται κίνδυνος.' Ἐκεῖνος δὲ αὐτίκα τὸ μελίπηκτον ἐδηδόκει. Καὶ

into the inn, and raped her; and they stole and ate the food that she was carrying. They left a little bit of the honey cake and, after forming the leftover bits into the shape of an elephant, they put it back into the basket without the woman noticing, and then they covered the basket. The woman picked up the basket, covered as it was before, and, unaware that the food in it had been eaten by those men, she took it off to her husband.

"When she set the basket before him, he immediately 79 uncovered it and saw that it contained nothing but the honey cake in the shape of an elephant. When he saw this, he said to his wife, 'What's this?' When she looked at what he had seen, she immediately realized what had happened to her, and said to her husband, 'While I was sleeping last night, I dreamed that I was riding an elephant, and then I slipped off and was trampled under its feet. When I awoke, I was gripped by a great fear and straightaway hurried off to the dream interpreter and told him what I had seen. He immediately interpreted the dream and instructed me: "You must make a honey cake in the shape of an elephant and take it to your husband to eat, so that this dream may be resolved with no danger to you." And look, I've acted, as you see, according to that man's instructions, but now you, my husband, must gobble it up so that no danger will come to me.' And straightaway her husband ate the honey cake. And

99

οὕτως ἡ γυνὴ πρὸς τὸν ἄνδρα προφασισαμένη τὸ ἀνύποπτον ἑαυτῇ ἐφ᾽ οἷς προεπεπόνθει παρὰ τῷ συνεύνῳ περιεποιήσατο· πᾶσι γὰρ οἷς λελάληκεν ἀναμφιλέκτως ἐκεῖνος πεπίστευκε.

80 "Λοιπὸν οὖν, ὦ βασιλεῦ, καὶ αὐτὸς ἐπίγνωθι τὸ ποικίλον τῶν γυναικείων μηχανημάτων καὶ ὅτι γε ὅπως ἂν καὶ βουληθεῖεν δυνατῶς πονηρεύεσθαι καὶ κατασκευάζειν ἔχουσιν." Τούτων πάλιν ὁ Κῦρος ἀκηκοὼς μὴ ἀποκτανθῆναι τὸν υἱὸν αὐτοῦ προσέταξεν.

81 Κατ᾽ αὐτὴν δὲ τὴν ἕκτην ἡμέραν σφόδρα ἡ γυνὴ ἐπὶ τῷδε τῷ προστάγματι τοῦ βασιλέως δεινοπαθήσασα, καθ᾽ ἑαυτὴν ἔλεγε ὡς· "Εἰ μὴ τὴν σήμερον τοῦ βασιλέως ὁ υἱὸς ἀποκτανθείη, τῇ αὔριον πάντως τῷ αὐτοῦ πατρὶ προσφθέγξεται καὶ εὐθέως διὰ τῆς ἐκείνου πρὸς τὸν βασιλέα ὁμιλίας τὰ τῆς ἐμῆς σκαιωρίας ἐλεγχθήσεται καὶ τῷ θανάτῳ παραδοθήσομαι. Χρὴ οὖν λοιπὸν ἐμαυτὴν διαχειρίσασθαι· οὐδαμῶς γάρ τι ἕτερον τῷ βασιλεῖ εἰρηκέναι τολμήσω." Ταῦτα ἐν ἑαυτῇ ἡ κακότροπος προσυλλογισαμένη καὶ τῷ φόβῳ δεινῶς ταραττομένη πρῶτα μὲν συνέλεξεν τὰ ὑπάρχοντα αὐτῇ καὶ τοῖς γνωστοῖς καὶ τοῖς γείτοσι διεμέτρησεν, εἶτα αὐτοὺς ἀξιοῖ ὕλην καυστικὴν αὐτῇ συναγαγεῖν. Οἱ δὲ αὐτίκα δαψιλῆ συναγείρουσι. Κἀκείνη διὰ ταύτης σφοδρὰν ἀνῆψε πυρκαϊάν· ἧς δὴ καὶ ἀναφθείσης ὥρμησεν ἡ γυνὴ τῇ καμίνῳ ἑαυτὴν ἐπεμβαλεῖν, ὅτιπερ ὑφωρᾶτο τῇ ἐπαύριον οὐ μικρὰν τὴν αἰσχύνην καὶ τὸν κατάγελων ἐπισπάσασθαι.

82 Καὶ ἐπείπερ ἤδη ἡ ἑβδόμη ἡμέρα ἐφίστατο, καθ᾽ ἣν ὁ παῖς τῷ βασιλεῖ προσφθέγξασθαι ἔμελλεν, ὥς γε κατ᾽

thus, by offering her husband an excuse, she kept him from suspecting what had really happened to her; for he believed everything that she had said without question.

"And so now, my king, you too must take note of the variety of feminine wiles and know that women are capable of behaving wickedly and fabricating stories however they wish." After hearing these things, Cyrus again ordered that his son not be killed. 80

On this sixth day, the woman suffered acutely because of the king's command, and she said to herself, "Unless the king's son is killed today, tomorrow he will relate everything to his father, and immediately, because of what he says to the king, my intrigue will be exposed and I will be condemned to death. I must, therefore, take my own life. For in no way will I dare to say anything else to the king." After speaking to herself in this way and becoming terribly fearful, the malicious woman first collected all her belongings and distributed them to her friends and neighbors. Then she asked them to collect firewood for her, and straightaway they gathered an abundant supply. And using this wood, she lit a great fire. And when this fire had been kindled, the woman was eager to throw herself into the furnace, because she suspected that on the next day she would attract great shame and ridicule. 81

And when the seventh day had arrived, on which the son was going to speak to the king, as his teacher had originally 82

ἀρχὰς ὑπὸ τοῦ διδασκάλου παρήγγελτο, διὰ τοῦτο ἡ γυνὴ λίαν ὡς εἰκὸς ἠγωνία καὶ ἐφρόντιζε καὶ μερίμναις καὶ ἀλγηδόσι τὴν καρδίαν ἐβάλλετο. Ἤιδει γὰρ ὡς ἡνίκα τῷ βασιλεῖ ὁ παῖς φθέγξηται, οὐ μόνον αὐτὴ καταισχυνθήσεται, ἀλλὰ καὶ ὀλέθρῳ μετὰ τῆς αἰσχύνης παραδοθήσεται ἐφ' οἷς πάντως τῷ παιδίῳ ἀτόπως λελάληκε.

83   Τοῦ γοῦν τοιούτου τῆς γυναικὸς χαλεποῦ βουλεύματος πολλαχοῦ γε τῇ φήμῃ θρυλλουμένου καὶ διαθέοντος ἔφθασεν καὶ εἰς τὰς τοῦ βασιλέως ἀκοάς. Καὶ δὴ τὸ τάχος τὴν γυναῖκα προφθάνει, καί φησιν αὐτῇ· "Τίνος χάριν, ὦ γύναι, πυρὶ σεαυτὴν παραδίδως;" Ἡ δέ, "Μὴ ὡς ἔδει με ἀπὸ τοῦ παιδός σου," ἔφη, "ἐξεδίκησας, οὔτε αὐτὸν καθὰ προσῆκεν ἀπέκτεινας." Ὁ δὲ βασιλεὺς ἅμα τῷ λόγῳ πίστεις αὐτῇ ἐνόρκους καὶ ἀσφαλεῖς δέδωκεν ὡς ἀναμφι-λέκτως τὸν παῖδα διαχειρίσεται. Ἡ δὲ μιαρὰ παλλακὴ τὸν λόγον ἀποδεξαμένη ἐπέσχεν ἑαυτὴν τοῦ τοιούτου ἐγ-χειρήματος. Καὶ αὐτίκα ὁ βασιλεὺς μετ' ὀργῆς ἀπεφήνατο ἀνυπερθέτως τὸν υἱὸν αὐτοῦ ξίφει ὑποβληθῆναι.

84   Τῆς οὖν τοιαύτης ἰταμωτάτης ἐξενεχθείσης ἀποφάσεως ὁ τοῦ βασιλέως ἕβδομος φιλοσοφώτατος σύμβουλος περὶ αὐτῆς ἐνωτισάμενος καὶ σὺν αὐτῷ οἱ ἕτεροι ἓξ τούτου συμφιλόσοφοι σφόδρα ἐπὶ τῷ γόνῳ τῆς πορφύρας ἤλγη-σαν, ὁρῶντες τὸν ἄκακον ὡς κακοῦργον κινδυνεύοντα, καὶ πορευθέντες ἐφίσταντο τῷ τοῦ βασιλέως σπεκουλάτωρι ἤδη τὸ ξίφος πρὸς τὴν σφαγὴν τοῦ παιδίου ἀνατείνοντι. Τούτῳ γοῦν ἐπιστάντες ἐπιμόνως αὐτὸν ἠξίουν ἐπ' ὀλίγον ὑπερθέσθαι τὴν τοῦ παιδὸς ἀναίρεσιν, ἄχρις ἂν ὁ τῶν φιλοσόφων ἕβδομος πρὸς τὸν βασιλέα εἰσέλθῃ ἅμα καὶ

ordered him, the woman, as might be expected, was very distressed on account of this and anxious, and her heart was beset with worries and pains. For she knew that once the son spoke to the king, not only would she be disgraced, but along with her disgrace she would also be condemned to destruction for the utterly improper suggestion she had made to the boy.

Now rumors of the woman's rash plan were quickly re- 83 peated and spread everywhere, and they even reached the king's ears. Then he swiftly caught her before she could act and said, "Why are you going to cast yourself into the fire?" And she said, "You have not avenged me against your son as you should have, nor have you killed him as was proper." As soon as the king heard this reply, he gave her sworn and unwavering assurances that he would, without question, have his son put to death. And the foul concubine accepted his word and held herself back from suicide. Then straightaway the king angrily declared that his son should be put to the sword without delay.

When this impetuous sentence had been pronounced, 84 the seventh of the king's most learned advisors heard about it, as did his six fellow philosophers, and they felt great pain over this child of the purple, because they saw the innocent boy exposed to danger as if he were a criminal. They went and stood over the king's executioner, who was already brandishing his sword to kill the boy. Then as they stood over him, they insisted that he put off the execution for a little while, until the seventh philosopher could go to the king

ἐξέλθῃ. Οὐ μὴν ἀλλὰ καὶ δώροις τὸν ἄνδρα ἐδεξιώσαντο. Ὁ δὲ τοὺς φιλοσόφους αἰδεσθεὶς συγκατανεύει τῇ αὐτῶν ἀξιώσει.

85 Εἶτα ὁ αὐτὸς τῶν φιλοσόφων ἕβδομος σύμβουλος πρὸς τὸν βασιλέα ἐκεῖθεν πορεύεται, καὶ εἰσελθὼν προσεκύνησεν αὐτὸν ἐπὶ τῆς γῆς, καί φησι· "Βασιλεῦ, εἰς τὸν αἰῶνα ζῆθι. Γινώσκειν σου τὸ κράτος ἐκδυσωπῶ, ὡς ἐξαίσιον ἅμα καὶ ἀνόσιον δρᾶμα πειρᾶσαι πεποιηκέναι, ὅτιπερ τὸν υἱὸν μαχαίρας ἔργον γενέσθαι προσέταξας ψιλῇ γυναικὸς ὑποθήκῃ οὕτως ἀνεξετάστως συναρπαγείς, καὶ ταῦτα μήπω ἐγνωκὼς κἂν ἀληθῆ σοι κἂν ψευδῆ λελάληκεν. Ἤκουσται δέ μοι καὶ τοῦτο, ὡς διὰ πολλῶν εὐχῶν, νηστειῶν τε καὶ εὐποιιῶν θεόθεν τοῦτον τὸν παῖδα σύ τε καὶ ἡ μήτηρ ἐξητήσασθε· καὶ διὰ γυναικὸς ῥῆμα ὀλέθρῳ αὐτὸν παραδίδως; Ἀλλ᾽ ὅμως μου τῶν ῥημάτων ἄκουσον.

86 "Ἀνὴρ γάρ τις ἦν πύθωνος πνεῦμα ἔχων καὶ τοῖς βουλομένοις τὰ μέλλοντα δῆθεν μαντευόμενος καὶ δαψιλῆ ἐντεῦθεν κέρδη ποριζόμενος· οὐ μὴν ἀλλὰ καὶ ἰατρικῆς τέχνης ὑπὸ τῆς μαντείας ἔμπειρος ἐτύγχανεν· ὅθεν καὶ πᾶσι τοῖς παρ᾽ αὐτοῦ περί τινων ἀδήλων πυνθανομένοις ἑτοίμους ἐποιεῖτο τὰς λύσεις. Οὕτως οὖν ὁ ἀνὴρ ἐπιστημόνως ἔχων οὐκ ὀλίγον ἑαυτῷ πλοῦτον ἐθησαύρισε. Μιᾷ γοῦν τῶν ἡμερῶν τὸ ἐνοικοῦν αὐτῷ μαντικὸν πνεῦμα πρὸς τὸν ἄνδρα εἰρήκει ὡς· "Ἔγωγε τοῦ λοιποῦ ὑπαναχωρῆσαί σου βούλομαι καὶ οὐκέτι ἕξεις με. Πλὴν πρὸ τῆς ἐκδημίας μου λόγους τρεῖς διαστελῶ σοι, καὶ δι᾽ ἑκάστου τούτων ὃ ἂν θεόθεν ἐξαιτήσῃ, αὐτίκα σοι παρασχεθήσεται.᾽

and come back; and they even rewarded the man with gifts. Out of deference to the philosophers, the executioner acquiesced to their request.

Then the same seventh learned advisor made his way 85 from there to the king, and having entered he prostrated himself before him on the ground and said, "*My king, may you live forever.* I entreat your majesty to understand that you are trying to perform an extraordinary and impious deed by ordering your son to die by the sword, because you have been beguiled so unquestioningly by a mere suggestion from a woman and, what is more, because you have not yet learned whether she has spoken truly or falsely. I have also heard that through many prayers, much fasting, and many good deeds, you and his mother beseeched God for this boy; do you now, then, hand him over to destruction on the word of a woman? But still, listen to my story.

"There once was a man who had a spirit of divination and 86 who supposedly prophesied the future to whoever wished to know it, and thereby made himself a good profit. Moreover, he was also skilled in the medical arts because of his prophetic power, from which he also offered ready solutions to all who asked him about uncertain matters. And so, because he possessed these types of knowledge, the man amassed no small amount of wealth for himself. Now one day the prophetic spirit that lived within him said to the man, 'I wish to go away from you from now on, and you will no longer have me. But before my departure, I will grant you three wishes, and through each of these, you will straightaway receive whatever you request from God.' And after

Καὶ ταῦτα αὐτῷ λέξαν τὸ τοῦ πύθωνος πνεῦμα καὶ τὰς τρεῖς ῥήσεις τῷ ἀνδρὶ δεδήλωκεν, εἶτα καὶ πόρρω αὐτοῦ παντελῶς ἐγεγόνει.

87 Ὁ δὲ τοῦ μαντικοῦ πνεύματος ἐξ αὐτοῦ ἀνακεχωρηκότος σὺν ἀθυμίᾳ πολλῇ οἴκαδε ἀφίκετο. Θεασαμένη δὲ αὐτὸν ἡ τούτου σύζυγος, 'Τί οὕτως,' ἔφη, 'στυγνὸς καὶ ὠχριῶν γέγονας;' Ὁ δὲ αὐτῇ ἀπεκρίνατο· 'Ὅτιπερ, ὦ γύναι, τὸ τοῦ πύθωνος ἐκεῖνο πνεῦμα, ὃ δὴ ἐγκατῴκει μοι, δι' οὗ ἐμαντευόμην καὶ αὐτὰς δὴ τὰς νόσους ἐθεράπευον, νῦν ἀπ' ἐμοῦ ἐξελθὸν τέλεον ὑπανεχώρησεν, καὶ τούτου ἐρημωθεὶς αὐτήν, γίνωσκε, τὴν ζωήν μου ἀπολέγομαι· ὑπ' αὐτοῦ γὰρ ἅπαντα τὰ ἀπόρρητα ἐδιδασκόμην καὶ δαψιλῆ διὰ τούτου κέρδη ἐποριζόμην.' Ἡ δὲ γυνὴ τὰ τοιαῦτα ῥήματα παρὰ τοῦ ἀνδρὸς ἀκούσασα σφόδρα κἀκείνη ἐπὶ τῷ συμβάντι ἤλγησεν. Ὁρῶν δὲ αὐτὴν πικρῶς ἀνιωμένην παρηγορεῖν ὡς ἐνὸν τῇ γυναικὶ ἐπεχείρησε, καὶ πρὸς αὐτὴν αὖθις εἴρηκεν· 'Θάρσει, ὦ γύναι, καὶ μὴ λυποῦ· τὸ γὰρ πνεῦμα ἐκεῖνο τρεῖς ῥήσεις μοι διεστείλατο, ὥστε δι' ἑκάστου τῶν τριῶν πᾶν εἴ τι θυμῆρές μοι θεόθεν ἐξαιτήσασθαι, καὶ δεδήλωκέν μοι ὡς εἴ τι δ' ἂν καὶ αἰτήσωμαι, εὐθέως μοι προσγενήσεται.' Τούτοις τοῖς λόγοις ἡ γυνὴ ἐπὶ τὸ εὐθυμότερον μετενεχθεῖσα, 'Αὐτάρκη σοι τὸ λοιπόν,' τῷ ἀνδρὶ ἀντέφησεν, 'ἐκεῖνα δὴ ἔστωσαν τὰ τρία ῥησείδια.' Ὁ δὲ ἀνὴρ αὖθις τῇ ὁμοζύγῳ λέγει· 'Τί οὖν συμβουλεύεις μοι ἐκ Θεοῦ αἰτήσασθαι;' Ἡ δὲ γυνὴ ἐκείνη λίαν οὖσα πονηροτάτη καὶ πρὸς ἀτάκτους ὁρμὰς καὶ παραλόγους ὀρέξεις ἐνδόσιμός τε καὶ φιλοσώματος, 'Οἶδας,' φησί, 'ὦ ἄνερ, καθὰ καὶ αὐτὴ ἐπίσταμαι, ὡς οὐδὲν συνουσίας τοῖς

saying this the spirit of divination granted him the three wishes, and then it went away from him forever.

"After the spirit of prophecy had left him, the man ar- 87 rived home in great despair. When his wife saw him, she said, 'Why are you so gloomy and pale?' He replied to her, 'Because that spirit of divination that used to live in me and through which I used to prophesy and treat diseases, has now left me and completely gone away. Now that it has deserted me, you should know that I am giving up on my life. For I used to learn all the secret things from it and thus made a good profit.' When the woman heard her husband's words, she too felt great pain at what had happened. And when he saw how bitterly distressed she was, he tried to console his wife as best he could, and he said to her in turn, 'Take heart and do not grieve. For that spirit granted me three wishes, so that I could ask God for anything I wanted with each of the three, and it revealed to me that whatever I ask for will immediately come true for me.' The woman became more cheerful when she heard these words, and she replied to her husband, 'May those three little wishes be sufficient for you for the rest of your life.' The man in turn said to his wife, 'What then do you advise me to request from God?' Now that woman was very wicked, prone to uncontrolled impulses and abnormal appetites, and given to sensuality, and so she said, 'You know, my husband, as I myself also understand, that nothing is dearer to humans than

ἀνθρώποις προσφιλέστερον· αἴτησαι τὸ θεῖον πολλοὺς τῷ σώματί σου ἰθυφάλλους ἐπιφυῆναι.' Ὁ δέ γε ματαιόφρων ἐκεῖνος τὴν τοιαύτην αὐτίκα δέησιν προέθετο καὶ ἅμα τὸ τούτου σῶμα ἰθυφάλλοις κατάκομον γέγονεν.

88 "Οὓς ἑωρακὼς ὁ δείλαιος ἑαυτὸν πικρῶς ἐμυσάττετο καὶ τὴν γυναῖκα θρασέως πλήττει καὶ καθυβρίζει, καὶ τοσοῦτον τῷ θυμῷ κατ᾽ ἐκείνης ἀγριαίνεται, ὡς καὶ ἀνελεῖν αὐτὴν ἀνηλεῶς βουλεύεσθαι. Καὶ ἔλεγε πρὸς αὐτήν· Αὕτη ἐστὶν ἡ ἐπωφελής σου συμβουλία, ὦ κατάρατε; Οὐκ ἠδέσθης τοιαύτης μοι ἀσχημοσύνης βουλὴν πονηρὰν ὑπο-θέσθαι;' Ἡ δὲ πρὸς αὐτὸν ἀντέφησεν· 'Τί τοσοῦτον ἐχαλέ-πηνας; Μηδὲν διαταραχθῇς περὶ τούτου τοῦ πράγματος· ἕτεροι γὰρ δύο ὑπελείφθησαν λόγοι. Αἴτησαι τοίνυν τὸ θεῖον διὰ τοῦ ἑνὸς ῥήματος τοὺς ἰθυφάλλους τούσδε ἀπὸ σοῦ ἀφανισθῆναι.' Ὁ δὲ τῇ συζύγῳ πεισθεὶς αἰτεῖται τοῦτο παρὰ Θεοῦ, καὶ εὐθὺς ἐκείνων μὲν ἀπηλλάγη τῶν ἰθυ-φάλλων, ἀπώλεσε δὲ τῇ τοιαύτῃ αἰτίᾳ καὶ ὅπερ δὴ γεν-νητὸν αἰδοῖον ἐκέκτητο. Αὖθις οὖν ἐπὶ πλέον τῆς γυναικὸς καταθρασύνεται καὶ αὐτὴν ἀποκτεῖναι ἐκ παντὸς τρόπου πειρᾶται. Ἡ δὲ γυνή, 'Ἵνα τί,' φησίν, 'ἀνελεῖν με σφαδάζεις; Μηδ᾽ ἐπὶ τούτῳ τῷ συμβάντι ἄσχαλλε· ἓν γάρ σοι ῥῆμα ὑπολέλειπται· λοιπὸν αἴτησαι τὸ θεῖον τὰ γεννητά σου ἀπολαβεῖν αἰδοῖα.' Ὁ δὲ τοῦτο ποιήσας μόλις τοῦ αἰτη-θέντος ἐπέτυχεν.

89 "Ἴδε οὖν, ὦ βασιλεῦ, οἷα ἐκείνῳ τῷ ἀνδρὶ συμβέβηκεν, ὅτιπερ ἀσυλλογίστως τῇ τῆς γυναικὸς πονηρᾷ βουλῇ ὁ μάταιος συγκατέθετο. Καὶ νῦν λοιπὸν μακροθύμησον, παρακαλῶ, καὶ μὴ κατεπείγου πρὸς τὴν ἄδικον τοῦ υἱοῦ

sexual intercourse: ask God to make many erect penises sprout from your body.' And he, fool that he was, straightaway prayed for this, and instantaneously his body was covered in erections.

"When he saw them, the poor man was deeply disgusted 88 with himself and impulsively began to strike and abuse his wife, and was so mad at her that he even wanted to kill her without mercy. And he said to her, 'This is your helpful advice, you accursed woman? Weren't you ashamed to give me such wickedly obscene advice?' She replied to him, 'Why are you so angry? Don't be upset about this since you still have two more wishes. Ask God for these erections to disappear from you with one of the wishes.' The man was convinced by his wife, and asked this from God, and immediately he was rid of his erections; but by making the request in this way he also lost his natural genitals. Then he insulted his wife still more and tried hard to kill her. But his wife said, 'Why are you trying to kill me? Don't be distressed at what's happened, since you still have one wish remaining: ask God to restore your natural genitals.' The man did this, and thus he got what he asked for, but only with difficulty.

"And so, you must observe, my king, what happened 89 to this man because the fool unthinkingly assented to the wicked counsel of his wife. And now be patient, I beg you, and do not rush to execute your son unjustly, nor be

σου ἀναίρεσιν, μηδὲ οὕτως ἀνεξετάστως συναρπαγῇς τῇ τῆς γυναικὸς τῆς μοχθηρᾶς σκαιωρίᾳ, καὶ μᾶλλον ὅταν ἡ διαβάλλουσα δεινὴ λίαν καὶ κακότροπος ᾖ. Καὶ ἄλλης δέ μου διηγήσεως ἄκουσον.

90 "Ἀνὴρ γάρ τις ἦν, ὃς ἔνορκον ἑαυτῷ ὅρον ἔθετο μὴ ὅλως ἠρεμῆσαι ἢ αὑτῷ δοῦναι ἄνεσιν μήτε μὴν ἀγαγέσθαι γυναῖκα, ἕως ἂν πᾶσι τοῖς τῶν γυναικῶν ἐπισταίη μηχανήμασι. Καὶ εὐθὺς τῆς πατρίδος ἐξελθὼν περιήρχετο τὰς χώρας πληρώσων τὸ σπουδαζόμενον. Ἕτερος δέ τις αὐτὸν κατὰ τὴν ὁδοιπορίαν συνήντησεν, καὶ μαθὼν παρ' αὐτοῦ τὴν κατεπείγουσαν χρείαν, ἔφη τῷ ἀνδρί· Ὀὐ δυνήσῃ, ὦ ἄνθρωπε, τοὺς τῶν γυναικῶν τρόπους κατανοῆσαι οὐδὲ τὸ πέρας αὐτῶν ἐφευρεῖν, ἕως ἂν σποδιὰν ἀγαγὼν καί τινα τόπον δι' αὐτῆς καταπάσας τεσσαράκοντα ἡμέρας καὶ τεσσαράκοντα νύκτας ἐπ' αὐτῆς διατελέσῃς καθήμενος καὶ μετρίας τροφῆς καὶ πόσεως μεταλαμβάνων· καὶ εἰθούτως δυνήσῃ ἀπαριθμῆσαι καὶ σημήνασθαι τὰς τῶν γυναικῶν πανουργίας.' Ὁ δὲ τούτων τῶν ῥημάτων ἀκούσας παρὰ τοῦ αὐτῷ συναντήσαντος ἐποίησε καθὼς ἐκεῖνος αὐτῷ ἐνετείλατο, καὶ διετέλει ἐπὶ σποδιᾶς καθήμενος καὶ εὐτελεῖ τῇ διαίτῃ χρώμενος καὶ παρ' ὅλας τὰς τεσσαράκοντα ἡμέρας καὶ τὰς τεσσαράκοντα νύκτας ἀπογραφόμενος τὰς τῶν γυναικῶν μηχανουργίας. Ἃς δὴ καὶ περαιώσασθαι ἐδόκει ἐσύστερον καὶ μηδὲν τούτων καταλιπεῖν ἄγραφον. Λαβὼν οὖν ἃς πεποιήκει ἀπογραφὰς πρὸς τὴν ἑαυτοῦ οἰκίαν ἐπανήρχετο.

91 "Πορευόμενος δὲ ἐπί τι χωρίον παρεγένετο, ἐν ᾧ καὶ κατέλυσεν. Ἦν δέ τις ἐν τῷ χωρίῳ ἐκείνῳ, ὃς καὶ

unquestioningly beguiled by the intrigue of that wicked woman, especially since that slanderer is very clever and malicious. Hear from me also another story.

"There once was a man who made a resolution that he 90 would by no means settle down or allow himself to relax or even take a wife until he understood all the wiles of women. And immediately he set out from his homeland and wandered the world to complete his study. Another man met him on his journey, and when he learned of the mission that was driving him, he said to him, 'You will not be able, sir, to comprehend the ways of women, nor to discover their limit, until you gather up some ashes and sprinkle them over a certain spot, and then spend forty days and forty nights sitting there, with limited food and drink. Only then will you be able to enumerate and record the wicked ways of women.' When he heard this advice from the man he had met, he did exactly what he had been instructed, and spent the whole of those forty days and forty nights sitting on the ashes, eating a simple diet, and making an inventory of the machinations of women. Afterward, when it seemed to him that he had finished his list and left none of these unrecorded, he took the inventory he had made and began his return home.

"As he was traveling, he came to a village where he found 91 lodging. There was in this village a man who had prepared a

παρασκευασάμενος ἑστίασίν τινα, τοὺς τοῦ χωρίου οἰκή-
τορας κέκληκεν, μεθ' ὧν κἀκεῖνον τὸν ἀπογραφέα εἰς
δεξίωσιν μετεκαλέσατο. Ὁ δὲ ἐλθὼν καὶ ἀναπεσὼν μετὰ
τῶν ἄλλων δαιτυμόνων οὐ παρομοίως ἐκείνοις ἐκ τῶν
παρατιθεμένων ἤσθιεν, ἀλλ' ἄσιτος ἐκαθέζετο. Φησὶ οὖν
πρὸς αὐτὸν ὁ ἑστιάτωρ· 'Πόθεν καὶ τίς εἶ, ὦ ἑταῖρε;' Ὁ δὲ
ἀπεκρίνατο· 'Ὁδίτης εἰμί, ὡς ὁρᾷς, καὶ ἐκ μακρᾶς παρα-
γίνομαι χώρας. Καὶ γὰρ τῆς ἐνεγκαμένης ἐξῆλθον τοῦ
σοφίαν ἐκμαθεῖν καὶ τὰ τῶν πονηρῶν γυναικῶν κατανοῆσαι
μηχανήματα.' Ταῦτα ἐκείνου εἰρηκότος, φησὶν ὁ ἑστιάτωρ
πρὸς τὴν ἑαυτοῦ σύζυγον ὡς· 'Ὁ ἀνὴρ οὗτος ξένος τοῦδε
τοῦ χωρίου πέφυκε καὶ οὐδὲν ὅλως ἔφαγεν, ἐξελθὼν δὲ
τῆς ἰδίας πατρίδος καὶ περιελθὼν τὰς χώρας ὅλας, τῶν
γυναικῶν πάσας ἐκμεμάθηκε μηχανουργίας καὶ ταύτας
γραφῇ παραδέδωκεν· ἀλλ' ἀναστᾶσα, γύναι, παρασκεύασον
αὐτῷ τὰ πρὸς βρῶσιν αὐτοῦ καὶ πόσιν ἁρμόζοντα, ὡς ἂν
παρ' ἡμῶν δεόντως φιλοφρονηθείη καὶ ἀναπαύσηται.' Ἡ
δὲ γυνὴ ἀναστᾶσα πεποίηκεν καθὼς ὁ ἀνὴρ αὐτῇ δι-
ετάξατο. Εἶτα τὸν ὁδοιπόρον ἐπηρώτα· 'Τί ἄρα πεποίηκας,
ἄνθρωπε; Γέγραφας πᾶσαν τὴν τῶν γυναικῶν πονηρίαν;'
Ὁ δέ, 'Ναί,' φησί, 'πάσας αὐτῶν τὰς πανουργίας ἀπεγραψά-
μην καὶ τοὺς αὐτῶν δόλους καὶ τὰς σκαιωρίας διελαβόμην,
μηδέν τι τούτων τὸ παράπαν ἐάσας ἀσήμαντον.'

92   'Ἐκείνη δὲ τούτων παρ' αὐτοῦ ἐνωτισαμένη ἔγνω ὡς
ματαιόφρων ὁ ὁδοιπόρος καὶ ἀσύνετος καθέστηκεν, καὶ
πρὸς αὐτὸν κατ' εἰρωνείαν ἀπεφθέγξατο· 'Καὶ ἐπείπερ, ὡς
φάσκεις, πάντα τὰ γυναικεῖα μηχανήματα γέγραφας,
ἀδύνατόν ἐστιν γυναικὶ εἴτε καὶ ἐμοὶ αὐτῇ τεχνάσασθαί τι

banquet and invited his fellow villagers, and he invited the inventory maker along with them as an act of hospitality. Though he went and reclined with the other dinner guests, he did not eat as they did from the dishes that were set out, but sat there without any food. Then the host said to him, 'Where are you from, and who are you, my friend?' And he answered, 'I'm a traveler, as you can see, and I come from a far-off land. For I left my native land to learn wisdom and to comprehend the wiles of wicked women.' At these words the host said to his wife, 'This man is a stranger in our village and hasn't eaten anything at all. He left his own country and traveled everywhere, and so he has learned all the machinations of women and committed them to writing. Now get up and prepare some suitable food and drink for him, so that he may be treated with proper kindness by us and get some rest.' His wife got up and did just as her husband had ordered her. Then she asked the traveler, 'What have you done, sir? Have you recorded all the wickedness of women?' And he replied, 'Yes, I've written down all their wicked ways and cataloged their tricks and their schemes, without omitting a single one.'

"Now when she heard what he had said, she realized that 92 the traveler was a witless fool, and said to him mockingly, 'Since, as you claim, you've recorded all the wiles of women, it is impossible for a woman, even me myself, to devise

πρὸς σὲ ἢ διὰ λόγου ἢ διά τινος πράξεως· πλὴν ἄκουσον τῶν ἐμῶν ῥημάτων· ἰδού, καθορᾷς τὸν ἐμὸν ἄνδρα ὡς εἰς βαθὺ γῆρας ἐλήλακεν, ἐγὼ δὲ νεᾶνις ἔτι, ὡς βλέπεις, καθέστηκα καὶ τῶν ἀνδρῶν συνουσίας πάνυ ἐφίεμαι, σὺ δ', ὡς ὁρῶ, νέος πέφυκας· καὶ ἰδοὺ ἔτυχες κατακόρως φαγὼν καὶ πιών, ἔτυχε δὲ καὶ ὁ ἐμὸς σύνευνος ἐν τοῖς ἔξω τανῦν τυγχάνων· ἐγερθεὶς οὖν τὴν ἔφεσίν μου αὐτός μοι ἐκπλήρωσον.' Ταῦτα εἰπούσης τῆς γυναικὸς πρὸς ἀπάτην τοῦ ὁδοιπόρου πείθεται τοῖς λόγοις αὐτῆς ὁ ἠλίθιος ἐκεῖνος καὶ ἀναστὰς τὴν ζώνην τοῦ ἰδίου φιμιναλίου ἔλυε τοῦ τῇ κλίνῃ ἐπαναβῆναι.

93   "Ἰδοῦσα δὲ ἡ γυνὴ τὸ τούτου πρὸς ἐπιμιξίαν ταχυρρεπές τε καὶ περισπούδαστον, τὰς χεῖρας τῇ ἑαυτῆς κεφαλῇ ἐπιθεῖσα μεγαλοφώνως ἐκραύγασεν. Εὐθὺς δὲ οἱ τοῦ χωρίου κάτοικοι ἐπὶ τῇ αὐτῆς κραυγῇ πρὸς τὴν οἰκίαν συνέδραμον, ὁ δέ γε ὁδοιπόρος—ἐκείνης οὕτω βοώσης κἀκείνων πρὸς αὐτὴν συντρεχόντων καὶ τῆς τραπέζης ἔτι πρὸ αὐτοῦ κειμένης—ἐκάθητο πάλιν σφόδρα δεδιὼς καὶ ἐρυθριῶν καὶ ἐν ἀμηχανίᾳ τυγχάνων. Εἰσελθόντες δὲ οἱ ἀγρῶται λέγουσιν τῇ γυναικί· 'Τίνος ἕνεκεν, ὦ γύναι, ἐπὶ τοσοῦτον ἐβόας;' Ἡ δὲ πρὸς αὐτοὺς ἀντέφησεν· 'Οὗτος ὁ ξένος παρ' ἡμῶν φιλοφρονούμενος καὶ ἀπὸ τῆσδε τῆς τραπέζης ἐσθίων ὑπό τινος θρύμματος τὸν φάρυγγα χαλεπῶς ἐπεσχέθη καὶ μικρὸν ὅσον ἐκινδύνευεν ἀπαγχονισθῆναι. Ἐγὼ δὲ αὐτίκα ἐπὶ τῷ συμβάντι τούτῳ ἀθρόον καιρίως ἀλγήσασα καὶ τὸν ἄνδρα παντελῶς ἐκλείπειν ὑποτοπάσασα οὕτως ὡς ἠκούσατε ἐκραύγασα. Νυνὶ δὲ τῆς τοῦ Θεοῦ ἀρωγῆς προφθασάσης ἀπηλλάγη ἐκείνης τῆς συνοχῆς καὶ τῆς

anything against you in word or deed. But listen to what I say. Look, you see how my husband has reached extreme old age, while I am still young, as you can see, and greatly desire to have sex with men. But you, as I can see, are a young man. And look, you've had your fill of eating and drinking, and my husband happens just now to be outside. So get up and fulfill my desire yourself.' The wife said these things to deceive the traveler, and that simpleton believed her words and, getting up, he loosened the belt of his pants to climb into the bed.

"When the woman saw his eagerness for sex and how 93 keen he was, she placed her hands on her head and shouted with a loud voice. As soon as they heard her shout, the villagers ran together to the house, and the traveler—with the wife having shouted so loudly, the villagers running to her aid, and the table still set in front of him—sat down again, fearful, blushing, and not knowing what to do. When the villagers arrived, they asked the wife, 'Why did you shout so loudly?' And she answered them, 'While our visitor was being entertained by us and was eating at this very table, he got a bit of food caught in his throat and came very near to choking. As for me, I was immediately distressed by what had happened to him so suddenly and, because I thought that all was lost for the man, I shouted, as you heard. But now that help from God has arrived in time, he has been delivered from that danger and has recovered his former

προτέρας εὐεξίας ἐν καταστάσει γέγονεν.' Ταῦτα εἰπούσης
ἐκείνης ἐξῆλθον τῆς οἰκίας οἱ ἐκεῖσε δραμόντες ἅπαντες.

94 "Ἡ δὲ γυνὴ ἐγγίσασα τῷ ὁδοιπόρῳ λέγει πρὸς αὐτόν·
Ἆρά γε τοῦτο ὅπερ εἰς σὲ διεπραξάμην ἔχεις ἀπογεγραμ-
μένον;' Ὁ δὲ ξένος, 'Οὐδαμῶς,' ἔφη. Ἡ δὲ, 'Μάτην λοιπόν,
ὦ ἄνθρωπε, τοὺς κόπους σου καὶ τὴν δαπάνην ἀνήλωσας·
πολλὰ γὰρ ἀγωνισάμενος ἀνηνύτοις ἐπεχείρησας καὶ τὰς
τῶν γυναικῶν μηχανουργίας οὔπω κατενόησας.' Ὁ δὲ ἅμα
τῷ λόγῳ ἐκείνῳ ἐγερθεὶς καὶ τὰ γραφέντα ἐνεγκὼν τῷ
πυρὶ ἐνέβαλεν καὶ θαυμάζων ἔλεγε ὡς· 'Οὐδεὶς ἀνθρώπων
διαγνῶναι δύναται τὰ τῶν γυναικῶν πανουργεύματα.'
Μετὰ δὲ ταῦτα διαπορούμενος καὶ μηκέτι προσθεὶς τὰ
γυναικεῖα συζητεῖν πρὸς τὴν ἰδίαν ἐπανῆκεν πατρίδα καὶ
ἀπεριέργῳ τῇ γνώμῃ νόμιμον αὐτῷ γυναῖκα ἠγάγετο.

95 "Ἐκ τούτων τοιγαροῦν, ὦ βασιλεῦ, τῶν τῷ κράτει σου
ἐξηγηθέντων παρὰ τῆς ἐμῆς εὐτελείας γνῶθι ἀκριβῶς ὡς
ἀπέραντος ἡ τῶν γυναικῶν μοχθηρία, καὶ μὴ οὕτως ἀσυλλογίστως πρὸς τὴν τοῦ υἱοῦ σου συναρπαγῆς διαχείρισιν
διὰ ψιλὴν γυναικὸς ὑποθήκην· εἰ γὰρ τὸν παῖδά σου
θανάτῳ ὑποβαλεῖς, τίς ἄρα ἔσται τὸ ἀπ' ἐκείνου ἐπὶ τῇ σῇ
πεποιθὼς προσπαθείᾳ;" Τούτων ὁ Κῦρος παρὰ τοῦ ἑβδό-
μου σοφωτάτου συμβούλου ἀκροασάμενος, εὐθὺς ἕνα τὸν
αὐτοῦ οἰκειότατον δορυφόρον προσεκαλέσατο καὶ τοῦτον
πρὸς τὸν σπεκουλάτωρα ἔστειλε κελεύων αὐτῷ μηδαμῶς
ἀποκτεῖναι τὸν ἑαυτοῦ υἱόν.

96 Εἶτα τῆς ὀγδόης ἐπιστάσης ἡμέρας λύεται μὲν τοῦ τῆς
σιωπῆς δεσμοῦ ἡ τοῦ παιδὸς γλῶττα, ἀρξάμενος δὲ φθέγγεσθαι λέγει πρός τινα κόρην πρὸ τῶν αὐτοῦ ὀφθαλμῶν

good health.' When she had said this, all those who had come running left the house.

"Then the wife came close to the traveler and said to him, 94 'Is what I've done to you recorded in your inventory?' The visitor said, 'No, not at all.' And she replied, 'Well, sir, you've wasted your effort and your money. For though you worked very hard, you undertook an impossible task and you still haven't grasped the machinations of women.' As soon as he heard this, he got up, carried his records to the fire, and tossed them in. Then with a sense of amazement he said, 'No man is able to discern the wicked ways of women completely.' After this, not knowing what to do and no longer applying himself to the study of the ways of women, he returned to his own country and took for himself a lawful wife without giving it too much thought.

"Therefore, my king, from this story, told to your majesty 95 by my humble self, you may know clearly that the wickedness of women is boundless, and so do not without due consideration be beguiled into killing your son because of the mere charge of a woman. For if you put your son to death, who will trust in your affection after that?" When Cyrus heard these words from his seventh very wise advisor, he immediately summoned his closest bodyguard and sent him to the executioner, ordering him by no means to kill his son.

Then as the eighth day dawned, the boy's tongue was 96 freed from its bond of silence. He began to speak by saying to a girl who happened to be standing right in front of him,

ἱσταμένην τυχαίως· "Ἀπελθοῦσα, νεᾶνι, κάλεσόν μοι τὸν τῶν φιλοσόφων τοῦ ἐμοῦ πατρὸς καὶ βασιλέως πρωτεύοντα." Ἡ δὲ τῆς φθογγῆς τοῦ νεανίσκου ἀσμένως ἀκούσασα, πορεύεται πρὸς τὸν φιλόσοφον ἐκεῖνον τὸν καὶ τῶν ἄλλων διαφορώτατον καὶ ἀπαγγέλλει αὐτῷ, λέγουσα ὡς· "Ὁ τοῦ βασιλέως υἱὸς φθέγγεσθαι ἀπήρξατο καὶ προσκαλεῖταί σε ὡς αὐτὸν παραγενέσθαι." Ὁ δὲ αὐτίκα δρομαῖος πρὸς τὸν παῖδα παραγίνεται καὶ τοῦτον χαριέστατα περιλαβὼν ποθεινότατα ἠσπάσατο. Εἶτα ὁ παῖς προσφθεγξάμενος τῷ φιλοσόφῳ ἀνακαλύπτει αὐτῷ ὅτου χάριν παρ' ὅλας τὰς ἑπτὰ ἡμέρας σιωπῶν διετέλει, ἀλλὰ μὴν καὶ ὅσα πρὸς αὐτὸν ἡ πονηρὰ τοῦ βασιλέως παλλακὴ ἀφρόνως λελάληκε δῆλα τῷ φιλοσόφῳ πεποιήκει καὶ προσέθετο λέγων· "Μεγάλας τὰς εὐχαριστίας ὑπέχω τῷ Θεῷ τε καὶ ὑμῖν, ὅτι με βιαίου καὶ ἀδίκου θανάτου τὸν ἀναίτιον ἐλυτρώσασθε καὶ τοῦ κινδύνου τῶν πρὸς τὸν βασιλέα καὶ πατέρα μου σκαιωριῶν τῆς μοχθηρᾶς γυναικὸς ἐξηρπάσατε. Ἀλλά μοι, κύριέ μου, πορεύθητι πρὸς τὸν βασιλέα καὶ γνώρισον αὐτῷ ὅσα σοι δεδήλωκα καὶ διωμίλησα, πρινὴ ἡ κακότροπος γυνὴ πρὸς αὐτὸν εἰσέλθοι καὶ τὰς τούτου διαφθείρη ἀκοὰς ὡς τὸ πρότερον." Ὁ δὲ φιλόσοφος τῷ παιδὶ ἀπεκρίνατο· "Γίνωσκε, ὦ νεανία, ὡς καὶ ὁ σὸς διδάσκαλος, ἅμα τῷ τὰ τῆς σῆς λαλιᾶς ἀκουτισθῆναι αὐτῷ, πρὸς τὸν βασιλέα παραγένηται." Ὁ δὲ παῖς, "Ἀληθῶς," εἶπε, "τοῦτο φής, κύριέ μου· τὴν σήμερον γὰρ κἀκεῖνος πρὸς τὸν βασιλέα ἐλεύσεται."

97 Τούτων οὕτω παρ' ἀμφοτέρων πρὸς ἀλλήλους λεχθέντων, ἐγείρεται ὁ φιλόσοφος μετὰ σπουδῆς καὶ πρὸς τὸν

"Go, young woman, and summon for me the chief philosopher of my father, the king." Glad to hear the young man's
voice, she went to that philosopher who far surpassed the
rest and announced to him, "The king's son has begun to
speak again and summons you to come to him." Straightaway he went to the boy at a run, and he embraced and
kissed him with great joy and love. Then the boy spoke to
the philosopher and revealed to him why he had kept his silence for seven whole days. Moreover, he made clear to him
all that the king's wicked concubine had imprudently said to
him, and then he added, "I owe great thanks both to God
and to all of you, because you both saved me, who was innocent, from a violent and unjust death, and rescued me from
the danger that came from the wicked woman's intrigues
against my father, the king. But please, my lord, go to the
king and tell him what I have revealed and communicated to
you, before that malicious woman gets to him and corrupts
his ears as she did before." The philosopher answered the
boy, "Young man, know that as soon as your teacher has
heard that you are speaking again, he will also go to the
king." The boy said, "You say this truly, my lord. For today
he, too, will go to the king."

After this conversation between them, the philosopher 97
quickly got up and made his way to the king. When he had

βασιλέα πορεύεται, καὶ εἰσελθὼν εἰς αὐτὸν καὶ τὴν συνήθη
τούτῳ ἀποδοὺς προσκύνησιν λέγει αὐτῷ· "Βασιλεῦ, ζῆθι
εἰς τὸν αἰῶνα, χαρᾶς σοι κομίζω εὐαγγέλια· σήμερον γὰρ ὁ
υἱός σου τῶν τῆς σιωπῆς δεσμῶν λέλυται καὶ φθέγγεσθαι
ἀδιακόπως ἤρξατο, καί με πρὸς τὸ σὸν ἔστειλε κράτος τοῦ
δηλῶσαι τῇ σκηπτουχίᾳ σου τὰ περὶ αὐτοῦ ἅπαντα."
Ταῦτα εἰπὼν διεσάφησε τῷ βασιλεῖ ὅσα παρὰ τοῦ παιδὸς
ἠκηκόει. Ὁ δὲ βασιλεὺς χαρᾶς ὅτι πλείστης ἐπὶ τῇ ἀγγελίᾳ
τοῦ φιλοσόφου πληρωθεὶς καὶ ὥσπερ ἄλλος ἐξ ἄλλου
ὑφ᾽ ἡδονῆς καταστάς, πρῶτα μὲν δώροις τὸν ἄνδρα τῶν
ἀγαθῶν ἕνεκεν ἀγγελιῶν ἐδεξιώσατο, εἶτα καί τινας τῶν
αὐτοῦ δορυφόρων ἀπέστειλε μετακαλούμενος τὸν παῖδα
σὺν πολλῇ ταχυτῆτι. Εὐθὺς δὲ παραγίνεται πρὸς τὸν βασιλέα ὁ παῖς καὶ εἰσελθὼν προσεκύνησεν αὐτόν. Ἀνέστη δὲ
τοῦ θρόνου ὁ βασιλεὺς ἐκ περιχαρείας καὶ τῷ υἱῷ χαριέντως
προσυπήντησεν καὶ τοῦτον περιλαβόμενος ποθεινότατα
ἠσπάσατο. Ὁ δὲ παῖς ἀνοίξας τὸ στόμα χαίρειν προσ-
φθέγγεται τῷ βασιλεῖ. Ὁ δὲ τῆς χειρὸς τοῦτον κρατήσας
συνεδριάζειν αὐτῷ ἐπὶ τῆς βασιλικῆς καθέδρας ἐκέλευσεν.

98   Εἶτά φησιν πρὸς τὸν φίλτατον υἱόν· "Τίς ἄρα ἡ αἰτία
ἐτύγχανεν, ὦ τέκνον ποθεινότατον, τῆς ἐπὶ ταῖς προλαβούσαις ἑπτὰ ἡμέραις τοσαύτης σου σιωπῆς καὶ ἀφωνίας
καὶ ὅτου χάριν οὐδόλως μοι ἐν αὐταῖς λελάληκας, ὡς κἀμὲ
διὰ τῆς σῆς σιγῆς ὑπὸ τῶν τῆς γυναικὸς ῥημάτων πρὸς
ὄλεθρόν σου συναρπάζεσθαι καὶ πειρᾶσθαί σε ἀνελεῖν;" Ὁ
δὲ νέος τῷ βασιλεῖ καὶ πατρὶ ἀπεκρίνατο· "Ὁ Θεός, ὦ
βασιλεῦ, ὅς ἐστιν ἀρωγὸς τῷ ἀνθρωπίνῳ γένει, οὗτός με
τῆς σφαγῆς διεφύλαττεν. Ὅτι δὲ μὴ ἐφθεγγόμην τῷ κράτει

come before him and performed the customary prostration, he said to him, "*My king, may you live forever.* I bring you tidings of joy. For today your son has been freed from the bonds of silence and has begun to speak without interruption, and he has sent me to your majesty to reveal to your royal highness everything that happened to him." After he had said this, he revealed to the king all that he had heard from the boy. Filled with the greatest possible joy at the philosopher's news and transformed by his delight, the king first of all honored the man with gifts in return for the good news, and then sent some of his bodyguards to summon the boy with the greatest urgency. Immediately the boy came to the king, and when he entered, he prostrated himself before him. The king stood up from his throne in his great joy and cheerfully went to meet his son and, embracing him, kissed him very lovingly. The boy opened his mouth and delivered his greetings to the king, who took him by the hand and ordered him to sit with him upon the royal throne.

Then the king said to his dearest son, "What was the reason, my most beloved son, for your prolonged silence and your speechlessness for these past seven days? Why did you not speak to me at all during that time? As a result of your silence, I was even tricked by the woman's words into ordering your execution and trying to kill you." The young man answered his king and father, "God, who helps the human race, protected me from death. As for the fact that I did not 98

121

σου ἐφ᾽ ὅλαις ταῖς προλαβούσαις ἑπτὰ ἡμέραις, γίνωσκε, ὦ δέσποτα, ὡς ὑπὸ τοῦ διδασκάλου μου Συντίπα ἐντεταλμένος ἐτύγχανον τοῦ μὴ τὸ παράπαν ἐντὸς τῶν ἑπτὰ ἡμερῶν λόγον τινὰ ἀποφθέγξασθαι. Ὅτι δὲ καὶ ἡ γυνὴ αὕτη πρὸς τὴν σφαγήν μου τὸ κράτος σου παρώρμα, γνωρίζω σοι, βασιλεῦ, καὶ περὶ ταύτης, ὡς ὅτε πρὸς σὲ μετὰ τὸ πέρας τῆς διδασκαλίας τοῦ ἐμοῦ μυσταγωγοῦ παραγέγονα καί με μετ᾽ ὀλίγον τῇ γυναικὶ ταύτῃ παραδέδωκας κἀκείνη με πρὸς τὴν αὐτῆς οἰκίαν ἀπήγαγεν, εὐθὺς ἡ γυνὴ—ἀκόλαστος, ὡς ἐῴκει, τυγχάνουσα—πρὸς συνουσίαν ἑαυτῆς με διηρέθιζε καὶ ᾑρεῖτο συγγενέσθαι με αὐτῇ. Ἐγὼ δὲ σφοδρῶς ἐπὶ τῷ ἀτόπῳ τοῦ πράγματος, ὡς ἔδει, χαλεπήνας καὶ κατ᾽ αὐτῆς ὀξύτατα θυμωθεὶς ὑπὸ τῆς κατεχούσης με τότε τοῦ θυμοῦ συγχύσεως καὶ ταραχῆς ἐπελαθόμην καὶ τῆς τοῦ διδασκάλου μου ἐντολῆς, ἥν μοι περὶ τῆς ἐν ταῖς ἑπτὰ ἡμέραις σιγῆς διεστείλατο, καὶ ἀποκριθεὶς ἔφην τῇ γυναικὶ ὡς· Ὀὐδὲν τό γε νῦν ἔχον περὶ ὧν μοι φῇς, ὦ γύναι, πρὸς σὲ ἀντιφθέγξομαι, ἄχρις ἂν ἑπτὰ ἡμέραι τὸ ἀπὸ τοῦδε παρέλθωσι, καὶ τούτων περαιουμένων, καθώς σοι προσήκει περὶ ὧν μοι λελάληκας ἀπολογήσομαι.᾽ Ταῦτα οὖν, ὦ βασιλεῦ, μόνον τῇ γυναικὶ τῷ τότε ἀντεφθεγξάμην μηδὲν ἕτερον μηκέτι προσθεὶς ἢ ἄλλο τέ τι φθεγξάμενος ἄχρι τῆσδε τῆς σήμερον ἡμέρας. Καθὸ δέ γε τὰ τῇ γυναικὶ ἀρεστὰ οὐδαμῶς ἐγὼ τότε διεπραξάμην, εὐθὺς ἐκείνη πολλῷ τῷ φόβῳ ληφθεῖσα κἀντεῦθεν κινδυνεῦσαι δι᾽ ἐμοῦ ὑφορωμένη ἔσπευδεν ἐντὸς τῶν ἑπτὰ ἡμερῶν ἀπωλείας με θέσθαι παρανάλωμα, καὶ σέ, ὦ βασιλεῦ, πρὸς τὴν σφαγήν μου παρεκίνει ἡ κακότροπος. Ἀλλὰ

speak to your majesty for the past seven whole days, know, master, that was because I had been commanded by my teacher Syntipas not to speak any word at all during the seven days. And as for the fact that this woman also incited your majesty to kill me, I will also tell you about her, my king. After I came to you at the end of my mentor's instruction and you, after a short time, handed me over to this woman and she led me off to her apartment, the woman immediately—because she is, as it appears, licentious—tried to goad me into having sex with her and wanted me to sleep with her. Then I became very angry, and rightly so, at the inappropriateness of this and was filled with great wrath against her. In the angry confusion and turmoil which were then overwhelming me, I even forgot the command that my teacher had given me about keeping silent during the seven days, and I said in response to the woman, 'I will not reply to you for the time being, woman, about what you're suggesting to me, until seven days pass from today, and when these days come to an end, I will defend myself, as you deserve, concerning what you've said to me.' That was all I said, my king, in reply to that woman, adding nothing more nor otherwise saying anything until today. Since at that time I did not in any way do what the woman desired, she was immediately seized with great fear and, suspecting that she was therefore in danger because of me, she rushed to have me condemned to death within the seven days. And so the malicious woman incited you, my king, to execute me. But the

τὸ μὲν τῆς ἐμῆς γε σιωπῆς αἴτιον ἤδη σοῦ τῇ σκηπτουχίᾳ
δεδήλωται· τοῦ λοιποῦ δέ, εἴπερ εὐδοκεῖ καὶ ἐθέλοι τὸ
κράτος σου, προστάξάτω ἱκανὸν ὄχλον συνελθεῖν καὶ πάντας τοὺς φιλοσόφους, ὅπως ἐπ' ἀκροάσει αὐτῶν ἀνακαλύψω
ἐπὶ τοῦ ἀνακτορικοῦ σου βήματος ἥν με διδασκαλίαν ὁ
φιλόσοφος Συντίπας ἐξεδίδαξεν."

99   Τούτων ἀκούσας τῶν ῥημάτων παρὰ τοῦ υἱοῦ ὁ βασιλεὺς ἐπὶ πλεῖον ἔχαιρε καὶ σφόδρα ἠγάλλετο, καὶ κελεύει
πάντας τοὺς φιλοσόφους καὶ εἰδήμονας συναθροισθῆναι,
ἀλλὰ μὴν καὶ αὐτοὺς τοὺς μεγιστᾶνας αὐτοῦ· καὶ δὴ
πάντες ἐπὶ τὸ αὐτὸ πρὸς τὸν βασιλέα συνῆλθον. Παραγίνεται δὲ πρὸς αὐτὸν καὶ ὁ τοῦ παιδὸς διδάσκαλος, καὶ
εἰσελθὼν προσεκύνησεν αὐτὸν ἐπὶ τῆς γῆς. Ὁ δὲ βασιλεὺς
ὑπολαβὼν ἔφη πρὸς αὐτόν· "Ποῦ ἦσθα μέχρι τοῦ νῦν,
σοφώτατε Συντίπα; Ὅτι γε διὰ τῆς σῆς ἀποδημίας μικροῦ
δεῖν τὸν υἱόν μου ἀπέκτεννον." Ὁ δὲ Συντίπας τῷ βασιλεῖ
ἀπεκρίνατο· "Ἐγώ, βασιλεῦ, τῷ υἱῷ σου ἐφ' ἡμέραις ἑπτὰ
σιγᾶν ἐνετειλάμην, καθότι τὰ περὶ τῆς αὐτοῦ τύχης δι'
ἀστρολογικῆς συζητήσεως ἐξερευνήσας, ἔγνων ὡς εἰ ἐντὸς τῶν ἑπτὰ ἡμερῶν φθέγξαιτο, εὐθὺς θανάτῳ ὑποβληθείη·
ὅθεν καὶ τοῦ σοῦ κράτους ἐμαυτὸν πόρρω πεποίηκα, ἕως
ἂν ἡ τῶν ἑπτὰ ἡμερῶν περαιωθείη διορία. Καὶ καλῶς ὁ
υἱός σου πεποίηκε μηδαμῶς σοι ἐν αὐταῖς φθεγξάμενος."
Ὁ δὲ βασιλεὺς ἔφη· "Χάρις μεγίστη λοιπὸν τῷ Θεῷ, ὅτι
μου τὸν υἱὸν τῆς σφαγῆς διεφύλαξεν· εἰ γὰρ ἐκεῖνον παρ'
ἐμοῦ ἀναιρεθῆναι συνέβη, ἐξαρθῆναι ἂν τῆς γῆς τὸ ἐμὸν
ἐκινδύνευεν ὄνομα."

100   Ταῦτα εἰπὼν ὁ βασιλεὺς προσκαλεῖται τοὺς φιλοσόφους,

reason for my silence, at least, has now been revealed to your royal highness. And now, if your majesty should consent and be willing, please order a sizable crowd, together with all the philosophers, to convene, so that in their hearing I may reveal from the royal dais the learning in which the philosopher Syntipas instructed me."

After hearing his son's story, the king rejoiced even more 99 and celebrated greatly; then he ordered all the philosophers and learned men, in addition to his noblemen, to be assembled. And they all convened together before the king. Then the boy's teacher also approached the king, and when he entered, he prostrated himself on the ground before him. In response, the king said to him, "Where have you been until now, most wise Syntipas? Because of your absence I came very close to killing my son." Syntipas answered the king, "I told your son to be silent for seven days, my king, because when I investigated his fortune through astrological inquiry, I learned that if he spoke within the seven days, he would immediately be subject to death. For this reason I also removed myself far away from your majesty, until the necessary seven days should pass. And your son did well in not speaking to you at all during that time." The king said, "Greatest thanks, then, to God, because he protected my son from death. For if I had succeeded in executing him, my name would likely have been wiped from the earth."

After he said this, the king summoned the philosophers 100

καὶ τούτους ἐγγυτέρω μετὰ καὶ τοῦ Συντίπα παραστησά-
μενος, τοῦ παιδὸς ἐκ δεξιῶν συνέδρου τῷ βασιλεῖ καθ-
εστηκότος, ἐπηρώτα τοὺς φιλοσόφους λέγων· "Γνωρίσατέ
μοι τανῦν, εἴπερ ἄρα τὸν ἐμὸν υἱὸν ἐντὸς τῶν ἑπτὰ ἡμερῶν
ἀνῃρηκέναι εἶχον, τίνι τὸ αἴτιον τῆς ἐκείνου σφαγῆς
ἐπεγράφετο, ἐμοί, τῷ υἱῷ μου ἢ τῇ γυναικί;"

101   Ἐγγίζουσι δὲ τῷ βασιλεῖ τέσσαρες τῶν φιλοσόφων, καὶ
ἀποκριθεὶς θάτερος αὐτῶν ἔφη· "Ἡ αἰτία αὕτη, ὦ βασιλεῦ,
τοῦ Συντίπα ἐτύγχανεν· ἐπειδὴ γὰρ ἐκεῖνος ἐγίνωσκεν ὡς
ἡ ἐντὸς τῶν ἑπτὰ ἡμερῶν τοῦ σοῦ παιδὸς λαλιὰ κίνδυνον
αὐτῷ ἐπάγει, ἵνα τί μὴ παρ' ἑαυτὸν τοῦτον ἐτήρει, ἀλλὰ
πρὸς τὸ σὸν κράτος ἀπέστειλεν;" Οὕτω τοῦ ἑνὸς φιλοσόφου
εἰπόντος, ὁ δεύτερος ἀπεκρίνατο· "Οὐ τοῦτό γε ὃ φάσκεις
εὐάρμοστον· οὐ γάρ τις αἰτία τῷ Συντίπα πρόσεστι, καθότι
οὐκ ἠδύνατο τὸν παρ' αὐτοῦ πρὸς τὸν βασιλέα ὑποσχεθέντα
ὅρον ἐλλεῖψαι ἢ πλεονάσαι οὔτε τῷ βασιλεῖ τὸ παράπαν
διαψεύσασθαι, καὶ διὰ τοῦτο μᾶλλον πόρρω τῶν αὐτοῦ
ἀπομακρύνας ὀφθαλμῶν ἑαυτὸν κατέκρυψε, τὸν δὲ παῖδα
πρὸς τὸν βασιλέα ἐξαπέστειλε. Τοιγαροῦν ἡ αἰτία τῷ τὴν
τοῦ παιδὸς ἀναίρεσιν ἐπιτάξαντι πρόσεστιν." Ἀποκριθεὶς
δὲ καὶ ὁ τρίτος φιλόσοφος ἔφησεν· "Οὐχ οὕτως ἐστὶ ὡς σὺ
λέγεις· οὐ γὰρ ὁ βασιλεὺς τοῦ πράγματος αἴτιος, ἀλλ'
ὥσπερ οὐδὲν ψυχρότερον τῆς τε καφούρας καὶ τοῦ ξύλου
ὅπερ καὶ σάνταλον ἡ συνήθεια οἶδε καλεῖν, ἀμφότερα δὲ
ἀλλήλοις παρά τινος συγκατατριβόμενα σπινθῆρας πυρὸς
μᾶλλον ἀποτελοῦσιν, οὕτω καὶ ἅπας ἀνήρ, κἂν ἄγαν εἴη
συνετὸς καὶ ἀγχίνους, ἅμα τῷ αὐτὸν γυναικὶ προσομιλῆσαι,
καὶ μᾶλλον τῇ παρ' ἑαυτοῦ ποθουμένῃ, εὐθὺς ὑπ' αὐτῆς

and assembled them, along with Syntipas, around himself, with the son seated on the right of the king. Then he asked the philosophers, "Tell me now, if I had been able to execute my son within the seven days, to whom would the blame for his death have been ascribed: to me, to my son, or to my concubine?"

Four of the philosophers approached the king, and one of them answered, "The blame, my king, would have belonged to Syntipas. For if he knew that your son would be in danger if he spoke within the seven days, why did he not keep him and watch over him himself rather than send him to your majesty?" When the first philosopher had spoken thus, the second one answered, "Your answer does not fit the situation. For no blame is attributable to Syntipas, because he was unable to shorten or lengthen the period of time that he promised the king or to lie to the king in any way, and for this reason he instead hid himself far from the king's eyes and sent the boy back. Therefore, the blame is attributable to the one who ordered the boy's execution." Then the third philosopher answered, "The situation is not as you say. For the king is not to blame for the act, but just as nothing is colder than camphorwood and the wood that in everyday language is called sandalwood, but then, when someone rubs these two types of wood together, they produce sparks of fire, so also every man, though he may be very intelligent and clever, as soon as he associates with a woman, and especially one that he desires, is immediately diverted by her

101

τοῦ ἰδίου σκοποῦ πρὸς τὸ ἐκείνης μεθέλκεται θέλημα. Ἡ γυνὴ τοίνυν τούτου ἐστὶν αἰτία τοῦ πράγματος, ὅτιπερ ψευδῶς τοῦ παιδὸς κατειποῦσα πρὸς ἀπώλειαν αὐτοῦ τὸν βασιλέα παρώτρυνε." Παρελθὼν δὲ καὶ ὁ τέταρτος φιλόσοφος ἔφη· "Οὐδ᾿ οὕτως ἔχει ὡς λέγετε· οὐδὲ γὰρ ἡ γυνὴ αἰτία καθέστηκεν, ἐπεὶ καὶ εἴωθεν ὡς τὰ πολλὰ ὄψις εὐειδοῦς νεανίσκου θέλγειν τὴν φύσιν τῆς γυναικὸς καὶ ὡς ἀπαλωτέραν θηρᾶσθαι, καὶ μᾶλλον εἰ τύχοι ὡς τὰ πολλὰ ἀλλήλοις αὐτοὺς καταμόνας ὡς φίλους προσομιλεῖν· τότε γὰρ ἡ γυνὴ ἐπὶ πλέον πρὸς τὴν τοῦ νέου γαργαλίζεται συνουσίαν καὶ διερεθίζει αὐτὸν εἰς ἐκπλήρωσιν τῆς ἰδίας ἐφέσεως, ὅθεν καὶ αὕτη ἡ γυνὴ τῷ αὐτῷ συνεσχέθη ἔρωτι. Ἐπεὶ δὲ οὐδαμῶς αὐτῇ ὁ τοῦ βασιλέως υἱὸς συγκατέθετο, ἀλλὰ μᾶλλον καὶ διαπειλεῖν αὐτῇ ἐδόκει, ἐδεδίει πάντως αὐτὸν ἡ γυνὴ καὶ ἑαυτὴν ἔσπευδεν ὑφορωμένου κινδύνου διατηρῆσαι, κἀντεῦθεν τὴν τοῦ νέου ἀναίρεσιν ὡς αὐτῇ συμφέρουσαν ἐπετηδεύετο. Λοιπὸν οὖν ἡ αἰτία τῷ νεανίσκῳ πρόσεστιν, ὅτι μὴ τὴν ἐντολὴν τοῦ διδασκάλου τετήρηκεν, ἀλλ᾿ ἐφθέγξατο τῇ γυναικὶ δειμαλέον καὶ ἀπότομον λόγον."

102   Ὑπολαβὼν δὲ καὶ ὁ Συντίπας λέγει· "Οὐκ ἔστιν οὕτως, ὡς ὑμεῖς φατε, οὐδὲ ὁ παῖς αἴτιος καθέστηκε· καὶ γὰρ οὐδὲν τῆς ἀληθείας μεῖζον, καὶ πᾶς ὃς φάσκει σοφιστικὸν ἑαυτὸν τυγχάνειν, διαψεύδεται δὲ μάλιστα, ἐξουδένωταί τε ὄντως πᾶσα ἡ αὐτοῦ σύνεσις, καὶ οὐκ ἔστιν σοφὸς ὁ τοιοῦτος οὔτε μοίρᾳ σοφῶν συνηρίθμηται, ἀλλὰ τῆς τῶν ψευδολόγων καὶ ὑποκριτῶν ὁμηγύρεως καθέστηκεν."

from his own aims and toward her will. The woman, therefore, is to blame for this situation, because by falsely denouncing the boy she incited the king to kill him." Then the fourth philosopher came forward and said, "The situation is not as you all say. For the woman is not to blame, either, since the sight of an attractive young man almost always charms a woman's nature and stalks it because it is weaker, and more so if it happens that the two of them frequently socialize with each other alone as friends; for at that time the woman is all the more tempted to have sex with the young man and she goads him into fulfilling her desires. This woman, therefore, was also held captive by the same erotic desire. And when the king's son refused to consent, but instead seemed even to be threatening her, the woman surely was afraid of him and rushed to protect herself from the danger she feared; therefore, she pursued the young man's execution as being beneficial to herself. And so, then, the blame is attributable to the young man, because he did not keep his teacher's command, but rather spoke to the woman with intimidating and brusque words."

Then Syntipas also responded, "The situation is not as 102 you all say, nor is the boy to blame. For indeed nothing is greater than the truth, and every man who claims to be wise but is actually mistaken finds that all his intelligence in reality comes to nothing, and he is not wise, nor to be numbered among the ranks of the wise, but rather has joined the company of liars and hypocrites."

103 Ὑπολαβὼν δὲ καὶ ὁ τοῦ βασιλέως υἱὸς λέγει τῷ πατρί·
"Δέσποτα βασιλεῦ, ἐπίτρεψον κἀμοὶ ἀπόλογόν τινα πρὸς
ταῦτα εἰρηκέναι." Ὁ δὲ βασιλεὺς ἐκέλευσεν καὶ τὸν υἱὸν
ἀποκριθῆναι. Κἀκεῖνος εὐθὺς τοῖς φιλοσόφοις φησίν· "Ἡ
ἐμὴ γνῶσις πρὸς τὴν ὑμετέραν σοφίαν ὡς μυῖα πρὸς
δράκοντα πέφυκεν, ἀλλ᾽ ὅμως μου τῶν ῥημάτων ἀκούσατε.
Ἦν γάρ τις ἀνὴρ ὃς ἑστίασίν τινα πολυτελῆ παρετοιμα-
σάμενος πολλοὺς δαιτυμόνας εἰς δεξίωσιν κέκληκεν, εἶτα
αὐτῶν ἀναπεσόντων καὶ ἐσθιόντων γάλα τούτους πεπωκέναι παρεσκεύαζεν. Ἔστειλεν οὖν πρὸς τὴν ἀγορὰν τὴν
ἑαυτοῦ δούλην τοῦ ὠνήσασθαι γάλα τοῖς κληθεῖσιν
ἀνδράσιν, ἡ δὲ λαβοῦσα τὴν χύτραν ἐπὶ τὴν ἀγορὰν
ἐπορεύθη καὶ ὠνήσατο γάλα· καὶ ἐπιθεῖσα τὴν χύτραν τῇ
ἑαυτῆς κεφαλῇ πρὸς τὴν τοῦ κυρίου αὐτῆς οἰκίαν ἐπανήρχετο, αὐτῆς δὲ πορευομένης λοῦπος ἄνωθεν καταπτὰς καί
τινα ὄφιν ἐπιφερόμενος ἐπὶ τὴν χύτραν κατέπαυσεν.
Σφοδρῶς δὲ συνεχόμενος ὑπὸ τῶν τοῦ λούπου ὀνύχων, ὁ
ὄφις ἀπὸ τῆς πολλῆς βίας τὸν ἰὸν ἐξήμεσε παρὰ τὸ τῆς
χύτρας στόμιον. Τοῦ δέ γε ἰοῦ λοιπὸν ἐν τῷ γάλακτι
ἐμεθέντος οὐκ ᾔσθετο περὶ τούτου τὸ παράπαν ἡ δούλη.
Ἀχθέντος οὖν εἰς τὸν οἶκον τοῦ τοιούτου γάλακτος
ἐπεπώκεσαν αὐτὸ οἱ δαιτυμόνες καὶ εὐθὺς πάντες τεθνή-
κασιν. Εἴπατε οὖν μοι, φιλόσοφοι, τίς τοῦ πράγματος ἐγεγόνει αἴτιος;"

104 Εἷς δὲ τῶν φιλοσόφων ὑπολαβὼν ἔφη· "Ὁ ἑστιάτωρ·
ἔδει γὰρ αὐτὸν πρὸ τοῦ τοὺς δαιτυμόνας πεπωκέναι ἐκ τοῦ
γάλακτος, ἐπιτρέψαι τῇ δούλῃ τοῦ ἐκείνην πρότερον
τούτου ἀπογεύσασθαι καὶ εἰθούτως τοῖς φίλοις αὐτοῦ

Then the king's son also responded to his father, "My 103
master and king, permit me also to defend myself against
these charges." The king told his son to respond, and immediately the son said to the philosophers, "My knowledge in
comparison with your wisdom is as a fly compared with a
dragon, but nonetheless listen to my words. There once was
a man who prepared a rich banquet and, as an act of hospitality, invited many dinner guests. The guests reclined, and
while they were eating, the man began preparing milk for
them to drink. And so, he sent his maidservant to the marketplace to buy milk for the men he had invited, and she,
taking a jug, made her way to the marketplace and bought
some milk. She placed the jug upon her head and began to
return to her master's house; but as she was making her way,
a bird of prey swooped down from above carrying a snake
and came to rest upon the jug. And the snake, which was
held fast by the talons of the bird, due to the squeezing spit
its venom into the mouth of the jug. Now the maidservant
had no idea that the venom had been spit into the milk, and
so when the poisoned milk was brought into the house, the
dinner guests drank it and immediately they all died. So, tell
me, philosophers, who was to blame for what happened?"

One of the philosophers responded, "The host, because 104
before the dinner guests drank of the milk, he ought to have
commanded his maidservant to taste it first and only then

μεταδοῦναι." Ἀποκριθεὶς δὲ ὁ ἕτερος τῶν αὐτῶν φιλοσόφων ἔφη· "Οὐχ οὕτως ἔχει τὰ τοῦ πράγματος· οὐ γὰρ ὁ ἑστιάτωρ κατά τι παραίτιος, ἀλλὰ τῷ ὄφει ἡ αἰτία πρόσεστιν." Ὑπολαβὼν δὲ ὁ ἕτερός φησιν· "Οὐδὲ οὕτως ἔχει ὥς φατε· οὐ γὰρ ὁ ὄφις μέμψεως ἐπάξιος, ἐπειδήπερ τῇ βίᾳ τῆς πιεζούσης αὐτὸν συνοχῆς, ὑφ᾽ ἧς καὶ ἀπαγχονισθῆναι ἠναγκάζετο, τὸν ἰὸν ἐξήμεσεν." Εἶτα καὶ ἄλλος τῶν φιλοσόφων ἀνταπεκρίνατο· "Ἡ αἰτία αὕτη τῷ λούπῳ μᾶλλον πρόσεστιν, ὅτιπερ ἐκείνου κραταιῶς τὸν ὄφιν συνέχοντός τε καὶ ἄγχοντος εἰς τὸ ἐμέσαι ὁ ὄφις συνηλάθη."

105   Παρελθὼν δὲ καὶ ὁ Συντίπας φησί· "Γνωστὸν ὑμῖν, ὦ ἄνδρες, ἔστω ὡς ἅπαν θεοδημιούργητον ζῷον δύναμιν ἔχον ζωτικὴν οὐδὲν ἕτερον ἐσθίει, ἀλλ᾽ ὅπερ αὐτοῦ τῇ φύσει ὁ Θεὸς ἀπέταξεν· τοιγαροῦν καὶ ὁ λοῦπος ἀπὸ τῶν τῆς γῆς ἑρπετῶν διατρέφεσθαι ταχθεὶς ἀναίτιος ἐπὶ τῷ συμβάντι καθέστηκεν."

106   Ὁ δὲ βασιλεὺς ταῦτα εἰπόντων τῶν φιλοσόφων ἐνατενίσας τῷ υἱῷ λέγει πρὸς αὐτόν· "Οἶμαι, ὦ υἱέ, ὡς οἱ παρόντες φιλόσοφοι οὐκ ἐπίστανται τίνι τόδε προσυπῆρχε τὸ αἴτιον. Πλὴν ἀλλὰ σὺ φράσον μοι· τίς ὁ γεγονὼς αἴτιος;" Ὁ δὲ παῖς τῷ βασιλεῖ ἀπεκρίνατο· "Οὐ κατά τι, ὦ δέσποτα βασιλεῦ, οἱ φιλόσοφοι σφάλλονται, οὐδ᾽ ὡς τῇ ἀληθείᾳ προσκρούοντες ἀλληνάλλως φάσκουσι· πλὴν ὁ τοῖς τὸ γάλα πεπωκόσι συμβεβηκὼς κίνδυνος ἀπέκειτο τῇ εἱμαρμένῃ αὐτῶν καὶ ἔμελλον ἐκεῖνοι τῷ τοιῷδε τρόπῳ τοῦ βίου ὑπεξελθεῖν."

107   Ὁ δὲ βασιλεὺς τὸν λόγον ὡς πάνυ δῆθεν εὐάρμοστον ἀποδεξάμενος ἥσθη λίαν ἐπὶ τῇ τοῦ υἱοῦ συνέσει καὶ τῇ

shared it with his friends." Another philosopher said in reply, "The matter is not like that. For the blame in no way lies with the host, but the blame belongs to the snake." Then another replied, "The matter is not as you say, either. For the snake does not deserve blame, since the force of the pressure that was squeezing and vigorously strangling it made it spit out its venom." Then yet another philosopher replied, "The blame for this belongs rather to the bird, because it had a powerful grip on the snake and was strangling it until the snake was compelled to spit."

Then Syntipas came forward and said, "You should know, gentlemen, that every living animal created by God eats only what God has ordained for it by nature. Therefore, since the bird of prey has been appointed to feed upon the earth's reptiles, it is free of blame for what happened." 105

When the philosophers had given their responses, the king fixed his gaze upon his son and said to him, "In my opinion, my son, these philosophers here before us do not understand who was to blame in this situation. But come now, you explain it to me. Who was to blame?" And the boy answered the king, "In no way, my master and king, do the philosophers err, nor do they give differing answers because they are opposed to the truth. Rather, the danger that befell those who drank the milk was reserved for them by fate, and they were destined to end their lives in precisely this manner." 106

The king approved of his son's speech and felt that it fit the situation perfectly, and he took great delight in his son's 107

αὐτοῦ συλλογιστικῇ τάχα καὶ σοφιστικῇ ἀποκρίσει. Καί φησιν πρὸς τὸν Συντίπαν· "Αἴτησαι ὃ ἂν θελήσῃς, καί σοι παρὰ τῆς ἐμῆς βασιλείας βραβευθήσεται· ἀλλὰ καὶ εἴ τις περισσοτέρα σοι πρόσεστι διδασκαλία, κἀκείνην τῷ υἱῷ μου ἐκδίδαξον." Ὁ δὲ Συντίπας τῷ βασιλεῖ ἔφη· "Γνωστὸν ἔστω σου τῷ κράτει, ὦ βασιλεῦ, ὡς οὐδὲν τῆς σοφιστικῆς τέχνης καὶ λογιότητος τὸ παράπαν ἐνέλιπον, ὅπερ μὴ τὸν υἱόν σου τὸ καθόλου ἐξεδίδαξα, ὡς καὶ πάντων τῶν ὑπὸ τὴν βασιλείαν σου φιλοσόφων ὑπέρτερον αὐτὸν καταστῆναι." Ὁ δὲ βασιλεὺς ὑπολαβὼν πρὸς τοὺς μεγιστᾶνας αὐτοῦ καὶ αὐτοὺς δὴ τοὺς ὑπ' αὐτὸν φιλοσόφους ἔφη· "Ἆρά γε ταῦτα φιλαλήθως ἡμῖν ὁ Συντίπας φθέγγεται;" Οἱ δὲ ἀπεκρίναντο· "Καὶ μάλα, ὦ δέσποτα." Ὁ δὲ τῷ υἱῷ αὐτοῦ ἐμβλέψας λέγει· "Σὺ δὲ τί φής, ὦ τέκνον; Ἐν ἀληθείᾳ ταῦτα περὶ σοῦ ὁ σὸς φάσκει διδάσκαλος;" Οἱ δὲ φιλόσοφοι ἀντὶ τοῦ παιδὸς ἀποκριθέντες εἶπον· "Οὐδεὶς ὡς ὁ υἱός σου ἐν τῇ τῶν λόγων διαπρέπει κομψότητι."

108   Λέγει οὖν καὶ ὁ παῖς τῷ βασιλεῖ· "Γνωρίζω σου τῷ κράτει, ὦ δέσποτα, ὡς εἴ τις τῶν ἀνθρώπων μὴ τελείαν σχοίη σύνεσιν, οὐκ ἀποδίδωσι ἀγαθὰ τοῖς εὐεργετήσασιν αὐτόν; τὸν μέντοι τοιοῦτον διάστροφον μᾶλλον καὶ ἀσύνετον χρὴ ὀνομάζεσθαι, μηδαμῶς δὲ ἀγχίνουν καὶ συνετόν. Ὁ οὖν διδάσκαλός μου Συντίπας ἐπιμόνως μου καὶ ἀκριβῶς ἐπιμελησάμενος δοκιμώτατόν με τῇ φιλοσοφίᾳ καὶ τῇ γνώσει κατέστησε, καὶ χρὴ τοῦτον παρὰ τῆς σῆς βασιλείας ἀξίαν τῆς ἐπιμελείας καὶ τὴν ἀμοιβὴν κομίσασθαι. Ἐπεὶ δέ, ὦ βασιλεῦ, καὶ οὗτοί σου οἱ φιλόσοφοι ἐπιμαρτυροῦσί μοι ὡς καὶ αὐτῶν δὴ τοῖς λόγοις ὑπερτερῶ, ἄκουσόν μου τῆς

intelligence and his logical and seemingly wise response. Then he said to Syntipas, "Ask for whatever you wish, and it shall be awarded to you by my majesty, and if you possess any additional teaching, instruct my son in that too." Syntipas replied to the king, "Your majesty should know, my king, that there is nothing else whatsoever that belongs to the art of wisdom and eloquent reasoning which I did not teach your son, so as to make him superior to all of the philosophers who are subject to your royal power." In response, the king said to his noblemen and also to the philosophers under him, "Has Syntipas spoken to me truthfully?", to which they replied, "Certainly, master." Then he turned to his son and said, "And you, my child, what do you say? Does your teacher speak truthfully about you?" But the philosophers responded on the boy's behalf, "There is no one as distinguished as your son for elegance in speaking."

Then the boy said to the king, "I will tell your majesty, 108 that if a man does not acquire perfect intelligence, he does not properly repay the gifts of his benefactors. Such a man ought rather to be labeled twisted and slow-witted, and by no means clever and intelligent. But my teacher Syntipas, because he attended to me so persistently and carefully and made me preeminent in learning and knowledge, ought also to receive from your majesty a reward worthy of his attentiveness and care. Since, my king, these philosophers of yours also bear witness that I am superior in speaking and

παρούσης διηγήσεως. Δύο γάρ τινα παιδία ἐτύγχανον, τὸ μὲν χρόνων πέντε, τὸ δὲ τριῶν. Ἦν δὲ καί τις ἀνὴρ γηραιὸς καὶ ἀνάπηρος ἅμα καὶ παράλυτος, ὃς συνέσει καὶ ἀγχινοίᾳ σὺν ἐκείνοις ὑπῆρχε κατάκομος." Ὁ δὲ βασιλεὺς τὸν εἱρμὸν ἀνακόπτων τοῦ διηγήματος λέγει τῷ υἱῷ· "Καὶ τίς ἦν, τέκνον, ἡ ἐκείνων ὑπόθεσις;" Ἀναλαβὼν δὲ ὁ παῖς τὸν λόγον ἄνωθεν διηγεῖτο λέγων.

109   "Ἀνήρ τις ἦν κίναιδος καὶ φιλήδονος λίαν, ὃς ἡνίκα περὶ γυναικὸς εὐειδοῦς ἠκηκόει, πρὸς ἐκείνην ἀκολασίας χάριν εὐθὺς ἐπορεύετο. Ἐδηλώθη γοῦν αὐτῷ ἐν μιᾷ περί τινος ὡραιοτάτης γυναικός, καὶ αὐτίκα πρὸς αὐτὴν ἀπελήλυθε συνουσίας ἕνεκεν. Εἶχε δὲ παῖδα ἡ γυνὴ ἐκείνη τριῶν ἐτῶν τῇ ἡλικίᾳ τυγχάνοντα, ὃς τῷ τότε τῇ μητρὶ ἔτυχε λέγειν· 'Παρασκεύασόν μοι, ὦ μῆτερ, ἔδεσμά τι τοῦ φαγεῖν.' Ἡ δὲ ὁρῶσα τὸν ἄνδρα ἐκεῖνον πρὸς τὴν μετ' αὐτῆς κατεπειγόμενον ἀκολασίαν λέγει πρὸς αὐτόν· 'Μικρόν με ἀνάμεινον, ἄνθρωπε, ἄχρις οὗ τῷ ἐμῷ παιδὶ βρώσιμόν τι παρασκευάσω.' Ὁ δὲ ὑπολαβὼν ἔφη τῇ γυναικί· 'Ἄφες, τό γε νῦν ἔχον, τὴν τοῦ παιδὸς φροντίδα καὶ τοῦτο δὴ τὸ ἡμέτερον ἐκπλήρωσον ἔργον, μήπως γένηταί μοι χρονίσαι ἐνταῦθα.' Ἡ δὲ ἀντέφησε τῷ ἀνδρί· 'Εἰ ᾔδεις, ὦ ἄνθρωπε, ὁποίαν οὗτος ὁ παῖς μου τὴν ἀγχίνοιαν κέκτηται, οὐκ ἂν τοιαῦτά μοι ἔλεγες.' Καὶ ταῦτα εἰποῦσα ἐγείρεται εὐθύς, καὶ ὅπερ ἦν ἐψήσασα ἔδεσμα ὀρύζιον τυγχάνον τῷ παιδὶ παρέθηκεν. Ὁ δὲ παῖς, εἰ καὶ μὴ πάντη νήπιος ἦν τῷ χρόνῳ, ἀλλ' οὖν ὀδυρόμενος διετέλει καὶ τὴν μητέρα ἠνάγκαζε περισσότερον αὐτῷ παρατεθεικέναι ὀρύζιον· 'Οὐ γὰρ κεκόρεσμαι ἔτι,' φησίν, 'ἀλλὰ πλείονος ὀρέγομαι.'

learning even to them, listen to this story. Once there were two children, one five years old, the other three. And there was also an old man who was lame and a paralytic, yet abounding in intelligence and cleverness." Then the king interrupted the train of his son's speech and said to him, "What, my child, is their story?" And the boy began to tell the story from the beginning.

"There was once a man who was a lecher and a hedonist; 109 whenever he heard about an attractive woman, he immediately went after her with licentiousness on his mind. Now one day he was informed about a very beautiful woman, and straightaway he set out to have sex with her. The woman had a three-year-old son, who at that moment happened to say to his mother, 'Mother, make me some food to eat.' Seeing that the man was eager to commit that licentious act with her, she said to him, 'Wait for me a bit, sir, until I've made my son something to eat.' He replied to the woman, 'Forget about taking care of your son for now and finish our business, so that I'm not delayed here.' She answered the man, 'If you knew how clever this son of mine was, you wouldn't speak to me like that.' After she said this, she immediately got up and served her son the food, which was rice that she had boiled. And even though the boy was not really an infant in terms of his age, he nevertheless kept whining and pressuring his mother to serve him more rice. 'I'm not full yet,' he said, 'and I want more.' Then the mother

Ἡ δὲ μήτηρ ἐποίησε κατὰ τὸ τοῦ παιδὸς θέλημα. Ὁ δὲ αὖθις καὶ ἑτέρας παραθήκης ἐφιέμενος ἐπὶ πλέον πρὸς τὴν μητέρα ὠλοφύρετο. Ὁ μέντοι ἀκόλαστος ἐκεῖνος ἀνὴρ δυσχεραίνων ἐπὶ τῇ ἀσελγείᾳ τοῦ παιδὸς καὶ τῷ τούτου ἀδιακόπῳ κλαυθμῷ λέγει πρὸς αὐτόν· Λίαν τῷ ὄντι ἀναιδὴς καὶ ἀκόρεστος πέφυκας καὶ οὐκ ἔνεστί σοι φρόνησις, ὡς ὁρῶ, τὸ παράπαν· εἰ γὰρ τὸ τοιοῦτον ἔδεσμα πέντε ἀνδράσι παρετέθη, δαψιλῶς ἂν αὐτοῖς εἰς κόρον διήρκεσεν.'

110   "Ὁ δὲ παῖς ὑπολαβὼν λέγει τῷ ἀνδρί· Ἐκεῖνος μᾶλλον πάσης ἀπεστέρηται φρονήσεως, ὃς τὸ παρὰ σοῦ νυνὶ ζητούμενον καὶ ἐμῇ μητρὶ ἀπρεπῶς λεγόμενον ἑαυτῷ ἐπιζητεῖ καὶ πρᾶξιν μεταδιώκει Θεῷ μεμισημένην· ἐν ἐμοὶ δὲ τί ὁρᾷς φρονήσεως ἐστερημένον; Ἀλλὰ καὶ ἀπὸ τοῦδέ μου τοῦ κλαυθμοῦ, ὅπερ ἀναίδειαν ἀποκαλεῖς, τίνα ὅλως ζημίαν ὑφίσταμαι; Μᾶλλον μὲν οὖν καὶ οἱ ὀφθαλμοί μου τοῖς δάκρυσι καθαρθέντες ἐπὶ πλεῖον διεφωτίσθησαν, καὶ οἱ μυκτῆρές μου τῆς ἐν αὐτοῖς ἀκαθαρσίας ἀπεσμήχησαν, καὶ τὸ παρατεθέν μοι ἔδεσμα προσετέθη μοι, καὶ διὰ τούτου τοῦ κλαυθμοῦ, εἴ τι δὴ καὶ ἤθελον, ῥᾳδίως μοι προσεγένετο.' Τούτων ὁ ἀνὴρ ἐκεῖνος τῶν συνετῶν ῥημάτων παρὰ τοῦ παιδὸς ἀκηκοὼς συνῆκεν ὡς ὁ παῖς ὑπέρκειται μᾶλλον αὐτοῦ τῇ ἰδίᾳ φρονήσει, καὶ αὐτίκα ἀναστὰς καὶ σχηματίσας τὰς χεῖρας προσεκύνησε τὸν παῖδα καί φησιν πρὸς αὐτόν· Μὴ μέμψῃ μοι, ἀξιῶ, περὶ ὧν σοι τανῦν ἀπεφθεγξάμην· οὐ γὰρ ᾔδειν ὡς τοιαύτην ἐκέκτησο φρόνησιν.' Καὶ τοῦτο εἰπών, εὐθὺς ἐκεῖθεν ὑπανεχώρησε, μηδὲν ἄτοπον ἐπὶ τῇ αὐτοῦ μητρὶ ἐργασάμενος.

111   "Ἄκουσον οὖν, ὦ δέσποτα βασιλεῦ, καὶ τῆς περὶ τοῦ

did as her son wished. But he wanted yet another serving, and cried to his mother even more. That licentious man, then, was annoyed at the boy's brattiness and his incessant crying, and said to him, 'You really are very shameless and insatiable, and I can see that you have no intelligence at all. For if this much food were set before five grown men, it would be more than enough to satisfy them.'

"Then the boy replied to the man, 'No, the man who 110 completely lacks intelligence is the one who seeks for himself what you now seek with your indecent suggestions to my mother, and who wants to do something that is hateful to God. What do you see in me that lacks intelligence? And what harm do I suffer at all from this crying of mine, which you call shameless? In fact, my eyes, washed by my tears, see all the more clearly, and my nostrils have been cleared of snot, and the food set before me has increased. By my crying, I easily got whatever I wanted.' When he heard these wise words from the boy, the man understood that the boy's intelligence was superior to his own. And straightaway he stood up and, making a gesture of supplication, prostrated himself before the boy and said to him, 'Don't blame me, I beg you, for what I said to you just now. For I didn't know that you possessed such intelligence.' And with these words he immediately withdrew from there, having done nothing improper to the boy's mother.

"Hear also, then, my master and king, the story about the 111

πενταετοῦς παιδὸς διηγήσεως. Ἄνδρες τινὲς ὑπῆρχον ἔμποροι τὸν ἀριθμὸν τρεῖς, οἳ καὶ ἀλλήλων κοινωνοὶ ἐτύγχανον, καὶ ἐπί τινα μακρὰν χώραν δι' ἐμπορίαν ἐστέλλοντο.
Τῆς δέ γε ὁδοιπορίας ἐχόμενοι εἴς τινα κώμην καταλαμ-
βάνουσιν, ἐν ᾗ καὶ παρά τινι γραΐδι τὴν κατάλυσιν ἔθεντο.
Μετὰ δὲ ταῦτα ἔδοξεν αὐτοῖς ἐπὶ τὸ βαλανεῖον ἀπελθεῖν
καὶ ἀπολούσασθαι, καὶ λέγουσι πρὸς τὴν γραΐδα· Ἑτοίμα-
σον ἡμῖν, ὦ γύναι, τὰ πρὸς τὸ βαλανεῖον χρειώδη σκεύη
καὶ ἐπιβλήματα.' Ἡ δὲ πάντα αὐτοῖς παρητοίμασε, μόνου
δὲ τοῦ κτενὸς ἐπελάθετο. Εἶτα ἐκεῖνοι ἐκβαλόντες ἅπερ
ἐφέροντο χρυσίου τρία βαλάντια, ὧν ἔνδοθεν τὸν ἑαυτῶν
κοινὸν θησαυρὸν ἐκέκτηντο, τῇ γραΐδι παραδεδώκασι, καὶ
διενετείλαντο αὐτῇ λέγοντες· Λαβοῦσα, ὦ γύναι, ταυτὶ τὰ
τρία τοῦ χρυσίου βαλάντια παρὰ σεαυτῇ φύλαττε, καὶ μὴ
πρός τινα ἡμῶν ἐπιδώσῃς τι τούτων, ἄχρις ὅτου ἡμᾶς γε
τοὺς τρεῖς ὁμοθυμαδὸν πρὸς σὲ παραγεγονότας θεάσῃ.'

112   Ταῦτα τῇ γραΐδι παραγγείλαντες ἐπὶ τὸ βαλανεῖον
ἐπορεύθησαν. Ἰδόντες δὲ ὡς κτένιον οὐκ ἐπεφέροντο,
στέλλουσι θάτερον αὐτῶν πρὸς τὴν γραΐδα ἐκείνην τοῦ
ἀγαγεῖν κτένιον. Ὁ δέ γε σταλεὶς ἐλθὼν πρὸς αὐτὴν ἔφη·
Οἱ κοινωνοί μου δι' ἐμοῦ δηλοῦσι, ὦ γύναι, λέγοντες·
"Στεῖλον ἡμῖν τὸ παρατεθέν σοι χρυσίον παρ' ἡμῶν."' Ἡ
δὲ λέγει τῷ ἀνδρί· Οὐδαμῶς σοί τι ἐπιδώσω, ἄχρις ἂν οἱ
τρεῖς πρός με ἐπὶ τὸ αὐτὸ παραγένησθε.' Ὁ δὲ λέγει τῇ
γυναικί· Ἰδοὺ κατ' ὄψιν τὴν σὴν οἱ κοινωνοί μου, ὡς ὁρᾷς,
ἑστήκασιν, εἰ καὶ πρὸς μακράν σου ἀπέχουσι· κἀκεῖνοί σοι
λέγουσι τὸ χρυσίον δεδωκέναι μοι.' Ταῦτα εἰπὼν φωνεῖ
πρὸς ἐκείνους περὶ τοῦ κτενὸς αὐτοῖς ἀνωνύμως καὶ

five-year-old child. There were some merchants, three in number, who were associates of each other and who once set out for a distant land on business. In the course of their travels they arrived at a certain town, where they took up lodging with an old woman. Afterward, they decided to go to the bath to wash themselves, and so they said to the old woman, 'Prepare for us the robes and the other things we need for the bath.' She made everything ready for them, forgetting only the comb. Then the merchants brought out three purses of gold that they were carrying with them, in which were stored their joint funds, and they handed them over to the old woman. Then they instructed her, 'Take these three purses of gold and keep them with you, and do not return them to any one of us until you see all three of us standing together before you.'

"After giving these instructions to the old woman, they 112 set out for the bath. But when they noticed that they did not have a comb, they sent one of their group back to the old woman to fetch it. Now the one who was sent back went to her and said, 'My associates are communicating through me, and they say, "Send us the gold we left with you."' And she said to the man, 'No way will I hand it over to you, until the three of you are standing in front of me, all together.' Then he said to the woman, 'Look, my associates are standing in your sight, as you can see, even though they're some way away from you, and they're telling you to give me the gold.' After he said this, he shouted to them, speaking about the comb without naming it or making clear what he meant

ἀδήλως οὑτωσὶ λέγων· Ὁὐδέν μοι ἡ γραῦς παρέχει, εἰ μὴ ὑμεῖς αὐτοὶ ἐπιτρέψοιτε.' Οἱ δὲ ἐφώνησαν πρὸς αὐτὴν λέγοντες· Πάρασχε, γύναι, αὐτῷ!' Ἡ δὲ εὐθὺς ἐκβαλοῦσα τὸ παρατεθὲν αὐτῇ χρυσίον ἐπιδέδωκεν αὐτῷ. Ἐκεῖνος δὲ τοῦτο εἰληφὼς εὐθὺς ἐκεῖθεν ἀπέδρα.

113 "Οἱ δέ γε τούτου κοινωνοὶ ἐπὶ πολὺ αὐτὸν διετέλουν προσμένοντες, εἶτα φωνοῦσι πρὸς τὴν γραῖδα· Ποῦ ἐστιν ὁ πρὸς σὲ σταλεὶς κοινωνὸς ἡμῶν, ὅτι μὴ ὅλως ἡμῖν ἀναφαίνεται;' Ἡ δὲ γραῦς ἔφησε τοῖς ἀνδράσιν ὡς· Τὸν θησαυρὸν ὑμῶν παρ' ἐμοῦ ἐπεζήτησε, καὶ κατὰ τὴν ὑμῶν προσφώνησίν τε καὶ προτροπὴν παραδέδωκα τοῦτον αὐτῷ, καὶ λαβὼν ὑπεχώρησε τῆς οἰκίας μου.' Οἱ δὲ ἀντεῖπον τῇ γυναικί· Ἡμεῖς κτένιον αὐτὸν ἀγαγεῖν ἡμῖν πρὸς σὲ ἀπεστάλκαμεν.' Ἡ δὲ γραῦς, Ἀλλ' ἐκεῖνος,' φησί, 'τὸ χρυσίον ὑμῶν ἐξ ἐμοῦ ἐπεζήτησεν ὡς ἀφ' ὑμετέρας προτροπῆς, κἀγὼ δὴ ἐσύστερον δοῦναι αὐτῷ ὑμῶν προτρεψάντων με ἐκβαλοῦσα τοῦτο πρὸς αὐτὸν ἐπιδέδωκα.'

114 "Ταῦτα οἱ ἔμποροι παρὰ τῆς γυναικὸς ἀπροσδοκήτως ἐνωτισθέντες καὶ πικρᾷ τῇ ἀθυμίᾳ συσχεθέντες, λαβόντες εὐθὺς τὴν γραῖδα ἀνάρπαστον πρὸς τὸν τῆς χώρας πορεύονται ἄρχοντα καὶ αὐτῷ τὰ τοῦ πράγματος περιπαθῶς ἐκτραγῳδοῦσιν. Ὁ δὲ ἄρχων ἔφη τῇ γυναικί· Ἀπόδος τοῖς ἀνδράσι τὸ παρατεθέν σοι παρ' αὐτῶν χρυσίον.' Ἡ δὲ γραῦς τῷ ἄρχοντι ἀπεκρίνατο· Ἐγώ, κύριέ μου, ἀποδέδωκα αὐτοῖς τὸν θησαυρὸν αὐτῶν.' Οἱ δὲ ἔμποροι πρὸς τὸν τοιοῦτον αὐτῆς ἀπόλογον ἀνθυπέφερον· Ἡμεῖς, ὦ δικαστά, τρεῖς τυγχάνοντες κοινωνοί, ὅτε ταύτῃ τῇ γραῖδι τὰ ἡμέτερα χρήματα παρεθέμεθα, εὐθὺς σὺν ἀκριβείᾳ

by saying, 'The old lady won't give me anything unless you yourselves tell her to.' And they shouted back to her, 'Give it to him!' And so, she immediately brought out the gold that had been left with her and gave it to the one man, who took it and immediately ran off.

"Now his associates, when they had been kept waiting for 113 a long time, shouted to the old woman, 'Where is our associate whom we sent to you? We've seen no sign of him.' And the old woman said to the men, 'He requested your money from me, and at your encouragement and bidding, I handed it over to him. And he took it and left my house.' They replied to the woman, 'We sent him back to you to get us a comb!' 'But he asked for your gold, and said that you were requesting it,' the old woman said, 'and when you did indeed urge me to give it to him, I took it out and handed it over to him.'

"When they heard the woman's surprising response, the 114 merchants were bitterly disappointed, and immediately they seized the old woman, went to the governor of that land, and explained the situation to him with great emotion and drama. Then the governor said to the woman, 'Give these men back the money that they left with you'; and the old woman replied to the governor, 'I did give them back their money, my lord.' But the merchants responded to this defense of hers, 'Judge, as we were three business associates when we deposited our money with this old woman, we

ἐνετειλάμεθα εἰπόντες ὡς· "Μηδαμῶς τῶν σῶν χειρῶν, ὦ
γύναι, ἡ τοιαύτη ἡμῶν ἐκβληθείη παρακαταθήκη, εἰ μή τί
γε ἡμᾶς τοὺς τρεῖς ἐπὶ τὸ αὐτὸ θεάσῃ ταύτην ἀπὸ σοῦ
ἐπιζητοῦντας."' Ὁ δὲ ἄρχων πάλιν πρὸς τὴν γραΐδα φησίν·
'Ἀπόδος τὸ χρυσίον τοῖς ἐμπόροις, ὦ γύναι, καὶ μηδὲν
μηκέτι πρὸς ταῦτα ἀμφίβαλλε.' Ἡ δὲ γραῦς ἐξῆλθεν ἐκ
προσώπου τοῦ ἄρχοντος πικρῶς ὀδυρομένη καὶ γοερὸν
ἀλαλάζουσα.

115   "Μετὰ μικρὸν δὲ παῖς τις ἐτῶν πέντε τυγχάνων τῇ γυναικὶ θρηνῳδούσῃ συναντᾷ, καὶ ταύτην κατοικτείρας τῆς
πικροτάτης οἰμωγῆς λέγει πρὸς αὐτήν· Τί οὕτως οἰκτρῶς,
ὦ γύναι, ὀλοφύρῃ;' Ἡ δὲ τῷ παιδὶ ἔφησεν· "Ἔασόν με, παῖ,
τὴν τάλαιναν ἀποδύρεσθαί μου τὴν συμφοράν.' Ὁ δὲ παῖς
ἐνέκειτο ἐκβιάζων αὐτὴν καὶ τὴν αἰτίαν τοῦ ὀδυρμοῦ πυν-
θανόμενος, καὶ οὐ πρότερον αὐτῆς ἀπέστη, ἄχρις οὗ
πάντα ἐκείνη αὐτῷ ὡς ἔχοι τὰ τοῦ πάθους διεσάφησεν. Ὁ
δὲ εὐθὺς ὑπολαβὼν τῇ γραΐδι ἔφησεν· "Ἔγωγε τῆσδε τῆς
κατεχούσης σε συμφορᾶς ἀπαλλάξω. Ἀλλ' εἰ βούλει τοῦτό
σοι ποιῆσαί με, δός μοι πρότερον ἄργυρον ἕνα, ἵνα δι' αὐτοῦ κάρυά μοι ἐξωνήσωμαι.' Ἡ δὲ γυνή, Ἔϊπερ με,' φησί,
'τῆς χαλεπῆς ταύτης συνοχῆς ἀπαλλάξεις, δώσω σοι τὸν
ἄργυρον.'

116   "Ὁ δὲ παῖς ἀποκριθεὶς λέγει πρὸς αὐτήν· 'Ὑπόστρεψον
λοιπὸν πρὸς τὸν ἄρχοντα καὶ λέξον αὐτῷ οὕτως· "Γνωρίζω
σοι, ὦ κύριέ μου, ὡς τρεῖς κοινωνοὶ ἐτύγχανον οἱ τὸ
χρυσίον μοι παραθέμενοι, καθὰ δὴ καὶ προεδηλώθη σου
τῇ ὑπεροχῇ, οἳ καὶ ἐνετείλαντό μοι λέγοντες· "Ὅρα μὴ
δώσῃς τινὶ ἐξ ἡμῶν τὰ παρατεθέντα σοι χρήματα, εἰ μὴ οἱ

immediately gave her precise instructions: "Do not hand over our deposit unless you see all three of us asking you to return it."' Once again, the governor said to the old woman, 'Give the merchants back their money, and don't stall any longer.' Then the woman left the governor's presence, lamenting bitterly and wailing aloud.

"A short while later a five-year-old boy met the woman as she was grieving. He took pity on her for her very bitter weeping, and said, 'Why are you mourning so sadly?' And she said to the child, 'Boy, leave me alone in my misery to lament my misfortune.' But the boy kept pressing her insistently and inquiring about the reason for her distress, and he did not stop until she had explained the whole story of her suffering to him. And then he responded immediately to the old woman, 'I will deliver you from the misfortune that has befallen you. But if you wish me to do this for you, first give me one silver coin, so that I may buy myself some nuts.' And the woman said, 'If you get me out of this mess, I'll give you the money.' 115

"The boy responded to her, 'Go back to the governor, then, and say this to him: "I'm telling you, my lord, that there were three merchants who left their gold with me, as has already been explained to your excellency, and they did give me these instructions: 'See that you do not give the money that we left with you to any one of us unless all three 116

τρεῖς ὁμοθυμαδὸν πρὸς σὲ παραγενώμεθα.᾽ Νῦν δέ, κύριέ μου, ἰδοὺ τὸ χρυσίον παρ᾽ ἐμοί ἐστιν· πρόσταξον τὸ λοιπὸν τοὺς τρεῖς κοινωνοὺς ἐπὶ τὸ αὐτὸ παραστῆναί μοι, καθὰ δὴ κἀκεῖνοι σὺν ἀκριβείᾳ παρηγγυήσαντο, καὶ εἰθούτως αὐτοῖς ὁ κοινὸς αὐτῶν θησαυρὸς παρ᾽ ἐμοῦ ἀποδοθήσεται.᾽᾽

Ἐπὶ ταύταις τοίνυν ταῖς τοῦ παιδὸς ἐκείνου πιθαναῖς ὑποθήκαις σφόδρα ἡσθεῖσα ἡ γυνὴ εὐθὺς ὑποστρέφει πρὸς τὸν ἡγεμόνα, καὶ τὰ παρ᾽ ἐκείνου ὑποτεθέντα αὐτῇ ὡς εὐσύνοπτα καὶ συνετὰ πρὸς αὐτὸν ἀπεφθέγξατο. Ὁ δὲ ἡγεμὼν εὐλογοφανῶς λέγειν διαγνοὺς τὴν γυναῖκα, μεταστέλλεται τοὺς ἐμπόρους καί φησι πρὸς αὐτούς· Δικαίως τανῦν ὑμῖν ἡ γραῦς ἀντιτίθεται. Λοιπὸν οὖν παραστήσατε μεθ᾽ ἑαυτῶν καὶ τὸν ἕτερον ὑμῶν κοινωνόν, καθὰ δὴ καὶ ὑμεῖς αὐτῇ ἐνετείλασθε, καὶ εἰθούτως οἱ τρεῖς ὁμοθυμαδὸν τὸ χρυσίον ἀπολήψεσθε.᾽

117 "Τῆς οὖν τοιαύτης ἀποφάσεως παρὰ τοῦ δικαστοῦ ἐκείνου ἐσύστερον ἐξενεχθείσης καὶ τῆς γυναικὸς μηκέτι παρὰ τῶν δύο ἀνδρῶν ἐκείνων καθελκομένης, συνῆκεν ὁ ἄρχων ὡς παρ᾽ ἑτέρου τινὸς ἡ ἐγκαλουμένη γραῦς τὸν ἔσχατον ἐκεῖνον ἀπόλογον ἐξεδίδακτο· καὶ ταύτην προσκαλεσάμενος ἐπυνθάνετο παρ᾽ αὐτῆς τίς ἄρα αὐτῇ τὴν πιθανὴν ἀντίθεσιν ἐκείνην ὑπέθετο. Ἡ δὲ ἀπεκρίνατο ὅτι· ᾽Παῖς μοι πενταετὴς ἐντυχὼν καὶ ὀδυρομένην με ἑωρακὼς ἐκεῖνός μοι ταύτην τὴν ἀντίθεσιν ὑπεσήμανεν.᾽ Ὁ δὲ ἡγεμὼν αὐτίκα τὸν παῖδα πρὸς ἑαυτὸν μετεστείλατο, καὶ τοῦτον ἐπηρώτα λέγων· ᾽Σύ, ὦ παῖ, τόνδε τὸν λόγον τῇ γραΐδι ὑπέθου;᾽ Ὁ δέ, ᾽Ναί,᾽ φησίν, ᾽ὦ κύριέ μου.᾽ Ὁ δὲ

of us stand before you together.' And now, my lord, look, I do in fact have their gold. So, order the three associates to appear before me all together, as they themselves so precisely specified, and then I will give them back their joint funds.'" Then the woman, who was very pleased with the boy's persuasive instructions, immediately returned to the ruler and said just what the boy had instructed her, believing his words to be clearly correct and smart. And the ruler determined that the woman was speaking convincingly, and so he summoned the merchants and said to them, 'The old woman has now made a fair counterproposal. So, appear before her now, you yourselves and your third associate, just as you yourselves instructed her, and then you three will receive your gold at the same time.'

"After this decision had been handed down by the judge 117 and the woman was no longer being accused by those two men, the governor realized that the accused woman had learned this perfect defense from someone else, and so he summoned her and asked her who had suggested this persuasive response to her. She replied, 'There was a five-year-old boy who saw me grieving, and he suggested this response to me.' The ruler straightaway summoned the boy and asked him, 'Did you suggest this speech to the old woman, my boy?' He answered, 'Yes, my lord.' Then the judge, amazed at

δικαστὴς ἐκπλαγεὶς ἐπὶ τῇ τοῦ παιδὸς συνέσει καὶ ἀγχινοίᾳ εὐθὺς αὐτὸν καθηγητὴν ῥητόρων καὶ φιλοσόφων προβάλλεται.

118 "Ἄκουσον δέ, ὦ δέσποτα καὶ βασιλεῦ, καὶ τῆς περὶ τοῦ γηραιοῦ ἀνδρὸς διηγήσεως. Ἀνὴρ γάρ τις ἦν, ὃς εἰωθὼς ἐμπορεύεσθαι, ἀρωματικὰ ξύλα εἰς ἐμπορίαν ὠνήσατο· καὶ δὴ μεμαθηκὼς περί τινος πόλεως ὡς σπανίως ἐν αὐτῇ τὰ τοιαῦτα ἐφευρίσκονται, εὐθὺς ἄρας τὰ ὠνηθέντα πρὸς ἐκείνην ἐπορεύθη τὴν πόλιν. Καταλαβὼν δὲ τὰ ἐκεῖσε, ἔξω τῆς πόλεως τὴν κατάλυσιν ἔθετο ὥστε μαθεῖν πρότερον πῶς ἐν αὐτῇ πιπράσκεται τὸ τοιόνδε ἀρωματικὸν ξύλον. Ἐν δὲ τῷ μεταξὺ γυνή τις δούλη τῶν ἐν τῇ πόλει τινὸς τυγχάνουσα τὸν ἔμπορον θεασαμένη, 'Πόθεν, ὦ ἑταῖρε;' πρὸς αὐτὸν ἔφη, 'Καὶ τίνα εἰσὶν ἃ ἐπιφέρῃ;' Ὁ δέ, ''Εμπορος ἐγώ,' ἀπεκρίνατο, 'καὶ ἃ ἐπιφέρομαι ξύλα εἰσὶν ἀρωματικά.' Ἡ δὲ εἰσελθοῦσα πρὸς τὸν αὐτῆς κύριον, πάντα δὴ τὰ κατ' ἐκεῖνον τὸν ἔμπορον αὐτῷ διεσάφησεν. Ὁ δὲ ποικίλος ὢν καὶ πανοῦργος τὸν τρόπον, αὐτίκα συναγαγὼν ἃ παρ' ἑαυτῷ ἀρωματικὰ ξύλα ἐκέκτητο τῷ πυρὶ ἔβαλεν. Καὶ τοῦτο αὐτοῦ ἐμφυσήσαντος πολλή τις ἐκεῖθεν εὐωδία ἐξεπέμπετο. Ἧς καὶ ὀσφρανθεὶς ὁ ἔξωθεν ἔμπορος λέγει τοῖς περὶ αὐτόν· 'Εὐωδίας πλήρης ἀρωματικῆς ὀσφραίνομαι· ἴδετε οὖν τὸ τάχος σὺν ἀκριβείᾳ πολλῇ μήπως τινὶ τῶν ἡμετέρων γόμων πυρκαϊά τις προσήγγισεν, καὶ ἡμέτερα ἀρώματα ὑποκαίονται.' Οἱ δὲ πρὸς αὐτὸν εἰρήκασιν· 'Οὐδαμῶς πυρκαϊά τις ἢ σπινθὴρ τὸ παράπαν τινὸς τῶν ἡμετέρων ἥψατο γόμων.'

119 "Πρωΐας δὲ γενομένης εἰσέδυ ἐκείνην τὴν πόλιν ὁ

the boy's intelligence and cleverness, immediately made him a teacher of rhetors and philosophers.

"Hear also, my master and king, the story about the old 118 man. There once was a merchant who made his living trading in aromatic wood. When he learned of a certain city where that kind of wood was rarely to be found, he immediately took his wares and made his way there. Upon his arrival, he found lodging outside the city, so he could first learn how to sell his aromatic wood inside. Meanwhile, a female slave who belonged to one of the citizens happened to see the merchant. 'Where are you from, my friend,' she said to him, 'and what are you transporting?' He replied, 'I'm a merchant, and am transporting aromatic wood.' Then she returned to her master and told him all about that merchant. Now the master was wily and wicked, and so he straightaway gathered all the aromatic wood he had and threw it into the fire. Then he blew on the fire, and a very fragrant scent arose from it. When the traveling merchant smelled the fragrance, he said to those around him, 'My nose is filled with the fragrance of aromatic wood. Make sure then, quickly and very carefully, that no fire has gotten close to any of our merchandise, and that our aromatic wood is not being burned up.' And they responded to him, 'No fire at all, not even a spark, has touched any of our merchandise.'

"When morning came, the merchant entered the city, 119

ἔμπορος. Καὶ εὐθὺς συναντᾷ αὐτῷ εἰσερχομένῳ ὁ τῆς
δούλης ἐκείνης δεσπότης· εἶτα καὶ πυνθάνεται παρ' αὐτοῦ
τί ἄρα εἶεν ἅπερ ἐν τῷ ἰδίῳ φόρτῳ ἐπιφέροιτο. Ὁ δὲ
ἔμπορος, Ἀρωματικά,' φησί, 'κομίζω ξύλα εἰς ὤνησιν τῶν
βουλομένων ἀπὸ τῶν τῆς πόλεως ταύτης κατοίκων.' Αὖθις
δὲ ἐκεῖνος· Τίς σε, ὦ ἄνθρωπε, κατηνάγκασε ταῦτα πρὸς
ταύτην διακομίσαι τὴν πόλιν καὶ τἄλλα δὴ τὰ ἐπικερδῆ σοι
εἴδη καταλιπεῖν; Ἴσθι γὰρ ἐν ἀκριβείᾳ ὡς τοῖς τοιούτοις
οἷα καυσίμῳ ὕλῃ οἱ ἐνταῦθα προσανέχουσι καὶ πρὸς τὴν
τῶν καμίνων ταῦτα καταχρῶνται ἔκκαυσιν.' Ἀλλ' ἐγώ,'
φησὶν ὁ ἔμπορος, 'ἠνώτισμαι μᾶλλον ὡς ὑπὲρ πάσας τὰς
πόλεις αὕτη ἐνδεὴς τῶν τοιούτων καὶ σπανίζουσα πέφυκεν.'
Ἀπεκρίνατο δὲ πρὸς αὐτὸν ὁ ἀνήρ· Οἱ ταῦτα εἰρηκότες
σοι μεγάλως σε ἐξηπάτησαν.' Τούτοις τοῖς λόγοις ὁ ἔμπορος τὴν καρδίαν πληγεὶς συνεσχέθη τῇ λύπῃ.

120   Ὁ δέ γε ἀνὴρ ἐκεῖνος ἀνίᾳ συσχεθέντα τοῦτον ἑωρακὼς λέγει πρὸς αὐτόν· Ὁρῶ σε δεινῶς, ἑταῖρε, γεγονότα
περίλυπον καί σε κατοικτείρω, ἴσθι, τῆς σφοδρᾶς ἀθυμίας.
Ἄγε δὴ λοιπὸν διάπρασόν μοι τὸν φόρτον σου ἅπαντα· καὶ
εἴ τι βούλει παράσχω σοι ἐν πλήρει πίνακι.' Ὁ δὲ ἔμπορος
συλλογισάμενος καθ' ἑαυτὸν ἔλεγε· Βέλτιόν μοι τοιγαροῦν, ὡς στοχάζομαι, πέφυκεν εἴ τι δή μοι δῴη ὁ ἀνὴρ
οὗτος εἰληφέναι ἐξ αὐτοῦ ἤπερ τὴν ἐμπορίαν μου παντελῶς
ἐαθῆναι ἀδιάπρατον.' Καὶ ταῦτα διανοησάμενος, αὐτίκα
διεπώλησεν ἐκείνῳ τῷ ἀνδρὶ τὸν ἑαυτοῦ φόρτον ἅπαντα,
συναρεσθεὶς ὑπὲρ τῆς τιμῆς ἐξ αὐτοῦ εἰληφέναι, εἴ τι δὴ
καὶ παρ' αὐτοῦ ἐπιζητήσειεν, ἐν πίνακι πεπληρωμένῳ.
Λαβὼν οὖν ὁ ἀνὴρ τὰ ὠνηθέντα παρ' αὐτοῦ εἰς τὴν ἰδίαν

and immediately as he was going in, that slave's master met him. When he inquired what goods he was transporting, the merchant replied, 'I'm bringing aromatic wood for sale to anyone living in this city who wishes to buy it.' Then the man said to him, 'Sir, who made you transport that stuff to this city and leave behind the things that would bring you a profit? You should understand clearly that the people here rely on such material for firewood, and they use it as fuel in their ovens.' The merchant said, 'But I was told just the opposite, that your city above all others lacked this type of wood and was in need of it.' And the man answered him, 'Those who told you that have greatly deceived you.' The merchant was struck to the heart by this news and overcome with sorrow.

"Now that man, when he saw the merchant overcome 120 with distress, said to him, 'I see, my friend, that you have become terribly sad; but, be assured, I'm taking pity on you for your great disappointment. So come, sell your entire inventory to me, and I'll give you a plate full of whatever you wish.' Contemplating this, the merchant said to himself, 'Well, whatever this man gives me, it will be better for me, I guess, to get that from him rather than to let my merchandise go completely unsold.' With that reasoning, the merchant straightaway sold his entire inventory to the man, having agreed that the price he would get would be a plate full of whatever he asked from him. After the man received the goods from the merchant, he transported them to his

διεκόμισεν οἰκίαν, μήτινος περὶ τούτου αἰσθομένου τὸ σύνολον. Ὁ μέντοι ἔμπορος τὴν πόλιν περιερχόμενος κατέλυσε ἅμα τοῖς αὐτοῦ κοινωνοῖς παρά τινι γραΐδι γυναικί. Εἶτα αὐτὴν ἐπερωτᾷ λέγων· 'Πῶς ἄρα, ὦ γύναι, τὰ ἀρωματικὰ ξύλα ἐν ταύτῃ ἀπεμπολοῦνται τῇ πόλει;' Ἡ δὲ ἔφη πρὸς αὐτόν· 'Ἰσοστάθμῳ αὐτοῖς χρυσῷ τὰ τοιαῦτα πιπράσκονται. Πλήν, ὦ ἔμπορε, ἰδοὺ λέγω σοι· προσεκτικῶς ἔχε ἀπὸ τῶν τῆσδε τῆς πόλεως κατοίκων· πανοῦργοι γὰρ ἅπαντες καὶ ποικίλοι πεφύκασιν, καὶ οὐκ ἔστι τὸν ἐνταῦθα παραγενόμενον μὴ παρὰ τῶν πολιτῶν αὐτῆς ὄλεθρον αὐτὸν σχεδὸν ὑφίστασθαι.'

121 "Ταῦτα εἰπούσης τῆς γραΐδος ἐκείνης γυναικός, ἐξῄει τοῦ οἰκίσκου αὐτῆς μετ' ὀλίγον ὁ ἔμπορος τὰ κατὰ τὴν πόλιν ὀψόμενος. Καὶ ὁρᾷ τρεῖς ἄνδρας τινὰς ἐπὶ τὸ αὐτὸ καθεζομένους, οἵσπερ καὶ θαμινὰ ἐνατενίζων εἰστήκει. Κἀκείνων δὲ τὸν ἔμπορον ἑωρακότων, θάτερος αὐτῶν πρὸς τοῦτον εἰρήκει· 'Δεῦρο, ὦ πάτερ, σύ τε κἀγὼ πρὸς ἀλλήλους διαλεχθῶμεν· καὶ ὃς ἂν τοῦ ἑτέρου τῇ τῶν λόγων περιγένοιτο πιθανότητι, ἐπιταξάτω τῷ ἡττηθέντι πεποιηκέναι ὅπερ ἂν ὁ νενικηκὼς βούλοιτο.' Ὁ δὲ ἔμπορος ἁπλοϊκῇ τῇ γνώμῃ καὶ ἀπεριέργῳ στοιχῶν, 'Ναί,' φησίν, 'καὶ γενέσθω καθὼς ἐκέλευσας.' Εἶτα ἐκαθέσθησαν πρὸς ἀλλήλους διαλεγόμενοι· καὶ νενίκηκε τὸν ἔμπορον ὁ μῖμος ἐκεῖνος καὶ πανοῦργος ἀνήρ, καὶ πρὸς αὐτὸν ἔφη· "Ἰδού, ὡς ὁρᾷς, τοῖς λόγοις περιεγενόμην σου· λοιπὸν οὖν ἐπιτρέπω σοι καταπιεῖν ἅπαντα τὰ τῆς θαλάσσης ὕδατα.' Ἐπὶ τούτοις οὖν ὁ ἔμπορος ἐν ἀθυμίᾳ καὶ ἀμηχανίᾳ γέγονε, μὴ δυνάμενός τινα εὐλογοφανῆ ἀντίθεσιν τῷ μίμῳ

own house, with no one having any idea at all what he was doing. Meanwhile the merchant, after wandering about the city, took lodging along with his companions at the home of an old woman. Then he asked her, 'How is aromatic wood sold in your city?' And she answered him, 'That product is sold for its weight in gold. But mark my words: beware of the inhabitants of this city. For they are all wicked and wily, and it is impossible for anyone who comes here not to be virtually destroyed at the hands of the citizens.'

"After the old woman said this, the merchant left her 121 house a short while later to look around the city. He saw three men sitting together, and he stood nearby and kept watching them. When they in turn noticed the merchant, one of them said to him, 'Come here, father, and let's you and I have a debate with each other, and whoever outdoes the other in the persuasiveness of his argument will tell the loser to do whatever he, the winner, wishes.' And the merchant, in keeping with his simple and straightforward mind, said, 'Sure, let's do just as you've said.' Then they sat down to debate each other, and that wicked charlatan defeated the merchant, and said, 'Look, as you can see, I've outdone you with my argument. Now, then, I'm ordering you to drink all of the water in the sea.' The merchant despaired and didn't know what to do about this outcome, for he was unable to

ἀντιπροβάλλεσθαι καὶ τοὺς αὐτοῦ βρόχους διαφυγεῖν. Ἦν δὲ ὁ ἔμπορος γλαυκόφθαλμος τὴν ὅρασιν· ἔτυχε δὲ καὶ ὁ ἕτερος τῶν τριῶν μίμων ἐκείνων μονόφθαλμος μὲν ὑπάρχων, γλαυκὸν δὲ τὸν ἕνα αὐτοῦ κεκτημένος ὀφθαλμόν. Κἀκεῖνος δὲ ἀναστὰς ἐπελάβετο ἰσχυρῶς τοῦ ἐμπόρου λέγων· 'Σύ μου τὸν ἕτερον ἐσύλησας ὀφθαλμόν· ἄγωμεν τοίνυν ἀμφότεροι πρὸς τὸν τῆς πόλεως ἄρχοντα, ὅπως δι' αὐτοῦ ἀποδώσεις μοι τὸν παρὰ σοῦ συληθέντα μου ὀφθαλμόν.'

122   "Ἠκηκόει δὲ ταῦτα καὶ ἡ τὸν ἔμπορον ὑποδεξαμένη γραῦς καὶ ὅτι πρὸς τὸν τῆς χώρας ἄρχοντα ὁ μῖμος ἐκεῖνος τὸν ἔμπορον εἷλκε· καὶ τούτοις ἀπερχομένοις συναντήσασα ἔφησε πρὸς τὸν μῖμον· "Ἔασον, ἀξιῶ, τὴν σήμερον ἐγγυητικῶς παρ' ἐμοὶ τὸν ἔμπορον· κἀγὼ αὐτὸν κατὰ τὴν αὔριον πρωΐαν, εἴπερ παρὰ σοῦ ζητηθῇ, αὖθις παραστήσω σοι.' Ὁ δὲ εἴξας τῇ τῆς γυναικὸς ἀξιώσει κατέλιπε παρ' αὐτῇ τὸν ἔμπορον. Καὶ λαβοῦσα αὐτὸν ἐκείνη πρὸς τὴν ἑαυτῆς ἐπανήγαγεν οἰκίαν· εἶτα λέγει πρὸς τὸν ἔμπορον· 'Πάντως σοι προκατήγγειλα προσεκτικῶς ἔχειν ἀπὸ τῶν ἐνταῦθα πολιτῶν, ὅτιπερ μῖμοι καὶ πονηροὶ τὴν φύσιν καὶ ποικίλοι καθεστήκασιν· μηκέτι οὖν εἰς τοὐμφανὲς αὐτῶν ἐξέλθῃς τὸ σύνολον. Καὶ ἐπεὶ τὸ πρότερον οὐκ ἐπείσθης μου τῇ παραινέσει, κἀντεῦθεν εὗρες τὰ τῆς παρακοῆς σου ἐπίχειρα, κἂν γοῦν τανῦν πείσθητί μοι περὶ οὗ σοι συναινέσαι βεβούλημαι. Γνωρίζω γάρ σοι ὡς οἱ τοιοῦτοι μῖμοι ἔχουσί τινα καθηγητὴν γηραιόν, ὃς καὶ τοῖς τῆς πονηρίας πλεονεκτήμασι μάλα τῶν ἄλλων διαφέρει καὶ ὑπερτερεῖ. Ὅθεν καὶ πάντες οἱ μῖμοι καθ' ἑκάστην ἑσπέραν παρ'

make any reasonable counterproposal to the charlatan and so escape his trap. Now the merchant was gray-eyed, and it so happened that another of those three charlatans had only one eye, and that one eye was also gray. And that man stood up and forcefully laid hold of the merchant, claiming, 'You stole my other eye! Let's go to the mayor of the city now, so that on his orders you'll give me back the eye that you stole.'

"Now the old woman who had received the merchant in 122 her home heard about what had happened, and that the charlatan was hauling the merchant before the mayor. She met them as they were setting off and said to the charlatan, 'I ask that you release this merchant into my custody for to-day, and tomorrow morning I'll present him to you, if you come looking for him.' He yielded to the old woman's re-quest and left the merchant with her. She took him and brought him back to her house, and then said to him, 'You know I told you beforehand to be wary of the citizens here, because they're charlatans and wicked and wily by nature. Now, don't go out again where they can see you at all. And since you didn't heed my advice before and so received the reward for your disobedience, this time trust me concerning the advice I want to give you. Let me tell you that these charlatans have an old man as their mentor, who greatly ex-ceeds and surpasses the rest in the extent of his wickedness. For this reason, all the charlatans go every evening to their

αὐτὸν ὡς καθηγητὴν προσφοιτῶσιν καὶ αὐτῷ τὰ ἑκάστῳ δι' ὅλης τῆς ἡμέρας εἰρημένα καὶ πεπραγμένα λεπτομερῶς ἀπαγγέλλουσι. Νῦν οὖν ἄκουσόν μου τῆς λυσιτελοῦς συμβουλίας, καὶ ἀναστὰς ἄμειψόν σου τὸ σχῆμα καὶ σαυτὸν ὡς ἕνα τῶν μίμων ἐκείνων ἀμφίασον καὶ σχημάτισον. Εἶτα ἀπελθὼν λάθρα ἐγκαταμίγηθι τῇ αὐτῶν ὁμηγύρει· πλὴν ὅρα μὴ φωραθῇς ὑπ' αὐτῶν· συμπορεύθητί τε αὐτοῖς πρὸς τὸν αὐτῶν καθηγητήν, καὶ πλησίον στὰς ἐκείνου, ἐν τῷ λεληθότι ὥσπερ τις τῶν τυχόντων καὶ κοινῶν τῆς πόλεως ἀνδρῶν, ἄκουσον ὧνπερ αὐτῷ ἀναγγελοῦσιν οἱ ὡμιληκότες σοι καὶ ὧν ἐκεῖνος πρὸς αὐτοὺς ἀποκριθήσεται. Καὶ πᾶν εἴ τι αὐτοῖς παρὰ τοῦ καθηγητοῦ λαληθήσεται σημείωσον ἐν τῇ διανοίᾳ σου, ὡς ἂν τὰς πρὸς ἐκείνους αὐτοῦ ἀποκρίσεις τοῖς πολεμοῦσί σε ἀντιπροθέμενος, κατὰ κράτος αὐτῶν τῆς πανουργίας περιγένοιο. Καί σοι ἐντεῦθεν μέγιστον προσγενήσεται κέρδος.'

123   Ὁ δὲ ἔμπορος ἐποίησεν ὡς παρὰ τῆς γραὸς ἐξεδίδακτο. Καὶ μετὰ τὸ ἀμεῖψαι τὸ αὐτοῦ σχῆμα στὰς ἔγγιστα τοῦ γηραιοῦ ἐκείνου, πρῶτα μὲν ἑωράκει πρὸς αὐτὸν παραγεγονότα τὸν τὰ ἀρωματικὰ ξύλα ὠνησάμενον, ὃς καὶ ἀπήγγειλε τῷ καθηγητῇ λέγων ὡς· Ἔγωγε συναντήσας τινὶ ἐμπόρῳ ξύλα εἰς διάπρασιν ἀρωματικὰ διακομίζοντι, πάντα τὸν αὐτοῦ φόρτον ἐξωνησάμην· πλὴν περὶ τῆς τῶν ὠνηθέντων τιμῆς συμπεφώνηκα δοῦναι αὐτῷ πίνακα πεπληρωμένον ὧν ἂν δόξῃ αὐτῷ ἐπιζητῆσαι παρ' ἐμοῦ εἰδῶν.' Ὁ δὲ καθηγητὴς ἀπεκρίνατο πρὸς αὐτὸν λέγων· Καὶ τίνα ἐστὶν τὰ παρὰ σοῦ συμφωνηθέντα; Ἆρά γε χρυσὸς ἢ ἄργυρος;' Ὁ δὲ μῖμος ἐκεῖνος, Οὐχί,' φησί, κύριέ μου,

mentor, and each of them reports to him in detail what they've said and done in the course of the whole day. Now listen to my good advice: get up, change your outfit, and dress and disguise yourself as one of those charlatans. Then go off and mingle undercover with their group, but just see that you're not detected by them. Go along with them to their mentor, stand next to him, as though you were a random and ordinary man from the city, and listen to what the men you met report to him and what he says in response without being noticed. And whatever their mentor says to them, make a mental note of it, so that by using his answers against the men who are attacking you, you'll overpower their wickedness. In this way you'll make the greatest profit.'

"Then the merchant did as the old woman had instructed him. After changing his clothing and standing near that old man, first he saw the man who had bought the aromatic wood come forward and report to his mentor and say, 'I met a merchant who was transporting aromatic wood for sale, and I bought his entire inventory. But as for the price of the merchandise I agreed to give him a plate full of whatever he should decide to ask from me.' His mentor responded to him, 'What did you agree upon? Gold or silver?' And the charlatan said, 'No, my lord, unnamed things, whatever that 123

ἀλλ᾽ εἴδη ἀνώνυμα, ἅπερ ἐκεῖνος βουληθείη ἐπιζητῆσαι,
πίνακα πεπληρωμένον.᾽ Ἔφη δὲ πρὸς αὐτὸν ὁ καθηγητής·
῾Μεγάλως σεαυτῷ ἐσφάλης. Ἔστω γὰρ τυχὸν ὅτιπερ δόξει
τῷ ἐμπόρῳ ψύλλους ἀπὸ σοῦ ζητῆσαι καθ᾽ ὅσον ὁ πίναξ
χωρήσειεν, ὧν τὸ μὲν ἥμισυ σμῆνος θῆλυ τυγχάνειν, ἄρσεν
δὲ τὸ ἕτερον ἥμισυ, ἀλλὰ μὴν ἴσως καὶ γλαυκοειδεῖς τούτους ὑπάρχειν προσαπαιτήσειεν ἀπὸ σοῦ· ἀρά γε σὺ
δυνήσῃ τοιαύτην δόσιν αὐτῷ παρασχεῖν; Πῶς ἔσται σοι
τοίνυν τῆς αὐτοῦ ὀχλήσεως ἀπαλλαγῆναι;᾽ Ὁ δὲ μῖμος
ὑπολαβὼν λέγει τῷ καθηγητῇ· ῾Οὐκ ἐπὶ τοσοῦτον, κύριέ
μου, ὁ ἔμπορος ἐκεῖνος σεσόφισται, οὐδὲ τοιαῦτα πανουρ-
γεύεσθαι ὁ αὐτοῦ νοῦς ἱκανός ἐστιν, ἀλλ᾽, ὡς οἶμαι, εἴτε
χρυσὸν εἴτε ἄργυρον ἐξ ἐμοῦ ἐπιζητήσειεν.᾽

124 ῾῾Προσελθὼν δὲ καὶ ὁ τῇ διαλέξει νενικηκὼς τὸν ἔμπορον ἀπήγγειλεν τῷ καθηγητῇ λέγων· ῾Κἀγώ, περὶ ὁμιλίας καὶ πλοκῆς λόγων τῷ ἐμπόρῳ ἐκείνῳ συναμιλληθεὶς
ἐπὶ αἱρέσει τοῦ τὸν ἡττηθησόμενον παρὰ τοῦ ἑτέρου ἐκπληρῶσαι εἴ τι δὴ καὶ παρὰ τοῦ νενικηκότος ἐπιταχθείη,
περιεγενόμην αὐτοῦ ἐν πάσῃ τῇ διαλέξει καὶ εὐθὺς
ἐπέτρεψα αὐτῷ καταπιεῖν ἅπαντα τὰ τῆς θαλάσσης ὕδατα.᾽
Ὁ δὲ καθηγητὴς ἀπεκρίνατο καὶ πρὸς ἐκεῖνον· ῾Οὐδὲ σὺ
καλῶς ἐποίησας. Ἔστω γὰρ ἴσως ὅτιπερ ἐκεῖνος ἀντείπῃ
σοι ὡς· ῾῾Ἄπιθι πρότερον καὶ ἀνάστειλον τοὺς τῇ θαλάσσῃ
ἐπιρρέοντας ποταμούς, καὶ εἰθούτως καταπίομαι τὰ τῆς
θαλάσσης ὕδατα, ἅπερ δὴ καὶ μόνα πεπωκέναι συνεθέμην
σοι.᾽᾽ Εἰ οὖν ταῦτα ὁ ἔμπορος ἀντιλέξει σοι, ἀρά γε σὺ
εὐχερῶς ἕξεις τοὺς ποταμοὺς ἀναχαιτίσαι τῆς ἐν τῇ
θαλάσσῃ ἐπιρροῆς;᾽ Ὁ δὲ μῖμος, ῾Ἀλλ᾽ ἴσθι,᾽ φησίν, ῾ὦ κύριέ

man might wish to ask for, a plate full.' Then his mentor said to him, 'You've made a huge mistake. What if, by chance, the merchant decides to ask for as many fleas as the plate will hold, half of the swarm female and the other half male, and maybe he also asks that they be gray in color? Will you be able to make such a payment? How will you escape from his pestering?' The charlatan said in reply to his mentor, 'That merchant, my lord, is not as clever as that, nor is his mind capable of contriving such things. I think he will ask me for either gold or silver instead.'

"Then the one who had defeated the merchant in debate 124 came forward and gave his mentor his report: 'After competing with that merchant in dialogue and the weaving of words, on the condition that the loser pay whatever the winner ordered, I defeated him in every aspect of the debate and immediately told him to drink all the water in the sea.' And his mentor answered him, 'You didn't do well, either. What if, by chance, he replies to you, "Go first and stop up the rivers that flow into the sea, and then I'll drink the waters of the sea, which are the only waters I promised to drink"? If the merchant makes this response to you, will you easily be able to prevent the rivers from flowing into the sea?' The charlatan said, 'Be assured, my lord, that the

μου, ὡς οὐκ ἐξικανοῖ ἡ τοῦ ἐμπόρου φρόνησις τὸν τοιοῦτόν μοι ἀντιφράσαι ἀπόλογον.'

125 "Εἶτα προσελθὼν τῷ καθηγητῇ καὶ ὁ μονόφθαλμος μῖμός φησι καὶ οὗτος αὐτῷ· Ἡμερον, κύριέ μου, ἑώρακα ἐν τῇ ἀγορᾷ ἄνδρα τινὰ ἔμπορον ξένον, ὃς ἦν γλαυκοειδεῖς τοὺς αὐτοῦ κεκτημένος ὀφθαλμούς. Καὶ τοῦτον κατασχὼν εἰρήκειν αὐτῷ ὡς· "Σύ τε κἀγὼ γλαυκοὶ τυγχάνομεν, καὶ σύ μου τὸν ἕνα ἐσύλησας ὀφθαλμόν· λοιπὸν οὖν οὐδαμῶς σου ἀπόσχωμαι, ἕως ἂν εἴτε τὸν ἕνα σου ἐξελκύσω ὀφθαλμόν, εἴτε αὐτὸν διὰ πάσης σου ἀναρρύσῃ τῆς περιουσίας."' Ὁ δὲ καθηγητής, 'Οὐδὲ σύ τι κατώρθωκας,' ἀπεκρίνατο. Εἰ γὰρ δόξει τῷ ἐμπόρῳ ἀντιφράσαι σοι ὅτι· "Πρότερον εἰς σύστασιν τῆς τοιαύτης σου προτάσεως ἔκβαλόν σου τὸν ἕνα τοῦτον ὃν ἔχεις ὀφθαλμόν, κἀγὼ ἐκβαλῶ θάτερον τῶν ἐμῶν ὀφθαλμῶν, καὶ ἀμφοτέρους σταθμίσωμεν· καὶ εἰ μὲν ἰσόσταθμοι ἀλλήλοις εὑρεθεῖεν, εὔδηλον ὅτι σός ἐστιν ὁ ἐμὸς εἷς ὀφθαλμός, εἰ δέ τις τῶν σταθμιζομένων δύο ὀφθαλμῶν βαρύτερος τοῦ ἑτέρου ἐν τῇ τοῦ ζυγοῦ φανείη πλάστιγγι, οὐχ ὑπάρχει σὸς ὁ θάτερός μου ὀφθαλμός, ἀλλὰ μᾶλλον καὶ ὑπὲρ τῆς αὐτοῦ ἐκβολῆς ἀξίως εὐθυνθήσῃ·" εἰ οὖν ταῦτά σοι ἀντιλέξει ὁ ἔμπορος, οὐχὶ πάντως ἐξ εὐλόγου ἀποπείσει σε τῆς ἀντιθέσεως; Καὶ τὸ δὴ χείριστον, ὅτι γε τούτου ἐπὶ σοὶ γενομένου, σὺ μὲν τέλεον ἀποστερηθήσῃ τῆς ὁράσεως καὶ πάντῃ γενήσῃ ἀόμματος, ἐκεῖνος δὲ ἕνα τῶν ἑαυτοῦ ὀφθαλμῶν ἐσύστερον ἔχων, πάλιν τὸ φῶς καθορῶν ἔσται.' Πρὸς ταῦτα ὁ μονόφθαλμος μῖμος ὑπολαβὼν λέγει τῷ καθηγητῇ· 'Ἀλλ' οὐκ ἐπὶ

merchant doesn't have the intelligence to articulate a defense like that.'

"Then the one-eyed charlatan approached his mentor, 125 and he gave his report: 'Today, my lord, I saw a foreign merchant in the marketplace, and he had gray eyes. And after I cornered him, I said, "You and I are both gray eyed, and you have stolen one of my eyes. Well, then, I won't let you go until I either pluck out one of your eyes or you ransom it with all your possessions."' His mentor answered, 'You haven't done well either. For the merchant may decide to respond to you like this, "First, to confirm this hypothesis of yours, pluck out the one eye that you do have, and I'll pluck out one of my eyes, and then let's weigh them. If they're found to be the same weight, it will be perfectly clear that my eye is yours, but if either of the two eyes turns out to be heavier than the other when we weigh them, then my eye is not yours, but rather you will have been called to account, and rightly so, thanks to its removal." If, then, the merchant makes this reply, won't he surely convince you to accept his very reasonable counterproposal? And this would be the worst outcome, because once you lose your eye, you'll be totally deprived of your sight and become completely blind, while that man will keep one of his eyes afterward and so will still have his vision.' In response to this, the one-eyed charlatan answered his mentor, 'But that merchant is not

τοσοῦτον πανοῦργος ὁ ἔμπορος ἐκεῖνος, ὡς τοιαύτην μοι πιθανὴν ἀντιπροθέσθαι ἀπολογίαν.'

126 "Τούτων οὕτω παρά τε τῶν μίμων καὶ τοῦ αὐτῶν καθηγητοῦ λαλουμένων τε καὶ ἀντιφθεγγομένων, ἠκροᾶτο λάθρα παρ᾽ ὅλην νύκτα ὁ ἔμπορος καὶ τῇ ἰδίᾳ ταῦτα συνετήρει καρδίᾳ. Πρωΐας δὲ γενομένης παραγίνεται πρὸς τὸν ἔμπορον ὁ τὰ ἀρωματικὰ ξύλα ὠνησάμενος. Εἶτά φησι πρὸς αὐτὸν ὁ ἔμπορος· Ἀπόδος μοι, ἑταῖρε, εἴ τί μοι συνεφώνησας παρασχεῖν ὑπὲρ τοῦ διαπραθέντος σοι φόρτου.' Ὁ δὲ μῖμος ἔφη πρὸς αὐτόν· Ζήτησον εἴ τι καὶ βούλει, κἀγὼ ἑτοίμως παράσχω σοι.' Ὁ δὲ ἔμπορος ἀπεκρίνατο· Θέλω ἵνα μοι δῷς ἐν τῷδε τῷ πίνακι ψύλλους καθ᾽ ὅσον χωρήσειεν, ὧν τὸ μὲν ἥμισυ στῖφος ἄρσεν, θῆλυ δὲ τὸ ἕτερον ἥμισυ, καὶ πάντας γλαυκοειδεῖς κατὰ πᾶσαν τὴν αὐτῶν ἰδέαν.' Οὕτως εἰπὼν τῷ μίμῳ ὁ ἔμπορος ἰσχυρῶς αὐτὸν διετέλει ἀπαναγκάζων καὶ πολλῇ τῇ βίᾳ πρὸς αὐτὸν κεχρημένος, ἄχρις ἂν ὁ μῖμος καὶ ἄκων ἐδεδώκει αὐτῷ πλείονα ποσότητα τῆς δικαίας τιμῆς τῶν ἀρωματικῶν αὐτοῦ ξύλων, καὶ εἰθούτως μόγις τῶν τούτου ἀπηλλάγη ὀχλήσεων. Ἐντυχὼν δὲ καὶ τοῖς ἑτέροις δυσὶ μίμοις, τῷ τε περὶ τοῦ ὀφθαλμοῦ διαμαχομένῳ καὶ τῷ τὴν θάλασσαν καταπιεῖν αὐτῷ ἐπιτρέψαντι, ἀπήτει κἀκείνους πεποιηκέναι ἅπερ λάθρα παρὰ τοῦ αὐτῶν καθηγητοῦ ἠκηκόει· καὶ διετέλει ἄγχων κἀκείνους, ἕως ἂν δι᾽ ὅσων δομάτων ὁ ἔμπορος ἐξ αὐτῶν ἠθέλησεν ἀπηλλάγησαν τῶν αὐτοῦ ὀχλήσεων.

127 "Καὶ νῦν, ὦ δέσποτα βασιλεῦ, ἐξ ὧν σοὶ διηγησάμην γίνωσκε ὡς οἵ τε δύο παῖδες ἐκεῖνοι, ὁ τριετής, φημί, καὶ

so crafty that he would counter me with such a persuasive defense.'

"As these reports and responses were thus being made by 126 the charlatans and their mentor, the merchant listened unnoticed the whole night long and guarded their words in his heart. When morning came, the man who had bought the aromatic wood came to the merchant. Then the merchant said to him, 'Pay me, my friend, what you agreed to give me for the merchandise that you bought.' The charlatan said to him, 'Ask whatever you wish, and I will readily provide it to you,' to which the merchant replied, 'I want you to give me as many fleas as this plate will hold, half of the swarm male, the other half female, and all of them completely gray in color.' After he said this to the charlatan, the merchant kept hounding him and applying great pressure, until the charlatan, unwillingly, gave him a sum of money that was greater than the fair market price for his aromatic wood, and thus barely escaped from his troubles. When he encountered the other two charlatans, the one who was challenging him about the eye and the other who had told him to drink up the sea, he demanded that they also do what he had secretly overheard from their mentor. And he kept on pressing them until they gave him whatever he wished in order to be freed from his pestering.

"And now, my master and king, from what I have narrated 127 to you, know that those two children, the three-year-old, I

ὁ πενταετής, περὶ ὧν προειρήκειν σοι, καὶ οὗτος ὁ γηραιὸς
καθηγητὴς πολλῇ τῇ γνώσει καὶ τῇ συνέσει κεκόσμηντο·
καὶ κατ᾽ ἐκείνους κἀμὲ ὁ ἐμὸς ἀπετέλεσεν διδάσκαλος."

128   Ὁ δὲ βασιλεὺς ὑπολαβὼν ἔφη τῷ υἱῷ· "Γνώρισόν μοι,
τέκνον, τοιγαροῦν πῶς ἐν μὲν τοῖς προλαβοῦσι τρισὶν
ἔτεσιν οὐ μεμάθηκας τὴν νῦν προσγενομένην σοι λογι-
ότητα, νυνὶ δὲ ἐν μόνοις τοῖς παρελθοῦσιν ἐξ μησὶν ἐπὶ
τοσοῦτον ἐσοφίσθης;" Ὁ δὲ παῖς τῷ βασιλεῖ ἀπεκρίνατο
ὡς· "Τῷ τότε, βασιλεῦ, ἔτι μου νηπιάζοντος, οὐ συνήργουν
ἀλλήλαις αἱ προσοῦσαί μοι τοῦ σώματος καὶ τῆς ψυχῆς
αἰσθήσεις· οὔτε γάρ μου τὸ σῶμα ἀφήλικος πάντη τυγχάνοντος οὔτε οἱ ὀφθαλμοὶ οὔτε ἡ γλῶττα οὔτε ἡ καρδία
ἀλλήλοις συνεκρότουν πρὸς τὴν τῆς διδασκαλίας μάθησιν·
οὐδὲ γὰρ δυνατόν ἐστι νηπιόφρονα πεφυκότα εὐχερῶς
γνῶσιν ἐκδιδάσκεσθαι, καθότι ἅπαν παιδίον ταῖς παιδιαῖς
καὶ τῇ ἀργίᾳ ἐνηδόμενον οὐ προσεκτικῶς τὸν νοῦν περὶ
τὴν διδασκαλίαν διατίθεται. Κἀγὼ δή, ὦ βασιλεῦ, τὸν αὐτὸν τρόπον τῷ τότε τῇ ἡλικίᾳ τε καὶ τῇ διανοίᾳ διακείμενος,
οὐδὲν ὅλως τῶν διδασκομένων ἠδυνάμην καρπώσασθαι,
ἅτε μὴ τούτοις τὸ παράπαν τὸν ἐμαυτοῦ νοῦν προσερείδων,
ἀλλ᾽ ὡς νηπιώδης διεσπαρμένον αὐτὸν ἔχων. Νυνὶ δὲ ὁ
διδάσκαλός μου Συντίπας τὸ νεάζον τῆς ἡλικίας μου περι-
σκοπῶν, οὐκ ἐμβριθῶς με ἐξεδίδασκεν, οὐδὲ τοῖς δυσχερέσι
κατ᾽ ἀρχὰς λόγοις πρός με ἐχρήσατο, ἵνα μὴ τῷ τῶν δυσ-
χερῶν καὶ δυσλήπτων βάρει ἐξ ἀρχῆς καταπονηθεὶς πάντα
τῆς ἐμῆς διανοίας ἀπορρίψω τὰ διδασκόμενα—καὶ γὰρ
ᾔδει μου ὁ διδάσκαλος ὅτιπερ, εἰ ἀμέτρως ἐξ ἀρχῆς με ἐκ-
διδάξειεν, εὐχερῶς εἶχον αὐτοῦ ἀφηνιάσαι καὶ ἀποστῆναι,

mean, and the five-year-old, about whom I told you earlier, and this aged mentor were adorned with great knowledge and intelligence. And my teacher has made me just like them."

The king replied to his son, "So, tell me, my child, how is it that in the prior three years you did not learn the eloquent reasoning that you have recently acquired, but now in only the past six months you have become so wise?" And the boy answered the king, "In the past, my king, since I was still a child, the senses of my body and soul did not cooperate with each other. For my body had not yet matured, and so my eyes, tongue, and heart were not working together to learn my lessons. For one who has a childish mind cannot be easily instructed in knowledge, because every child delights in play and idleness rather than focusing his mind attentively on his education. Since at that time, my king, I was equally immature in both my age and my intellect, I could reap no fruit from what I was being taught. I was not fixing my mind on my lessons, but I was scatterbrained like a child. But now my teacher Syntipas, since he carefully observed my youth, did not teach me with severity or use difficult words at first, so that the weight of difficult and incomprehensible lessons would not crush me from the very start and cause me to reject from my mind everything that I was being taught—for indeed my teacher knew that, if he were to instruct me too intensely from the beginning, I would easily rebel and revolt

128

ἅτε βασιλέως τυγχάνων υἱός—ἀλλὰ κατὰ μικρὸν τοῖς λόγοις με διαρρυθμίζων, οὕτω με δεξιῶς εἰς τὸ τέλειον τῆς
φιλοσοφίας ἀνήγαγε. Κἀγὼ δὲ τελεωτέρας ἐφαπτόμενος
φρονήσεως συνετήρουν ἐν τῇ καρδίᾳ πάντα δὴ τὰ παρ᾽
αὐτοῦ μοι ἐκδιδασκόμενα, καὶ συναγαγὼν τὸν πρῴην μου
διασπαρέντα λογισμὸν τά τε ὦτα συντείνας πρὸς ἀκοὴν
καὶ τὴν γλῶτταν πρὸς λόγων μελέτην τε καὶ πλοκὴν καὶ
τὰς χεῖρας πρὸς διάστιξιν συλλαβῶν, οὕτως ἐπὶ καιρὸν
τῶν ἓξ καὶ μόνων μηνῶν πάντα δὴ τὰ διδαχθέντα μοι
ἀκριβέστατα κατέλαβον καὶ ἐν μεθέξει πάσης φιλοσοφίας
καὶ συνέσεως γέγονα, συναραμένης πάντως καὶ τῆς θείας
δυνάμεως ἐμοί τε καὶ τῇ περὶ ἐμὲ τοῦ μυσταγωγοῦ
σπουδῇ."

129   Τούτοις ὁ βασιλεὺς τοῖς τοῦ παιδὸς ῥήμασι σφόδρα τὴν
καρδίαν ἡσθεὶς εὐχαριστηρίους τῷ Θεῷ λόγους ἀνέπεμπεν, καὶ τὴν τοῦ παιδὸς σύνεσιν καὶ φιλοσοφίαν ἐκθειάζων
διετέλει τὰ μέγιστα, καὶ τῷ Συντίπᾳ μεγάλας ὁμολογεῖ τὰς
χάριτας. Εἶτα κελεύει παραστῆναι αὐτῷ τὴν πονηρὰν ἐκείνην γυναῖκα, ἥτις τὸν αὐτοῦ υἱὸν ἀπολέσαι ἐμηχανᾶτο.
Καὶ ταύτης παραστάσης λέγει πρὸς αὐτὴν ὁ βασιλεύς·
"Ἀνακάλυψόν μοι, ὦ γύναι, μηδὲν κατὰ φόβον ὑποστει-
λαμένη, τίνος χάριν τὸν ἐμὸν υἱὸν ἀπολέσαι ἔσπευδες καὶ
τίς ἦν ὁ τρόπος τῆς τοιαύτης σου σκαιωρίας;" Ὑπολαβοῦσα
δὲ ἡ γυνὴ ἔφη· "Οἶδας, ὦ κράτιστε βασιλεῦ, ὡς οὐδέν τινι
τῶν ἀνθρώπων τῆς ἰδίας ζωῆς καθέστηκεν προσφιλέστε-
ρον· κἂν γάρ τις πενίᾳ εἴη συζῶν ἢ καί τινι βιωτικῇ
περιπετείᾳ πιέζοιτο, ἀλλ᾽ ὅμως καὶ οὗτος τῆς οἰκείας ζωῆς
περιέχεται. Ἐγὼ τοίνυν τὸν παῖδά σου τούτου χάριν τῷ σῷ

against him, since I was the king's son. Instead, he acclimated me gradually to his teachings and thus skillfully guided me to perfection in learning. As I was gaining a more perfect intelligence, I also kept in my heart everything that he had taught me. I collected my formerly scattered thoughts, and I directed my ears toward listening, my tongue toward the study and the composition of speeches, and my hands toward formal handwriting. And thus, in a period of only six months, I grasped everything that was taught to me with great precision, and I came to possess all learning and intelligence. Of course, the power of God also supported me and assisted my mentor's zealous efforts on my behalf."

Exceedingly and deeply delighted by the boy's response, 129 the king offered up a prayer of thanksgiving to God and went on effusively praising the boy's intelligence and learning, and he also acknowledged his great gratitude to Syntipas. Then he ordered that wicked woman who had contrived to kill his son to appear before him. And when she arrived, the king said to her, "Tell me, woman, and hold nothing back out of fear: why were you eager to kill my son and how did your scheme come about?" The woman replied, "You know, mightiest king, that nothing is dearer to any human being than his own life. For even if someone is living in poverty or is oppressed by one of life's reversals of fortune, nevertheless even this man clings to his own life. And so, by your command I took your son off alone with me, so that as a

προστάγματι πρὸς ἐμαυτὴν ἔλαβον, ὡς διὰ τὴν τοῦ κράτους σου θεραπείαν καταμόνας παρ' αὐτοῦ διαγνῶναι, ὑπὸ ποίας τῆς αἰτίας ἐπεχόμενος οὐ φθέγγεται. Καὶ διετέλουν παντοιοτρόποις πεύσεσι καὶ θωπείαις τοῦτον ὑπερχομένη καὶ τὸ τῆς σιγῆς αὐτοῦ σκληρὸν μειλιχίοις τοῖς λόγοις διαλεαίνουσα, ἄχρις ὅτου παρεσκεύασα τοῦτον ἕνα λόγον μοι ἀποκρίνασθαι. Ὃν δὴ καὶ ὀργίλως καὶ ἀποτόμως φθεγξάμενος εἰρήκει πρός με ὡς· Οὐδέν σοι, γύναι, τό γε νῦν ἔχον, ἀποκριθήσομαι, ἄχρις ὅτου ἑπτὰ ἡμέραι τὸ ἀπὸ τοῦδε παρέλθωσιν, καὶ εἰθούτως κατ' ἀξίαν σοι ἀπολογήσομαι.' Ἐγὼ δὲ τούτῳ τῷ λόγῳ σφόδρα ἐκθροηθεῖσα καὶ περιδεὴς λίαν καταστᾶσα καὶ κινδύνῳ παρὰ τοῦ παιδὸς ὑποβληθῆναι ὑφορωμένη, συνεῖδον μηχανικῶς τὸν ἐξ αὐτοῦ διαφυγεῖν ὄλεθρον, κἀντεῦθεν ὑπὸ σατανικῆς ἐνεργείας παρορμηθεῖσα κατεψευσάμην τοῦ παιδός σου καὶ δολερῶς αὐτοῦ ἐπὶ τοῦ κράτους σου κατηγόρησα. Καὶ τὸ ἁμαρτηθέν μοι ἐπίσταμαι καὶ φανερῶς τοῦτο καθομολογῶ μὴ κατά τι τόδε ἀπαρνουμένη. Τὸ λοιπόν, ὦ μέγιστε βασιλεῦ, τὰ δοκοῦντά σοι πρᾶξον ἐπ' ἐμοί, καθὼς ἂν εὐδοκήσειε τὸ θεοκυβέρνητον κράτος σου."

130   Ὁ δὲ βασιλεὺς ἐμβλέψας τοῖς παρισταμένοις μεγιστᾶσιν αὐτοῦ, λέγει πρὸς αὐτούς· "Ὁποίαν ὑμεῖς παρέχετε βουλὴν τῇ βασιλείᾳ μου περὶ τοῦ τοιούτου πράγματος, καὶ ὁποίας ἡ γυνὴ αὕτη τῆς τιμωρίας ἀξία πέφυκεν;" Εἷς δὲ τῶν μεγιστάνων ὑπολαβὼν λέγει τῷ βασιλεῖ· "Δίκαιόν ἐστιν, ὦ βασιλεῦ, χεῖρας καὶ πόδας τῆς γυναικὸς ταύτης ἀποτμηθῆναι." Ἕτερος δὲ ἀπεκρίνατο λέγων· "Οὐχ οὕτως ἔχει τὸ δίκαιον, ὡς σὺ λέγεις, ἀλλὰ προσήκει ζώσης αὐτῆς

service to your majesty I might discover from him in private what was preventing him from speaking. And I kept fawning on him with all kinds of questions and flatteries and smoothing the harshness of his silence with gentle words, until I made him speak one sentence to me. This he uttered angrily and brusquely: 'I will not reply to you for the time being, woman, until seven days pass from today, and then I will defend myself against you as you deserve.' I became very worried and frightened by his response, and suspected that I would find myself in danger from your son, and so I deviously came to see his destruction as a means of escape. Then, urged on by a satanic power, I spoke falsely against your son and deceitfully accused him to your majesty. I understand my sin and confess it openly, and I do not deny it at all. And so, greatest king, do to me as you think best, just as your divinely guided majesty sees fit."

And then the king, looking at the noblemen standing 130 around him, said to them, "What sort of counsel do you offer my majesty concerning this matter, and what sort of punishment does this woman deserve?" One of the noblemen replied to the king, "It is just, my king, for this woman's hands and feet to be cut off." Another answered, "The just thing to do is not what you have said, but rather it is

ἐξορυχθῆναι τὴν καρδίαν." Ἕτερος δὲ πάλιν τῶν μεγιστάνων ἔφη· "Τὴν γλῶτταν αὐτῆς ἐκκοπῆναι χρεών ἐστιν."
131 Ἡ δὲ γυνὴ τῶν τοιούτων ἀκρωμένη ἀποφάσεων καὶ
οἵας περὶ αὐτῆς τῷ βασιλεῖ τὰς τιμωρίας ὑποτιθέασιν,
τοιοῦτόν τινα μῦθον πρὸς ἐκείνους ἀπεφθέγγατο· "Ἔοικεν,
ὦ μεγιστᾶνες," λέγουσα, "τά τε παρ' ὑμῶν ἀποφαινόμενα
κατ' ἐμὲ παράδειγμά τινος ἀλώπεκος, ἥτις νυκτὸς εἴς τινα
πόλιν εἰσήρχετο. Ἦν δὲ ἡ αὐτῆς εἰσέλευσις διὰ θυρίδος
οἰκίσκου γινομένη ἀνδρός τινος σκυτέως· ὁσάκις δὲ δι'
αὐτῆς τὴν ἐκείνου οἰκίαν εἰσήρχετο, τὰ τούτου κατήσθιεν
δέρματα. Εἶτα ὁ σκυτεὺς ἐκεῖνος ἑωρακὼς τὰ γεγονότα ἐν
τοῖς αὐτοῦ δέρμασι σπαράγματα, εὐθὺς αὐτῇ παγίδα ἰσχυ-
ροτάτην ἵστησιν. Ἡ δὲ ἀλώπηξ μετὰ ταῦτα κατὰ τὸ αὐτῆς
σύνηθες εἰσερχομένη δι' ἐκείνης πάλιν τῆς θυρίδος, παραχρῆμα τῇ παγίδι συλλαμβάνεται. Πονηρὰ δὲ ἡ κερδὼ καὶ
ποικιλότροπος τυγχάνουσα, διά τινος εὐμεθόδου μηχανῆς
τὴν περιέχουσαν αὐτὴν παγίδα διέφυγε, καὶ περιήρχετο
πᾶσαν ἐκείνην τὴν πόλιν τοῦ ἐντυχεῖν τινι ἑτέρᾳ θυρίδι, δι'
ἧς δυνηθείη ἐξελθεῖν τῆς πόλεως, <ἡ δὲ> πανταχόθεν περι-
τετείχιστο, καὶ παρ' ὅλην τὴν νύκτα κοπιάσασα οὐδόλως
τινὰ ἔξοδον εὑρηκέναι ἴσχυσε. Τῆς δέ γε ἡμέρας διαυγα-
ζούσης διελογίσατο καθ' ἑαυτὴν καὶ εἶπεν ὡς· Εἴπερ ἡ
ἡμέρα ἐπιστῇ, πάντως ὑπὸ τῶν κυνῶν θεαθήσομαι, καὶ οὐ
πρότερόν μου ἀπόσχωνται, μέχρις ἄν μου τὰς σάρκας δια-
μερίσονται. Ἀλλ' ἔγωγε οἶδα τί με δεῖ πεποιηκέναι.'
132 "Καὶ ταῦτα εἰποῦσα πορεύεται ἐπὶ τὴν πύλην τῆς
πόλεως, καὶ ἑαυτὴν ἐγγὺς τῆς φλιᾶς ἔσωθεν ἐκτανύσασα
προσεποιεῖτο νεκρὰ καὶ ἄπνους τυγχάνειν· τούτῳ δὲ τῷ

appropriate to rip out her heart while she is still alive." Another of the noblemen in turn said, "Her tongue should be cut out."

When she heard these judgments and the sorts of punishment that they were suggesting to the king, the woman told them the following story: "Noble men," she said, "the punishments you suggest for me resemble the example of a fox that would enter a certain city by night, coming in through a small opening in the wall of a little house belonging to a cobbler. Every time it entered his house through the opening, it would eat the cobbler's shoe leather. And so the cobbler, when he saw the shreds among his leather, immediately set a very sure trap for the fox. Later, as it was entering yet again as usual through the opening, the fox was instantly caught in the trap. Now that wily fox was wicked and resourceful, and so by means of a well-conceived scheme it escaped the trap that was holding it. Then it wandered throughout the entire city to find some other window through which it could get out. The city was walled in on all sides, however, and though the fox tried hard all night long, it could find no way out. As day was breaking, the fox reasoned to itself, 'If day dawns, I will surely be detected by the dogs, and they will not let go of me until they divide my flesh among themselves. But I know what I must do.'

"With these words, the fox made its way to the city gate, where it stretched itself out near the doorpost and pretended to be dead and lifeless. Employing this trick, it

131

132

τρόπῳ ἐχρήσατο, προσμένουσα διανοιγῆναι τὴν πύλην καὶ
εὐθὺς ἑαυτὴν ἀθρόον δι' αὐτῆς φυγάδα ἐξαγαγεῖν καὶ τοῦ
ὑφορωμένου ἀπαλλαγῆναι κινδύνου. Οὕτω δὲ αὐτῆς ὡς
νεκρᾶς ἀναπεσούσης καὶ τῆς πύλης ὑπὸ τὴν ἕω συνήθως
διανοιγομένης, ἑωράκει τις ταύτην καὶ πρὸς ἑαυτὸν εἰ-
ρήκει· "Ὄντως ἡ κέρκος τῆς ἀλώπεκος ταύτης λίαν ἐστὶν
χρησιμεύουσα εἰς ἕτοιμον σπόγγον μυλικοῦ ἐργαστηρίου.'
Καὶ τοῦτο εἰπών, εὐθὺς τὴν ἑαυτοῦ σπασάμενος μάχαιραν,
ἀπέτεμεν αὐτήν. Ἡ δὲ ἀλώπηξ τῆς οὐρᾶς αὐτῆς ἀποτμη-
θείσης σιωπῶσα γενναίως ὑπήνεγκεν. Εἶτά τις ἕτερος παρερχόμενος καὶ ταύτην ἑωρακὼς ἔλεγεν καὶ οὗτος· Ἀκοῇ
ἀκήκοα ὡς εἴπερ τις τῶν νηπιαζόντων παίδων ἐπὶ πολὺ
διατελοίη κλαυθμυρίζων, οὐδὲν ἕτερον αὐτῷ εἰς θεραπείαν
καὶ ἀπόπαυσιν τοῦ πολλοῦ αὐτοῦ κλαυθμοῦ ὀνησιφόρον
καθίσταται ὡς ὦτα ἀλώπεκος, ἅπερ εἴ γε παρὰ τοῦ παιδίου
διηνεκῶς ἐπιφέρεται, οὐκέτι ἐπὶ πλεῖστον ὁ κλαυθμὸς
αὐτῷ παραγίνεται.' Καὶ ταῦτα εἰπών, εὐθὺς τὰ τῆς ἀλώπεκος ἐκείνης ὦτα μαχαίρᾳ ἀπέκοψεν. Ὃ καὶ τοῦτο γενναίως ἡ ἀλώπηξ ἤνεγκεν διὰ τὴν τῆς νεκρότητος αὐτῆς
ὑπόκρισιν καὶ προσποίησιν. Ἕτερος δέ τις ἐκεῖσε τὴν
διέλευσιν ποιούμενος, Κἀγώ,' φησίν, 'ὦ ἄνδρες, ἠνώτισμαι
ὡς εἴπερ τις τοὺς ὀδόντας ἀλγῶν ἔσται καὶ ὀδυνώμενος,
ὀφείλει ἀλώπεκος ἄγειν ὀδόντα καὶ τῷ πάσχοντι ἐπιτιθέ-
ναι ὀδόντι· καὶ εὐθὺς τῆς τοῦ πάθους θεραπείας τεύξεται.'
Οὕτως οὖν κἀκεῖνος ὁ ἀνὴρ εἰρηκώς, αὐτίκα λίθον ἀράμενος, πάντας τοὺς ἐκείνης ὀδόντας συνέτριψεν· κἀκείνη δὲ
καὶ ταύτην γενναίως ὑπήνεγκε τὴν τιμωρίαν.

133   "Καὶ οὕτω διετέλει τὰ ἀλγεινὰ ὑπομένουσα, ἄχρις ὅτου

waited for the gate to be opened so that it could immediately run out swiftly and escape the danger that it feared. And so, when it had lain down as though dead and the gate was being opened as usual at dawn, someone saw it and said to himself, 'Truly this fox's tail is very useful as a handy sponge in a mill.' After he said this, he immediately drew his knife and cut off the tail. Now the fox, although its tail had been cut off, bravely endured in silence. Then someone else came along, and when he saw the fox, he said, 'I have heard it said that if an infant goes on crying for a long time, nothing else is as effective at treating and calming its wailing as the ears of a fox; if the child wears them all the time, it no longer cries so much.' And having said this, he immediately cut off the fox's ears with his knife. This too the fox bravely endured on account of its playacting and pretending to be dead. Then another passerby said, 'I too, gentlemen, have heard that if someone has a toothache and is experiencing pain, he should take a fox's tooth and apply it to his own aching tooth. And immediately he will get relief from his suffering.' And so, when this man too had spoken in this way, straightaway he picked up a rock and shattered all of the fox's teeth, but it bravely endured this punishment as well.

"And in this way, it went on enduring its pains, until an- 133

ἕτερός τις ἀνὴρ παρερχόμενος ἔφη ὡς· Κἀγὼ ἀκήκοα
ὅτιπερ εἰς πᾶν ὅ τι οὖν ἀκεσώδυνον φάρμακον ἡ τῆς ἀλώπεκος χρησιμεύει καρδία, καὶ ὅτι πάσαις ταῖς νόσοις θερα-
πευτική ἐστιν.' Οὕτως οὖν κἀκεῖνος εἰπών, εὐθὺς μάχαιραν
σπασάμενος ἐξορύξαι τὴν αὐτῆς ἐπειρᾶτο καρδίαν. Κατ'
ἐκείνην δὲ τὴν ὥραν ἔτυχεν καὶ τὴν πύλην τοῦ τείχους
διηνοιγμένην ὑπάρχειν· καὶ αὐτίκα ἡ ἀλώπηξ ἀθρόον ἐκ-
πηδήσασα, πολλῷ τῷ τάχει διὰ τῆς πύλης ἐξέδραμε καὶ
τὸν ἐπηρτημένον διέφυγε κίνδυνον. Κἀγὼ δὴ τανῦν, ἡ
τάλαινα, ὦ βασιλεῦ, πάντα μὲν τἆλλα ἅπερ οἱ τοῦ κράτους
σου μεγιστᾶνες συμβουλεύουσι τῇ σκηπτουχίᾳ σου ἑτοίμως ἔχω ὑπομεῖναι, τὸ δὲ τὴν καρδίαν μου ἐξορυχθῆναι
ὑπενεγκεῖν οὐ δεδύνημαι· θανάτου γὰρ βιαίου τοῦτο παραίτιον πέφυκε."

134   Ἐπὶ τούτοις οὖν ἀποκριθεὶς ὁ τοῦ βασιλέως υἱὸς λέγει
τῷ πατρὶ καὶ τοῖς παρεστηκόσι μεγιστᾶσιν· "Ἀληθῶς ἡ
γυνὴ καὶ πρεπόντως φησίν· οὐ χρὴ γὰρ τοὺς τῶν ἀνδρῶν
συνετοὺς καὶ φρενήρεις τὰ παρὰ τῶν γυναικῶν σφαλλό-
μενα ὑπὸ μέμψιν πολλὴν καὶ αἰτίασιν τιθέναι. Λοιπὸν οὖν
οὐδὲ ταύτῃ τῇ γυναικὶ τιμωρίας καὶ ποινῆς προσήκει ἀπό-
φασις· ἀλλὰ τοῦτο μόνον δέον ἐπ' αὐτῇ γενέσθαι, ἵνα ἡ
αὐτῆς κεφαλὴ ἀποξυρισθῇ καὶ ἡ ὄψις αὐτῆς ἀσβόλῃ περι-
χρισθῇ, κώδωνά τε τοῦ αὐτῆς τραχήλου ἐξαρτήσωσιν, εἶτα
καὶ ὄνῳ ἀντιστρόφως αὐτὴν ἐποχεῖσθαι παρασκευάσαντες,
ἀνὰ πᾶσαν θριαμβεύσωσι τὴν πόλιν, ἔμπροσθέν τε αὐτῇ
δύο συμπεριέρχωνται κήρυκες, ὁ μὲν εἷς αὐτῶν προπορευ-
όμενος, ὁ δὲ ἕτερος ὄπιθεν ἐπακολουθῶν, οἳ καὶ ὀφείλουσιν
βοᾶν εἰς ἐπήκοον πάντων ὅπερ ἡ γυνὴ ἐξηργάσατο

other man came along and said, 'I have also heard that the fox's heart is useful as a pain-relieving drug for every ailment, and that it is a remedy for all diseases.' And so, when this man too had spoken thus, he immediately drew his knife and tried to rip out the fox's heart. At that moment it happened also that the gate of the city wall was standing wide open. Straightaway the fox suddenly leaped up, ran out through the gate with great speed, and escaped the impending danger. I too, wretch that I am, my king, am now ready to endure whatever your majesty's noblemen suggest to your lordship, but I cannot endure having my heart ripped out. For this would lead to a violent death."

Then in response to this speech the king's son said to 134 his father and the noblemen standing nearby, "The woman speaks truly and fittingly. For intelligent men of sound mind should not subject the failures of women to excessive blame and accusation. And so, a sentence of punishment and penalty is not appropriate, even for this woman. Rather, this alone should be her fate: her head should be shaved and her face smeared with soot, and your men should hang a bell from her neck; then, after setting her backward upon an ass, they should parade her in infamy through the whole city. Two heralds should accompany her, one of them walking in front and the other following behind, and they should shout for all to hear what wickedness the woman brought about."

ἀτόπημα." Οὕτως εἰπόντος τοῦ παιδός, ἥσθη ὁ βασιλεὺς ἐπὶ τοῖς λαληθεῖσι, συνεμαρτύρουν δὲ καὶ οἱ μεγιστᾶνες ἀποδεχόμενοι τὴν γνώμην. Καί φησι πρὸς τὸν παῖδα ὁ βασιλεύς· "Ἄριστα, ὦ τέκνον, λελάληκας καὶ συνετῶς τῷ ὄντι ἡμῖν συμβεβούλευκας. Γενέσθω λοιπὸν ἐπὶ τῇ γυναικὶ ὅπερ ὁ ἐμὸς υἱὸς ἡμῖν συνεβούλευσε." Καὶ διεπράχθη ἐπὶ τῇ πονηρᾷ καὶ σκολιᾷ γυναικὶ ὅπερ ὁ τοῦ βασιλέως υἱὸς τῷ πατρὶ περὶ αὐτῆς συνήνεσεν.

135   Εἶτά φησιν ὁ βασιλεὺς τῷ φιλοσόφῳ Συντίπᾳ· "Ἀνακά-λυψόν μοι, ὦ φιλόσοφε, καὶ ἀριδήλως παράστησον, πόθεν ἡ τοσαύτη σύνεσις καὶ φιλοσοφία τῷ υἱῷ μου προσεγένετο; Μή τοι ἐξ αὐτῆς τῆς γεννήσεως φυσικὴν ἔσχε τὴν λογι-ότητα; Ἢ μᾶλλον διὰ τῆς σῆς ἐπιμελείας σεσόφισται;" Ὑπολαβὼν δὲ ὁ Συντίπας λέγει τῷ βασιλεῖ· "Ἡ τοῦ υἱοῦ σου σύνεσις ἅμα καὶ γνῶσις, ὦ βασιλεῦ, ἄνωθεν αὐτῷ ἐν πρώτοις κεχορήγηται· ἀλλὰ καὶ αὐτὴ ἡ τῆς γεννήσεως αὐτοῦ τύχη τὸ τῆς γνώσεως προτέρημα, ὡς οἶμαι, πεπλού-τηκεν· ἔπειτα δὲ καὶ ὑπὸ τῆς ἐμῆς πάντως ἐπιμελείας καὶ σπουδῆς τὸ ἐν γνώσει ἀπαράμιλλον ἔσχηκεν· πλὴν περὶ τούτου καί τινός μου διηγήσεως, ὦ βασιλεῦ, ἄκουσον." Ὁ δὲ βασιλεύς, "Φράσον ὃ βούλει," φησί, "σοφώτατε Συν-τίπα." Ὁ δὲ τοιαύτης πρὸς αὐτὸν ἐξηγήσεως ἀπήρξατο.

136   "Βασιλεύς τις ἦν ἐν τοῖς ἔκπαλαι χρόνοις, ὃς δὴ καὶ πλείστους ὑφ' ἑαυτὸν φιλοσόφους ἐπλούτει, ὧν ὁ εἷς ἐτύγ-χανε τῶν ἄλλων μάλα διαφορώτατος. Ἦν δὲ ἐκείνῳ τῷ βασιλεῖ καί τις ἕτερος ἀνὴρ τὴν ἀστροθεάμονα τέχνην ἄκρως ἐξησκημένος. Τῷ γοῦν πρωτεύοντι ἐκείνῳ τοῦ βασιλέως φιλοσόφῳ υἱὸς τότε γεννᾶται, περὶ οὗ δὴ καὶ τῷ

When the boy said this, the king was delighted with his suggestion, and the noblemen also approved his opinion and added their support. And the king said to his son, "You have spoken very well, my child, and truly you have advised us intelligently. Now let what my son has advised be done to the woman." And what was recommended by the king's son to his father was done to the wicked and crooked woman.

Then the king said to the philosopher Syntipas, "Reveal to me, philosopher, and show me clearly, where did my son get such great intelligence and learning? He did not receive his eloquent reasoning naturally when he was born, did he? Or did he instead become wise through your attentiveness?" Syntipas answered the king, "Your son's intelligence and knowledge, my king, have in the first place been bestowed on him from heaven above. But also, in my opinion, the good fortune that came from his birth has enriched the superiority of his knowledge. And finally, he obtained his unparalleled knowledge through my complete attention and zealous effort. But concerning his development hear a story from me too, my king." The king said, "Say whatever you wish, most wise Syntipas." And Syntipas began to narrate the following story to him. 135

"There was once a king in olden times, who had an abundance of philosophers under his command, one of whom was preeminent by far over the rest. That king also had another man who was highly skilled in the art of observing the stars. Now at that time a son was born to the king's chief philosopher. The birth was announced to the king, who 136

βασιλεῖ ἀνηγγέλη. Ὁ δὲ εὐθὺς τὸν ἀστρολόγον ἐκεῖνον προσεκαλέσατο καὶ τοῦτον περὶ τοῦ τεχθέντος τῷ φιλοσόφῳ παιδὸς <ἀνηρώτα. Ὁ δὲ ἀστρολόγος τὴν γέννησιν> πρότερον μεμαθηκώς, ἐξήτασε περὶ τῆς αὐτοῦ τύχης· καὶ τῷ βασιλεῖ δεδήλωκεν ὡς· "Ὁ παῖς οὗτος, ὦ δέσποτα, ἐξ ὧν με οἱ τῶν ἀστέρων δρόμοι διδάσκουσι, τὴν τῶν λῃστῶν καὶ κακούργων πονηρὰν τύχην κέκτηται, καὶ ἐπὶ μακροὺς βιοτεύσει χρόνους, ἀλλὰ καὶ κατ' αὐτὴν τὴν τρεισκαιδεκαετίαν τῆς αὐτοῦ ζωῆς μεγίστην κακουργίαν καὶ κλοπὴν διαπράξεται.' Τούτων δὲ οὕτως παρὰ τοῦ ἀστρολόγου ἐκείνου ῥηθέντων, λέγει πρὸς αὐτὸν ὁ τοῦ τεχθέντος πατήρ· 'Πάντως ἤδη φιλαλήθως δῆθεν τῷ βασιλεῖ τὰ τῆς τύχης τοῦ τεχθέντος μοι παιδὸς ἐγνώρισας;' Ὁ δέ, 'Ναί,' φησίν, 'ὦ φιλόσοφε· ἀκριβῶς γὰρ τὰ περὶ αὐτοῦ ἐξετάσας καὶ συζητήσας, εὗρον ὅτιπερ λῃστὴς γενήσεται καὶ λῃστῶν ὁ χαλεπώτατός τε καὶ ὀλεθριώτατος.' Ὑπολαβὼν δὲ ὁ φιλόσοφος λέγει ἐκείνῳ τῷ βασιλεῖ· "Ἔγωγε λοιπὸν τὸν ἐμὸν παῖδα ῥυθμίσω τε καὶ ἐκπαιδεύσω τοῦ μή τινα τοιαύτην αὐτὸν πρᾶξιν νενοσηκέναι, ἀλλὰ μᾶλλον τῶν ἀπηγορευμένων αὐτὸν πρακτέων ἀπέχεσθαι.'

137   "Ὁ μέντοι γεννηθεὶς παῖς ὀκτὼ μῆνας τῆς ἡλικίας ἀνύσας, τῆς μὲν τοῦ μητρῴου μαζοῦ θηλῆς εὐθὺς ἀποτέμνεται. Τοῦτον δὲ μετὰ ταῦτα ὁ πατὴρ ἐντὸς οἰκίσκου τινὸς ἐγκατακλείει, καὶ ἤρξατο αὐτὸν διά τινων ἁπαλῶν καὶ λυσιτελῶν ἐδεσμάτων ἐκτρέφειν τε καὶ ἀνατρέφειν, οὐ μὴν ἀλλὰ καὶ πᾶσαν αὐτὸν ἀρετὴν ἐκδιδάσκειν καὶ σεμνότητα. Καὶ οὕτω σὺν ἀκριβείᾳ τὸν υἱὸν ἀνατρέφων, οὐκ εἴα τινὰ τὸ παράπαν πρὸς αὐτὸν εἰσέρχεσθαι οὔτε ἔξωθεν τοῦ

immediately summoned the astrologer and asked him about the child. The astrologer had learned about the birth ahead of time and had already inquired into the child's fortune. And so he revealed to the king, 'From what the courses of the stars teach me, master, this boy possesses the wicked fortune of bandits and criminals, and although he will live for many years, in the thirteenth year of his life he will commit a very great crime and a theft.' When the astrologer had said this, the child's father asked him, 'Did you just now really and truly reveal to the king the fortune of the child who was born to me?' He said, 'Yes. Upon examining and investigating his life in detail, I found that he will become a bandit, and among bandits he will be the cruelest and most dastardly.' Then the philosopher replied to the king, 'Then I will train and educate my son so that he does not become sick with criminal activity, but rather refrains from illegal actions.'

"And so, when the boy born to him reached eight months 137 of age, he was immediately separated from the nipple of his mother's breast. Then his father confined him to a room and began to rear and raise him on simple and nourishing foods, and moreover to teach him dignity and every virtue. And raising his son in this way with great care, he neither allowed anyone at all to approach him, nor permitted the boy to go

οἰκίσκου τὸν παῖδα προέρχεσθαι, ἀλλ' οὐδὲ τῶν πονηρῶν
τοῦ ἀνθρωπίνου βίου πράξεων γνώριμόν τι τούτῳ καθίστα
τὸ σύνολον. Καὶ οὕτως ὁ παῖς ἀνατρεφόμενος καὶ τοῖς
χρόνοις προβαίνων τῆς πεντεκαιδεκαετοῦς ἡλικίας ἥψατο.
Εἶτά φησιν πρὸς αὐτὸν ὁ φιλοσοφώτατος τούτου πατήρ·
Αὔριον, ὦ τέκνον, πρὸς τὸν βασιλέα πορεύσομαι καὶ σὲ
μεθ' ἑαυτοῦ ἀπαγαγεῖν πρὸς αὐτὸν βεβούλημαι, ὡς ἂν χαίρειν αὐτῷ προσφθέγξῃ καὶ ὡς δεόντως τούτῳ προσομιλή-
σῃς μετά γε τὴν συνήθη καὶ δουλοπρεπῆ προσκύνησιν.'
Οὕτω μὲν ὁ φιλόσοφος τῷ ἑαυτοῦ ἔλεγεν υἱῷ.

138 "Καὶ ἦν τοῦτον ἄκρως τῇ διδασκαλίᾳ ἐκπαιδεύσας, ἅτε
σπεύδων ψευδῆ ἐναποδεῖξαι τὸν ἀστρολόγον ἐν τῇ ἐκείνου
περὶ τούτου προρρήσει. Ὁ δέ γε νεανίας ἀκηκοὼς ὅτιπερ
αὐτὸν εἰς τὸν βασιλέα εἰσαγαγεῖν ὁ πατὴρ ἐβούλετο, ἠγωνία μᾶλλον ἐπὶ τῷ ἀκούσματι, καὶ λογισμοῖς συνεστρέφετο,
λέγων ὡς· Οὐδέποτε ἄλλοτε βασιλέα τεθέαμαι. Καὶ νῦν
ἐπείπερ ὁ ἐμὸς πατὴρ εἰς τόνδε με τὸν βασιλέα εἰσαγαγεῖν
βούλεται, χρὴ κἀμὲ μυρεψικὰ καὶ ἀρωματικὰ εἴδη αὐτῷ
προσενεγκεῖν καὶ τῇ αὐτῶν προσαγωγῇ τὸ κράτος αὐτοῦ
ὡς τὸ εἰκὸς ἐγκωμιάσαι· πλὴν ἀλλ' ἐρυθριῶ τοιαῦτά τινα
εἴδη ἀπὸ τοῦ ἐμοῦ πατρὸς ἐπιζητῆσαι. Ἐπίσταμαι δ' οὖν
ὅμως τί με δεῖ πεποιηκέναι.' Καὶ ταῦτα εἰπὼν τῇ ἐπιούσῃ
νυκτὶ ἐξέρχεται λάθρα τῆς πατρῴας οἰκίας καὶ πορεύεται
πρὸς τὸ τοῦ βασιλέως παλάτιον· εἶτα διορυγήν τινα κατὰ
τοὺς κλέπτας ἐν τῷ τούτου τείχει ποιησάμενος, εἰσέδυ τὰ
βασίλεια ἕως αὐτοῦ τοῦ βασιλικοῦ κοιτῶνος. Καὶ αὐτίκα
ὁ βασιλεὺς ἔξυπνος γενόμενος ἀθρόον αὐτὸν ἑωράκει, καὶ
τῇ αὐτοῦ θέᾳ δειλίᾳ συνεσχέθη. Καὶ θροούμενος τὰ

outside the room, and so he kept the boy completely ignorant of the wicked deeds that are part of human life. And the
boy, raised in this way and advancing in years, reached his
fifteenth year. Then his father, the king's most learned philosopher, said to him, 'Tomorrow, my child, I will go to the
king, and I want to take you along with me, so that you may
address greetings to him and converse with him properly after making the customary and servile prostration.' This is
what the philosopher said to his son.

"Now the philosopher had given his son an excellent education because he was eager to prove the astrologer's prediction false. But when the young man heard that his father
wished to take him to the king, he agonized at the news and
wrapped himself in his thoughts: 'I've never seen a king before. And now since my father wants to introduce me to this
king, I should also offer perfumes and spices to him, and
with these offerings praise his majesty as is proper. But I'm
embarrassed to ask my father for these things. So, I know
what I must do.' He said this to himself and, when night fell,
he secretly left his father's house and made his way to the
king's palace. Then he dug a hole, as thieves do, through the
king's wall and sneaked into the palace, going as far as the
royal bedchamber itself. Straightaway the king woke up and
suddenly saw him, and at the sight of him was gripped by
cowardice. And since he was very scared, he said to himself,

μέγιστα, καθ' ἑαυτὸν ἔλεγεν ὡς· 'Εἰ μὴ πλεῖστον οὗτος ἐφ'
ἑαυτῷ τὸ θάρσος ἐκέκτητο, οὐκ ἂν οὕτως ἀωρὶ τῶν νυκτῶν
τῆς ἐνθάδε κατετόλμησεν εἰσελεύσεως· καὶ εἴπερ αὐτῷ
ἀντικαταστῆναι πειράσομαι, ἴσως ἀνελεῖν ἐπιχειρήσει με.'
Ταῦτα οὖν ὁ βασιλεὺς ἐκεῖνος συλλογισάμενος καὶ ἡσυ-
χάσας μᾶλλον, παραχωρεῖ τῷ νέῳ ἐκεῖθεν εἰληφέναι εἴ τι
δὴ καὶ βουληθείη. Καὶ δὴ ἐκτείνας ἐκεῖνος τὰς χεῖρας, τῶν
ἐκεῖσε κειμένων βασιλικῶν ἥψατο ὑφασμάτων, καί τινα
τούτων σινδόνα ἐξείλκυσε πολλοῦ γε τιμωμένην. Ἦν δὴ
καὶ μόνην λαβὼν καὶ τοῦ παλατίου ἐξελθών, εὐθὺς ταύτην
ἀπεμπόλησε, καὶ ἐκ τῆς τιμῆς μυρσίνης ἀρώματα καὶ ἕτερα
μυρεψικὰ εἴδη δαψιλῶς ὠνήσατο. Ὁ μέντοι βασιλεὺς
οὐδενὶ τὴν τοῦ νέου νυκτερινὴν ἐπιστασίαν τὸ παράπαν
ἐγνώρισεν.

139   '"Ἕωθεν οὖν ὁ φιλόσοφος τὸν ἑαυτοῦ παῖδα παραλαβών,
πρὸς τὸν βασιλέα πορεύεται· καὶ εἰσελθόντες, ἐπὶ τῆς γῆς
αὐτὸν προσεκύνησαν. Καὶ εὐθὺς ὁ παῖς τὰ ὠνηθέντα
ἐκεῖνα εὐώδη καὶ τερπνότατα εἴδη τῷ ἀνάκτορι προσήνεγ-
κεν, καὶ δι' αὐτῶν τῆς προσαγωγῆς τοῦτον ἐγκωμιάζειν
ἀπήρξατο. Ἔφη δὲ καὶ ὁ φιλόσοφος πρὸς αὐτόν· 'Βασιλεῦ,
ζῆθι εἰς τὸν αἰῶνα. Ἰδού, ὡς ὁρᾷς, τῷ κράτει σου τουτονί
μου τὸν παῖδα παρέστησα, ὃν ὁ σὸς ἀστρολόγος περὶ αὐτὴν τὴν τρεισκαιδεκαετίαν τῆς αὐτοῦ ζωῆς ληστρικῆς
ἐργασίας μέλλειν κατάρξασθαι προηγόρευσε. Καὶ ἰδοὺ
νῦν πεντεκαιδεκαετὴς γέγονεν, καὶ οὐδαμῶς κλοπὴν
ἐξηργάσατο· λοιπὸν οὖν ψευδὴς ὁ ἀστρολόγος ἤδη πε-
φώραται, καὶ αἱ τούτου προρρήσεις ληρώδεις ἀπεδείχθη-
σαν.' Ὁ δὲ βασιλεὺς ἐκεῖνος περιέργως τῇ ὄψει τοῦ

'If this man were not extremely courageous, he would not have dared to enter my room like this in the dead of night. If I attempt to confront him, he might try to kill me.' And so the king, reasoning in this way, chose to remain quiet and allowed the young man to take from his room whatever he wished. Then the young man stretched out his hands and laid hold of the royal robes that were lying there, and he pulled out a very expensive linen one. Taking only this garment and leaving the palace, he immediately sold it, and from the proceeds bought spices of the myrtle tree and other perfumes in great quantities. The king, as it happened, did not report the young man's nighttime incursion to anyone at all.

"When dawn arrived, the philosopher took his son and 139 made his way to the king. And when they came into the king's presence, they prostrated themselves before him on the ground. And immediately the boy offered the ruler those fragrant and most delightful perfumes and spices that he had bought, and as he offered them he began to praise the king. Then the philosopher said to him, '*My king, may you live forever.* Look, as you see, I have presented your majesty with this son of mine, whom your astrologer proclaimed would begin the work of a bandit in about the thirteenth year of his life. And look, now he is fifteen years old, and he has committed no theft at all. And so, then, the astrologer has now been proved false, and his predictions have been revealed to be nonsense.' But the king, gazing inquisitively at

νεανίσκου ἐνατενίσας, ἐπέγνω ὡς ἐκεῖνος ἦν ὁ τὴν διορυ-
γὴν τῇ νυκτὶ ἐργασάμενος κλέπτης καὶ τολμηρῶς εἰσδὺς
τὰ βασίλεια καὶ τὴν ἐν τῷ κοιτῶνι αὐτοῦ κλοπὴν ποιησάμενος. Καὶ ὑπολαβών, 'Οὗτός ἐστιν,' ἔφη, 'ὁ κατὰ τῆς
βασιλείας μου εἰσεληλυθὼς κλέπτης.' Καὶ ἐπιστώθη μᾶλλον ἐπ᾽ αὐτῷ ἡ τοῦ ἀστρολόγου προαγόρευσις.

140   "'Εκ ταύτης μου τῆς διηγήσεως, ὦ κράτιστε βασιλεῦ,
γνῶθι ὅτι ἑκάστου τῇ γεννήσει ἰδία τις ἀπόκειται παρὰ
Θεοῦ ἔκβασις εὐτυχίας καὶ ἀτυχίας· ὥσπερ ἐν μὲν τῇ τοῦ
σοῦ υἱοῦ γεννήσει ἀπέβη αὐτῷ ἐσύστερον τὰ εὔχρηστα
καὶ ἐπαινετὰ καὶ εὐτυχίας ἄναμεστα, ἐν δὲ τῇ γεννήσει τοῦ
τεχθέντος παιδὸς τῷ φιλοσόφῳ τοῦ βασιλέως ἐκείνου,
περὶ οὗ προδιελαβόμην σοι, ἀπέβη τὰ ἄχρηστα καὶ φευκτέα
καὶ ἀπόβλητα καὶ ἀτυχίας πεπληρωμένα."

141   Ταῦτα τῷ βασιλεῖ Κύρῳ τοῦ Συντίπα διηγησαμένου,
φησὶν ὁ βασιλεὺς πρὸς τὸν ἑαυτοῦ παῖδα· "Φράσον μοι,
περιπόθητον τέκνον, πῶς ἄρα καὶ ποίῳ τρόπῳ ὁ σὸς
μυσταγωγὸς Συντίπας τὴν τοσαύτην σε φιλοσοφίαν ἐξεδίδαξεν;" Ὁ δὲ παῖς τῷ πατρὶ ἀπεκρίνατο· "Ἐπειδήπερ
εἰσέτι, ὦ δέσποτα, περὶ τούτου μαθεῖν συζητεῖς, γνωρίζω
αὖθις τῷ κράτει σου ὡς παραλαβών με ἀπὸ σοῦ ὁ ἐμὸς
διδάσκαλος καὶ εἰς τὸν αὐτοῦ οἶκον ἀπαγαγών, εὐθὺς
οἰκίσκον νεωστί μοι ἐδείματο· καὶ τοῦτον ἔσωθεν κοσμίως
περιχρίσας καὶ λευκότητι καταγλαΐσας, πάντα ὅσα ἔμελλεν
ἐκδιδάξαι με ἐν τοῖς τοῦ οἰκίσκου τοίχοις ἀνιστόρησε καὶ
γράμμασιν διεστίξατό τε καὶ ἀκριβῶς ἀνετάξατο, οὐ μὴν
ἀλλὰ καὶ τὸν ἥλιον καὶ τὴν σελήνην καὶ τοὺς ἀστέρας ἐν
τούτοις ἀνεζωγράφησεν.

the young man's face, recognized that he was the thief who had dug the hole through the wall in the night, boldly sneaked into the palace, and committed the theft in his bed-chamber. And he replied, 'This is the thief who entered my palace!' And so, rather than being refuted, the astrologer's prediction about him was confirmed.

"From this story, mightiest king, know that God sets 140 aside an individual destiny of good or bad fortune at each person's birth. Just as by the birth of your son the events of his life later turned out advantageous, praiseworthy, and full of good fortune, so also by the birth of that son born to the king's philosopher, about whom I just told you, the events of his life turned out detrimental, reprehensible, worthless, and full of bad fortune."

After Syntipas narrated this story to king Cyrus, the king 141 said to his son, "Tell me, much-beloved child, how and in what way did your mentor Syntipas impart to you so much learning?" The boy answered his father, "Since you still seek to learn about this, master, I will tell your majesty again that my teacher, after he received me from you and took me away to his house, immediately built a new room for me. And when he had beautifully painted the interior and made it a brilliant white, he sketched everything that he intended to teach me on the walls of the room, writing it out formally and arranging it very carefully. Not only that, but he also painted the sun, moon, and stars on the walls.

142 "Ἐνεχάραξε δὲ τοῖς αὐτοῖς τοῦ οἰκήματος τοίχοις καὶ τὰ δέκα κεφάλαια τῆς τε σοφίας καὶ τῆς γνώσεως καὶ τῆς διδασκαλίας. Ὧν τὸ πρῶτον κεφάλαιον περὶ σκαιοῦ τε καὶ λοιδόρου παρεισάγει ἀνδρός, ὃς ὢν μεταξὺ δύο τινῶν εἴτε ὁμαιμόνων εἴτε προσφιλῶν διενέξεις τε καὶ διαμάχας ἀναρριπίζει. Τὸ δεύτερον κεφάλαιον περὶ φιλοσόφου παρίστησιν ἀνδρός, ὃς πολλὴν τῷ ἑαυτοῦ προσφιλεῖ ἐμποιεῖ τὴν ὠφέλειαν. Τὸ τρίτον κεφάλαιον περὶ δολιόφρονος ἀνδρὸς εἰσηγεῖται, ὃς οὐκ ἐπινυστάζει τῷ κακῷ πώποτε, δόλους καὶ σκαιωρίας κατὰ τοῦ ἑτέρου συρράπτων, ἐκείνου μὴ εἰδότος. Τὸ τέταρτον κεφάλαιον περὶ ἀνδρός ἐστιν ἀπρεπῶς ἑτέρῳ προσονειδίζοντος τὴν ἐκείνου τῷ σώματι ἐνυπάρχουσαν ἐκ λέπρας ἴσως ἀσχημοσύνην. Τὸ πέμπτον κεφάλαιον περὶ τοῦ μὴ δεῖν ἀποφαίνεσθαί τινα περί τινος πράγματος ἢ κατηγορίας, πρινὴ τὴν ταύτης διαβεβαιωθείη ἀλήθειαν. Τὸ ἕκτον κεφάλαιον περὶ τοῦ μὴ δεῖν τινα ἐπὶ ἄφρονι ἀνδρὶ καὶ ἰδιωτικῶς ἔχοντι πεποιθέναι. Τὸ ἕβδομον κεφάλαιον περὶ φθονεροῦ ἀνδρὸς ἐκδιδάσκει ζηλοτύπως πρὸς ἑτέρους ἄνδρας ἔχοντος διὰ τὸ ἐκείνους χρηστοῦ τινος ἐπαπολαύειν ἢ ἀξιεπαίνου τινὸς προτερήματος ἐν μετουσίᾳ τυγχάνειν· ὃς δὴ καὶ βασκαίνων ἐκείνοις ἀνιᾶται μὲν καθ' ἑαυτὸν καὶ τῷ φθόνῳ τήκεται, τοὺς δέ γε διαφθονουμένους κατ' οὐδένα τρόπον ἐντεῦθεν λυμαίνεται. Τὸ ὄγδοον κεφάλαιον πέφυκεν περὶ τοῦ δεῖν τινα πάντας ἀγαπᾶν καὶ μηδαμῶς τῷ κακοποιήσαντι ἀποδιδόναι τὰ ὅμοια. Τὸ ἔνατον κεφάλαιον παρίστησιν ὅτι χρὴ καθώς τις θέλει ἵνα ποιῇ αὐτῷ ἕτερος, καὶ αὐτὸν ἐκείνῳ ποιεῖν ὁμοίως. Τὸ δέκατον κεφάλαιον δηλοῖ περὶ τοῦ μὴ δεῖν τινα

"He also inscribed on the walls of the room the ten chap- 142
ters of wisdom, knowledge, and education. The first of these
chapters is about a malicious and abusive man who gets between two relatives or friends and stirs up quarrels and con-
tention. The second chapter is about a philosopher who
provides a great benefit to his beloved friend. The third
chapter is about a treacherous man who is always vigilant in
his evil as he stitches together deceits and intrigues against
another man behind his back. The fourth chapter is about a
man who inappropriately criticizes another man for the dis-
figurement of his body that might have come from leprosy.
The fifth chapter is about how one must not render a decision about any matter or accusation before he has confirmed
the truth of it. The sixth chapter is about how one must not
put his trust in a man who is foolish and idiotic. The seventh
chapter teaches about an envious man who is jealous toward
other men because they enjoy some good thing or possess
some praiseworthy advantage; this man, because he is jealous of them, is troubled in himself and wastes away from
envy, but he in no way harms the objects of his envy by doing
so. The eighth chapter is about how one must love everyone
and in no way repay in kind someone who has done him
wrong. The ninth chapter is about the principle that one
should treat others just as he wishes to be treated by them.
The tenth chapter explains that one must not befriend and

φιλιοῦσθαι καὶ ἀδελφὰ φρονεῖν τοῖς ἀσεβῶς τῶν πράξεων
καὶ τυραννικῶς ἔχουσι καὶ ἀδικίαις καὶ πλεονεξίαις χρω-
μένοις." Ταῦτα οὕτως ὁ βασιλεὺς ταῖς ἀκοαῖς παρὰ τοῦ
υἱοῦ ἐνηχηθείς, εὐχαριστηρίους τῷ Θεῷ λόγους ἀνέπεμπεν
καὶ τὸν Συντίπαν διετέλει ἐγκωμιάζων, οὐ μὴν ἀλλὰ καὶ
δώροις τὸν ἄνδρα φιλοτίμοις ἐδεξιοῦτο.

143   Εἶτα λέγει πρὸς τὸν παῖδα οὑτωσί· "Γνώρισόν μοι,
τέκνον ποθεινότατον· ἀρά γε τὰ συμβαίνοντά τινι ἐξ εἱ-
μαρμένης καὶ τύχης συμβαίνειν εἰώθασιν;" Ὁ δὲ παῖς ἔφη
τῷ βασιλεῖ· "Τοῦτο μὲν οὕτως ἔχειν, ὦ δέσποτα, πολλοὶ
τῶν ἀνθρώπων οἴονται· πλὴν τὸ αἴτιον τῶν συμβαινόντων
λυπηρῶν ἐκ τῆς τῶν ἀνθρώπων γίνεται μοχθηρίας. Οὐ
γὰρ δικαίως χρῶνται ταῖς πράξεσιν, ἀλλὰ σκολιῶς καὶ
ἀδίκως. Ἔθος γάρ ἐστιν αὐτοῖς, ὅταν τινὶ τῶν φιλοσόφων
ἀνδρῶν ἐντυγχάνωσι, τῷ τὰ χρηστὰ καὶ δέοντα καὶ
λυσιτελῆ συμβουλεύοντι, εἰ μὴ καὶ πλούτῳ κομῶν καὶ τιμῇ
διαπρέπων ὁ τοιοῦτος ὑπάρχει, περιφρονεῖν μᾶλλον αὐτὸν
καὶ ὡς ἰδιωτικὸν παρορᾶν καὶ μὴ ἕνα τοῦτον ἡγεῖσθαι τῶν
φιλοσόφων· διὸ οὐδὲ τὸ οὖς τοῖς ἐκείνου λόγοις τὸ
παράπαν ὑποκλίνουσιν. Εἰ δέ τις κατὰ τὸν βίον εὐπραγῶν
εἴη καὶ εὐθηνούμενος καὶ τιμῆς παρὰ πάντων ἀξιούμενος,
σοφίας δὲ καὶ συνέσεως παντελῶς ἀπεστέρηται, ἐκείνῳ
μᾶλλον οἱ ἄνθρωποι προσανέχουσι, κἂν ἰδιωτικῶς τοῦ
νοὸς ἔχει. Οὐ καλῶς τοίνυν τοῦτο δρῶσιν οἱ ἄνθρωποι,
ἀλλὰ καὶ μάλα κακοτρόπως."

144   Αὖθις οὖν ὁ βασιλεὺς τὸν υἱὸν ἐπηρώτα· "Τίνι ἄρα τὸ
βασιλεύειν προσήκει;" Ὁ δὲ παῖς, "Τῷ συνετῷ," φησί, "καὶ
ἐχέφρονι, ὡς ἂν ἐντεῦθεν καὶ τὸ ὑπήκοον καλῶς

think brotherly thoughts toward those who are impious and tyrannical in their actions and who practice injustice and greed." When the king had heard all this from his son, he offered up prayers of thanksgiving to God and continuously praised Syntipas, and moreover he honored the man with generous gifts.

Then he said to his son, "Tell me, most beloved child: are 143 fate and fortune usually the cause of whatever happens to us?" And the boy said to the king, "Many people think so, master. But the cause of the grievous things that happen to us is in fact people's wickedness. For they do not behave justly, but crookedly and unjustly. For whenever they meet a philosopher who advises what is good and necessary and beneficial, unless that man both abounds in wealth and is eminent in honor, they usually despise him instead, disregard him as lacking understanding, and do not consider him to be a philosopher. And so, they do not even incline their ear to his words. However, if someone is flourishing and successful and is thought worthy of honor by everyone, but is also utterly bereft of wisdom and intelligence, people devote themselves to him instead, even though his mind lacks understanding. People, therefore, act dishonorably, and moreover very maliciously."

Then again the king questioned his son, "For whom is 144 kingship fitting?" And the boy said, "For the intelligent and sensible man: so that his subjects may consequently be well

διακυβερνᾶται, καὶ μηδέν τι ἄδικον ὑπό τινος συγχωρῆται γίνεσθαι, μηδ᾽ αὖ ὁ βασιλεύων πρὸ τοῦ τὴν ἀλήθειαν ἐννόμως βεβαιοῦσθαι καταδίκῃ τινὰ καθυποβάλλῃ, καὶ ὅπως τοῖς μὲν εὐθέσι καὶ ἀγαθοῖς ἀγαθὰ ἀποδίδωσι, τοῖς δὲ σκαιοῖς καὶ κακοτρόποις τὰ ἀναλογοῦντα λυπηρά, τόν τε τοῦ Θεοῦ φόβον πρὸ ὀφθαλμῶν ἔχῃ καὶ μηδὲν τοῦ δικαίου λογίζηται προτιμότερον." Ἔφη δὲ πάλιν ὁ βασιλεὺς τῷ υἱῷ· "Ποία βασιλεία, ὦ τέκνον, ἀσφαλεστέρα καθέστηκεν;" Καί φησιν ὁ παῖς· "Ἡ τὸν Θεὸν εὐλαβουμένη καὶ τὸ δίκαιον μεταδιώκουσα, ἥτις καὶ τοὺς πένητας οἰκτείρει καὶ τοὺς κακῶς ἔχοντας τῶν ὑπηκόων καὶ βιωτικαῖς περιπετείαις πιεζομένους ἀνακτᾶται καὶ εὐεργετεῖ." Ὁ δὲ βασιλεὺς ἔφη· "Καὶ ὁποίᾳ δὴ τῇ βασιλείᾳ οἱ ἄνθρωποι ἐπιτέρπονται;" Ὁ δὲ παῖς, "Τῇ ἐκ θείας προνοίας γεγενημένῃ," φησί, "καὶ τῇ δικαίως πολιτευομένῃ καὶ πάσης ἀγαθοεργίας πρὸς τοὺς ὑπ᾽ αὐτὴν ἀντεχομένῃ."

145   Αὖθις δὲ ὁ βασιλεὺς παρὰ τοῦ υἱοῦ ἐπυνθάνετο· "Ἆρά γε, ὦ τέκνον, ἡ σοφιστεία τῶν φιλοσόφων τῆς τῶν ἑτέρων περιγίνεται πανουργίας;" Ὁ δὲ υἱὸς ἔφη τῷ βασιλεῖ· "Σφόδρα τῆς πανουργίας ἡ γνῶσις περιγίνεται καὶ ἐφ᾽ ἅπασιν αὐτῆς ὑπερτερεῖν δύναται, ἅτε τὰς τῶν πράξεων διαφορὰς ἀσφαλῶς διακρίνουσα καὶ τὰ φύσει καλὰ τῶν ἐναντίων διαιροῦσα· ἡ γὰρ ἐνυπάρχουσά τισι πανουργία οὐ συνέσεως καὶ σοφίας καθέστηκεν, ἀλλὰ ψιλῆς διανοίας τε καὶ προθέσεως καὶ φρονήσεως." Ὁ δὲ βασιλεὺς πάλιν ἐπηρώτα· "Τίνος χάριν οὐκ αἰδοῦνταί τινα τὸ παράπαν οἱ φιλόσοφοι, ἀλλ᾽ ἰταμῶς τὴν αὐτῶν διδασκαλίαν τοῖς πᾶσι προτείνονται;" Ὁ δὲ παῖς ὑπολαβὼν ἔφησεν· "Τούτου χάριν, βασιλεῦ, τὸ

governed, and none of them may be allowed to do anything unjust, nor in turn may the king inflict a penalty on anyone before the truth is lawfully confirmed; and so that he may repay righteous and good people with good things, and crooked and malicious people with correspondingly griev-ous things, and he may keep the fear of God before his eyes and consider nothing more valuable than justice." Once again the king said to his son, "What sort of kingship, my child, is most secure?" And the boy said, "The one that re-veres God and pursues justice, and both pities the poor and restores and shows kindness to those subjects who are suf-fering and oppressed by life's reversals of fortune." Then the king said, "In what sort of kingship do people take delight?" And the boy said, "In the one that is born from divine provi-dence, justly administered, and devoted to doing every good deed for its subjects."

Once again the king inquired of his son, "My child, is the 145 wisdom of the philosophers superior to the wickedness of other men?" And the son said to the king, "Knowledge is far superior to wickedness and is able to surpass it in every way, because it unfailingly distinguishes the differences between actions and separates those that are naturally good from those that are not. For the wickedness that exists within some people comes not from intelligence and wisdom, but from an intellect, will, and understanding that are superfi-cial." Once again the king asked, "Why do the philosophers feel no shame before anyone at all, but boldly offer their in-struction to everyone?" And the boy replied, "Because, my

ἀναιδὲς ἔχουσιν, ἐφ' ᾧ διδάσκειν πάντας ἐπιποθοῦσι καὶ μάλιστα τοὺς συνετωτέρους καὶ τῆς σοφίας ἐφιεμένους." "Τίνες οὖν," φησὶν ὁ βασιλεύς, "ὑπάρχουσιν οἱ παρὰ τῶν φιλοσόφων μισούμενοι;" Ὁ παῖς ἀπεκρίνατο· "Πάντες ὅσοι μὴ γνώμης εὐθύτητι τὴν τούτων διδασκαλίαν προσίενται, ἀλλὰ τοὺς αὐτῶν ἐλέγχους πικρῶς ὑποφέρουσιν, ὡς τῇ ἀληθείᾳ προσκρούοντες."

146 Καὶ ὁ βασιλεὺς πάλιν ἔφη· "Ποῖος θησαυρὸς τῶν ἄλλων ἐστὶν κρείσσων;" Ὑπολαβὼν ὁ υἱὸς αὐτοῦ εἶπεν· "Ὁ τῶν ἀγαθῶν ἔργων." Ὁ βασιλεὺς λέγει· "Τίνος τις χρῄζει κατὰ τῶν ἀντιπάλων;" Ὁ δὲ παῖς, "Τῆς ἐπὶ τῷ Θεῷ," φησί, "πεποιθήσεως." Ὁ βασιλεὺς λέγει· "Τίς τῷ ὄντι πλουσιώτατος πέφυκεν;" Ὁ δὲ παῖς ἔφη· "Ὃς πέποιθεν ἐπὶ τὸ θεῖον καὶ ἀγαθοεργίαν κέκτηται."

147 Ὁ βασιλεὺς εἶπε· "Ποῖός ἐστιν ὁ τὴν κρείττονα κεκτημένος ἀνάπαυσιν;" Ὁ δὲ παῖς ἔφη· "Ὁ μὴ βασκαίνων τινί, καὶ ἑαυτῷ μὲν ἐπιμεμφόμενος, ἕτερον δὲ μὴ κατακρίνων." Ὁ βασιλεὺς εἶπεν· "Τίς ἄφρων ὄντως τυγχάνει;" Ὁ δὲ παῖς λέγει· "Ὁ μὴ συνιεὶς τὸ ἑαυτοῦ παράπτωμα καὶ μὴ πειθόμενος τῷ τὰ χρηστὰ αὐτῷ συμβουλεύοντι." Ὁ βασιλεὺς ἔφη· "Τίς τῶν ἀνθρώπων ἀρίστην ἔχει καὶ φιλικὴν τὴν διάθεσιν;" Ὁ δὲ παῖς φησιν· "Ὁ μή τινα τὸ παράπαν ἀνιῶν, μηδὲ ζηλοτύπως πρός τινα διακείμενος."

148 Ὁ βασιλεὺς εἶπεν· "Ποῖος λογισμὸς τῷ Θεῷ καθέστηκε βδελυκτός;" Ὁ δὲ υἱὸς αὐτοῦ ἔφη· "Ὃς ἐστιν ὑπερήφανος καὶ ἀλάζων. Ἀλλὰ μὴν μεμίσηται αὐτῷ καὶ ἀφροσύνη καὶ λόγων ἀπρεπῶν ἀδολεσχία." Ὁ βασιλεὺς λέγει· "Ποία τῶν αἰσχρῶν πράξεων πλέονι τῇ ἁμαρτίᾳ περιβάλλει τὸν

king, they have no reason to be ashamed of what they desire to teach everyone, especially those who are exceptionally intelligent and who long for wisdom." "Whom, then," said the king, "do the philosophers hate?" And the boy answered, "All those who do not accept their teaching straightforwardly in their minds, but endure their reproaches bitterly out of hostility to the truth."

And once again the king said, "What sort of treasure is 146
better than all others?" His son replied, "The one that comes from good deeds." The king said, "What does someone need against his rivals?" And the boy said, "Trust in God." The king said, "Who is truly the richest?" And the boy said, "He who trusts in God and does good deeds."

The king said, "What sort of man enjoys the best re- 147
pose?" And the boy said, "He who does not disparage anyone, and who finds fault with himself but does not judge another." The king said, "Who is truly a fool?" And the boy said, "He who does not understand his own transgression and does not obey the one who gives him good counsel." The king said, "Who has an excellent and friendly disposition?" And the boy said, "He who vexes no one at all and is not disposed to be jealous of anyone."

The king said, "What sort of reasoning is abominable to 148
God?" And his son said, "That which is arrogant and boastful. But foolishness and indecent words are also especially hateful to him." The king said, "Which shameful action involves the doer in greater sin?" The young man said, "Envy

χρώμενον;" Ὁ νέος ἔφη· "Φθόνος καὶ ψευδομαρτυρία,
ἀπληστία τε καὶ πλεονεξία, καὶ τὸ πορεύεσθαί τινα ὀπίσω
τῶν ἑαυτοῦ θελημάτων διὰ τὸ μήτε τὸν Θεὸν φοβεῖσθαι
μήτε ἄνθρωπον αἰσχύνεσθαι ἐφ᾽ οἷς ἀλόγοις πλημμελεῖ τε
καὶ ἁμαρτάνει. Αὗται δὴ αἱ πράξεις τοῦ ἐφαμάρτου βίου
πεφύκασιν." Ὁ βασιλεὺς λέγει· "Καὶ τίς ἐστιν ὁ μὴ ταῦτα
συνιείς;" Ὁ νέος ἔφη· "Ὃς ἐστιν ἀκόρεστος ἐν πᾶσι καὶ
λίαν φιλάργυρος."

149   Ὁ βασιλεὺς εἶπεν· "Τίνα ὀφείλει τις δεδοικέναι καὶ ὑπο-
τρέμειν;" Ὁ δὲ παῖς λέγει· "Τὸν μὴ φοβούμενον τὸ θεῖον,
μήτε ὑπερέχουσαν ἐξουσίαν εὐλαβούμενον, μηδὲ δικαίως
κρίνοντα. Ἀλλὰ μὴν πτοεῖσθαι δεῖ καὶ φίλον δολιόφρονα
καὶ ὑποκριτήν, ὃς ἄλλα μὲν τῷ στόματι φθέγγεται, ἄλλα
δὲ τῇ καρδίᾳ πονηρῶς συλλογίζεται."

150   Ὁ βασιλεὺς ἔφη· "Πῶς ἄρα οἱ ἄνθρωποι ἐπὶ πλέον
ἀλλήλοις ἐχθραίνονται ἤπερ τὴν φιλίαν ἀσπάζονται;" Ὁ
δὲ παῖς λέγει· "Ἐφ᾽ ᾧ ἡ μὲν τῆς ζημίας πρᾶξις εὐχερὴς τῷ
πράττοντι καθίσταται, ἡ δὲ τῆς εὐποιΐας δυσχερὴς ἐς τὰ
μάλιστα."

151   Αὖθις δὲ ὁ βασιλεύς· "Πῶς ὁ μὲν νοσῶν ἡδέως τὰς τῶν
ἰατρῶν ἐντολὰς προσίεται, κἂν ἐπαχθεῖς εἶναι δοκῶσιν, οἱ
δὲ ἄνθρωποι, ὅταν αὐτοῖς ἡ ἀλήθεια φθέγγηται, βαρέως
ταύτην φέρουσιν;" Ὁ δὲ υἱὸς ἔφη τῷ βασιλεῖ· "Ὅτιπερ ὁ
μὲν νοσῶν τὰ τούτῳ προσφερόμενα φάρμακα, κἂν ἀηδῆ
πως καὶ πικρότατα πέφυκεν, ἀλλ᾽ ὡς ὑγείας καὶ χαροποιοῦ
εὐεξίας πρόξενα ἡδέως προσδέχεται· ὁ δὲ ἄφρων ἀνὴρ καὶ
ἀσύνετος, ὅταν αὐτῷ ἀληθῆ τε καὶ δέοντα λέγωνται,
βαρέως ταῦτα φέρει καὶ δυσχεραίνει ἐπ᾽ αὐτοῖς, καθότι

and false witness, insatiable desire and greed, and for someone to pursue his own will, because he neither shows fear of
God nor respect for humanity in the foolish ways in which
he offends and sins. These are the actions of the sinful life."
The king said, "And who is the one who does not understand
these things?" The young man said, "He who is insatiable in
everything and very miserly."

The king said, "Who should make a man fear and trem- 149
ble?" And the boy said, "He who does not fear God and re-
vere his superior authority, and who does not judge justly.
Moreover, one must be frightened both of a friend with a
deceitful mind and of a hypocrite, who says one thing with
his mouth but wickedly reasons another thing in his heart."

The king said, "How is it that people hate each other 150
more than they welcome each other's friendship?" And the
boy said, "Because doing harm is easy for the one who does
it, but doing good is extremely difficult."

Once again the king said, "How does the sick man gladly 151
follow a doctor's orders, even if they seem burdensome, but
whenever someone speaks the truth, people take it hard?"
And the son said to the king, "Because, even if the drugs offered to the sick man are somehow distasteful and very bitter, he gladly welcomes them because they promote health
and joyful vigor. But whenever true and necessary things are
said to the foolish and unintelligent man, he takes them
hard and is annoyed at them, because unlike the sick man,

οὐχ ὑπό τινος βίας εἴτε ὀδύνης ὥσπερ ὁ νοσῶν συνωθεῖται πρὸς τὰ ἁρμόζοντα. Διὰ γὰρ τοῦτο καὶ γέγραπται· Ἔλεγχε σοφὸν καὶ ἀγαπήσει σε, καὶ μὴ ἔλεγχε ἄφρονα, ἵνα μή σε μισήσῃ.'"

152   Ἔφη πάλιν ὁ βασιλεὺς τῷ υἱῷ· "Πῶς ἄρα ὁ μὲν δαψιλῶς ἐσθίων εὐθὺς καὶ κορέννυται, ὁ δὲ χρημάτων ἐρῶν ἀκόρεστον ἔχει τὴν περὶ ταῦτα ἔφεσιν;" Ὁ παῖς ἀπεκρίνατο· "Ἡ μὲν τὰ ὄψα δεχομένη τοῦ ἀνδρὸς γαστὴρ μετὰ τὴν τούτων δαψιλῆ μετάληψιν πάντως καὶ κόρον αὐτῶν, κἂν μὴ βούλοιτο, λαμβάνει· ὀφθαλμὸς δὲ λίχνος καθ᾽ ὅσον ὁρᾷ τὰ χρήματα, κατὰ τοσοῦτον καὶ αὐτῶν ἐφίεται καὶ ἀκορέστως πρὸς ταῦτα ἔχει, μέχρις ἂν διὰ θανάτου ὑπὸ τὸν χοῦν ἡ αὐτοῦ ὄψις, ὡς ἔθος, καλυφθείη."

153   Φησὶν οὖν αὖθις ὁ βασιλεύς· "Ὁποῖος ἀποβαίνει ἄρα ὁ τοῦ πονηροῦ ἀνδρὸς καὶ βασκάνου θάνατος;" Καὶ ὁ υἱὸς ἀπεκρίνατο· "Θάνατος ἀνδρὸς τοιούτου κέρδος τοῖς ἑτέροις γίνεται· οὐδὲν γὰρ τῶν ἀθέσμων πράξεων χεῖρον τῆς βασκανίας καθέστηκεν. Καὶ χρὴ πάντα ἄνθρωπον θερμῶς αἰτεῖσθαι τὸ θεῖον, ὅπως ὁ φθόνος τῆς ἑαυτοῦ καρδίας ἐξαρθείη τέλεον. Γνῶθι δέ, ὦ βασιλεῦ, ὡς ἅπας μὴ βασκαίνων ἄνθρωπος ἡδέως πάνυ ἐσθίει, ἡδέως τε πίνει καὶ ἡδέως ὑπνώττει· ἡ γὰρ αὐτοῦ διαγωγὴ φροντίδος ἀπήλλακται, ὁ βίος αὐτοῦ ἀνώδυνος τέτακται, ἡ καθέδρα ἀμέριμνος καὶ ἡ στάσις ἄπονος. Ταῦτα οὖν, ὦ κράτιστε βασιλεῦ, ἅπερ παρ᾽ ἐμοῦ ἀκήκοας, αὐτάρκη πεφύκασιν εἰς διαγωγὴν ἀρίστην καὶ βίον ἀκατάγνωστον τοῖς ἐχέφροσι κατὰ σὲ καὶ συνετοῖς ἀνδράσι καὶ φιλοσοφίας ἐφιεμένοις."

he is not pushed to do the right thing by some force or pain. For this reason, it is also written, '*Refute a wise man and he will love you,* and *do not refute* a foolish man, *lest* he *hate you.*'"

Once again the king said to his son, "How is it that some- 152 one who eats a lot is immediately filled, while someone who covets money has an insatiable desire for it?" The boy answered, "The man's stomach receives food, and after getting a lot of it is surely satisfied, too, even without wishing to be full. But a greedy eye longs for however much money it sees and is not satisfied even with that, until death draws a veil over its sight beneath the earth, as happens to us all."

And then once again the king said, "What happens when 153 a wicked and jealous man dies?" And the son answered, "The death of such a man is a gain for everyone else, because nothing is worse than lawless actions that come from jealousy. And every man ought to beseech God fervently, so that envy is completely removed from his own heart. For know, my king, that every man who feels no jealousy eats with great pleasure and drinks with pleasure and sleeps with pleasure. For his way of living is free of anxiety, his life is ordered so as to be free of pain, his sitting is free of worry, and his standing is free of toil. And so, mightiest king, the advice that you have heard from me is all that is needed to live a life that is virtuous and beyond reproach, for men like you, who are sensible and intelligent, and who possess a desire for learning."

154   Τέλος σὺν Θεῷ τῆς περὶ τοῦ βασιλέως Περσῶν Κύρου
καὶ τῆς αὐτοῦ πονηρᾶς τῶν ἄλλων καὶ κακοτρόπου γυναικὸς καὶ τοῦ γνησίου τούτου παιδὸς καὶ τῶν αὐτοῦ ἑπτὰ
φιλοσόφων καὶ τοῦ διδασκάλου τοῦ υἱοῦ αὐτοῦ, ᾧ ὄνομα
Συντίπας, λεπτομεροῦς διηγήσεως. Ἧς αἱ παραβολικαὶ
ὁμιλίαι ιδ', τῆς γυναικὸς σὺν τῷ μύθῳ τῆς ἀλώπεκος ϛ', τοῦ
παιδὸς σὺν τῇ ἐξηγήσει τῶν δέκα κεφαλαίων, ὧν ἐδιδάχθη,
καὶ ταῖς βιωφελέσι πρὸς τὸν πατέρα ἑαυτοῦ ἀποκρίσεσιν
ὁμιλίαι ϛ', καὶ τοῦ Συντίπα μία· πάντων ἐξηγήσεις κζ'.

With God's help, this is the end of the intricate narrative 154
about Cyrus, king of the Persians, and one of his many wives,
who was wicked and malicious, and his legitimate son and
his seven philosophers and his son's teacher, whose name
was Syntipas. It contains fourteen parables, in addition to
six told by the woman, including the story of the fox; six told
by the son, including the story of the ten chapters, in which
he was instructed, and the responses to his father that are
useful for life; and one told by Syntipas. Altogether, then,
there are twenty-seven stories.

THE FABLES OF SYNTIPAS

Συντίπα τοῦ Φιλοσόφου ἐκ τῶν Παραδειγματικῶν αὐτοῦ Λόγων

I

Ὄνος ἀκούσας φωνῆς τέττιγος ἡδέως αὐτῇ ἐπετέρπετο, καὶ τὸν τέττιγα ἐπηρώτα λέγων· "Τί ἄρα τρεφόμενος οὕτω γλυκεῖαν ἔχει‹ς› τὴν φωνήν;" Ὁ δὲ τέττιξ τῷ ὄνῳ ἀντέφησεν· "Ἡ ἐμὴ τροφὴ ἀήρ ἐστι καὶ δρόσος." Ὁ δὲ ὄνος τούτου ἀκούσας τοῦ ῥήματος ἐνόμισε μέθοδον εὑρηκέναι δι᾽ ἧς ὁμοίαν τῷ τέττιγι σχοίη φωνήν· καὶ τὸ στόμα εὐθὺς ἀνοίξας πρὸς τὸν ἀέρα κεχήνωτο ὡς δεξόμενος δῆθεν δρόσον εἰς διατροφήν, ἕως οὗ τῷ λιμῷ διεφθάρη.

2 Οὗτος ὁ μῦθος δηλοῖ ὅτι οὐ δεῖ τινα τὰ φυσικὰ τοῖς παρὰ φύσιν ἐξομοιοῦν καὶ τοῖς ἀδυνάτοις ἀφρόνως ἐπιχειρεῖν.

2

Ἄνθρωπός τις ἦν πένης, ὃς καὶ ξύλων γόμον ἐπὶ τῶν νώτων ἐβάσταζε. Κατὰ δὲ τὴν ὁδοιπορίαν ἰλιγγιάσας ἐκαθέσθη καὶ τὸν γόμον κατέθετο καὶ τὸν Θάνατον οἰκτρῶς ἀνεκαλεῖτο, λέγων· "Ὦ Θάνατε." Αὐτίκα γοῦν ὁ

FROM THE EXEMPLARY STORIES
OF SYNTIPAS THE PHILOSOPHER

I

An ass heard the song of a cicada and was enjoying it with great pleasure, and so he asked the cicada, "What do you eat that causes you to have such a sweet voice?" The cicada answered the ass, "My food is air and dew." When he heard this reply, the ass believed that he had found a way to get the same voice as the cicada. And so he immediately opened his mouth and remained there gaping at the air and expecting to be fed by the dew, until he died of starvation.

This fable shows that people must not assimilate their 2 natural behaviors to behaviors that are unnatural and foolishly attempt what is impossible.

2

There was once a poor man who was carrying a load of wood on his back. He felt faint during his journey, and so he sat down and set his load aside. Then he called out sadly to Death, "Please, Death." Death arrived straightaway and

Θάνατος ἔφθασε καὶ πρὸς αὐτὸν ἔφη· "Τίνος χάριν ἐκάλεσάς με;" Λέγει πρὸς αὐτὸν ὁ ἀνήρ· "Ἵνα τὸν γόμον ἀπὸ τῆς γῆς συνεξάρῃς μοι."

2   Οὗτος δηλοῖ ὅτι πάντες ἄνθρωποι φιλόζῳοι τυγχάνουσιν, εἰ καὶ θλίψεσι καὶ ἀνάγκαις συνέχονται.

3

Χελιδὼν καὶ κόραξ περὶ κάλλους ἀλλήλοις ἐμάχοντο. Καί φησιν ὁ κόραξ τῇ χελιδόνι· "Τὸ σὸν κάλλος ἐν μόνῳ τῷ ἔαρι καταφαίνεται, ἐν δὲ τῷ τοῦ χειμῶνος καιρῷ οὐ δύναται πρὸς τὸ ψύχος ἀντισχεῖν· τὸ δὲ ἐμὸν σῶμα καὶ τῷ κρύει τοῦ χειμῶνος καὶ τῷ καύσωνι τοῦ θέρους γενναίως ἀνθίσταται."

2   Οὗτος δηλοῖ ὅτι ὑγεία καὶ ἰσχὺς σώματος κρείττων κάλλους καὶ ὡραιότητος πέφυκε.

4

Ποταμοὶ συνῆλθον ἐπὶ τὸ αὐτὸ καὶ τὴν θάλασσαν κατῃτιῶντο, λέγοντες αὐτῇ· "Διὰ τί ἡμᾶς, εἰσερχομένους ἐν τοῖς ὕδασι καὶ ὑπάρχοντας ποτίμους καὶ γλυκεῖς, ἁλμυροὺς ἀπεργάζῃ καὶ ἀπότους;" Ἡ δὲ θάλασσα, ἰδοῦσα

asked him, "Why did you call me?" The man replied, "So that you might help me lift my load up from the ground."

This fable shows that all people love life, even when they 2 are suffering under affliction and duress.

3

A swallow and a crow were quarreling with each other over their beauty. The crow said to the swallow, "Your beauty is only apparent in spring, but in the wintertime it cannot stand the cold. My body, however, bravely withstands both winter's icy cold and summer's burning heat."

This fable shows that the body's health and strength are 2 naturally superior to beauty and attractiveness.

4

Some rivers gathered together and scolded the sea: "We enter your waters drinkable and sweet. Why, then, do you make us salty and undrinkable?" When she saw that the

ὅτι αὐτῆς καταμέμφονται, λέγει πρὸς αὐτούς· "Μὴ ἔρχεσθε καὶ μὴ γίνεσθε ἁλμυροί."

2   Οὗτος παρίστησι τοὺς ἀκαίρως τινὰς αἰτιωμένους καὶ παρ' αὐτῶν μᾶλλον ὠφελουμένους.

5

Γαλῆ τις ἐν χαλκευτικῷ εἰσελήλυθεν ἐργαστηρίῳ, κἀκεῖσε ῥίνον εὑροῦσα σιδηροῦν τοῦτον ἱκανῶς ἀνέλειχεν, ὥστε τὴν ἑαυτῆς ἀποτρίβεσθαι γλῶτταν καὶ δεινῶς ἐκδαμάζεσθαι καὶ ῥοὴν αἵματος ἀφιέναι. Ἡ δὲ γαλῆ μᾶλλον ἐτέρπετο, δοκοῦσα δῆθεν τὸν σίδηρον ἐκβιβρώσκειν, ἕως ἡ ταύτης γλῶττα παντελῶς ἐκδεδαπάνηται.

2   Οὗτος ὁ μῦθος δηλοῖ ὅτι πράττων τις ἔργον ἀλυσιτελὲς ὡς ἐπωφελές, μᾶλλον καὶ τούτῳ δυσαποσπάστως προσκεί-μενος, ἐς ὕστερον ὑπ' αὐτοῦ καταλυμαίνεται.

6

Ἀνήρ τις θηρευτής, λύκον θεασάμενος προσβάλλοντα τῇ ποίμνῃ καὶ πλεῖστα τῶν προβάτων ὡς δυνατὸν δια-σπαράττοντα, τοῦτον εὐμηχάνως θηρεύει καὶ τοὺς κύνας αὐτῷ ἐπαφίησι, φθεγξάμενος πρὸς αὐτόν· "Ὦ δεινότατον

rivers were criticizing her, the sea said to them, "So, don't come in and don't become salty."

This fable shows how people make ill-timed accusations 2 against others who are in reality benefiting them.

5

A cat entered a metalworking shop and found an iron file there. She licked the file so much that she wore down her tongue, making it terribly tender and releasing a stream of blood. But the cat was delighted, mistakenly believing that she was devouring the file, until her tongue was completely gone.

This fable shows that when someone performs an 2 unprofitable task as though it were beneficial and, what is more, applies himself to it unceasingly, he is in the end completely destroyed by it.

6

When a hunter saw a wolf attacking his flock and killing as many of the sheep as he could, he skillfully hunted down the wolf and set his dogs on him, saying, "You terrible beast,

θηρίον, ποῦ σου ἡ προλαβοῦσα ἰσχύς, ὅτι τοῖς κυσὶν ὅλως ἀντιστῆναι οὐκ ἠδυνήθης;"

2 Οὗτος δηλοῖ ὡς τῶν ἀνθρώπων ἕκαστος ἐν τῇ ἰδίᾳ τέχνῃ καθέστηκε δόκιμος.

7

Δύο ἀλέκτορες ἀλλήλοις ἐμάχοντο. Καὶ ὁ μὲν εἷς ἡττηθεὶς τόπῳ τινὶ ἐν παραβύστῳ ἀπεκρύβη, ὁ δὲ ἕτερος, τὴν νίκην ἀράμενος, ἐφ' ὑψηλοῦ τινος ἔστηκε δωματίου τὰ μεγάλα φρυαττόμενος καὶ τῇ νίκῃ ἐγκαυχώμενος, ἕως ἀετὸς καταπτὰς τοῦτον ἐκεῖθεν ἀνήρπασεν.

2 Οὗτος δηλοῖ ὡς οὐ χρή τινα ἐπ' εὐτυχίᾳ καὶ δυνάμει μέγα φρονεῖν καὶ ἀφρόνως σοβαρεύεσθαι.

8

Περιστερά τις σφόδρα ἐδίψα καὶ ἐφ' ὕδατος ζήτησιν τῇδε κἀκεῖσε περιήρχετο. Ἰδοῦσα δὲ ἔν τινι τοίχῳ ἐζωγραφημένην ὑδρίαν ἐδόκει ἀληθῶς ὁρᾶν ὕδατος σκεῦος μεστόν, καὶ ἐλθοῦσα τοῦ πιεῖν τῷ τοίχῳ προσέκρουσε καὶ αὐτίκα τοῦ ζῆν ἀπερρήγνυτο. Ὅτε δὲ πρὸς τελευταίαν ἐγγίσασα ἀναπνοὴν ἦν, ἐν ἑαυτῇ ἔλεγεν ὅτι· "Δυστυχὴς

where now is the strength you used to have? For you haven't
been able to offer any resistance to my dogs."

This fable shows that every man proves himself worthy in 2
his own particular skill.

7

Two roosters were fighting each other. The loser hid himself away somewhere in secret, while the winner stood up
high on top of a house, crowing loudly and priding himself
on his victory, until an eagle swooped down and snatched
him up.

This fable shows that one should not be arrogant and 2
foolishly put on airs due to success and power.

8

A dove was very thirsty and was flying here and there in
search of water. When she saw the image of a water jar
painted on a wall, she thought that she was really seeing
a vessel full of water. But when she went to take a drink,
she collided with the wall and straightaway lost her life. As
she was near her final breath, she said to herself, "I really am

ὄντως ἐγὼ καὶ ἀθλία, ἐφ᾽ ᾧ ὕδατος γλιχομένη μὴ θανάτου ἐμνημόνευον."

2   Οὗτος δηλοῖ ὡς πολὺ κρείττων ἡ μακροθυμία τῆς ἀλογίστου σπουδῆς καὶ ταχυτῆτος.

9

Κόραξ ἀετὸν ἐθεάσατο ἄρνα τῆς ποίμνης ἀφαρπάζοντα καὶ ἠθέλησε δῆθεν τοῦτον ἐκμιμήσασθαι. Ἰδὼν δὲ ἐν τῇ ποίμνῃ κριόν, ἐπειράθη τοῦτον ἁρπάσαι. Τῶν δὲ ὀνύχων αὐτοῦ τῷ τοῦ κριοῦ συσχεθέντων ἐρίῳ, φθάσας ὁ ποιμήν, καὶ τοῦτον πλήξας, ἀπέκτεινεν.

2   Οὗτος δηλοῖ ὡς ἀνίσχυρος ἀνήρ, τῷ δυνατωτέρῳ ἑαυτοῦ ἀφομοιοῦσθαι πειρώμενος, οὐ μόνον ἀσθενὴς εἶναι καὶ ἀφελὴς ἀπελέγχεται, ἀλλὰ καὶ κακῶς ἐξ ἀφροσύνης ἀποθνήσκει.

10

Λαγωός τις ἐδίψα καὶ ἐν φρέατι κατῆλθε τοῦ ὕδωρ πιεῖν, ἀφ᾽ οὗ καὶ ἡδέως πολὺ ἐπεπώκει. Ὅτε δὲ ἐκεῖθεν ἀνελθεῖν ἔμελλεν ἀμηχανίᾳ συνεσχέθη περὶ τὴν ἄνοδον, καὶ τὰ μέγιστα ἠθύμει. Ἀλώπηξ δὲ ἐλθοῦσα κἀκεῖσε τοῦτον

unfortunate and wretched because, while I was longing for water, I was not mindful of death."

This fable shows that patience is much better than ² thoughtless haste and speed.

9

A crow saw an eagle snatching a lamb from its flock and wanted to imitate him. And so, when the crow spied a ram in the same flock, he tried to snatch it. But as soon as his claws grabbed the ram's fleece, the shepherd was there to strike and kill him.

This fable shows that when a puny man tries to act like ² someone stronger than himself, he not only proves himself weak and naïve, but he also dies a miserable death because of his foolishness.

IO

A hare was thirsty and descended into a well to drink water. He drank deeply from the well with pleasure, but when it was time to make his ascent, he had no idea about how to go back up, and so he became extremely disheartened. Then

εὑροῦσα ἔφη πρὸς αὐτόν· "Μεγάλως ὄντως ἐσφάλης· πρότερον γὰρ ὤφειλες βουλεύσασθαι πῶς ἔσται σοι τοῦ φρέατος ἀνελθεῖν, εἶθ' οὕτως ἐν αὐτῷ κατελθεῖν."

2   Οὗτος ἐλέγχει τοὺς αὐτοβούλως πράττοντας καὶ μὴ συμβουλευομένους.

II

Ταῦρος εὑρηκὼς κοιμώμενον λέοντα, τοῦτον κερατίσας ἀπέκτεινεν. Ἐπιστᾶσα δὲ ἡ ἐκείνου μήτηρ πικρῶς αὐτὸν ἀπεκλαίετο. Ἰδὼν δὲ αὐτὴν σύαγρος ὀλοφυρομένην, μακρόθεν ἑστὼς ἔφη πρὸς αὐτήν· "Ὦ πόσοι ἄρα τυγχάνουσιν ἄνθρωποι θρηνοῦντες, ὧν τὰ τέκνα ὑμεῖς ἀπεκτείνατε."

2   Οὗτος δηλοῖ ὅτι ἐν ᾧ μέτρῳ μετρεῖ τις ἀντιμετρηθήσεται αὐτῷ.

12

Ποιμήν τις ἀπολέσας ἓν τῶν προβάτων ἐδεήθη τοῦ θεοῦ συνθήκας ποιούμενος ὡς εἴ γε τοῦτο ἐφεύροι, ἕτερον ὑπὲρ αὐτοῦ εἰς θυσίαν προσάξει. Περιερχόμενος δὲ ὁρᾷ τὸ αὐτὸ πρόβατον ὑπὸ λέοντος βιβρωσκόμενον, καὶ τοῦτο

a fox came along and found him there, and she said to the hare, "You've really made a huge mistake. For you should have first considered how you would climb up out the well, and only then have climbed down into it."

This fable condemns those who act of their own accord   2
and without seeking advice.

II

A bull found a sleeping lion and gored him to death. Then the lion's mother stood over him, weeping bitterly. When a wild boar saw her mourning, he stood at a distance and said to her, "Alas, how many humans are in mourning because you lions have killed their children."

This fable shows that *in the same measure that* someone   2
measures out, so shall it be measured out to him *in return.*

12

When a shepherd lost one of his sheep, he prayed to God, promising that if he found it, he would offer another sheep as a sacrifice in return. As he searched about, he saw that very same sheep being eaten by a lion. When he had

ἰδὼν ἐν ἑαυτῷ ἔλεγεν ὡς· "Εἰ μόνον τὸν τοῦ θηρίου δια-
δράσαιμι κίνδυνον, καὶ ἕτερον πρόβατον εἰς λύτρου δῶρον
προσενέγκοιμι."

2   Οὗτος δηλοῖ ὡς τὴν ἰδίαν ζωὴν πάντες ἄνθρωποι
παντὸς κέρδους καὶ πλούτου προτιμοτέραν ἔχουσιν.

13

Λέων προσβαλὼν ταύροις δυσὶν ἐπειρᾶτο τούτους κατα-
θοινήσασθαι. Οἱ δὲ τὰ ἑαυτῶν κέρατα ἐπίσης αὐτῷ ἀντι-
παρατάξαντες οὐκ εἴων τὸν λέοντα μέσον αὐτῶν παρελθεῖν.
Ὁρῶν τοίνυν ἐκεῖνος ὡς ἀδυνάτως ἔχει πρὸς αὐτοὺς κατ-
εσοφίσατο τοῦ ἑνός, καὶ πρὸς αὐτὸν ἔφησεν ὡς· "Εἴ γε τὸν
σὸν ἑταῖρον προδώσεις μοι, ἀβλαβῆ σε διατηρήσω." Καὶ
τούτῳ τῷ τρόπῳ ἀμφοτέρους τοὺς ταύρους ἀνῄρηκεν.

2   Οὗτος δηλοῖ ὡς καὶ πόλεις καὶ ἄνθρωποι ἀλλήλοις
ὁμονοοῦντες οὐ συγχωροῦσιν αὐτῶν τοὺς ἐχθροὺς περι-
γίνεσθαι· τῆς δ' ὁμονοίας καταφρονοῦντες εὐχερῶς ἄρδην
τοῖς ὑπεναντίοις ἁλίσκονται.

seen this, he said to himself, "If only I could escape the danger of this beast, I would offer yet another sheep as the price of my ransom!"

This fable shows that all men regard their own lives as 2 more valuable than any profit or riches.

13

A lion attacked two bulls and tried to make a feast of them. But they lined up their horns in tandem against the lion and did not allow him to get between them. So, when the lion saw that it was impossible to beat the two bulls, he devised a trick against one of them, saying, "If you betray your companion to me, I'll leave you unharmed." And in this way the lion killed both bulls.

This fable shows that when cities as well as men are uni- 2 fied, they do not allow their enemies to get the better of them, but when they disregard unity, they are easily and utterly conquered by their adversaries.

14

Ἀλώπηξ καὶ πίθηξ ἐπὶ τὸ αὐτὸ ὡδοιπόρουν. Παρερχόμενοι δὲ διά τινων μνημείων, ἔφη ὁ πίθηξ τῇ ἀλώπεκι ὡς· "Πάντες οἱ νεκροὶ οὗτοι ἀπελεύθεροι τῶν ἐμῶν γεννητόρων ὑπάρχουσιν." Ἡ δὲ ἀλώπηξ λέγει τῷ πίθηκι· "Εὐχερῶς ἐψεύσω· οὐδεὶς γὰρ τῶν ἐνταῦθα ταφέντων ἀπελέγξαι σε δύναται."

2   Οὗτος παριστᾷ τὸν τοὺς ψευδολόγους ὀρθῶς διελέγχοντα, καὶ τοὺς προδήλως τὸ ψεῦδος ἀντὶ ἀληθείας προσφέροντας.

15

Ἔλαφός τις διψῶσα κατῆλθεν ἐπί τινα πηγὴν τοῦ ὕδωρ πιεῖν. Ἰδοῦσα δὲ ἐν τῷ ὕδατι τὸ τοῦ ἰδίου σώματος ὁμοίωμα, τῇ μὲν τῶν ποδῶν λεπτότητι ἀπηρέσκετο, τῇ δὲ τῶν κεράτων μορφῇ ἐπετέρπετο. Ἄφνω δέ τινες ἐφίστανται θηρευταὶ καὶ ταύτην ἐδίωκον. Καὶ καθ' ὅσον μὲν ἐπὶ τῆς πεδιάδος ἔτρεχε τῶν διωκόντων ὑπερεγίνετο, φθάσασα δὲ εἰς ἕλος ἀπροσδοκήτως εἰσελθεῖν, τῶν αὐτῆς κεράτων τοῖς κλάδοις συμπλακέντων, ὑπὸ τῶν διωκόντων καταλαμβάνεται καὶ στενάξασα ἔφη· "Οἴμοι τῇ ταλαιπώρῳ, ὅτι ἐφ' οἷς ἀπηρεσκόμην ὑπ' αὐτῶν μᾶλλον διεσῳζόμην, οἷς δὲ ἐνεκαυχώμην, ὑπ' αὐτῶν δὴ καὶ ἀπόλλυμαι."

2   Οὗτος δηλοῖ ὡς οὐ χρή τινα τῶν ἐν ἑαυτῷ ἐπαινεῖν, εἰ μὴ τὰ εὔχρηστα καὶ ἐπωφελῆ.

14

A fox and a monkey were traveling to the same place. As they were passing by some tombs, the monkey said to the fox, "All these dead men were freed slaves that belonged to my ancestors." Then the fox said to the monkey, "It's easy to lie now, since no one buried here can prove you wrong."

This fable presents the man who correctly refutes liars 2 and people who offer obvious lies instead of the truth.

15

A thirsty deer went down to a spring to drink water. When he saw the image of his body in the water, he didn't like the slenderness of his legs but was delighted by the shape of his antlers. Suddenly some hunters came upon him and began chasing him. As long as the deer ran on level ground, he got the better of his pursuers, but as soon as he ran unexpectedly into a swamp, his antlers became entangled in branches. He was caught by the pursuers, and he said with a groan, "How miserable I am! I was being saved by what displeased me, but now I'm being destroyed by what made me feel proud."

This fable shows that one should not praise one's own 2 attributes, unless they are useful and beneficial.

16

Ἦν τις κύων χαλκέων τινῶν ἐν οἰκίᾳ διάγων. Κἀκείνων μὲν ἐργαζομένων οὗτος εἰς ὕπνον ἐτρέπετο, εἰς ἑστίασιν δὲ καθεζομένων ἐγίνετο ἔξυπνος καὶ τοῖς ἑαυτοῦ κυρίοις χαριέντως προσεπέλαζεν. Οἱ δὲ πρὸς αὐτὸν ἔλεγον· "Πῶς τῷ μὲν ψόφῳ τῶν βαρυτάτων σφυρῶν οὐδ᾽ ὅλως ἐξυπνίζῃ, τῷ δὲ βραχυτάτῳ κρότῳ τῶν μυλοδόντων ταχέως διεγείρῃ;"

2   Οὗτος δηλοῖ ὡς καὶ ἄνθρωποι ἀνήκοοι, ἐφ᾽ οἷς δῆθεν ὠφελεῖσθαι καραδοκοῦσι, ταχέως τούτοις καὶ ὑπακούουσιν, ἐν οἷς δ᾽ ἀπαρέσκονται ἀπαθεῖς πάντῃ καθίστανται.

17

Ἀλώπηξ θεασαμένη ἐγκάθειρκτον λέοντα, καὶ τούτου στᾶσα ἐγγύς, δεινῶς αὐτὸν ὕβριζεν. Ὁ δὲ λέων ἔφη πρὸς αὐτήν· "Οὐ σύ με καθυβρίζεις, ἀλλ᾽ ἡ προσπεσοῦσά μοι ἀτυχία."

2   Οὗτος δηλοῖ ὡς πολλοὶ τῶν ἐνδόξων δυσπραγίαις περιπίπτοντες ὑπὸ εὐτελῶν ἐξουθενοῦνται.

16

There was a dog who lived in a house with some blacksmiths. While the smiths were working, the dog would usually sleep, but when they sat down to eat, he would wake up and joyfully approach his masters. And so, the smiths would say to the dog, "How is it that you always sleep through the crash of our heaviest hammers, but at the slightest sound of our chewing, you swiftly wake up?"

This fable shows that even people who do not usually listen will swiftly give ear to whatever they expect will benefit them, while they remain utterly indifferent to whatever they dislike. 2

17

A fox saw a lion in a cage, and after coming up close, began to insult him terribly. Then the lion said to the fox, "You're not insulting me; this misfortune that I've fallen into is what's insulting me."

This fable shows that many important people, when they fall into misfortune, are scorned by insignificant people. 2

18

Ὄφις τις ἕρπων παρὰ πολλῶν συνεπατεῖτο, πορευόμενος δὲ εἰς τὸ τοῦ Ἀπόλλωνος εἰδωλεῖον εἰσελήλυθεν.
Ὁ δὲ Ἀπόλλων εὐθὺς ἔφη πρὸς αὐτόν· "Εἰ ὤλεσάς γε τὸν
πρῶτόν σε συμπατήσαντα, οὐδεὶς ἂν τῶν ἑτέρων κατατε-
τόλμηκέ σου."

2   Οὗτος δηλοῖ ὡς οἱ προλαβόντως σφαλέντες εἴπερ εὐθὺς
σωφρονίζοιντο, οἱ ἕτεροι δι' ἐκείνων κατάφοβοι γίνονται.

19

Λέοντος δορὰν κύνες εὑρόντες διεσπάραττον ταύτην.
Τούτοις δὲ ἀλώπηξ ἰδοῦσα ἔφη· "Εἰ οὗτος ὁ λέων τοῖς ζῶσι
συνῆν, εἴδετε ἂν τοὺς αὐτοῦ ὄνυχας ἰσχυροτέρους τῶν
ὑμετέρων ὀδόντων."

2   Οὗτος δηλοῖ πρὸς τοὺς τῶν ἐνδόξων καταφρονοῦντας,
ὅταν τῆς ἀρχῆς καὶ δόξης ἐκπίπτωσι.

18

A snake was being trampled by many people as he crawled along, and so he made his way to the shrine of Apollo and went inside. Then Apollo immediately said to the snake, "If you had killed the first person to step on you, none of the others would have dared to do it."

This fable shows that if the first people to commit a 2 transgression are immediately taught a lesson, the rest will be intimidated by their example.

19

Some dogs found the hide of a lion and began to tear it apart. A fox saw them and said, "If this lion were still among the living, you would realize that its claws are more powerful than your teeth."

This fable criticizes those who show contempt for im- 2 portant people once the latter have lost their power and fame.

20

Ἔλαφος νόσῳ περιπεσοῦσα ἐπί τινος τόπου πεδινοῦ κατακέκλιτο. Τινὰ δὲ τῶν θηρίων εἰς θέαν αὐτῆς ἐλθόντα τὴν παρακειμένην τῇ ἐλάφῳ νομὴν κατεβοσκήθησαν· εἶτα ἐκείνη τῆς νόσου ἀπαλλαγεῖσα τῇ ἐνδείᾳ δεινῶς κατετρύχετο, καὶ τῇ νομῇ τὸ ζῆν προσαπώλεσεν.

2 Οὗτος δηλοῖ ὡς οἱ περιττοὺς καὶ ἀνονήτους κτώμενοι φίλους ἀντὶ κέρδους ὑπ' αὐτῶν ζημίαν μᾶλλον ὑφίστανται.

21

Ἀνὴρ θηρευτὴς παρερχόμενον κύνα ἰδὼν διηνεκῶς αὐτῷ ψωμοὺς προσεπέρριπτε. Λέγει οὖν πρὸς τὸν ἄνδρα ὁ κύων· "Ἄνθρωπε, ἄπιθι ἐξ ἐμοῦ· ἡ γὰρ πολλή σου εὔνοια μᾶλλόν με τὰ μέγιστα θροεῖ."

2 Οὗτος δηλοῖ ὡς οἱ πολλὰ δῶρά τισι παρεχόμενοι δῆλοί εἰσι τὴν ἀλήθειαν ἀνατρέποντες.

20

A deer fell ill and lay down on a plain. Some of the other animals came to see her, and they grazed on the pasture that surrounded the deer. When the deer recovered from her illness, she suffered terribly from want of food, and so she lost her life along with her pasture.

This fable shows that those with too many useless friends   2
suffer loss at their hands rather than gain.

21

A hunter saw a dog passing by and kept throwing bread to him. Then the dog said to the man, "Get away from me, man, for your great kindness really worries me."

This fable shows that those who give many gifts to other   2
people are in truth acting falsely.

22

Λαγωοί τινες πρὸς ἀετὸν πόλεμον συγκροτοῦντες τὰς ἀλώπεκας εἰς συμμαχίαν προσεκαλοῦντο. Αἱ δὲ πρὸς αὐτοὺς εἶπον· "Ἑτοίμως ἂν εἴχομεν συμμαχεῖν ὑμῖν, εἰ μὴ ᾔδειμεν τίνες τέ ἐστε καὶ τίνι διαμάχεσθε."

2 Οὗτος ἐλέγχει τοὺς τοῖς ἰσχυροτέροις προσκρούοντας καὶ ἑαυτοῖς ἐξ αὐτῶν κίνδυνον ἐπάγοντας.

23

Παῖς τις εἰσελθὼν ἐπί τινα ποταμὸν ἀπολούσασθαι, καὶ μὴ εἰδὼς νήχεσθαι, ἐκινδύνευεν ἀποπνιγῆναι. Καί τινα παρερχόμενον ἄνδρα ἰδὼν εἰς βοήθειαν τοῦτον ἐκάλει. Ὁ δὲ ἄνθρωπος τοῦτον διασῴζων ἐκεῖθεν ἔλεγεν αὐτῷ· "Ἵνα τί, μὴ νήχεσθαι εἰδώς, τῆς τοσαύτης κατατετόλμηκας πλημμύρας;" Ὁ δὲ παῖς αὐτῷ ἔφη· "Τέως νῦν βοήθει μοι, καὶ μετὰ ταῦτα ὀνείδισον."

2 Οὗτος δηλοῖ ὡς ὁ ἐν περιστάσει τινὰ προσονειδίζων ἀκαίρως αὐτοῦ καὶ ἀπρεπῶς καταμέμφεται.

22

Some hares were provoking a war with an eagle and invited the foxes to be their allies. But the foxes said to them, "We would gladly be your allies, if we didn't know who you were and whom you're fighting."

This fable condemns those who bring danger upon them- 2 selves by provoking people who are stronger than they are.

23

A boy went into a river to bathe, but since he did not know how to swim, he came close to drowning. When he saw a man passing by, he called to him for help. As he was rescuing the boy from the river, the man said to him, "If you don't know how to swim, why did you venture into such deep waters?" And the boy answered, "Help me now, and scold me later."

This fable shows that a person who scolds someone in the 2 midst of a crisis is criticizing him inopportunely and inappropriately.

24

Ἀετός τις τῇ ἀλώπεκι φιλιωθεὶς τοὺς αὐτῆς μετὰ ταῦτα καταβέβρωκε σκύμνους. Ἡ δὲ πρὸς αὐτὸν μὴ δυναμένη, τῆς θείας δίκης ἐδέετο κατ' αὐτοῦ. Μιᾷ γοῦν συμβέβηκε θυσίαν τινὰ ἐπὶ βωμοῦ κατακαίεσθαι, ὁ δὲ ἀετὸς καταπτὰς βρῶμα ἐκεῖθεν ζέον ἐξήρπασε καὶ τοῖς ἑαυτοῦ νεοσσοῖς διαδέδωκεν. Οἱ δὲ νεοσσοὶ ἐσθίοντες ὑπὸ τῆς ζέσεως εὐθὺς διεφθάρησαν.

2 Οὗτος δηλοῖ ὡς οἱ τῶν ἀνθρώπων δυνάσται καὶ ἄδικοι, εἰ καὶ παρὰ τῶν ἀδικουμένων μηδὲν πάσχουσιν, ἀλλά γε ταῖς ἐκείνων ἀραῖς θείαν ἀγανάκτησιν ἐπισπῶνται.

25

Ὥρᾳ χειμῶνος ἔχις τις πλησίον ὁδοῦ κατέκειτο καὶ τῇ τοῦ ψύχους σφοδρότητι ἐκινδύνευε διαφθαρῆναι. Ἀνὴρ δέ τις παρερχόμενος καὶ ταύτην ἰδὼν κατῴκτειρε, καὶ ἄρας τῆς γῆς τῷ ἰδίῳ κόλπῳ ἐναπέθετο. Ἡ δὲ ἔχις διαθερμανθεῖσα εὐθὺς καιρίῳ δήγματι τὸν ἄνδρα ἀπέκτεινεν.

2 Οὗτος δηλοῖ ὡς ὁ φύσει κακός, κἂν ἀγαθόν τι παρὰ τινοσοῦν ἐπισπάσαιτο, τῷ εὐεργέτῃ μᾶλλον κακὰ ἀποδίδωσιν.

24

An eagle made friends with a fox, but later he devoured the fox's cubs. Since the fox had no power against the eagle, she prayed for divine justice. Then one day it happened that a sacrifice was being burned upon an altar, and the eagle latched onto the seething-hot food and snatched it away, and then he gave the food to his own nestlings. These nestlings were immediately killed by the heat as they ate the food.

This fable shows that powerful and unjust people, even if 2 they do not suffer at the hands of those they have treated unjustly, still bring upon themselves divine wrath as a result of their victims' prayers.

25

A viper was lying beside a road during wintertime and was on the verge of dying from the severe cold. A man came along, and when he saw the viper, he took pity on it, and so he picked it up off the ground and tucked it away in his pocket. When the viper had warmed up, it immediately killed the man with a bite.

This fable shows that a person who is evil by nature, even 2 if someone does him a good turn, repays his benefactor with evil.

26

Ἀνήρ τις ἰξευτὴς κατέσχε τινὰ πέρδικα καὶ εὐθὺς αὐτὴν καταθῦσαι ἠθέλησεν. Ἡ δὲ πέρδιξ, τῆς ἰδίας ζωῆς ἀντεχομένη, πρὸς τὸν ἰξευτὴν συνέθετο ὡς· "Εἴ με τῶν δεσμῶν ἐλευθερώσεις, πολλοὺς πέρδικας ἐκμειλιξαμένη προσαγάγω σοι." Ὁ δὲ ἰξευτής, τῷ ταύτης λόγῳ μᾶλλον μανείς, ταύτην αὐτίκα ἀνῄρηκεν.

2   Οὗτος δηλοῖ ὡς ὁ ἑτέρῳ παγίδα ἱστῶν αὐτὸς ἐν αὐτῇ ὡς σκαιὸς ἐμπεσεῖται.

27

Ἀνήρ τις ὄρνιν ἐκέκτητο χρυσοῦν ᾠὸν καθ᾽ ἑκάστην αὐτῷ τίκτουσαν. Ὁ δὲ μὴ τῷ καθημερινῷ ἐκείνῳ ἐπαρκούμενος κέρδει, ἀλλ᾽ ἀφρόνως τοῦ πλείονος ὀρεγόμενος, τὴν ὄρνιν κατέθυσεν· ἐδόκει γὰρ ἐν τοῖς ἐγκάτοις αὐτῆς θησαυρῷ τινι ἐντυχεῖν. Καὶ μηδὲν ὅλως ἐφευρὼν καθ᾽ ἑαυτὸν ἔλεξεν ὡς· "Ἐλπίδι θησαυροῦ ἐπερειδόμενος, καὶ τοῦ ἐν χερσὶ κέρδους ἐξέπεσον."

2   Οὗτος δηλοῖ ὡς οἱ πολλοί, τῶν πλειόνων ὀρεγόμενοι, καὶ τῶν ὀλίγων ἐκπίπτουσι.

26

A fowler caught a partridge and wished to kill it immediately. Clinging to her life, the partridge offered a bargain to the fowler: "If you free me from captivity, I'll bring you many more partridges to appease you." But the fowler instead became enraged at the bird's offer and killed her straightaway.

This fable shows that one who sets a trap for another will 2 fall into it himself because of his wickedness.

27

A man once had a hen that laid a golden egg for him every day. He was not satisfied with his daily profit, however, and so, foolishly grasping at more, he killed the hen, for he believed that he would find a treasure inside her. And when he found absolutely nothing, he said to himself, "Because I was relying on the hope of a treasure, I even lost the profit that was already in my hands."

This fable shows that most people, when they grasp at 2 more, lose even the little that they have.

28

Κύων ἁρπάσας βρῶμα ἐκ μακελλίου ᾤχετο φυγὰς ἐκεῖθεν καὶ ἔφθασεν ἐπί τινα ποταμόν. Περαιούμενος δὲ αὐτὸν ὁρᾷ ἐν τοῖς ὕδασι τὴν τοῦ βρώματος σκιὰν πολλῷ οὖσαν, οὗ ἔφερεν, εὐμεγεθεστέραν, καὶ τοῦ στόματος ἀπορρίψας τὸ βρῶμα ἐπὶ τὴν ὁραθεῖσαν αὐτοῦ σκιὰν κατηπείγετο. Τῆς δὲ ἀφανοῦς γενομένης, στραφεὶς ὁ κύων τὸ ἀπορριφθὲν ἆραι, οὐδὲν ἐφεῦρε τὸ σύνολον· καὶ γὰρ ἐκεῖνο παρά τινος καταπτάντος κόρακος εὐθὺς ἡρπάγη καὶ κατεβρώθη. Εἶτα ὁ κύων ἑαυτὸν ἐταλάνιζε, "Τί ἄρα πέπονθα;" λέγων, "Ὅτι ὃ εἶχον ἀφρόνως καταλιπὼν ἐφ᾽ ἕτερον ἀφανὲς ἠπειγόμην, κἀκείνου ἀποτυχὼν καὶ τοῦ προτέρου ἐξέπεσον."

2   Οὗτος δηλοῖ περὶ τῶν ἀκορέστως ἐχόντων καὶ τῶν περιττῶν ὀρεγομένων.

29

Ὄνος καὶ ἵππος ὑπῆρχον ἀνθρώπῳ τινί, καὶ ἕκαστος αὐτῶν ἰδίαν ὑπηρεσίαν ἐπλήρου. Ἀλλ᾽ ὁ μὲν ἵππος ἀνέσεως πολλῆς παραπολαύων δαψιλῶς ἐτρέφετο· χαίτην τε καὶ πλοκάμους ὑπὸ τῶν ἱπποκόμων ἐκαλλωπίζετο καὶ ὁσημέραι τοῖς ὕδασιν ἀπελούετο. Ὁ δὲ ὄνος διόλου ἀχθοφορῶν

28

A dog snatched some meat from a butcher's shop and, as he was making his escape, arrived at a river. While he was crossing, he saw that the reflection of the meat in the water was much larger than what he was carrying. And so, he threw away the meat that was in his mouth and chased after the reflection he had seen. When it disappeared, the dog turned around to pick up what he had thrown away, but he could not find it anywhere, for it had been immediately snatched up and devoured by a crow that had swooped down. Then the dog blamed himself: "What happened to me? I foolishly threw away what I had in order to chase after an illusion and, when I failed to get that, I also lost what I had before."

This fable reveals the truth about those who are insati- 2
able and grasp at too much.

29

A man had an ass and a horse, and each animal performed its own particular service. The horse received many treats and was fed lavishly, and the grooms made him beautiful by braiding his mane and washed him every day with water. But the ass was always loaded down and exhausted by the weight

τῷ τῶν γόμων βάρει κατετρύχετο. Μιᾷ γοῦν ὁ τοῦ ἵππου κύριος ἐπιβὰς αὐτοῦ ἐπί τινα πόλεμον ἀπῄει, καὶ μάχης συγκροτηθείσης ὁ ἵππος πληγεὶς ἀνῃρέθη. Ἰδὼν δὲ τὴν αὐτοῦ ἀπώλειαν ὁ ὄνος ἑαυτὸν μᾶλλον τῆς πολυμόχθου ἐμακάριζεν ὑπηρεσίας.

2   Οὗτος δηλοῖ ὡς ὁ πενιχρὸς βίος ἀνεπίφθονος τυγχάνων πολλῷ μᾶλλον τοῦ πλούτου, ὡς κινδυνώδους, προτιμότερος.

30

Ὄναγρος ὄνον ἰδὼν βαρὺν γόμον ἐπαγόμενον, καὶ τὴν δουλείαν αὐτῷ ἐπονειδίζων, ἔλεγεν· "Εὐτυχὴς ὄντως ἐγώ, ὅτι ζῶν ἐλευθέρως καὶ διάγων ἀκόπως αὐτοσχέδιον καὶ τὴν νομὴν ἐν τοῖς ὄρεσι κέκτημαι· σὺ δὲ δι' ἄλλου τρέφῃ, καὶ δουλείαις καὶ πληγαῖς καθυποβάλλῃ διηνεκῶς." Συνέβη γοῦν αὐθωρὸν λέοντά τινα φανῆναι καὶ τῷ μὲν ὄνῳ μὴ προσπελάσαι, ὡς συνόντος αὐτῷ τοῦ ὀνηλάτου, τῷ δὲ ὀνάγρῳ, μεμονωμένῳ τυγχάνοντι, σφοδρῶς ἐπελθεῖν καὶ αὐτὸν θέσθαι κατάβρωμα.

2   Οὗτος δηλοῖ ὡς οἱ ἀνυπότακτοι καὶ σκληροτράχηλοι, τῇ αὐτοβουλίᾳ φερόμενοι καὶ βοηθείας τινὸς μὴ δεόμενοι, αὐθωρὸν πτῶμα γίνονται.

of his burden. Then one day the horse's master mounted him and rode him off to war, and when battle was joined, the horse was struck and killed. When the ass saw that the horse had been killed, he considered himself more blessed on account of his own toilsome service.

This fable shows that the impoverished life, though it is unenviable, is preferable by far to the wealthy life, which is dangerous. 2

30

A wild ass saw a domesticated ass carrying a heavy burden, and he scolded the ass for his servility: "I am truly fortunate, because I live freely, enjoy an easy life, and have whatever pasture I choose in the mountains. But you are fed by someone else, and you are continuously subjected to servitude and beatings." It happened that a lion appeared at that very moment, and while he did not approach the domesticated ass because his driver was there with him, he fiercely attacked the wild ass, who was standing alone, and made a meal out of him.

This fable shows that insubordinate and stubborn people, swept away by their obstinance and refusal to ask anyone for help, become a corpse in an instant. 2

31

Συκῆ τις, ὥρᾳ χειμῶνος τὰ ἑαυτῆς ἀποβαλοῦσα φύλλα, ὑπό τινος ἐλαίας πλησιαζούσης τὴν γύμνωσιν ὠνειδίζετο, λεγούσης ὡς· "Ἐγὼ καὶ χειμῶνος καὶ θέρους τοῖς φύλλοις μου κεκαλλώπισμαι καὶ ἀείφυλλος πέφυκα, σὺ δὲ μόνῳ τῷ θέρει πρόσκαιρον ἔχεις τὸ κάλλος." Οὕτω δὲ αὐτῆς καυχωμένης, κεραυνὸς ἄφνω θεόθεν κατηνέχθη καὶ ταύτην κατέφλεξε· τῆς δὲ συκῆς τὸ παράπαν οὐχ ἥψατο.

2   Οὕτως οἱ τῷ πλούτῳ καὶ τῇ τύχῃ ἐγκαυχώμενοι ἐξαίσιον πτῶμα ὑφίστανται.

32

Ἀνήρ τις κηπουρόν τινα θεασάμενος τῶν λαχάνων ἀρδείαν ποιούμενον ἔφη πρὸς αὐτόν· "Πῶς τὰ μὲν ἄγρια φυτά, μήτε φυτευόμενα μήτε ἐργαζόμενα, ὡραῖα πεφύκασι, τὰ δὲ τῆς ὑμῶν φυτηκομίας πολλάκις ξηραίνεται;" Ὁ δὲ κηπουρὸς ἀντέφησεν ὡς· "Τὰ ἄγρια τῶν φυτῶν μόνῃ τῇ θείᾳ προνοίᾳ ἐφορᾶται, τὰ δὲ ἡμέτερα ὑπὸ χειρὸς ἀνθρωπίνης ἐπιμελεῖται."

2   Οὗτος δηλοῖ ὡς κρείττων ἡ τῶν μητέρων ἀνατροφὴ πέφυκε τῆς τῶν μητρυιῶν ἐπιμελείας.

31

When a fig tree shed her leaves in wintertime, a nearby olive tree chided her for her nakedness: "I am adorned with beautiful leaves in both winter and summer, and I am naturally evergreen, but you possess a temporary beauty only in the summer." While the olive tree was boasting in this way, a thunderbolt from heaven suddenly struck her and burned her up, but did not touch the fig tree at all.

Thus those who boast of their wealth and fortune suffer a 2 sudden fall.

32

A man saw a gardener watering his vegetables and said to him, "How do wild plants, which are neither sown nor tended, naturally ripen in their proper season, while the plants under your care often wither?" The gardener replied, "Wild plants are watched over by divine providence alone, while our plants are cared for by human hands."

Thus the fable shows that a mother's rearing is naturally 2 better than a stepmother's care.

33

Κύων ἐν μακελλίῳ εἰσελθὼν καρδίας βρῶμα ἐκεῖθεν ἀφήρπασεν. Ὁ δέ γε μακελλεὺς ἐπιστραφεὶς ἔλεγεν αὐτῷ· "Οὐ καρδίαν ἥρπασας, ἀλλὰ καρδίαν ἐνέθου μοι· εἰ γὰρ αὖθις ἐνταῦθα εἰσέλθῃς, ἐγώ σοι τὰ τῆς ἁρπαγῆς ἐπιδείξω ἐπίχειρα."

2 Οὗτος δηλοῖ ὡς ἐν τῷ παθεῖν τις ἐπισπᾶται τὸ μαθεῖν καὶ προσεκτικῶς ἔχειν.

34

Κύων κηπουροῦ τινος εἰς φρέαρ ἐμπέπτωκεν. Ὁ δὲ κηπουρὸς κατελθὼν αὐτὸν ἐκεῖθεν ἀνελκύσαι, δεινῶς ὑπ᾽ αὐτοῦ ἐδήχθη, δόξαντος μᾶλλον τὸν ἄνδρα βούλεσθαι αὐτὸν ἐπὶ πλέον καταβυθίσαι τῷ ὕδατι. Ὁ δὲ κηπουρὸς ὑπὸ τοῦ κυνὸς δηχθείς, "Δικαίως," ἔφη, "πέπονθα, ὅτι σὲ τοῦ φρέατος ἐκβαλεῖν ἐσπουδακὼς χαλεπῶς μᾶλλον ὑπὸ σοῦ τετραυμάτισμαι."

2 Ὁ μῦθος οὗτος τοὺς ἀχαρίστους καὶ ἀγνώμονας ἐλέγχει.

33

A dog entered a butcher's shop and stole a heart to eat. The butcher turned around and said, "You haven't stolen a heart; no, you've given me heart. For if you come in here again, I'll show you the wages of theft."

This fable shows that through suffering one gains knowl- 2
edge and attentiveness.

34

A gardener's dog fell into a well. The gardener went down to pull him out, but the dog bit him badly because he thought that the man wanted to push him down deeper into the water instead. After he was bitten by the dog, the gardener said, "I've gotten what I deserve because, although I hurried to get you out of the well, I've been seriously wounded by you instead."

This fable condemns those who are thankless and un- 2
grateful.

35

Ἀνδρός τινος ἡ γαστὴρ τοῖς ἑαυτοῦ ποσὶ περὶ ἰσχύος διεφέρετο. Οἱ μέντοι πόδες ἔλεγον τῇ γαστρὶ ὡς· "Ἡμεῖς σοῦ ἐσμεν ἰσχυρότεροι, ἅτε δὴ καὶ διαβαστῶντές σε." Ἡ δὲ γαστὴρ τοῖς ποσὶν ἀντέφησεν ὡς· "Εἰ μὴ ἐγὼ τὰς βρώσεις ἐδεχόμην, ὑμεῖς ἀδυνάτως ὅλως στῆναι εἴχετε ἄν."

2 Οὗτος δηλοῖ ὡς καὶ ἅπαν στράτευμα πρὸς τὴν μάχην ἀδόκιμον γίνεται, εἰ μὴ πρότερον ὑπὸ τοῦ στρατηλάτου γυμνάζοιτο καὶ παραθαρρύνοιτο.

36

Νυκτερίς, κέπφος καὶ βάτος πρὸς ἀλλήλους κοινωνίαν ἔθεντο, τοῦ ἐπί τινα δῆθεν ἐμπορίαν ἀπελθεῖν. Καὶ ἡ μὲν χρυσόν, ὁ δὲ χαλκόν, ἡ δὲ ὑφάσματα δανειακῶς ἐξελάβοντο καὶ ἐν πλοίῳ ἀποθέμενοι τοῦ πλοὸς εὐθὺς εἴχοντο. Ἄφνω δὲ ζάλη καὶ καταιγὶς διαπνεύσασα εἰς κλύδωνα μέγιστον τὸ πέλαγος ἦρε, καὶ τὸ σκάφος διασπαράξαν τὰ ἐν αὐτῷ πάντα τῷ βυθῷ παραδίδωσιν. Ἐξ ἐκείνου δὲ ἡ μὲν νυκτερίς, τοὺς δανειστὰς πτοουμένη καὶ δεδιῶσα καὶ ἑαυτὴν ὑποστέλλουσα, μόνῃ τῇ νυκτὶ ἐξέρχεται· ὁ δὲ κέπφος ἐπὶ τῆς θαλάσσης τὰς διατριβὰς ἔχει, ἀναζητῶν τὸν χαλκόν· ἡ δὲ βάτος τοῖς ἱματισμοῖς τῶν παραπορευομένων συμπλέκεται, τὰ ὑφάσματα εὑρεῖν δι' ὅλου σπουδάζουσα.

35

A man's stomach was quarreling with his feet about their strength. The feet were saying to the stomach, "We're stronger than you are, given that we carry you around." The stomach replied to the feet, "If I didn't take in food, you wouldn't be able to stand at all."

This fable shows that every army is worthless for battle,   2 unless it is first trained and encouraged by its commander.

36

A bat, a petrel, and a bramble bush made a partnership with each other to sell merchandise abroad. The bat borrowed gold, the petrel bronze, and the bramble bush cloth, and after stowing it all on board a ship they immediately began their voyage. Suddenly a violent storm blew up and swelled the sea into an enormous wave, which tore the ship to pieces and sent all its cargo into the deep. Since that time, the bat has been scared and afraid of lenders and keeps to itself, flying out only at night. The petrel spends his time at sea, searching for his bronze. And the bramble bush entangles herself in the clothing of passersby, always eager to find her own cloth.

2   Οὗτος ὁ μῦθος δηλοῖ ὡς τῶν ἀνθρώπων ἕκαστον χρή, μετὰ τὴν ἔκβασιν τῶν ἐπικινδύνων πράξεων, προσεκτικῶς ἔχειν, ὥστε μὴ αὖθις τοῖς ἐκ τούτων ὁμοίοις κακοῖς περιπετεῖς γίνεσθαι.

37

Λέων γηράσας τις καὶ ἀτονήσας, καὶ ἑαυτὸν μὴ δυνάμενος διατρέφειν, ἐπειρᾶτο μηχανικῶς διαζῆν. Νοσεῖν οὖν προσποιούμενος κατέκλινεν ἑαυτὸν ἔν τινι σπηλαίῳ· εἶτα τῶν ἄλλων θηρίων εἰς ἐπίσκεψιν αὐτοῦ παραγινομένων, εὐθὺς ἕκαστον αὐτῶν ἁρπάζων κατήσθιε. Γνοῦσα δὲ ἡ ἀλώπηξ τὴν αὐτοῦ πανουργίαν οὐκ ἤθελε πρὸς αὐτὸν ἀνελθεῖν, ἀλλὰ μακρόθεν ἑστῶσα ἐπηρώτα τὸν λέοντα ὅπως δῆθεν τὰ κατ᾽ αὐτὸν ἔχει. Ὁ δὲ πρὸς αὐτὴν ἔλεγε· "Τίνος χάριν οὐκ εἰσέρχῃ πρός με;" Ἡ δὲ ἀλώπηξ ἀντέφησεν ὡς· "Πολλῶν ἴχνη ἐνταῦθα ἑώρακα εἰσελθόντων μέν, μὴ ἐξελθόντων δέ."

2   Οὗτος δηλοῖ ὡς καὶ τοὺς ἀνθρώπους ὑφορᾶσθαι δεῖ τὰ τῶν πρακτέων ἐπικίνδυνα καὶ ἐξ αὐτῶν ἀποδιδράσκειν, ἀσφαλίζεσθαι δὲ καὶ ἀπὸ τῶν δόλῳ καὶ ὑποκρίσει φιλίας πειρωμένων ἑταίρους λυμαίνεσθαι.

This fable shows that everybody ought to be cautious in 2
the aftermath of dangerous endeavors, so that they may not
fall victim again to similar misfortunes.

37

A lion that grew old, tired, and unable to feed himself
was trying to stay alive by trickery. And so, feigning illness,
he lay down in a cave. Then, when the other animals came
by to visit, he would immediately grab each one and gobble
it up. A fox recognized the lion's wickedness and refused to
come close to him, but instead stood far off and asked the
lion how he was doing. The lion said to her, "Why won't you
approach me?" And the fox replied, "I've seen the footprints
of many animals going in, but none coming out."

This fable shows that people must be wary of actions that 2
are dangerous and avoid them, and that they must protect
themselves against those who attempt to harm companions
through deceit and the pretense of friendship.

38

Κύων καταδιώκων λύκον ἐφρυάττετο τῇ τε τῶν ποδῶν ταχυτῆτι καὶ τῇ ἰδίᾳ ἰσχύϊ, καὶ ἐδόκει φεύγειν τὸν λύκον δι᾽ οἰκείαν δῆθεν ἀσθένειαν. Στραφεὶς οὖν ὁ λύκος ἔφησε πρὸς τὸν κύνα· "Οὐ σὲ δέδοικα, ἀλλὰ τὴν τοῦ σοῦ δεσπότου καταδρομήν."

2   Οὗτος δηλοῖ ὡς οὐ δεῖ τινα ἐγκαυχᾶσθαι τῇ τῶν ἑτέρων γενναιότητι.

39

Νεανίσκος τις ἐν τοῖς ἐξωτάτοις καὶ ἐρημικωτάτοις τόποις ἀκρίδας ἠπείγετο κατασχεῖν, καὶ ἰδὼν μέσον αὐτῶν σκορπίον ἐδόκει κἀκεῖνον ἀκρίδα ὄντως τυγχάνειν. Καὶ δὴ τὴν χεῖρα ἐκτείνας ἐξᾶραι αὐτὸν τῆς γῆς ἔμελλεν. Ὁ δὲ σκορπίος τὸ αὐτοῦ κέντρον πρὸς τὸ νύξαι τὸν νέον ἰθύνας, ἔφη πρὸς αὐτὸν ὡς· "Εἰ ὅλως τετόλμηκάς μου καθάψασθαι, παρεσκεύασα ἄν σε ἀπολῦσαι καὶ ἃς κατέσχες ἀκρίδας."

2   Οὗτος δηλοῖ ὡς οὐ χρὴ καὶ τοῖς σκαιοῖς ἀνδράσι καὶ τοῖς ἀγαθοῖς ἐπίσης ἐντυγχάνειν, ἀλλ᾽ ἑκάστῳ πρὸς τὴν ἰδίαν γνώμην δεόντως προσομιλεῖν.

38

A dog that was chasing down a wolf was feeling arrogant because of the swiftness of his feet and his own strength, and he thought the wolf was fleeing through its own weakness. Then the wolf turned around and said to the dog, "I'm not afraid of you, but the attack of your master."

This fable shows that one must not pride oneself on 2 someone else's bravery.

39

A young man was trying hard to catch grasshoppers in a very remote and deserted place. When he saw a scorpion in their midst, he thought that it was actually a grasshopper, too, and so he stretched out his hand and was about to pick it up from the ground. But the scorpion raised its stinger to sting the youth and said to him, "If you even dare to touch me, I'll make you lose the grasshoppers that you've caught as well."

This fable shows that one ought not to associate with 2 wicked men and good men in the same way, but rather one should deal with each as his character demands.

40

Ταῦρος λέοντά τινα ἀποδιδράσκων ἔν τινι σπηλαίῳ τὴν καταφυγὴν ἔθετο. Ἐν αὐτῷ δὲ ἔτυχεν ἀγρίας αἶγας τυγχάνειν, αἳ δὴ καὶ τὸν ταῦρον εὐθὺς ἐκεράτιζον. Ὁ δὲ πρὸς αὐτὰς ἔλεγεν ὡς· "Οὐχ ὑμᾶς δέδοικα, ἀλλὰ τὸν τοῦ σπηλαίου ἔξωθεν ἑστηκότα."

2 Οὗτος δηλοῖ ὡς τοῖς ἐν δυσπραγίαις ὑπὸ δυναστῶν περιπίπτουσι πάντες οἱ ἐντυγχάνοντες μισητῶς ἐπεμβαίνουσιν.

41

Ἀνήρ τις, ἑωρακὼς Αἰθίοπά τινα Ἰνδὸν λουόμενον ἔν τινι ποταμῷ, ἔφη πρὸς αὐτόν· "Μὴ συνταράσσῃς καὶ θολοποιῇς τὸ ὕδωρ· οὐδέποτε γὰρ λευκὸς γενήσῃ τῷ σώματι."

2 Οὗτος δηλοῖ ὡς οὐδὲν τῶν φυσικῶν πραγμάτων τοῖς φυσικοῖς μεταβάλλεται.

40

A bull was fleeing from a lion and took refuge in a cave, where there happened to be some wild goats. They immediately started butting the bull, who said to them, "I'm not afraid of you, but the one standing outside the cave."

This fable shows that whenever people encounter someone who has run afoul of those in charge, they attack him with hatred. 2

41

When a man saw a black-skinned Indian washing himself in a river, he said to him, "Don't stir up the water and make it muddy, since you'll never make your body white."

This fable shows that nothing that occurs naturally can be changed by natural means. 2

42

Γυνή τις χήρα ὄρνιν ἐκέκτητο ἓν ᾠὸν αὐτῇ καθ᾽ ἑκάστην ἡμέραν τίκτουσαν, ἣν καὶ δαψιλῶς διέτρεφεν ἡ γυνή, δοκοῦσα ὡς τοῖς πλείοσι σιτίοις δύο ἔσται γεννῶσα ᾠά. Ἡ δὲ ὄρνις ὑπὸ τῆς πλησμονῆς ἐμβριθὴς γενομένη οὐδὲ τὸ ἓν ᾠὸν γεννᾶν, ὡς τὸ πρότερον, ἠδύνατο.

2   Οὗτος δηλοῖ ὡς οἱ τῶν πλειόνων ὀρεγόμενοι καὶ τῶν ἐν χερσὶν ὀλίγων στερίσκονται.

43

Μύρμηξ τις ὥρᾳ χειμῶνος ὃν θέρους συνήγαγε σῖτον καθ᾽ ἑαυτὸν ἤσθιεν. Ὁ δὲ τέττιξ προσελθὼν αὐτῷ ᾐτεῖτο μεταδοθῆναι αὐτῷ ἐκ τῶν αὐτοῦ σιτίων. Ὁ δὲ μύρμηξ ἔφη πρὸς αὐτόν· "Καὶ τί ἄρα πράττων διετέλεις ἐφ᾽ ὅλῳ τῷ τοῦ θέρους καιρῷ, ὅτι μὴ συνέλεξας σῖτον ἑαυτῷ εἰς διατροφήν;" Ὁ δὲ τέττιξ ἀντέφησεν αὐτῷ ὡς· "Τῷ μελῳδεῖν ἀπασχολούμενος τῆς συλλογῆς ἐκωλυόμην." Τῇ γοῦν τοιαύτῃ τοῦ τέττιγος ἀποκρίσει ὁ μύρμηξ ἐπιγελάσας, τὸν ἑαυτοῦ σῖτον τοῖς ἐνδοτέροις τῆς γῆς μυχοῖς ἐναπέκρυψε καὶ πρὸς αὐτὸν ἀπεφθέγξατο ὡς· "Ἐπεὶ τότε ματαίως ἐμελῴδεις, νυνὶ λοιπὸν ὀρχήσασθαι θέλησον."

2   Οὗτος παρίστησι τοὺς ὀκνηρούς τε καὶ ἀμελεῖς, καὶ τοὺς ἐν ματαιοπραγίαις διάγοντας κἀντεῦθεν ὑστερουμένους.

42

A widowed woman had a hen that laid one egg for her each day. The woman fed the hen excessively, believing that with more food it would lay two eggs. But the hen became fat from overfeeding and was unable to lay even the one egg, as before.

This fable shows that those who grasp for more are deprived even of the little that they already possess. 2

43

An ant was by himself in wintertime, eating the food that he had gathered during the summer. A cicada approached him and asked him to share some of his food. The ant said to him, "What were you doing for the entire summer, that you didn't gather food to feed yourself?" The cicada replied, "I was busy singing, which prevented me from gathering." Laughing at the cicada's reply, the ant concealed his food in the innermost recesses of the earth and replied to him, "Since you sang in vain then, go ahead and dance now."

This fable depicts those who are lazy and negligent, and 2 who waste their time in fruitless pursuits and find themselves in need because of it.

44

Αἰγός τινος ἐπὶ πέτρας ὑψηλῆς νεμομένης, λύκος ἐπιστὰς κάτωθεν ἐπειρᾶτο αὐτὴν κατασχεῖν καὶ βεβρωκέναι· μὴ δυνάμενος δὲ ὅλως ἐπαναβῆναι τῇ πέτρᾳ, ἑστὼς κάτωθεν πρὸς τὴν αἶγα ἔφησεν· "Ὦ ταλαίπωρε, ἵνα τί καταλιποῦσα τοὺς πεδινοὺς τόπους καὶ τοὺς λειμῶνας ἐπὶ τῆς πέτρας ταύτης τὴν νομὴν πεποίησαι; Ἢ πάντως ἵν' ἐντεῦθεν κινδυνεύσῃς διαφθαρῆναι;" Ἡ δὲ πρὸς τὸν λύκον ἀπεκρίνατο· "Οἶδα ὡς πολλάκις ἐμοῦ ἕνεκεν ἀργὸς διετέλεσας, καὶ δοκεῖς κατενεγκεῖν με τῆς πέτρας καὶ σεαυτῷ θέσθαι κατάβρωμα."

2   Οὗτος δηλοῖ ὡς πολλοὶ τῶν ἀνθρώπων βουλὴν ἑτέροις παρέχουσι τὴν ἐκείνοις μὲν ὀλεθρίαν, ἑαυτοῖς δὲ ἐπικερδῆ καὶ ὠφέλιμον.

45

Ἀνήρ τις ἐπωχεῖτο ἵππῳ τινὶ θηλείᾳ ἐγκύῳ οὔσῃ, καὶ ὁδοιποροῦντος αὐτοῦ ἡ ἵππος πῶλον ἀπέτεκεν. Ὁ δὲ πῶλος κατόπιν αὐτῆς εὐθὺς πορευόμενος καὶ ταχέως ἰλιγγιάσας πρὸς τὸν τῆς ἰδίας μητρὸς ἐπιβάτην ἔλεγεν· "Ἰδού, ὁρᾷς με βραχύτατον καὶ πρὸς πορείαν ἀδύνατον· γίνωσκε δέ, ὡς εἰ ἐνταῦθά με καταλίπῃς, αὐθωρὸν διαφθείρομαι, εἰ δ' ἐντεῦθεν ἄρῃς με καὶ ἀπαγάγῃς ἐν οἴκῳ καὶ ἀνατραφῆναι

44

A goat was grazing on a high cliff when a wolf came upon her from below and tried to catch and eat her. Because there was no way he could climb up the cliff, he stood below and said to the goat, "You miserable goat, why have you left the plains and meadows and made this cliff your pasture? Just to risk being killed by falling down from there?" The goat answered him, "I know that you've often been too slow to catch me, and now you think that you can bring me down from this cliff and make me your dinner."

This fable shows that many people offer advice that is destructive to others, but profitable and beneficial to themselves. 2

45

A man was riding on a mare that was pregnant, and in the course of his journey the mare gave birth to a colt. This colt immediately began walking behind them, but it quickly felt faint and so it said to the man riding his mother, "Look, you see that I'm very small and unable to travel. You should realize that if you leave me here, I'll perish immediately, but if

ποιήσῃς, οὕτως αὐξυνθεὶς ἐν ὑστέρῳ ἐποχεῖσθαί μοι ποιήσω σε."

2 Οὗτος δηλοῖ ὡς ἐκείνους εὐεργετεῖν χρή, ὑπὲρ ὧν καὶ ἡ ἀντάμειψις τῆς εὐποιΐας ἐλπίζεται.

46

Ἀνήρ τις ἁλιεὺς παρὰ τὴν θάλασσαν ἄγραν ἰχθύων ἐποίει. Πίθηξ δέ τις αὐτὸν κατιδὼν ἐκμιμήσασθαι ἠβουλήθη. Τοῦ δὲ ἀνδρὸς ἀποβάντος ἔν τινι σπηλαίῳ ἐπὶ τῷ διαναπαύσασθαι, τὸ δὲ δίκτυον παρὰ τὴν ἠϊόνα καταλιπόντος, ἐλθὼν ὁ πίθηξ καὶ τοῦ δικτύου λαβόμενος ἀγρεῦσαι δῆθεν δι᾽ αὐτοῦ ἐπεχείρει. Ἀγνώστως δὲ τῇ τέχνῃ καὶ ἀσυντάκτως χρώμενος, καὶ τῷ δικτύῳ περισχεθείς, ἐπὶ τῆς θαλάσσης εὐθὺς πέπτωκε καὶ ἀπεπνίγη. Ὁ δὲ ἁλιεὺς καταλαβὼν αὐτὸν ἤδη ἀποπνιγέντα ἔφη· "Ὦ ἄθλιε, ὤλεσέ σε ἡ ἀφροσύνη σου καὶ ἡ ματαία ἐπίνοια."

2 Οὗτος δηλοῖ ὡς οἱ τὰ ὑπὲρ αὐτοὺς μιμεῖσθαι πειρώμενοι, ἑαυτοῖς ἐντεῦθεν ἐπάγουσι κίνδυνον.

you pick me up, take me home, and raise me, later, when I'm grown, I'll let you ride me."

This fable shows that one ought to be kind to those who   2
they hope will repay their good deed.

46

A fisherman was fishing by the sea. A monkey saw him and wanted to imitate him. When the man went off into a cave to rest and left his net on the shore, the monkey came and grabbed the net to try his hand at fishing. But he was ignorant and disorganized in the art of fishing, and so he became entangled in the net, fell straight into the sea, and drowned. The fisherman got hold of the monkey after he had already drowned and said, "You wretched monkey, your folly and your foolish thinking have destroyed you."

This fable shows that those who try to imitate things that   2
are beyond them bring danger on themselves.

47

Κ ώνωψ τις ἐλθὼν ἐπὶ κέρατος ἔστη ταύρου τινός, πειρώμενος δῆθεν αὐτῷ ἄχθος ἐμποιῆσαί τι. Τοῦ δὲ ταύρου
παρ᾽ οὐδὲν αὐτὸν λογιζομένου, βουλόμενος ὁ κώνωψ ἐξ
αὐτοῦ ἀποπτῆναι, καὶ βιάζων αὐτόν, ἔφη ὡς· "Εἴπερ
ἐπαχθής σοι πέφυκα, πετασθήσομαι ἀπὸ σοῦ." Καὶ ὁ ταῦρος ἔφη τῷ κώνωπι· "Οὔτε ἐλθόντος σοῦ ᾐσθόμην, οὔτε
ὑποχωροῦντά σε γνώσομαι."

2 Οὗτος δηλοῖ ὡς καὶ ἄνθρωποί τινες, εὐτελεῖς ἅμα καὶ
ἄφρονες προδήλως τυγχάνοντες, δοκοῦσι καθ᾽ ἑαυτοὺς
τῶν ἐν τιμῇ τε καὶ συνέσει διαπρεπόντων ὑπερέχειν.

48

Ἀ νήρ τις τῶν εὐλαβῶν τυγχάνων τάχα καὶ τοῖς πρα-
κτέοις σεμνός, ἐπὶ χρόνον ἱκανὸν εὐμαρῶς τοῖς ἰδίοις παισὶ
συμβιοτεύων, μετὰ ταῦτα ἐνδείᾳ περιπίπτει ἐσχάτῃ. Καὶ
τὴν ψυχὴν καιρίως ἀλγῶν ἐβλασφήμει τὸ θεῖον καὶ ἑαυτὸν
ἀνελεῖν ἠναγκάζετο. Λαβὼν γοῦν σπάθην ἐπί τινα τῶν
ἐρημικῶν τόπων ἔξήει, θανεῖν μᾶλλον ἑλόμενος ἤπερ ζῆν
κακῶς. Καὶ πορευόμενος λάκκον τινὰ βαθύτατον ἔτυχεν
εὑρηκώς, ἐν ᾧ χρυσίον οὐκ ὀλίγον παρά τινος τῶν γιγαν-
τιαίων ἀνδρῶν ἀπετέθειτο, ᾧ Κύκλωψ ἦν τὸ ὄνομα. Ἰδὼν
δὲ ὁ δῆθεν εὐλαβὴς ἀνὴρ τὸ χρυσίον φόβου εὐθὺς καὶ

47

A mosquito came along and landed upon the horn of a bull in an attempt to make himself a burden to the animal. But when the bull considered the insect to be nothing, the mosquito wished to fly off and tried to pressure the bull: "If I'm burdensome to you, I'll fly away." The bull responded, "I didn't feel your arrival, and I won't notice your departure either."

This fable shows that some people, even though they are obviously insignificant and foolish, believe in their own minds that they excel others who are distinguished in honor and intelligence. 2

48

There once was a man who was pious and seemingly respected for his deeds, and for a long time he lived an easy life together with his children. Later, however, he fell into extreme poverty. He felt a mortal pain in his soul, and so he began to blaspheme God and felt compelled to take his own life. Taking up a sword, then, he went off to a deserted place, having decided to die rather than go on living in misery. As he was making his way, he came across a very deep cistern, in which he discovered an enormous stash of gold, which had been stored away by one of the gigantic men who was called a Cyclops. When the supposedly pious man saw the gold, he

χαρᾶς ἀνάπλεως γίνεται, καὶ ῥίπτει μὲν τῆς χειρὸς τὸ
ξίφος, αἴρει δὲ τὸ χρυσίον ἐκεῖθεν, καὶ ἄσμενος ἐπὶ τὴν
οἰκίαν καὶ τοὺς παῖδας αὐτοῦ ἐπανέρχεται. Εἶτα ὁ Κύκλωψ
ἐπὶ τὸν λάκκον ἐλθὼν καὶ τὸ μὲν χρυσίον μὴ εὑρηκώς,
ἀντ' αὐτοῦ δὲ κείμενον ἐκεῖσε τὸ ξίφος ἑωρακώς, αὐτίκα
τοῦτο σπασάμενος ἑαυτὸν διεχειρίσατο.

2   Ὁ λόγος οὗτος δηλοῖ ὡς τοῖς σκαιοῖς ἀνδράσιν ἀκο-
λούθως τὰ κακὰ ἐπισυμβαίνει, τοῖς δὲ ἀγαθοῖς καὶ εὐλαβέσι
τὰ ἀγαθὰ ταμιεύεται.

49

Ἀνήρ τις θηρευτής, λαγωὸν κατασχὼν καὶ τοῦτον
ἐπιφερόμενος, τῆς ὁδοιπορίας εἴχετο. Καί τινι προσυπαν-
τηθεὶς ἐφίππῳ ἀνδρί, ἐζητεῖτο παρ' αὐτοῦ τὸν λαγωὸν ἐν
προσχήματι ἀπεμπολήσεως. Λαβὼν οὖν ὁ ἱππεὺς τὸν λαγωὸν ἀπὸ τοῦ θηρευτοῦ, εὐθὺς δρομαῖος ᾤχετο. Ὁ δὲ
θηρευτὴς κατόπιν αὐτοῦ τρέχων φθάσαι αὐτὸν δῆθεν
ἐδόκει· τοῦ δὲ ἱππέως ἐκ πολλοῦ τοῦ διαστήματος μακρὰν
ἐκείνου ἀπέχοντος, ὁ θηρευτὴς καὶ ἄκων φωνεῖ πρὸς αὐτὸν καί φησιν· "Ἄπελθε λοιπόν· ἐγὼ γὰρ ἤδη τὸν λαγωὸν
ἐδωρησάμην σοι."

2   Οὗτος δηλοῖ ὡς πολλοὶ ἀκουσίως τὰ ἴδια ἀφαιρούμενοι
προσποιοῦνται δῆθεν ἑκοντὶ ταῦτα δωρεῖσθαι.

was immediately filled with fear as well as joy, and he cast the sword from his hand, lifted the gold out of there, and joyfully returned to his home and children. Then the Cyclops came to the cistern. He found no gold, but lying there in its place he saw the sword. And straightaway he drew it and killed himself.

This fable shows that evils befall wicked men as a matter 2 of course, while good things are reserved for those who are good and pious.

49

A hunter had caught a hare and was carrying it as he was going on his way. He met a man on horseback, who asked him for the hare under the pretense of buying it. Then, when the horseman had gotten the hare from the hunter, he set off immediately at full gallop. The hunter ran behind him, supposing that he could catch him. But when the horseman was far ahead of him at a very great distance, the hunter grudgingly yelled to him, "Go, then! For I just gave you the hare as a present."

This fable shows that many people, when they have been 2 deprived of their personal property against their will, pretend to have willingly given it away.

50

Κύων λαγωοῦ κατατρέχων καὶ τοῦτον καταλαβών, ποτὲ μὲν αὐτὸν ἔδακνε, ποτὲ δὲ τὸ ἐντεῦθεν ἀπορρέον αὐτοῦ αἷμα ἀνέλειχεν. Ὁ δὲ λαγωὸς ἐδόκει τὸν κύνα μᾶλλον καταφιλεῖν αὐτόν, καὶ ὑπολαβὼν ἔφη πρὸς αὐτόν· "Ἢ ὡς προσφιλὴς περιπτύσσου με, ἢ ὡς ἐχθρὸς καὶ πολέμιος κατάδακνε."

2   Οὗτος δηλοῖ ὡς καὶ ἄνθρωποί τινες, ἔξωθεν μὲν φιλίαν ὑποκρίνονται, ἔσωθεν δὲ κακίας καὶ ἀπηνείας πεπλήρωνται.

51

Γαλαῖς ποτε καὶ μυσὶ μάχη συνεκροτεῖτο. Ἡττώμενοι δὲ κατὰ κράτος οἱ μύες, καὶ γνόντες ἐξ ἀτονίας πάντως καὶ δειλίας ἡττᾶσθαι, σατράπας ἑαυτοῖς καὶ τῆς μάχης ἀρχηγοὺς κεχειροτονήκασιν. Οἱ δὲ σατράπαι ἐμφανέστεροι θελήσαντες καὶ θαρραλεώτεροι τῶν ἄλλων μυῶν καθίστασθαι, κέρατα ταῖς ἑαυτῶν κορυφαῖς περιέθεντο. Εἶτα πάλιν αἱ γαλαῖ τοῖς μυσὶ προσβαλοῦσαι εἰς φυγὴν πάντας τρέπουσι· καὶ οἱ μὲν ἄλλοι μύες φυγάδες γενόμενοι πρὸς τὰς ἑαυτῶν καταδύσεις εὐθὺς ῥᾳδίως εἰσέδυσαν, οἱ δὲ τούτων προέξαρχοι, μέχρι τῶν ὀπῶν καὶ οὗτοι ἐν τῷ φεύγειν φθάσαντες, τῆς ἐν αὐταῖς εἰσελεύσεως ὑπὸ τῶν κεράτων ἐκωλύοντο. Καὶ τούτους αἱ γαλαῖ καταλαβοῦσαι ὀλέθρῳ παραδεδώκασιν.

50

A dog was chasing down a hare and caught him. Then one moment he was biting the hare, but in the next he was licking up the blood that flowed from his wound. The hare thought that the dog was instead kissing him, and so he said in response, "Either embrace me as my friend, or keep on biting me as my opponent and enemy."

This fable shows that some people, though they act 2 friendly on the outside, are filled with evil and cruelty on the inside.

51

Once a battle broke out between cats and mice. The mice were being overpowered, and when they realized that they were being defeated by their cowardice and utter lack of resistance, they elected satraps and generals for themselves. Now the satraps wanted to be more conspicuous and inspire more confidence than the other mice, and so they placed horns on their heads. Then once again the cats attacked the mice and routed them all. The ordinary mice fled immediately to their lairs and easily slipped inside, but their leaders, although they also reached their own holes in their retreat, were prevented from entering by their horns. And so, the cats captured and killed them.

2   Οὗτος δηλοῖ ὡς οἱ τοῖς ὅπλοις ἑαυτῶν τεθαρρηκότες, καὶ μὴ τὴν θείαν συμμαχίαν ἐπικαλεσάμενοι, ὑπ᾿ αὐτῶν δὴ καὶ τὸν κίνδυνον ἐπισπῶνται.

52

Λύκος ἁρπάσας χοῖρον καὶ ἀπάγων αὐτὸν συνήντησε λέοντι. Ὁ δὲ εὐθὺς τὸν χοῖρον ἀφήρπασεν. Ἀφαιρεθεὶς δὲ αὐτὸν ὁ λύκος ἐν ἑαυτῷ ἔλεγε· "Πάντως καὶ αὐτὸς ἐθαύμαζον, πῶς ἂν καὶ διέμεινε παρ᾿ ἐμοὶ τὸ ἐξ ἁρπαγῆς μοι προσγενόμενον."

2   Οὗτος δηλοῖ ὡς καὶ τὰ ἀλλότρια πράγματα, πλεονεκτικῶς τισι καὶ βιαίως ἐπικτώμενα, τοῖς ταῦτα ἁρπάζουσιν οὐκ εἰς τέλος παραμένουσιν.

53

Ποτὲ τῶν πτηνῶν εἰς κοινὴν βουλὴν ἐπὶ τὸ αὐτὸ συνελθόντων, ἕκαστον αὐτῶν, τίνι τῶν ἄλλων ἐφαρμόζει τὸ βασιλεύειν, πρὸς ἀλλήλους ἐβουλεύοντο. Ὁ δὲ ταῶς ἔφη τοῖς λοιποῖς ὡς· "Ἔμοιγε μᾶλλον προσήκει ἡ βασιλεία, ἅτε κάλλει καὶ ὡραιότητι σεμνυνομένῳ." Τῶν δὲ ἑτέρων πτηνῶν ἐπαρεσθέντων τῷ ταῶνι, παρελθὼν εἰς μέσον ὁ

This fable shows that people who take courage from their   2
weapons but fail to summon God as their ally bring danger
upon themselves through those very weapons.

52

A wolf snatched a pig and while carrying it away met a
lion, which immediately snatched the pig away from the
wolf. After being robbed of it, the wolf said to himself, "Oh,
well. I was wondering myself how long I would keep the
thing that I got by stealing."

This fable shows that other people's property, when it is   2
acquired greedily and by force, does not remain forever with
those who steal it.

53

Once the birds, one of every type, came together in a
common meeting and were deliberating among themselves
about which of them was best suited to be king. And the
peacock said to the rest, "The kingship suits me best,
because I pride myself on my beauty and loveliness."
When the other birds expressed their satisfaction with the

κόραξ ἀντέφησεν· "Ἐὰν σὺ τὴν βασιλείαν παραλάβῃς,
ἆρά γε, τοῦ ἀετοῦ ἡμῖν ἐπερχομένου, δύνασαι ἡμᾶς τῆς
ἐκείνου ἐξελέσθαι προσβολῆς;"

2   Οὗτος δηλοῖ ὡς τὸ βασιλεύειν οὐ τοῖς κάλλει φαιδρυ-
νομένοις ἁρμόττει, ἀλλὰ τοῖς ῥωμαλέοις καὶ γενναιότητι
διαπρέπουσιν.

54

Νεανίσκος τις ὁδοιπορῶν ἐν ἡμέρᾳ καύσωνος ἐντυγχάνει γυναικί τινι γραΐδι, ἥτις καὶ αὐτὴ τὴν αὐτὴν ὁδὸν τῷ
νεανίσκῳ συνεπορεύετο. Ὁρῶν δὲ αὐτὴν ἐκεῖνος τῷ τε
καύσωνι καὶ τῷ τῆς ὁδοιπορίας καμάτῳ δεινῶς ἰλιγγιῶσαν,
κατῴκτειρε τῆς ἀσθενείας, καὶ μηκέτι ἐξισχύουσαν ὅλως
πορεύεσθαι, ἄρας ταύτην τῆς γῆς ἐπὶ τῶν νώτων αὐτοῦ
διεβάσταζε. Ταύτην δὲ ἐπιφερόμενος λογισμοῖς τισιν
αἰσχροῖς δεινῶς ἐταράττετο, ὑφ᾽ ὧν καὶ πρὸς οἶστρον
ἀκολασίας καὶ σφοδρὸν ἔρωτα ὁ αὐτοῦ ἦρτο ἰθύφαλλος·
εὐθὺς δὲ τῇ γῇ καταθεὶς τὴν γραῖδα, ταύτῃ ἀκολάστως
συνεγένετο. Ἡ δὲ πρὸς αὐτὸν ἁπλοϊκῶς ἔλεγε· "Τί ἐστιν
ὃ ἐπ᾽ ἐμοὶ ἐργάζῃ;" Ὁ δὲ αὐτῇ ἔφη ὡς· "Βαρεῖα πέφυκας,
καὶ τούτου χάριν ἀπογλύψαι σου τῆς σαρκὸς διανενόημαι."
Καὶ ταῦτα εἰπών, καὶ εἰς τέλος αὐτῇ συμφθαρείς, πάλιν
τῆς γῆς ταύτην ἐξάρας ἐπὶ τῶν ἑαυτοῦ νώτων ἐπέθετο.
Καὶ μήκος ὁδοῦ τινος διελάσαντος αὐτοῦ, ἔφη πρὸς αὐτὸν

peacock, the crow came into their midst and objected, "If you assume the kingship, can you save us from the eagle's attack when he swoops down upon us?"

This fable shows that kingship is not suited to those who stand out for their beauty, but to those who are distinguished by strength and courage. 2

54

A young man was traveling on a hot day and happened upon an old woman, who herself was traveling the same road as the young man. When he saw that she was terribly faint from the heat and toil of the journey, he took pity on her infirmity, and when she could no longer walk at all, he picked her up from the ground and began to carry her on his back. As he carried her along, he was aroused by some terribly wicked thoughts, which brought on a mighty lust and an urge to behave licentiously and gave him an erection. Immediately, then, he set the old woman on the ground and lustily had sex with her. And she said to him in all innocence, "What are you doing to me?", to which he replied, "You're heavy, and so I had in mind to chisel off some of your flesh." After he said this, and when he had finished having sex with her, he picked her up again from the ground and put her on his back. When he had gone some distance down the road,

ἡ γραῦς· "Εἰ ἔτι βαρεῖά σοι καὶ ἐπαχθὴς πέφυκα, πάλιν με καταγαγὼν πλέον ἐξ ἐμοῦ ἀπόγλυψον."

2   Οὗτος δηλοῖ ὡς τῶν ἀνθρώπων τινές, τὴν ἰδίαν πληροῦντες ἐπιθυμίαν, προφασίζονται ὡς ἐξ ἀγνοίας τὸ γεγονὸς διεπράξαντο, δόξαντες δῆθεν μὴ ἐκεῖνο, ἀλλ' ἕτερόν τι τῶν δεόντων μᾶλλον πεποιηκέναι.

55

Ὁ Ἥλιος καὶ ὁ Βορρᾶς ἄνεμός ποτε ἤριζον πρὸς ἀλλήλους, ποῖος ἐξ ἀμφοῖν τὸν ἄνθρωπον ἀπογυμνοῦν δύναται. Ἤρξατο οὖν πρῶτος ὁ Βορρᾶς σφοδρῶς πνέειν κατὰ τοῦ ἀνθρώπου. Ὁ δὲ ἄνθρωπος, καθόσον ἐψύχετο, τοῖς ἱματίοις ἑαυτὸν περιέσκεπε καὶ κραταίως αὐτῶν περιείχετο, μή πως τῇ σφοδροτάτῃ τοῦ ἀνέμου προσβολῇ ἐκ τοῦ σώματος αὐτοῦ ἀναρπασθῶσιν· ὅθεν καὶ κατ' οὐδὲν ὁ Βορρᾶς τὸν ἄνδρα παρέβλαψεν, οὔτε τῶν περικειμένων αὐτῷ ἀμφίων ἀπογυμνῶσαι αὐτὸν ἠδυνήθη. Εἶτα καὶ ὁ Ἥλιος αὐτῷ ἐπιλάμψας, καὶ τὸν ἀέρα τῆς ἡμέρας σφόδρα καταθερμάνας, εὐθὺς τὸν ἄνδρα τὰ ἱμάτια ἀποδύσασθαι παρεσκεύασε καὶ ἐπ' ὤμων ταῦτα ἐπιφέρεσθαι.

2   Οὗτος δηλοῖ ὡς τὸ ταπεινοφρονεῖν τοῦ ματαίως κομπάζειν ἐνεργέστερον ἐπὶ πᾶσι καὶ πρακτικώτερον πέφυκεν.

the old woman said to him, "If I'm still heavy and a burden to you, put me down again and chisel some more off me."

This fable shows that some people, when they satisfy 2 their own desire, make the excuse that they did so out of ignorance, imagining, perhaps, that they did not do what they actually did, but some other thing that had to be done.

55

The Sun and the North Wind were once contending with each other to see which of the two could make a man take off his clothes. First, the North Wind began to blow mightily against the man, who, as he grew colder, shielded himself with his clothes and wrapped them tightly around himself, so that they would not be somehow snatched off his body by the mighty blast of the wind. And so, the North Wind caused the man no harm at all, and was unable to strip him of the clothes he was wearing. Next, the Sun shone down upon him, and once he had intensely heated the daytime breeze, he immediately made the man take off his clothes and carry them on his shoulders.

This fable shows that humility is always more effective 2 and practical than empty boasting.

56

Ἀνήρ τις ὑπὸ κυνὸς καιρίως δηχθεὶς ἐζήτει τὸν τὴν πληγὴν αὐτοῦ θεραπεύσοντα. Ἕτερος δέ τις αὐτῷ συναντήσας ἔφη πρὸς αὐτόν· "Τοῦτο προσήκει ποιῆσαί σε· ἀπὸ τοῦ τῆς πληγῆς αἵματος ἐπισταλάξαι τῷ ψωμῷ καὶ τῷ δακόντι κυνὶ τὸν ψωμὸν ἐπιρρίψαι φαγεῖν, καὶ οὕτως ἡ πληγή σου θεραπευθήσεται." Ὁ δὲ δηχθεὶς ἀντέφη αὐτῷ· "Εἰ τοῦτο ποιήσω, ὑπὸ πάντων τῶν ἐν τῇ πόλει ταύτῃ κυνῶν ἔσομαι δακνόμενος."

2   Οὗτος ὁ λόγος δηλοῖ ὡς εἰ καὶ τὸν σκαιὸν ἄνθρωπον τιμήσειέ τις καὶ δεξιώσαιτο, ἀλλ᾽ οὐκ ἐκεῖνος αὐτὸν τὸν τιμήσαντα, ἀλλὰ τοὺς ὁμοίους αὐτῷ κακοὺς μᾶλλον ἀγαπᾷ.

57

Ὄρνις τις εὑροῦσα ᾠὰ ὄφεως ἐσχόλαζε τῇ τούτων διατριβῇ, καὶ ταῦτα ἐπῳάζουσα ἐπεκάθητο. Χελιδὼν δέ τις αὐτὴν θεασαμένη, "Ὦ μωρὰ καὶ ἀναίσθητε," ἔφη, "τίνος χάριν ὄφεως περιέπεις γεννήματα; Εἰ γὰρ αὐξηθῶσι, σοὶ πρότερον ἐμποιήσουσι τὸν ὄλεθρον, καὶ μετέπειτα ἑτέροις."

2   Οὗτος δηλοῖ ὡς οὐ χρή τινα ἐπὶ διαθέσει ἀνοσίου ἀνδρὸς πεποιθέναι πώποτε, κἂν πολλὴν αὐτῷ τὴν εὔνοιαν ἐπιδείξηται.

56

A man received a serious bite from a dog and was seeking someone to treat his wound. Another man met him and said, "This is what you should do: drip some blood from your wound on to some bread, and then throw the bread to the dog that bit you, for him to eat. In this way, your wound will be healed." The man who had been bitten said in response, "If I do that, I'll be bitten by every dog in town."

This fable shows that even if someone pays respect to a 2 wicked man and treats him kindly, that man does not love the one who has respected him, but rather those who are evil like himself.

57

A hen found the eggs of a snake and, since she had time to spend with them, sat down to hatch them. A swallow saw her and said, "You stupid fool, why are you caring for a snake's young? If they hatch, first they will kill you, and then they will go after others."

This fable shows that one must never trust the disposi- 2 tion of unholy men, even if one has shown them great kindness.

58

Στρουθός τις ἐπὶ μυρσίνης διέτριβε, καὶ διὰ τὸ ἡδὺ τῆς τοῦ δένδρου διαίτης οὐδ' ὅλως αὐτοῦ ἀφίστατο. Ἰξευτὴς δέ τις τοῦτον παρατηρησάμενος κατέσχε τε καὶ κατέθυσεν. Ὁ δὲ στρουθὸς μέλλων ἀποσφαγῆναι πρὸς ἑαυτὸν ἔλεγεν· "Οἴμοι τῷ ταλαιπώρῳ, ὅτι διὰ τροφῆς ἀφορμὴν καὶ μικρὰν ἡδονὴν τοῦ ζῆν ἀπορρήγνυμαι."

2   Οὗτος δηλοῖ ὡς καὶ ἄνθρωποί τινες, δι' ἔφεσιν τρυφῆς καὶ ἁβρότητος περὶ τὸ ζῆν πολλάκις, ὡς μοχθηροί, κινδυνεύουσι.

59

Κάμηλος κεράτων ἐφιεμένη ἐδέετο τοῦ Διὸς ἑαυτῇ ταῦτα προσγενέσθαι· ὁ δὲ Ζεύς, ὀργισθεὶς μᾶλλον ἐπὶ τῇ αὐτῆς ἀπληστίᾳ, καὶ τὰ ταύτης ὦτα ἠλάττωσεν.

2   Οὗτος δηλοῖ ὡς οἱ τοῦ πλείονος ὀρεγόμενοι καὶ ὧν ἔχουσιν ἀποστεροῦνται.

58

A sparrow was living in a myrtle tree, and because his diet in that tree was so sweet, he never left it. Now a fowler observed the bird, and caught and killed him. As the sparrow was about to be slaughtered, he said to himself, "Alas, poor me! I'm losing my life for the sake of food and a little pleasure."

This fable shows that some people, being good-for-nothings, often risk their lives out of a desire for luxury and splendor. 2

59

A camel desired to have horns, and so she prayed to Zeus to have them added to her. But Zeus became angry at the camel's greed, and made her ears smaller instead.

This fable shows that those who grasp at more are deprived of what they already have. 2

60

Κύκνοι καὶ χῆνες ἀλλήλοις φιλιωθέντες ἐπὶ τῆς πεδιάδος ἐξῆλθον, καὶ νεμομένων αὐτῶν ὁμοθυμαδὸν θηρευταὶ αὐτοῖς ἐπήεσαν. Καὶ οἱ μὲν κύκνοι διὰ τὴν τοῦ σώματος ὠκύτητα, εὐθὺς πετασθέντες ἔφυγον· αἱ δὲ χῆνες, τῇ ἑαυτῶν φυσικῇ βραδυτῆτι ἐπεχόμεναι, ὑπὸ τῶν θηρευτῶν κατεσχέθησαν.

2   Οὗτος ὁ λόγος παριστᾷ τοὺς μὴ ὁλοτρόπως τοῖς ἑαυτῶν φίλοις προσανέχοντας, ἀλλ᾽ ἐν καιρῷ περιστάσεως τούτων ἀφισταμένους.

61

Λύκοι τινὲς ἔν τινι ποταμῷ δέρματα βοῶν ἑωρακότες, καὶ ταῦτα σπουδάζοντες ἐκεῖθεν ἀνελκύσαι, τῆς τοῦ ποταμοῦ πλημμύρας βαθείας οὔσης κατατολμῆσαι οὐκ ἠδύναντο· ὅθεν ἐβουλεύσαντο καθ᾽ ἑαυτοὺς πρότερον τὰ ὕδατα καταπιεῖν, καὶ εἶθ᾽ οὕτω τὰ δέρματα φθάσαι καὶ ἀναλαβεῖν. Ἀνὴρ δέ τις ὑπολαβὼν ἔφη πρὸς αὐτούς· "Εἰ ὅλως πειραθῆτε τὰ τοσαῦτα καταπιεῖν ὕδατα, εὐθὺς διασπασθέντες καὶ τῆς ζωῆς στερηθήσεσθε."

2   Ὁ μῦθος οὗτος ἐλέγχει τοὺς τοῖς ἀνηνύτοις ἐξ ἀφροσύνης ἐπιχειροῦντας.

60

Some swans and geese became friends and went out upon a plain. While they were foraging together, some hunters ambushed them. Now the swans, thanks to the swiftness of their bodies, immediately escaped by flying away, while the geese, held back by their natural sluggishness, were captured by the hunters.

This fable portrays those who are not entirely devoted to 2 their friends, but who desert them in a moment of crisis.

61

Some wolves saw some oxhides in a river and rushed to drag them out, but they could not brave the river's waters, which were deep. And so, after deliberating among themselves they decided first to drink down the water, and then go and get the hides. In response to this, a certain man said, "If you really try to drink that much water, you'll immediately burst and lose your lives."

This fable condemns those who undertake impossible 2 tasks out of foolishness.

62

Τέττιξ, ἄνδρα τινὰ θεασάμενος κατασχεῖν αὐτὸν μη-
χανώμενον, ἔφη πρὸς αὐτόν· "Ἐκείνοις τοῖς ὀρνέοις ἐπέρ-
χου, παρ' ὧν σοι καὶ ὄφελός τι προσγενήσεται· ἐμὲ γὰρ εἰ
κατάσχοις, οὐδὲν ἐξ ἐμοῦ τὸ παράπαν κερδανεῖς."

2   Οὗτος δηλοῖ ὡς οὐ χρή τινα τῶν ἀχρήστων καὶ ἀνο-
νήτων ἐφίεσθαι.

62

A cicada saw a man who was planning to catch him and said, "Go after those birds, since you'll get some benefit from them. For if you catch me, you'll gain nothing at all."

This fable shows that one should not desire useless and ² unprofitable things.

Abbreviations

Boissonade = Jean François Boissonade, *Syntipas: De Syntipa et Cyri filio Andreopuli narratio* (Paris, 1828)

BSP = *The Book of Syntipas the Philosopher*

Fables = *The Fables of Syntipas*

Hausrath–Hunger = August Hausrath and Herbert Hunger, eds., *Corpus fabularum Aesopicarum,* vol. 1, *Fabulae Aesopicae soluta oratione conscriptae* (Leipzig, 1959)

Jernstedt–Nikitin = Viktor Jernstedt and Petr Nikitin, eds., *Mich. Andreopuli Liber Syntipae* (Saint Petersburg, 1912)

ODB = Alexander P. Kazhdan, Alice-Mary Talbot, Anthony Cutler, Timothy E. Gregory, and Nancy P. Ševčenko, eds., *Oxford Dictionary of Byzantium,* 3 vols. (New York, 1991)

Perry, *Aesopica* = Ben Edwin Perry, *Aesopica: A Series of Texts Relating to Aesop or Ascribed to Him or Closely Connected with the Literary Tradition that Bears His Name,* vol. 1, *Greek and Latin Texts* (Urbana, Ill., 1952)

Perry, *Babrius and Phaedrus* = Ben Edwin Perry, ed., *Babrius and Phaedrus,* Loeb Classical Library 436 (Cambridge, Mass., and London, 1965)

Note on the Texts

Our text of the *BSP* is based on Jernstedt–Nikitin, who used three manuscripts labeled ABC. Manuscripts A and C also contain the *Fables* and were used by Perry, *Aesopica;* see below.

A = *Mosquensis Bibliothecae Synodalis gr.* 298 (*Vladimir* 436), written in two hands. Folios 1–349, written in the second half of the thirteenth century (Charis Messis and Stratis Papaioannou, "Translations I: From Other Languages into Greek, III. Arabic," in *The Oxford Handbook of Byzantine Literature,* ed. S. Papaioannou [Oxford and New York, forthcoming], appendix) or the fourteenth century (Jernstedt–Nikitin, ii; Perry, *Aesopica,* 511), include the *BSP* with its dedicatory poem (section 1) and summarizing epilogue (section 154).

B = *Vaticanus gr.* 335, written in the fourteenth century (Messis and Papaioannou, "Translations I," appendix) or the fourteenth to fifteenth century (Jernstedt–Nikitin, ii).

C = *Monacensis gr.* 525, fourteenth century. This manuscript contains only the text beginning from our section 76 (Jernstedt–Nikitin, 56.2), "He said then" (λέγει οὖν) to the end.

We made several changes to the text based on Boissonade's edition of the *Retractatio,* which Jernstedt–Nikitin print in parallel with their text of the *BSP.*

Our text of the *Fables* is based almost entirely on Perry, *Aesopica,* with occasional preference given to Hausrath–

Hunger. Perry used four manuscripts. The first of these contains two copies of the *Fables* by two different hands at different dates and is thus treated as two separate manuscripts:

A B = Mosquensis Bibliothecae Synodalis gr. 298 (*Vladimir* 436), written in two hands and containing two copies of the *Fables*. Folios 1–349, written in the second half of the thirteenth century (Messis and Papaioannou, "Translations I," appendix) or in the fourteenth century (Jernstedt–Nikitin, ii; Perry, *Aesopica,* 511), include one copy of the *Fables* (232v–46v) (= B). Folios 350–576, written in the fifteenth century, include a second copy of the *Fables* (531–550) (= A).

M = Monacensis gr. 525, fourteenth century.

V = Vindobonensis phil. gr. 166, sixteenth century.

The Greek text presented in this volume is not a full critical edition, and we have not personally inspected the manuscripts. In formatting the text, we have corrected typographical errors, made changes to capitalization, divided paragraphs differently, and added section numbers. We have also changed punctuation to correct errors and to clarify the interpretation of the Greek, but we have not attempted to repunctuate the entire text. Accentuation of enclitics has been normalized according to Herbert Weir Smyth, *Greek Grammar for Colleges* (New York, 1920), 42–43. A few manuscript readings relegated by Jernstedt–Nikitin to the *apparatus criticus* have been restored to the main text. In our Notes to the Texts we have listed significant deviations from Jernstedt–Nikitin and Perry, *Aesopica.*

Notes to the Texts

THE BOOK OF SYNTIPAS THE PHILOSOPHER

9 &ἔχοντα τὸν παῖδα *Beneker–Gibson*: ἔχοντα [τὸν παῖδα] *Jernstedt–Nikitin*

σφοδρότερον τοῦ πατρὸς *Beneker–Gibson*: σφοδρότερον [τοῦ πατρὸς] *Jernstedt–Nikitin*

12 βασιλεῦ οὐ *Beneker–Gibson*: βασιλεῦ ἔφη οὐ *Jernstedt–Nikitin*

31 οὖν τῆς κόρης *Beneker–Gibson*: οὖν φησίν τῆς κόρης *Jernstedt–Nikitin*

43 ὤμοσε *Beneker–Gibson*: ὄμοσε *Jernstedt–Nikitin*

61 αὐτὸν ἐκλαφύξαι *Beneker–Gibson*: αὐτῷ ἐκφυλάξαι *Jernstedt–Nikitin*

67 ἐνεχείρισα *Beneker–Gibson*: ἐνεχείρησα *Jernstedt–Nikitin*

68 ἐνεχείρισεν *Beneker–Gibson*: ἐνεχείρησεν *Jernstedt–Nikitin*

72 τοῦτον ἀπέκτεινε καὶ *Boissonade*: <...> *Jernstedt–Nikitin*

88 ἄσχαλλε *Beneker–Gibson*: ἀσχάλλου *Jernstedt–Nikitin*

91 τοῦδε τοῦ χωρίου πέφυκε *Beneker–Gibson (compare* τοῦδε τοῦ χωρίου πεφύκει *C)*: τούτου πέφυκε χωρίου *Jernstedt–Nikitin*

100 συνέδρου *Beneker–Gibson*: συνεδρίου *Jernstedt–Nikitin*

101 τύχοι *Beneker–Gibson*: τύχοιεν *Jernstedt–Nikitin*

φίλους *Beneker–Gibson, based on Jernstedt–Nikitin's conjecture*: φιλεῖ *Jernstedt–Nikitin*

107 μεγιστᾶνας *Beneker–Gibson*: μεγιστάνους *Jernstedt–Nikitin*

115 κάρυα *Boissonade*: κάρα *Jernstedt–Nikitin*

120 ὁ δέ γε ἀνὴρ *C*: ὁ δέ γε ὁ ἀνὴρ *Jernstedt–Nikitin*

122 αὐτῇ *Beneker–Gibson*; ἑαυτῇ *Jernstedt–Nikitin*

124 τοὺς τῇ θαλάσσῃ *C*: τοὺς τῆς θαλάσσης *Jernstedt–Nikitin*

131   πόλεως ἡ δὲ πανταχόθεν C: πόλεως <...> πανταχόθεν *Jernstedt–*
       Nikitin
132   καὶ ἑαυτὴν ἐγγὺς C: καὶ αὐτὴν ἐγγὺς *Jernstedt–Nikitin*
136   ἀνηρώτα ὁ δὲ ἀστρολόγος τὴν γέννησιν *Beneker–Gibson:* <...>
       Jernstedt–Nikitin
138   τῷ νέῳ C: τὸν νέον *Jernstedt–Nikitin*
140   προδιελαβόμην C: προεδιελαβόμην *Jernstedt–Nikitin*
142   τῆς τε σοφίας καὶ τῆς γνώσεως *Beneker–Gibson (compare* τῆς σο-
       φίας καὶ τῆς γνώσεως *Boissonade):* τῆς τε σοφίας τῆς γνώσεως
       Jernstedt–Nikitin
144   ἔχῃ *Beneker–Gibson (from the correction* η *written above* ἔχειν *in C):*
       ἔχειε *Jernstedt–Nikitin*
       λογίζηται *Beneker–Gibson (from the correction* τ(αι) *written above*
       λογιζη *in C):* λογίζεται *Jernstedt–Nikitin*

The Fables of Syntipas

29.2   ἀνεπίφθονος *Hausrath–Hunger:* ἀνεπίφοβος *Perry,* Aesopica
34.2   ὁ μῦθος οὗτος τοὺς ἀχαρίστους καὶ ἀγνώμονας ἐλέγχει
       Hausrath–Hunger: οὗτος δηλοῖ κατὰ τῶν ἀχαρίστων καὶ ἀγνω-
       μόνων ἐλέγχους *Perry,* Aesopica
37.2   ὑφορᾶσθαι *Hausrath–Hunger:* ἀφορᾶσθαι *Perry,* Aesopica
51.2   τὸν κίνδυνον *Hausrath–Hunger:* τῶν κινδύνων *Perry,* Aesopica
61.1   φθάσαι καὶ ἀναλαβεῖν *Hausrath–Hunger:* φθάσαι ἀναλαβεῖν
       Perry, Aesopica

Notes to the Translations

title   *The Book of Syntipas the Philosopher*: The title is not found in the manuscripts but is Jernstedt–Nikitin's conjecture (p. i) from what appears to be a title in section 2.

1   *Syntipas . . . Michael Andreopoulos . . . Gabriel*: See the Introduction.

   the least of the grammarians: Andreopoulos refers to himself as a *grammatikos*. For more about his training and occupation, see the Introduction.

   city named for honey: Melitene, modern Malatya in Turkey. Andreopoulos derives its name from the Greek word *meli* (honey).

   the Romans' books: The Byzantines considered themselves Romans.

2   *Cyrus, king of the Persians*: Cyrus II of Persia, called "The Great," founded the Persian empire and ruled ca. 557 BCE until his death in 530. He is praised as a good king in Xenophon's *Cyropaedia* and as the deliverer of the Jews from captivity in the Hebrew Bible (Isaiah 45:1).

   Mousos the Persian: The ninth-century Arabic scholar Mūsā b. ʿĪsā al-Kisrawī.

3   *for many long years, as the saying goes*: This does not appear to be a Greek proverb.

4   *after six months and two hours*: By adding the two hours, Syntipas is saying that when the six months have passed, he will return the king's son at the second hour of the day, which by modern reckoning is about eight o'clock in the morning.

5   *very spacious room*: A unique example of such a classroom has been preserved in Egypt. The walls were plastered with white gypsum, and literary texts, including poems exhorting the students to study hard, were inscribed on them with red ink. See Raffaella Cribiore and Paoli Davoli, "New Literary Texts from Amheida, Ancient Trimithis (Dakhla Oasis, Egypt)," *Zeitschrift für Papyrologie und Epigraphik* 187 (2013): 1–14.

16   *Hagarenes*: A term for Arabs, and in general for Muslims.

      which in everyday language is called a parrot: For similar glosses, see sections 37, 38, and 101. Andreopoulos must have felt his audience would need these explanatory glosses, which he assigned to characters in his translation.

22   *My king, may you live forever*: Daniel 2:4, 3:9, 5:10, 6:7, 6:22. This formula, with slight variations, is also found below in sections 34, 46, 59, 74, 85, 97, and 139 but is not noted each time.

23   *white loaves . . . cleanliness*: There is a wordplay in the Greek here that is hard to render in English; the loaves are καθαροί ("pure" or "clean," but also, in the plural in this context, "white"), and the servant of the merchant, who never eats unclean food, is thus pleased by their cleanliness (καθαρότης).

27   *Draw your sword*: The Greek verb here, ἀπογύμνωσον, means literally "to strip naked." This may be one of several humorous double entendres, concluding with the unsuspecting husband's compliment to his cheating wife on the "greatest kindness" she has done to the slave.

31   *lamia*: An ancient monster or demon that preyed on young children. In some stories, as here, a *lamia* was a ghost that took the form of a beautiful young woman to seduce young men and feed upon them.

      that other inn: Literally, "that other such and such (δεῖνα) inn." This is a common feature of Persian and Arabic (but not Greek) storytelling, in which the specific names of people, places, and things are omitted because they are thought to be insignificant to the story. See also section 43, "King So-and-So . . . another King So-and-So."

37   *which in everyday language is called rice*: See note in section 16.

38   *which in everyday language is called a very-fine-grained sieve*: See note in section 16.

43   *whose son are you*: It is odd that the vinedresser refers to him as "son," since the boy has been transformed into a woman.

King So-and-So . . . another King So-and-So: For this storytelling feature, see note in section 31.

immediately transformed into a woman: The story does not explain how the vinedresser was transformed into a woman or how the king's son was transformed back into a boy.

50   *There was once a woman . . . lawful husband*: This is the beginning of the second story told by the fourth advisor. The usual introduction (a formula like "Let me relate for you also another story which I have heard") appears to have been lost or omitted in the Greek text.

63   *bedspread*: In this story the woman's husband is wearing a bedspread as a robe. In the Greek, the bedspread is called a robe (πέπλος), but also a woven item (ὕφασμα) and a home furnishing item (ἔπιπλον), both of which we translate as "blanket."

71   *They arrived at an inn*: This inn is a roadside lodging that evidently has an enclosure for pack animals.

night watchman: The lion's great fear of the man could reflect an earlier version of the story, in which the lion thought the man was a demon figure instead of a human being. In a later Old Spanish version that was translated from an Arabic version, the lion says to himself, "This is the (demon) Tempest that men speak of": Domenico Comparetti, trans., *Researches Respecting the Book of Sindibad* (London, 1882), 144.

74   *at the sixth hour*: Around noon in the modern reckoning of time.

82   *And when the seventh day . . . she had made to the boy*: Jernstedt–Nikitin (critical apparatus, p. 60 on lines 3–8) suggest that Andreopoulos added this paragraph later, because the end of it does not transition smoothly to the beginning of the next paragraph, but that he was still working from a Syriac source.

84   *child of the purple*: A royal child.

92   *pants*: This rare word, φιμινάλιον, is typically used in the plural, φιμινάλια.

101   *that in everyday language is called sandalwood*: See note in section 16.

      they produce sparks of fire: Byzantine medical writers considered camphor and sandalwood to be cold by nature, and they prescribed medicines made from them to treat illnesses that make the body warm; see, for example, the section "Περὶ μύρων" in the anonymous and undated treatise *On the Potency of Foods* (Anonymi Medici, Περὶ τροφῶν δυνάμεως); *Anecdota Atheniensia et alia*, ed. Armand Delatte (Liège and Paris, 1939), vol. 2, 475.27–476.5.

108   *who was lame and a paralytic*: When the king's son later tells this story, he does not portray the charlatans' mentor as disabled.

114   *governor of that land*: In this story the same man is variously called "governor," "ruler," and "judge."

117   *rhetors*: The rhetor was responsible for the third and highest level of schooling in Byzantium.

118   *the old man . . . a merchant*: The old man (who is not mentioned again until section 122) and the merchant are different individuals.

132   *if the child wears them all the time*: Perhaps the ears were hung around the child's neck as an amulet.

      a fox's tooth: In the *Cyranides* 2.2.33–34, fox teeth are said to help with teething pains in children; ed. Dimitris Kaimakis, *Die Kyraniden* (Meisenheim-am-Glan, 1976), 116.

133   *the fox's heart*: The *Cyranides* 2.2.32–33 suggests that wearing a fox's heart will prevent envy; ed. Kaimakis, *Die Kyraniden*, 116.

134   *what wickedness the woman brought about*: This punishment appears to be similar to the Byzantine "parade of infamy," a ritualized shaming that was prescribed for various offenses, including improper conduct within a family. See further "infamy" in *ODB*.

137   *his father confined him to a room*: The story of Barlaam and Ioasaph includes a similar story about the birth of Ioasaph; see chapter

3 in [*John Damascene*]: *Barlaam and Ioasaph*, ed. and trans. G. R. Woodward and H. Mattingly, Loeb Classical Library 34 (Cambridge, Mass., and London, 1967).

139   *thirteenth year of his life . . . fifteen years old*: It is unclear why the discrepancy about the age at which the boy would begin his long criminal career is included and even emphasized, as it seems to undermine Syntipas's claim about the astrologer's accuracy.

142   *ten chapters*: For comparative material from ancient and medieval western Asia and Persia, see Ben Edwin Perry, "The Origin of the Book of Sindbad," *Fabula* 3 (1959): 78–80.

       in no way harms the objects of his envy: This is a direct refutation of the "evil eye," the belief that envious people could harm others by their gaze. See Richard Greenfield, "Magic and the Occult Sciences," in *The Cambridge Intellectual History of Byzantium*, ed. A. Kaldellis and N. Siniossoglou (Cambridge, 2017), 215–33, at 221, with further bibliography.

143   *Then he said to his son*: The king and his son begin to engage in a question-and-answer form of philosophical dialogue known in Byzantium as *erotapokrisis* (see *ODB*). See Perry, *Origin*, 82–83, for comparative material from ancient and medieval western Asia and Persia.

151   *Refute a wise man . . . lest he hate you*: See Proverbs 9:8: "Do not refute evil men, lest they hate you; refute a wise man and he will love you."

154   *fourteen parables*: Delivered by the seven philosophers, who each tell two stories.

THE FABLES OF SYNTIPAS

11.2   *in the same measure . . . measured out to him in return*: See Matthew 7:2 and Mark 4:24.

21.1   *kept throwing bread to him*: The hunter is trying to entrap the dog, probably to become his master and use him for hunting.

34.1   *I've been seriously wounded by you instead*: This version of the myth

has the gardener making a confusing statement. Other versions have him asking himself why he bothered to attempt to save the ungrateful dog.

36.1   *petrel*: A type of seabird.

41.1   *black-skinned*: Literally, "Ethiopian," which means "with burned face."

51.1   *satraps*: Satrap was a Persian term for a governor.

54.2   *some people*: The lesson of this fable is aimed at the actions of the old woman, who accepts the young man's false excuse and seeks to indulge her sexual desire.

Concordance of Fables

The table below lists the fables of Syntipas and their corresponding numbers in the catalog of Ben Edwin Perry, *Babrius and Phaedrus,* Loeb Classical Library 436 (Cambridge, Mass., and London, 1965), 419–610. We have supplied titles based on our translation. An asterisk (*) indicates that a fable is unique to the collection attributed to Syntipas.

Syntipas	Perry	Title
1	184	The ass and the cicada
2	60	The poor man and Death
3	229	The swallow and the crow
4*	412	The rivers and the sea
5	59	The cat and the file
6*	404	The hunter and the wolf
7	281	The two roosters and the eagle
8	201	The thirsty dove
9	2	The crow that imitated an eagle
10*	408	The hare in the well and the fox
11*	414	The bull, the lioness, and the wild boar
12	49	The shepherd and the lion
13	372	The lion and the two bulls
14	14	The fox and the monkey

Syntipas	Perry	Title
15	74	The deer at a spring and the hunters
16*	415	The dog and the blacksmiths
17*	409	The caged lion and the fox
18	198	The trampled snake
19*	406	The dogs that carried a lion's hide
20	305	The sick deer
21*	403	The hunter and the dog
22	256	The hares and the foxes
23	211	The bathing boy
24	1	The eagle and the fox
25	176	The man who picked up a viper
26	265	The fowler and the partridge
27	87	The hen that laid golden eggs
28	133	The dog that carried meat
29	357	The ass that considered a horse to be blessed
30*	411	The wild ass and the domesticated ass
31*	413	The fig tree and the olive tree
32	119	The gardener who watered his vegetables
33	254	The dog and the butcher
34	120	The gardener and the dog
35	130	The stomach and the feet
36	171	The bat, the petrel, and the bramble bush
37	142	The old lion and the fox
38*	407	The dog that chased a wolf
39	199	The young man who hunted grasshoppers and the scorpion

Syntipas	Perry	Title
40	217	The bull and the wild goats
41	393	The black-skinned man
42	58	The woman and the bird
43	373	The ant and the cicada
44	157	The wolf and the goat
45*	401	The colt
46	203	The monkey and the fisherman
47	137	The mosquito and the bull
48*	405	The Cyclops
49*	402	The hunter and the horseman
50	136	The dog and the hare
51	165	The mice and the cats
52	347	The wolf and the lion
53	219	The peacock and the crow
54*	410	The young man and the old woman
55	46	The Sun and the North Wind
56	64	The man who was bitten by a dog
57	192	The hen and the swallow
58	86	The sparrow in the myrtle tree
59	117	The camel that desired horns
60	228	The swans and the geese
61	135	The wolves that drank from a river
62	387	The cicada and the man

Bibliography

Editions and Translations

Conca, Fabrizio. *Novelle Bizantine: Il libro di Syntipas.* Milan, 2004.

Daly, Lloyd W. *Aesop without Morals: The Famous Fables and a Life of Aesop.* New York, 1961.

Gibbs, Laura. *Aesop's Fables.* Oxford, 2002.

Hausrath, August, and Herbert Hunger. *Corpus fabularum Aesopicarum.* Vol. 1, *Fabulae Aesopicae soluta oratione conscriptae.* Leipzig, 1959.

Jernstedt, Viktor, and Petr Nikitin. *Mich. Andreopuli Liber Syntipae.* Saint Petersburg, 1912.

Maltese, Enrico V. *Il libro di Sindbad: Novelle persiane medievali.* Turin, 1993.

Perry, Ben Edwin. *Aesopica: A Series of Texts Relating to Aesop or Ascribed to Him or Closely Connected with the Literary Tradition That Bears His Name.* Vol. 1, *Greek and Latin Texts.* Urbana, Ill., 1952.

Πούλος, Κώστας E. *Το Βιβλίο των Εφτά Σοφών.* Athens, 2000.

Further Reading

Translations of Other Eastern Versions of the Sinbad Story

Clouson, William Alexander. *The Book of Sindibād, or the Story of the King, His Son, the Damsel, and the Seven Vazīrs.* Glasgow, 1884. [from Persian and Arabic]

Comparetti, Domenico. *Researches Respecting the Book of Sindibad.* London, 1882. [from Old Spanish]

Epstein, Morris. *Tales of Sendebar. [Mishle Sendabar.]* Philadelphia, 1967. [from Hebrew]

Gilleland, Brady B. *Johannes de Alta Silva: Dolopathos, or the King and the Seven Wise Men.* Binghamton, N.Y., 1981. [from Latin]

Gollancz, Hermann. "The History of Sindban and the Seven Wise Masters." *Folk-Lore: Transactions of the Folk-Lore Society* 8 (1897): 99–130. [from Syriac]

Related Stories

Perry, Ben Edwin. *Babrius and Phaedrus.* Loeb Classical Library 436. Cambridge, Mass., and London, 1965.

Thackston, Wheeler. *Nasrullah Munshi: Kalila and Dimna.* Indianapolis, 2019.

Woodward, G. R., and H. Mattingly. *[John Damascene]: Barlaam and Ioasaph.* Loeb Classical Library 34. Cambridge, Mass., and London, 1967.

Index